Necropolis

*Book III
of the Royal Sorceress series*

Necropolis

Book III
of the Royal Sorceress series

Christopher G. Nuttall

Elsewhen Press

Necropolis
First published in Great Britain by Elsewhen Press, 2014
An imprint of Alnpete Limited

Elsewhen Press, PO Box 757, Dartford, Kent DA2 7TQ
www.elsewhen.press

British Library Cataloguing in Publication Data.
A catalogue record for this book is available from the British Library.

ISBN 978-1-908168-62-7 Print edition
ISBN 978-1-908168-72-6 eBook edition

To Elspeth and Catherine Nuttall

Prologue

Written for publication in *The Times*, London, 1831. Article suppressed at the request of His Majesty's Government.

It is with great dismay that we report an attack on Cavendish Hall, home of His Majesty's Royal Sorcerers Corps. The incident was spearheaded by an explosion in one of the training compartments, which apparently served as a diversion to allow the actual attack to take place without interruption. As far as can be determined, the aim of the attack was the kidnap of OLIVIA CRICHTON, adopted daughter of LADY GWENDOLYN CRICHTON, the Royal Sorceress. The kidnappers succeeded in removing OLIVIA CRICHTON from Cavendish Hall and, as of writing, she has not been recovered.

Large parts of OLIVIA CRICHTON'S past are a mystery. It is known she was adopted after the Swing, with several people suggesting that she is the daughter of either Master Thomas or Master Jack, but there are no records of her existence prior to that time. Nor is there any clear reason why LADY GWENDOLYN CRICHTON chose to adopt her, despite being barely of marriageable age herself. The only reasonable assumption seems to be that MISS CRICHTON possesses powerful magic of her own. If she is indeed the daughter of a Master Magician, she may well be a Master herself.

LADY GWENDOLYN CRICHTON flatly refuses to comment on the affair. However, her father, LORD RUDOLF CRICHTON states that OLIVIA CRICHTON has been accepted into the family, suggesting that she may well have an aristocratic birth, even if the records are sealed.

Speaking in the House of Commons, HIS MAJESTY'S PRIME MINISTER, THE DUKE OF INDIA, stated that the attack would not be allowed to hamper His Majesty's Government's preparations for war with France, which is expected at any moment. The Royal Sorcerers Corps, in common with the other military arms of this great nation, will stand shoulder to shoulder against any threat. However, with an attack that has apparently caused a considerable amount of damage, the reputation of the Royal Sorcerers Corps has been badly dented at the worst possible time.

Inspector LESTRADE of Scotland Yard was unwilling to comment, but sources within the government have suggested that the kidnapping was intended to put pressure on LADY GWENDOLYN CRICHTON, who would be expected to lead the Royal Sorcerers Corps into battle, despite being a woman. COLONEL SEBASTIAN, who has rejoined his old unit, was unavailable for comment, but other disgruntled magicians have warned of the dangers of female emotions interfering with military operations. If LADY GWENDOLYN CRICHTON is threatened with her daughter being killed or otherwise hurt, how will she react under such pressure?

The timing of the incident appears dire. With war against France seemingly days or even hours away, and the Russians apparently reluctant to commit to either side, we can only pray that OLIVIA CRICHTON is recovered as soon as possible. Indeed, the fate of Great Britain and her Empire might depend on her safe return.

Chapter One

livia Crichton fought her way back to wakefulness through a haze of pain.

Her memories made no sense. She'd been in the library, studying – again – with her tutor, trying to master boring Latin grammar she knew she'd never use outside Cavendish Hall. Apparently, educated ladies were supposed to know Latin; privately, she figured that she'd forget it as soon as she had impressed her tutor and he moved on to something more interesting. And he'd given her a drink of water. And ...

She swallowed hard, cursing her own carelessness. Six months off the streets and she'd lowered her guard long enough to take a drink from a near-stranger, a man who hadn't tried to hide his disdain for the street child Lady Gwen had adopted. There had to have been something in the water, she realised slowly, something to knock her out. And then she'd been transported somewhere else.

Carefully, without opening her eyes, she felt out her surroundings. She was lying facedown on something soft, her hands were firmly tied behind her back. The environment felt as if it were rocking slightly, reminding her of the first time she'd sailed on a boat up the Thames with Jack, before the Swing. She could hear nothing, apart from a thrumming sound that seemed to come from below her. And, as far as she could tell, she was alone. Bracing herself, she opened her eyes.

She was in a cabin, she realised at once. It was barren, apart from a mattress and a tiny porthole that shone bright light into the room. The walls were blank metal; the door seemed strong enough to resist an army. But she knew better than to stay where she'd been put. A childhood in the Rookery had taught her that being helpless was *never* a good idea. She twisted slightly, testing her bonds, then started to press against the knots. It didn't feel as though she was bound tightly enough to prevent her from carefully working her way free.

The other girls at the Hall would be helpless by now, she thought, with a flicker of contempt and bitter amusement. *Their perfumes and social graces wouldn't get them out of this mess.*

She smiled, darkly, as she managed to loosen the ropes enough to pull her hands free. In theory, she was an aristocrat herself, the adopted daughter of the Royal Sorceress. But in practice, no one took her seriously, apart from Lady Gwen and the senior magicians, some of whom viewed her and her magic with barely-concealed horror. She simply didn't have the noble blood of the other women at Cavendish Hall, let alone the endless lessons in etiquette that had been drilled into their heads since they were old enough to tell the difference between a knife and a fork. There was no one at the hall she could really talk to, not as a friend. But then, in the Rookery, friendship had often been secondary to bare survival. A friend could hurt you more effectively than a stranger.

Her hands came free. She let out a sigh of relief, remembering the first time she'd been captured and tied up by an older man who hadn't realised she was a girl. Not that that would have saved her, she knew; his tastes might have run to young boys, but there were plenty of others on the streets who preferred young girls. She might well have been sold to one of the brothels and never been seen again, or simply wound up with her throat cut in an alleyway. But she'd escaped the bastard and she would escape this new prison too.

She undid the bonds on her legs, then stood up, gingerly. Her legs felt weak, as if the drug hadn't worked its way completely out of her body. She shuddered, then staggered over to the porthole and looked outside. There was a seemingly endless stretch of water outside but, in the distance, she could see land. She pulled at the porthole, trying to open it up, but rapidly discovered that it was impossible. It was firmly sealed against escape.

Gritting her teeth, she walked over to the door and tested it. It was hard to open, but it wasn't locked. Olivia blinked in surprise, then decided not to look a gift horse in the mouth and crept outside. In the distance, she could hear someone talking in a language she didn't recognise, but there was no one in sight. They must have believed that the bonds were enough to secure her, she thought with another flicker of contempt. If she'd been a born noblewoman, she reminded herself, they would probably have been right.

The floor – the deck, she told herself – was silvered, reflecting her own face back at her. She scowled darkly as she saw her torn dress and long blonde hair, knowing that there was no way she could still hope to pass for a young boy. She'd filled out alarmingly ever since coming to Cavendish Hall and feeding regularly, growing breasts and a thick mane of hair which took far too long to prepare every morning. If it hadn't been for the maids, Olivia would have cut her hair as short as Lady Gwen. But they'd been insistent and Olivia hadn't wanted to defy them, even though she was technically their social superior. They'd helped save her from all manner of social embarrassments in the time she'd been at the Hall.

She brushed her hair out of her face, looking down at her dress. It still bothered her to know that it had cost enough money to feed a dozen families in the Rookery for six months, both because of the expense and because it made her a target. Wearing something expensive in the Rookery was just *asking* to be robbed, unless one happened to be so well known and fearsome that everyone else was scared instead. And to think that it was one of the *cheaper* dresses in Cavendish Hall! She should have worn trousers instead, she told herself tartly, even if Gwen would have disapproved. It would have been far more practical than the damned dress ...

Olivia froze as she heard someone coming down the corridor towards her. She glanced around hastily, looking for somewhere to hide, but saw nothing apart from unbroken metal. There was no time to get back to her cabin-prison before he came into view ... she braced herself, then ran forward, cursing the dress under her breath. The man gaped at her as she charged him, then raised his hands, too late. Olivia rammed her fist into his chest with all of her strength, then chopped at his throat. He dropped to the deck, choking and gasping for breath.

Idiot, Olivia thought, with a certain amusement. Growing up in the Rookery had taught her how to fight – and fight properly, not like the aristocrats and their obsession with fair fights with stupid rules. And most of the girls she had to study with at Cavendish Hall would have refused to fight, even if they'd been threatened with rape and murder. The very thought of being without male protection would have shocked them, even as half of the silly cows railed against being taken for delicate and dependent women. They wouldn't have lasted a day in the Rookery.

She tore at her dress, abandoning modesty in favour of movement, then started to run towards a ladder leading up to the next level. Another man was coming down the ladder, carrying a large metal box in one hand; Olivia ran forward and punched him, as hard as she could, in the groin. He staggered, then fell, screaming in pain. Olivia cursed her own mistake – the entire boat would hear the racket – and then scrambled up the ladder as quickly as she could. Outside, sea air slapped at her face; she heard the sound of gulls calling as she came out of the hatch and ran towards the railing. But when she saw the water, she froze. Land was so far away that it was barely a strip of green on the horizon.

Ladies weren't normally taught to swim. Gwen had insisted she learn, and she'd taken to her lessons far better than any of the aristocratic girls, but she'd only ever swum in the large pool at Cavendish Hall, wearing one of the absurd bathing costumes that covered almost everything, apart from her face and hair. The idea of swimming in the sea made her hesitate a moment too long, just long enough for someone to wrap their arms around her and yank her backwards. Olivia gasped in pain as he squeezed, then lifted her foot and kicked him in the leg as hard as she could. He grunted, but ignored it. She screamed and he clamped a hand over her mouth, precisely as she had hoped. Opening her mouth, she bit him as hard as she could, biting down until she drew blood. He gasped, his grip on her loosening. Taking advantage of his distraction, she pulled herself free and started to run.

But where could she go? She'd seen a handful of boats, but this one didn't look large enough for her to hide long enough to be rescued, if anyone knew where she was. Gwen would look for her – Olivia had no doubt of that – but how would Gwen knew where to start looking? And could she even catch up with the boat in time to save Olivia? The kidnappers, whoever they were, might well take their humiliation out on their captive, who had dared to try to escape. Olivia had heard enough stories from the Rookery to know she didn't dare let herself be recaptured.

She reached the stern of the boat, stared down at the choppy water, and started to scramble over the railing. It would be a long swim; probably a very dangerous swim, but at least she would take her destiny in her own hands. She was midway over her railing when she heard a voice behind her.

"Stop," it ordered. "STOP!"

Olivia's body froze before her mind quite caught up with what was happening. For a long moment, she teetered on the railing, as if she were about to fall over the edge and plummet into the water, then strong hands gripped her and pulled her back onto the boat. She was rolled over and found herself looking up into the eyes of a tall thin man with short dark hair and an incredibly pale face. Even if she hadn't felt his magic, she liked to think she would have deduced what he was from his expression alone. There was a hint of arrogance in his face that all such magicians seemed to have in common, the belief that they were superior to their fellow men, even their fellow magicians.

A Charmer, she realised, numbly. *Wonderful.*

"That was unwise," the Charmer said, evenly. "There are dangerous currents in these waters, young lady. You would have been very lucky if your body was ever recovered."

There was no longer any magic in his voice, but Olivia cringed inwardly anyway. She *hated* Charmers. Very few people actually liked having such magicians who could influence their thoughts or compel someone to obey, anywhere near them. And some of the Charmers in training at Cavendish Hall loved playing tricks on their fellow students. All magicians seemed to have a sense of playfulness in common, but Charmers were often nasty rather than playful.

"Now, *listen*," he added. Magic ran through his voice, demanding her complete attention. "You will obey all orders I give you. You will remain calm at all times. You will remain in your cabin unless escorted by myself or one of my crew. You will not attempt to jump into the water again or to escape by any other means as long as you are on this vessel."

Olivia cursed inwardly as she felt the commands sinking into her mind. Ropes and chains were one thing – she had already escaped one set of ropes – but mental commands were quite another. There was no attempt to be *subtle*, no attempt to influence her thoughts without her being aware of the influence, yet it hardly mattered. The commands would last for days, perhaps weeks, before she finally managed to break free. And he would presumably renew them every few days. She was trapped, bound by her own mind, far more solidly than she would be by handcuffs or shackles.

The Charmer leaned down until his dark eyes held hers firmly. "Do you understand me?"

"Yes, sir," Olivia said. She felt helpless and weak, a feeling she hated ... but the anger was curiously muted, dampened by his magic. He knew that strong emotion would help her to break the spell and had taken steps to prevent her from getting angry. "I understand."

"Very good," the Charmer said. He stood upright and smiled down at her, a glint of amusement in his cold eyes. "Stand."

Olivia felt her body obey at once. She tried to glare at him as she rose to her feet, but the numbness seemed to press down on her emotions, making it harder for her to do anything more than stand there like a damnable opium addict. The thought was terrifying; she'd seen men and women venture into the opium dens and slowly fade away into nothingness, hooked on the drug that was slowly destroying their lives. Even if she'd had the money, she liked to think she wouldn't have walked into a den willingly ...

But that wasn't the worst of it, she knew. A Charmer's influence could be almost as addictive as any drug. At some point, their victims moved from hating the compulsion to loving it and demanding to surrender their minds to the magician controlling them. She swore to herself that she would never let that happen, yet she knew it wouldn't be easy to resist. Unscrupulous Charmers were among the worst of magicians. Their victims often ended up in Bedlams, unable even to care for themselves. And he would want her to be completely under his control.

She found her voice. "What do you want from me?"

The Charmer smiled. "What do you think?"

Olivia swallowed. She had two things that were largely unique, as far as anyone knew. She was Lady Gwen's daughter ... and she was a Necromancer. But anyone who wanted to kidnap her purely for the ransom wouldn't have taken her out of Britain. No, they would have preferred to keep her somewhere she could be traded quickly for whatever ransom they demanded. Lady Gwen was a wealthy woman in her own right. They could have demanded a vast sum of money with the reasonable certainty that they would be paid.

But if they wanted her because she was a Necromancer ...

She felt sick as she remembered the final moments of the Battle of London. The shambling hordes of undead monsters advancing towards her, the eerie whispering running through her mind that had grown louder and louder as the undead had grown in strength ... and the moment she'd finally managed to stop their advance. They would have destroyed London, then the entire country if they hadn't been stopped. She had saved Britain from a doom unleashed by one of her foremost defenders. And even that hadn't been enough to save her from a death sentence, purely for being what she was. It had taken her adoption by Lady Gwen to convince the government to let her live.

"You must never use your powers again, unless ordered to do so," Gwen had said. Olivia hadn't needed much convincing. Unlike the other forms of magic, even Charm, received wisdom claimed that Necromancy was impossible to use for any decent purpose. "And you must not even tell people what you are."

Olivia shuddered. Someone had clearly found out anyway – and kidnapped her.

"You know," the Charmer said. "Don't you?"

Her words came unwillingly to her lips. "You want me to raise the dead."

"Something like that," the Charmer said. "Follow me."

He stood and strode back towards the hatch. Olivia followed him, unwillingly. She tried to struggle against the mental commands, but they were too strong to break. And yet, she knew that if she didn't struggle, the commands would only sink further and further into her head until she would no longer be able to separate them from her own thoughts. He'd have her completely in his power when she thought she was serving him willingly.

The cabin looked as unprepossessing as before, but this time she felt herself trapped the moment she stepped back inside. The Charmer nodded to the mattress, then smiled at her mischievously. Olivia glowered at him, then sat down with all the dignity she could muster in her underclothes. She should definitely have worn trousers.

"You will be fed, of course," the Charmer said. "You will eat and drink each day. You will not attempt to harm or kill yourself – or anyone else onboard this vessel."

He smirked at her expression. She hadn't considered suicide, at least not as a serious possibility, but he was clearly moving ahead of her. Olivia knew the potential consequences of an outbreak of undead monsters far better than anyone who hadn't witnessed one such occurrence – and the knowledge she could cause one was terrifying. Suicide might have seemed the only reasonable solution if escape wasn't a possibility. But he'd already ensured she couldn't end her own life.

"Thank you," she said, sourly.

The Charmer nodded, then walked over to the door and stepped outside. He paused, then turned to face her. "I suggest you sleep," he added. "We have quite a long journey ahead of us."

It wasn't a command, but her mind insisted on interpreting it as one. Olivia felt her eyelids suddenly grow heavier. It was all she could do to lie down before her eyes closed and she plunged into darkness ...

... And, when she dreamed, she dreamed of the horror she knew was to come.

Chapter Two

wen could see smoke rising in the distance as the carriage raced towards Willingham Hall, the driver cracking the whip as if the hounds of hell were after them. The message had been urgent, and she knew it needed to be dealt with, but she also knew that Lord Mycroft had deliberately arranged for her to go in hopes of distracting her from her worries about Olivia. Where the hell was she?

It had been a week since the attack on Cavendish Hall. No one, not even Mycroft's brother, had managed to trace the kidnappers, which suggested that Olivia had been taken out of the country. The French seemed the most likely suspect – Britain had been on the brink of war with France for the last two weeks – but they wouldn't say anything, she knew, if they *had* managed to kidnap her daughter. The last living Necromancer was a weapon, first and foremost. It was why Olivia had been permitted to live.

The carriage rocked as it passed through the gates and headed up towards the hall. Gwen peered towards the towering building, admiring the strange mixture of styles that had been worked into the hall, from Indian and Chinese influences to good old-fashioned British concepts from the Elizabethan era. It was no fortress, she noted, but it showed off both the wealth and global reach of the Willingham Family. Lord Willingham and his family had made their money through trade and, no matter how the older families might sneer, trade was the backbone of the British Empire. The least they deserved was to have any troubles they might encounter taken seriously by the government.

She sucked in her breath as she saw the flames burning through the west wing of the giant house, flickering with an unearthly light. They weren't natural flames – the horde of men carrying buckets of water towards the manor could have put them out by now if they'd been normal – but flames caused by magic. Gwen could *feel* the heat even from a short distance away, yet the flames didn't seem to be interested in spreading further. A Blazer with a remarkable level of both power and control had damaged but not destroyed the building.

"Your Ladyship?" the driver called. "Do you want me to wait here?"

"Yes, please," Gwen said, as she reached for her stick. "I'll need you to take me back to London afterwards."

She jammed her top hat, a memento of Master Thomas, on her head, then opened the door and jumped lightly down to the ground, using magic to ensure she landed gently. The men fighting the fire barely even glanced at her, probably without realising that she was a girl, but the assembled womenfolk stared at her in silent disbelief. Gwen fought down the urge to smile in a most inappropriate fashion. In her top hat, male suit and carrying a cane, she defied all of the strictest ideas of what a woman should wear, particularly at her age. It was clear that no one at Willingham Hall had ever even *heard* of the trouser brigade.

And to think that I am far from the only woman who wears trousers, she thought, as she looked around to see who was in charge. There was normally at least one intensely practical woman in charge of the female servants, if the Lady of the House wasn't around or had suffered a fainting fit. She would be old enough to be a mother, old enough to command respect, but not old enough to be a grandmother.

"Lady Gwen," a voice said. It was intensely formal, so carefully aristocratic that Gwen just *knew* the speaker hadn't been born an aristocrat, or at least not a very high-ranking noblewoman. "We thank you for coming."

Gwen turned to see an older woman making her way towards the carriage and sighed, inwardly. Lady Elizabeth Willingham was tall, alarmingly thin, with long dark hair that was slowly starting to go grey. The older woman glanced over Gwen's appearance and shook her head, so minutely that a man might not have even noticed the slight motion of disapproval. If Gwen had been a normal girl in society, Lady Elizabeth's disapproval would have been disastrous to her prospects. Instead, it was merely annoying. She just *knew* they weren't going to get on.

"You're welcome," she said, calmly. If there was one lesson she'd learned from her mother, it was how to be polite to someone she would much rather stab with a knife. "I came as soon as I heard."

"Lady Gwen," another voice said. Gwen looked past Lady Elizabeth to see a younger woman, only five or six years older than Gwen, staggering towards them. She looked tired and worn – and deeply worried. "I'm so glad you're here."

Gwen nodded, studying the younger woman. She would be Lady Fanny, if she recalled correctly, the wife of Lord Willingham. Lady Elizabeth would be her mother-in-law. Gwen felt a flicker of sympathy for Lady Fanny, who clearly looked harried. A mother-in-law who expected everything to be absolutely perfect would be an absolute nightmare. God knew Gwen's own mother had been quite unbearable at times to Gwen's sister-in-law. And there was little recourse when the men of the household weren't expected to meddle in the female sphere.

"It's all right," Gwen said, as comfortingly as she could. "Now, tell me what happened and –"

"It isn't a suitable story for your ears," Lady Elizabeth said. "We thank you for coming ..."

Lady Fanny gave her mother-in-law a look of absolute despair. Gwen felt nothing, but amused disbelief. There was a fire, clearly of magical origin, burning through the manor house, several people might well have been killed or badly hurt ... and Lady Elizabeth was clinging to her preconceptions about what young women should or should not hear! Like so many others Gwen had met, she was perfectly capable of denying reality if it suited her to do so. Even the unavoidable truths of female existence were simply ignored by the older women.

"I will hear it," Gwen said, purposely looking past the older woman. "Tell me what happened, please."

Lady Fanny looked as if she couldn't quite believe what Gwen had done. This far from London, Lady Elizabeth's will would reign supreme. If she wanted to ignore reality, there was no one who could tell her otherwise, particularly with her son out of the country. Indeed, from the notes Lord Mycroft had given her, Lady Elizabeth held some control over the property that wouldn't relax until her death. Judging by the way she treated her daughter-in-law, Gwen wouldn't be too surprised if her death came sooner rather than later.

"I don't quite know where to begin," Lady Fanny said. "I was in the sewing room, knitting blankets for the troops, when there were cries of fire."

"And then the west wing started to burn," Lady Elizabeth put in. "They dragged a body out of the flames before they became too intense to handle."

Gwen's eyes narrowed. "A body? Just *one* body?"

"Yes," Lady Elizabeth confirmed. "The Governess."

Lady Fanny looked up, meeting Gwen's eyes for the first time. "My daughter is missing," she insisted, despite the look she received from Lady Elizabeth. "Where has she gone?"

"You don't need to make a fuss," Lady Elizabeth said, tartly. "Your daughter will return to us, of that I am sure."

Gwen felt her temper start to fray. There were more important matters than maintaining the proper appearances and conduct at all times. If Lady Fanny's daughter was missing, it was hard to blame her for being worried, just as Gwen herself was worried about Olivia. But older women tended to ensure that their children were brought up by governesses rather than doing the hard work of childrearing themselves. They preferred to maintain an emotional distance between themselves and their children, just in case the children died when they were very young.

"You have given her too much freedom," Lady Elizabeth continued, blithely. "She has no doubt run out into the forest where she will hide for a few hours, before returning to us."

Gwen looked over at Lady Fanny, purposefully ignoring the older woman. "Take me to the Governess," she ordered. "I need to see the body."

"It isn't a fit sight for a young woman," Lady Elizabeth said, as Lady Fanny started forward. "I think it would be better if ..."

"I have seen more bodies in the last year then most soldiers see in their entire lives," Gwen snapped. She had no idea if that was actually true, but she *had* seen far too many dead bodies in her short career. Some of them had even reanimated and tried to kill her. "And you will hold your tongue or I will see to it that you are socially blacklisted everywhere in High Society."

Lady Elizabeth opened her mouth and shut it again with a loud snap. Gwen was the Royal Sorceress, Master Thomas's designated heir ... and someone who had the ear of a great many important personages. *And* she was the person who had earned the eternal gratitude of most of High Society by destroying blackmail material that would otherwise be used against them ...

"Stay here," Gwen ordered. No doubt Lady Elizabeth would eventually convince herself that she hadn't heard what she'd heard, but for the moment she'd stay quiet. Gwen looked over at Lady Fanny and winked. "Take me to the body."

She eyed the younger woman carefully as Lady Fanny led her away from the manor, towards a copse of trees where the female servants had gathered. Most of them were young, young enough to be easy to dominate, although a handful were clearly older and tougher. But Lady Fanny looked almost as beaten down as some of the younger servants, despite being a born aristocrat. It was clear that Lady Elizabeth had wasted no time imposing her authority on her new daughter-in-law.

"You don't have to put up with her, you know," Gwen said, softly. It was strange to realise that she might have ended up in the same boat, if she hadn't been born with magic. Her marriage would have been arranged for best advantage and she would have been expected to simply accept whatever her father decided. "There are places to go."

"Not for me," Lady Fanny said, so quietly that Gwen could barely hear her. "My family would never take me back."

"I'm sorry," Gwen said. The Swing had caused a number of changes in society, but there was still so much injustice and mistreatment at all levels. It was far from unknown for servants to be regularly beaten by their masters, even though it was technically illegal. And Lady Elizabeth could ensure that they never worked again, if they left her. "I'm truly sorry."

They stopped in front of a blanket covering a body. Gwen knelt down, ignoring the gasp from Lady Fanny, and drew the blanket back, revealing a woman she vaguely recognised. She was tall, almost skeletally thin, with a tart disapproving face and an expression that suggested she was permanently sucking on a lemon. Her hair was drawn back into a tight bun, so tight that Gwen knew she spent too much time each day pinning it firmly into place. And her right shoulder was missing completely, along with her arm and parts of her throat.

"A Blazer did this," Gwen muttered, as she examined the wound. The heat had been sufficient to seal the damage or the woman would have bled to death, although it was clearly immaterial. She doubted anyone could have survived such wounds long enough to reach a Healer, assuming there was one in the area. "Who is this woman?"

"Madame Constant," Lady Fanny said. "She came with *very* high recommendations."

Gwen shuddered. She'd only met Madame Constant once, but it had ended badly for both of them. Madame Constant believed, beyond a shadow of a doubt, that children needed a firm hand to guide them along the path to adulthood, with every small deviation punished intensely. Lady Mary, Gwen's mother, had hired Madame Constant as one of the endless series of governesses that had tried to bring up the young Gwen. But Madame Constant had taken one look at Gwen's magic and resigned on the spot. If half the stories Gwen had heard about how she brought up children were true, it was hard to blame her.

"She would have done," Gwen said. She looked up, sharply. "And you trusted your daughter with her?"

"Lady Elizabeth chose her," Lady Fanny said. "I wasn't consulted."

"This is your daughter's education," Gwen said. "Your daughter's *life*. You shouldn't let your mother-in-law supervise the development of a girl far too young to stand up for herself."

She shuddered, again. Madame Constant was – had been – a firm believer in the concept that sparing the rod spoilt the child. Gwen had no doubt that she would have been very harsh to Lady Fanny's daughter, all in the interests of making her a proper young lady. She'd occasionally seen the victims of constant beatings at Cavendish Hall. They flinched away from every sharp noise and were suspicious of comforting words. And they were often so scared of the magic within them that they repressed it until it burst out and wreaked havoc.

She straightened up and looked back at the manor. Had Lady Fanny's daughter developed magic?

It was simple enough to identify a magician, although she had no idea if Susan Willingham had ever been tested, but almost impossible to predict when a magician might actually come into his or her powers. Gwen herself still flinched in horror from the memory of the day her magic had come to life, even though she had continued to learn as much as she could without guidance from anyone else. Other magicians had developed their powers when stressed, threatened with death ... or, in one case, drinking himself into a stupor. That particular development had been *nasty*. It had taken days to clean up the mess.

"So," she said, as evenly as possible, "how did Madame Constant treat your daughter?"

"I thought she was doing a good job," Lady Fanny said. "She was hired to teach reading and writing, Latin and history ... and music. Susan was doing well ... I didn't see any problems."

Gwen felt her face harden. She hadn't seen any problems either, not with how she'd treated the servants in Crichton Hall or with the more generalised treatment of the poor and powerless in London. It had taken Jack to open her eyes and show her just how badly the latter had suffered under the aristocracy. There were far too many others in the aristocracy who never saw it at all.

Or think the poor deserve it for being born poor, Gwen thought, bitterly. Even now, it was hard for someone to climb out of the gutters and into the middle class, let alone the aristocracy. There was just so much weighted against them.

"Of course you didn't," Gwen said. "Was Susan the only person Madame Constant was teaching?"

"Well ... Susan was the only person she was hired to teach," Lady Fanny said. "But Jo, Susan's personal maid, would often join the lessons."

Gwen lifted her eyebrows. It wasn't uncommon for the servants to join the lessons, particularly the servants who were no older than the children of the house, but it sounded oddly charitable for Madame Constant. If the woman had ever had a charitable thought in her life Gwen would have been astonished. She'd always seemed more interested in hammering her idea of how to behave into her victims' heads.

Maybe I misjudged her, she thought, sourly. *She didn't try to teach me for very long.*

She looked down at the body again, studying the damage. Up close, it was clear that Madame Constant hadn't ever had children of her own. Gwen was no medical expert – most of the textbooks she'd devoured had actually concealed truths, rather than revealed them – but the older woman looked too thin to ever have children. A nasty thought struck her, but a quick check revealed that Madame Constant was definitely female. Embarrassed, she ignored the coughing sound from Lady Fanny and straightened up. If *she* could pass for a man from time to time, why couldn't a man pass for a woman?

It's harder to fool women than men, she reminded herself, sharply.

"I think hiring her was a mistake," she said, as she looked down at the dead body. "And your daughter is likely to carry the scars for a long time to come."

Lady Fanny blanched.

Gwen ignored her as she turned back towards the fire. The firemen had intensified their efforts, yet the flames had neither faded away nor spread to the rest of the house. She fought down the urge to laugh as she realised the truth, then started to walk towards the flames, Lady Fanny scampering after her as if she didn't quite believe what Gwen was doing. Up close, the heat was almost overpowering. Gwen felt sweat trickling down her back as she walked closer to the flames.

"Stay here," she ordered.

Bracing herself, she pushed forward, closing her eyes and concentrating her mind. The heat grew even hotter, but it didn't burn her flesh. Smirking to herself, she kept walking forward, feeling the heat fading away to nothingness. An illusion, she told herself, as she opened her eyes. Someone with more power than skill had created a small fire and an illusion of a very large one. There was almost no real damage at all.

Outside, she heard shouting from the firemen, none of whom seemed to be able to believe their eyes. Gwen felt a moment of sympathy for them – they'd probably be blamed for soaking the house in their struggle against the illusory fire, once the illusion stopped affecting them too – then she stepped forward, into the schoolroom.

Inside, she was greeted by a scene from hell.

Chapter Three

he schoolroom itself wasn't too different from the study Gwen had used when she'd been a child, working her way through an endless succession of tutors. There was a pair of desks, a larger desk for the teacher and a blackboard, which had been badly marred by the fire. A shattered cane lay on the floor, smashed into a dozen pieces. One cupboard lay smashed open, revealing dried food and bottled water. She looked over towards the shattered window and winced, inwardly, as she saw the blood and the mangled remains of Madame Constant's arm. Her body had been blown right out of the window.

Should have asked where they found the body, stupid, Gwen told herself, as she searched the room quickly and efficiently. There was no sign of where the children – both children – had gone, but someone could easily have taken a small amount of dried food from one cupboard and a bottle of water from another. It suggested that there had been no preplanning before they'd fled, Gwen noted, although it was impossible to say for sure. The whole affair might have been carefully planned in advance.

Pushing the thought aside, she looked over towards the other door and realised that it led to a second room. Peeking through, she discovered the mangled remains of a Grand Piano – one that had probably cost more than Gwen made in a year – lying on the floor, ripped to pieces. It didn't look as though it had been blasted by a Blazer, something that worried Gwen more than she cared to admit. If Susan was displaying more than one kind of magic, it suggested she was a Master Magician, just like Gwen. Finding another Master would be a relief, but it would also be a major problem. The elements within the Royal Sorcerers Corps that hated the idea of *Gwen* leading them would have a collective fit when they realised that her successor would also be female.

And not a very patient one, she thought, remembering her own music lessons. *Those* hadn't lasted very long. She simply hadn't had the patience to learn to play anything, not even the penny whistle Dave had given her as a joke. But then, the whistle hadn't lasted any longer than the short time it had taken Lady Mary to realise she had it and confiscate it, despite their joint complaints. Anyone would have thought she considered whistle-playing undignified for a young lady.

Gwen smiled at the thought, then walked out of the door and onto the grass. Ahead of her, there was a forest. It was nowhere near deep and dark enough to hide someone indefinitely, Gwen noted, but a child might not realise that. Gwen felt a moment of envy – she would have loved to run through the woods as a little girl – and kept walking until she was at the very edge of the forest. Closing her eyes, she concentrated on her magic, trying to feel out where the children might be hiding. But there was so much life running through the woods that it was impossible to detect them ... if, of course, they hadn't run further. Gwen silently prayed they hadn't as she opened her eyes and walked into the woods. A great many things could happen to children in the countryside, few of them good.

She smiled again, feeling an odd sense of relaxation as she strode deeper and deeper into the small forest. Birds sang in the trees overhead, reminding her just how much she enjoyed her few excursions out of London. A sudden bitter pang tore at her heart as she recalled that *Olivia* had loved those excursions too, the chance to be alone together. But Gwen's work didn't allow her much time to merely enjoy herself.

I'll find you, she promised silently. *And whoever took you will not live to regret it.*

She paused as she heard the sounds of birds flapping away from a distant corner of the forest. Something had scared them ... and birds in the countryside were smart enough to be afraid of humans. Hunting was a common pastime, even for the poorest in the land; a bird could feed a family if it was caught in a trap or even shot down with a shotgun. She turned and walked towards the sound, not bothering to conceal her approach. If the children tried to run, she could catch them with her magic. And besides, they would probably react better if she was clearly not trying to sneak up on them.

There was a sudden sound ahead of her, followed by a shape darting from a hiding place and running away from her. Gwen reached out with her magic and caught at the figure, then felt a sudden surge of resistance; frighteningly powerful, but utterly unfocused. Susan had no real training, Gwen noted, as she lost her grip on the girl. And then a burst of magic flashed out of a bush and over Gwen's head. She ducked, almost a moment too late, as part of the mystery unravelled itself in front of her. There were two children and both of them had magic.

"Enough," she called, putting as much command into her tone as she could. Her mother had taught her how to issue commands to children and inferiors, after all, warning the young Gwen never to even *hint* that she thought they might not obey. Weakness invited challenges and attacks. "We need to talk."

There was another burst of magic, stronger this time. Gwen caught it on her own magic and watched as the flash of light broke up harmlessly. She gritted her teeth, then pushed as much Charm into her voice as she could. If her growing suspicions were correct, neither of the girls would have any real defence against blunt Charm.

"Come here," she ordered, feeling the magic rippling through the air. "Now."

There was a long pause, then two young girls appeared from the undergrowth, staggering towards her as if they were trying to resist her command. One of them was wearing a fine dress that looked as though it had seen better days; it was muddy, torn and ripped ... and probably completely beyond repair. Gwen shuddered to think of what Lady Mary would have said if she'd ruined a dress that cost upwards of twenty pounds. She looked enough like Lady Fanny that Gwen had no hesitation in placing her as Susan Willingham.

The other wore a tattered dress that seemed to have survived the brief excursion to the forest better than Susan's.

She was smaller and thinner, with a nasty scar on her cheek that looked to have been made recently, perhaps within the last few hours. Her dark face and plainly braided hair suggested a poorer origin than Susan, although it was clear by the way the two girls clung together that they were definitely friends. Gwen felt a cold sensation in her chest as she worked out the remainder of the story, recalling the damage she'd seen in the schoolroom.

"You must be Jo," Gwen said, trying to appear as unthreatening as possible. Inspector Lestrade's methods for interrogating suspects might work on burly men, but they would probably reduce young children to tears. "My name is Gwen. I'm the Royal Sorceress."

Susan's eyes went wide. "You're *her*?"

Gwen smiled, then levitated herself a few inches above the ground. "Yes," she said, simply.

Susan's face went very dark. "I'm not going back," she said. Raw sparks of magic flickered around her face, each one glittering with deadly energy. "I won't go back."

"Probably not," Gwen said. She sat down on the ground, heedless of the mud staining the seat of her trousers, then motioned for the girls to sit down too. "But I do need to know what happened today."

Jo looked alarmed. "It was my fault," she said, softly. "Everything was my fault."

"No it wasn't," Susan snapped. She caught Jo's hand and held it, tightly. "It was the crone's fault."

Gwen smiled. "Madame Constant?"

"Yeah," Susan said, rebelliously. She would probably have been told off for slurring her words like that, if she'd been in the schoolroom. "It was all her fault."

"Then tell me what happened," Gwen urged. "Start from the beginning, then go on until the end."

The two girls exchanged helpless glances, then Susan started to talk. "We were supposed to learn together," she said. "Jo was meant to learn too. But every time I made a mistake, the crone punished Jo. Look at her face."

Gwen gritted her teeth. A whipping boy ... girl, in this case. She'd read about them in books, but she'd never heard of anyone actually trying in real life. An aristocratic boy would be given a friend from the poorest level of society, someone who could be whipped if the young aristocrat acted badly. In theory, the aristocrat would be overcome with guilt at watching his friend get punished and stop acting badly. Gwen suspected that, based on some of the more entitled aristocratic magicians she had to deal with as Royal Sorceress, the noble youth would as likely watch and laugh as his friend suffered. Not everyone was moved by someone else's pain, particularly those who had never been taught basic empathy in the first place.

"Jo could make things move," Susan said. "I used to love watching her make our dolls dance, but when the crone found out she struck her across the face. And then I ... I ..."

Her voice trailed away. Susan and Jo might have come from very different places in society, but their shared magic – even if they weren't completely aware of it – would have brought them together. Gwen felt another sudden stab of envy, wishing she'd had a magical friend, even if she'd only been a serving girl. But she'd never met another magician until Master Thomas strode into her life and recruited her to serve as his successor.

"Your magic burst out," Gwen said, softly. "What happened?"

"There was fire everywhere," Susan said. "The crone fell backwards, her shoulder was burning; Jo threw her out the window, but the flames kept spreading. And we ran ..."

"You can't run any longer," Gwen said. She stood up, using magic to sweep the mud off her trousers. "But I don't think you will be staying here either."

Susan stepped in front of Jo protectively. "I won't let you take her to jail," she said, with an icy firmness that reminded Gwen of several much older girls. "I *won't!*"

Gwen was tempted to point out that it had been *Susan* who'd killed Madame Constant, but held her tongue. Susan had been conditioned to believe that her friend would pay the price for her misdeeds; even now, even after someone had died, she still clung to the fear of her friend being punished. Perhaps the whole concept of the whipping girl worked after all ... Gwen considered it briefly, then shook her head. It was cruel, heartless and thoroughly unpleasant.

"She won't go to jail," Gwen assured her. In crimes involving magic, it was *her* judgement that was final. Besides, it was an established point of law that accidental magic, unleashed when the magician first came into his or her powers, wasn't a criminal offence. "But neither of you can stay here. You'll both come back with me to Cavendish Hall."

Susan's eyes lit up. "You'll teach me how to use magic?"

"Someone definitely will," Gwen said. The British Empire needed all the magic-users it could get, even if they happened to be born female. Besides, Susan was clearly powerful if she'd managed to create such a realistic illusion and leave it in place for several hours. "And you won't have to worry about Madame Constant ever again."

She watched as the two girls shared a long hug, knowing that one day they would realise that they'd actually killed someone, no matter how unpleasant she'd been. Gwen herself hadn't handled the knowledge very well, other magicians had merely taken it in their stride or had a few rough nights before they came to terms with the simple fact that they'd ended a person's life. It wouldn't be easy for them at Cavendish Hall – they'd be younger than most of the students there – but it was the best place for them. Besides, it would be a good chance for them to catch up on their education in other matters too.

"Come on," she said. "The carriage is waiting."

The two girls followed her out of the forest, muttering excitedly to one another. Gwen smiled, remembering her own enthusiasm when she'd finally been allowed to attend Cavendish Hall, then schooled her face into a blank expression when she saw Lady Elizabeth striding across the lawn towards them. Her face was set in grim lines that Gwen recognised from her own mother, the absolute certainty that she was in the right combined with a reluctance to listen to anyone else. Gwen gritted her teeth in cold determination, then stepped forward. There was no point in handing someone like Lady Elizabeth the chance to get their word in first.

"I will be taking the girls back with me to Cavendish Hall," she said, shortly. "Susan and Jo will each be allowed to bring one bag of clothing and a handful of treasured possessions. Any ... paperwork relating to Jo will be transferred to me and handled by my lawyers. There will be time, later on, for Lady Fanny to visit her daughter, but for the moment it is vitally important that she finds her feet at Cavendish Hall."

Lady Elizabeth's mouth fell open. No sounds emerged.

"Go get a bag of clothing each," Gwen ordered the girls. She waited for them to run past Lady Elizabeth and into the manor, then looked back at Lady Elizabeth. "Madame Constant's body is to be placed in a sealed coffin and shipped to Cavendish Hall for disposal, along with any personal possessions she might have. I shall expect to receive them within the next two days."

"But ..." Lady Elizabeth finally managed to stammer.

Gwen gave her a completely sweet, completely fake smile. "You will say nothing about the affair here to anyone," she continued. Lady Elizabeth could probably be relied upon to cover the whole affair up, but it was well to make sure of it. "The firemen will be dismissed, with enough money to ensure they hold their tongues. I do not want a single *word* to get into the broadsheets. Do you understand me?"

Lady Elizabeth stared at her helplessly. She would have been less surprised, Gwen suspected, if Gwen had slapped her across the face. The whole idea of a young woman, someone younger than her, actually issuing orders was preposterous, at least to her mindset. Young ladies were there to be guided by their superiors, taught how to think and act and not to question those who happened to be significantly older. And, if a young lady dared to act independently, her reputation could be ruined.

But Gwen was immune to all such threats. Lady Elizabeth had nothing to threaten her with ... and they both knew it.

"Yes," she said, finally. She drew herself up to her full height and glowered at Gwen. "You will see to it that the serving girl does not return?"

Gwen thought about pointing out that Susan was also a magician, but kept the thought to herself. Lady Elizabeth was probably old enough to remember when magic was new and freakish, a feared change in the world ... and she probably still believed that it was almost exclusively a male domain. It was stupid, Gwen knew; there had been female magicians long before she'd come into her own powers. But people like Lady Elizabeth were very good at ignoring things that didn't fit into their worldview. Clearly, she'd never even realised that Jo was a magician until the truth had been rubbed in her face.

"Yes," she said, instead. Jo's existence produced other problems, but they could be handled, particularly with the help of a good lawyer. "You will send me all the documentation concerning her, of course."

Lady Elizabeth nodded, without arguing. Gwen was surprised. Jo's youth suggested that she had been bought from her family, as easily as one would sell a dog or a cat. The thought made Gwen sick, even though she knew that Master Thomas had effectively done the same thing when he'd convinced Gwen's family to let him take her to Cavendish Hall. But while Gwen had been groomed to be the Royal Sorceress, Jo had been treated as a slave. It was illegal, now, to sell children. And yet, it wasn't enough to stop the trade.

And Jo was lucky, Gwen thought, remembering some of the places Jack had shown her. It had been a bitter education, an introduction to a world she'd never known existed. *There are far worse places to be than here.*

Gwen stepped away from Lady Elizabeth, had a brief conversation with Lady Fanny, then waited for the two girls to come running back into the open. Susan had a small leather case of clothes, but Jo was carrying hers in a cloth bag. Somehow, Gwen wasn't surprised. No matter the letter of the law, Jo's owners had been under no obligation to do more than provide her with the bare minimum. It was sickening, but it was legal.

"Get into the carriage," she ordered, then followed them in herself. "Cavendish Hall, please."

The driver cracked the whip. Moments later, the carriage shuddered to life and started to take them away from Willingham Hall. Gwen sat back in her seat, then sighed inwardly. The brief diversion had helped her to forget Olivia, but now the incident was over she remembered her missing daughter. Looking at the two girls in front of her, she couldn't help wondering if she'd have to adopt them too. And yet the thought was almost a betrayal of her first daughter.

She looked down at her pale hands, shivering. Just where *was* Olivia?

Chapter Four

Well," Ivan said. "Did you enjoy your voyage?"

Olivia glared at him, but the Charmer only laughed. He'd kept her in her cabin most of the time, bound by chains far harder to escape than ropes or handcuffs. She knew, intellectually, that she should be screaming with rage or fear, but instead she felt nothing apart from a damnable coolness that provided no impetus to break his commands. He'd done a very good job of binding her to him.

He held out a hand as the ship rocked, slightly. "Come with me," he ordered. "I have some surprises for you."

Olivia followed him, helplessly. She didn't want to know what a Charmer might consider a nice surprise – she'd met too many Charmers to believe that any of them were decent people – but he wasn't giving her a choice. Outside, she heard the sound of people calling out in the same language she'd heard every day, one that remained frustratingly impenetrable to her. And then she shivered as a gust of wind blew down the corridor, setting her teeth to chattering madly. She'd slept in the open in London in winter, when she hadn't stolen enough money to get a place to stay in the Rookery, but this was far colder. She couldn't help wondering if she was about to freeze to death.

"In here," Ivan said, as the boat rocked again. "I think we found the right size of clothes for you."

Olivia frowned as she saw a set of clothes on the bed. Most of them looked heavier than anything she'd seen in London, including a coat that seemed to be made of fur. She stepped closer, wonderingly, and saw a bathtub at the far side of the room. It was steaming so enthusiastically that she realised the temperature was dropping rapidly.

"Have a wash, then dress," the Charmer ordered. "Make sure you put on everything, including the coat and gloves. The weather outside is colder than anything you might have experienced in London."

Olivia opened her mouth to ask, even as her body went to work, if he was going to watch her undressing. Instead, before she could ask, he stepped out of the hatch and locked it behind him. Olivia muttered a word she'd learned in the Rookery under her breath, then undressed and dumped her clothes in the corner, cursing her own weakness. Once, she would have thought nothing of wearing the same clothes for weeks, without washing them. But that had been a different life in the Rookery, where being smelly and generally disgusting could save a person's life.

She washed herself as thoroughly as she could, then sorted through the clothes, trying to figure out in what order to put them on. The aristocratic girls at Cavendish Hall had their own ideas about wearing underwear, even though no one actually saw them wearing it, but she had never bothered to try to follow their fashions. Even though Gwen had given her an allowance for buying clothes, she rarely used it. Instead, she'd salted it away in various places, just in case. It had been months before she'd managed to stop hiding food too.

In the end, she pulled them on in what seemed the most suitable order, leaving the fur coat and gloves until last. The outfit felt alarmingly hot after she'd washed herself, but she had a feeling that it would be necessary. Two minutes after she'd finished, the door opened and Ivan looked her up and down. She must have passed muster, because he beckoned for her to follow him rather than suggesting she change her clothes. A moment later, they were climbing up the ladder to the deck.

The cold hit her like a sledgehammer, despite the coat and gloves. Olivia felt herself shivering helplessly as she staggered over to the rail and looked around. There were actual pieces of ice floating in the water! She stared in frank disbelief – she'd never seen ice before, at least not floating on the water – and then looked towards the looming city in the distance. One look was quite enough to tell her it wasn't London. The style of buildings was completely different.

She sucked in her breath sharply, the icy air stinging her throat. Some of the buildings at the water's edge looked like slums, if more firmly built than any of the slums outside London, but others looked strange, almost alien to her eyes. Many of them were topped with onion-shaped structures, painted gold so they reflected the light of the sun. The boat shuddered slightly as it altered course, taking them past an island that held a brooding fortress. Olivia had seen the defences built along the Thames to defend London, but these were different. Guns pointed in all directions, including towards the city itself. It struck her, suddenly, that the fortress was intended to oppress the city as much as defend it.

It wasn't the only visible defence, either. Hundreds of guns were placed on both sides of the river, in position to engage any warship planning to raid the city. Behind them, soldiers wearing dark uniforms marched and drilled, intent on keeping themselves warm through constant motion. Olivia remembered snowy days in London and shivered in sympathy, wondering just how long the snow remained on the ground ... wherever she was. The soldiers couldn't have a very easy time of it.

Ivan came up beside her and leaned against the railing, staring out over the city. Olivia looked across at him, then remembered she was allowed to ask questions. He hadn't tied up her tongue, merely told her never to speak to anyone apart from him or someone he introduced to her. Shaking her head, she opened her mouth and posed the question he'd so far refused to answer.

"Where are we?"

"St. Petersburg," Ivan said. Clearly, he'd decided there was no point trying to keep her in the dark any longer. "Russia."

A piece of ice struck the boat gently as his words sank in. Olivia knew little about geography outside London, but she had seen the map that hung on Gwen's wall. Russia was beyond the Franco-Spanish Empire, separated from the French by a handful of German states. If London was a tiny dot on that map, Russia had to be thousands of miles from Britain ... she found herself shivering again as the sheer distance they'd travelled sank in, piece by piece. She couldn't stay with them, not when she knew what they intended to do with her. If they'd just wanted to hurt Gwen, they would have killed Olivia by now. But even if she broke free, where would she go?

"Oh," she said, cursing the damnable coolness once again. "And what are we doing here?"

"Closest safe port," Ivan assured her. The boat shuddered as it hit yet another piece of ice, which was nudged aside by the impact. "I don't think the ice poses much danger."

He straightened up and pointed towards a large wharf, near yet another gun emplacement. A handful of men wearing large fur hats and carrying rifles were waiting for them, standing beside a number of horses. Olivia smiled at their appearance – horsemen seemed to share the same sense of arrogance and daring-do, wherever they were – but then realised that they were her escort. They would take her to her final destination. And then ... she didn't know precisely what would happen, but she was sure it would be nothing good.

She thought desperately as the boat made its slow way towards the pier, but nothing occurred to her. Russia ... she didn't know the language and knew no one who did, apart from Ivan and his crew. She knew a little French and Latin, thanks to the tutors Gwen had hired, but she knew no Russian at all. If she broke free, she wouldn't be able to talk to anyone, no matter who they were. Unless there was a British Embassy somewhere in the city ... Gwen *had* been charged with assigning magicians to embassies, and St. Petersburg *was* a capital city, so it was likely that there *was* an embassy somewhere close by. But where?

A dull thump echoed through the ship as it docked. A handful of men, who were shirtless despite the cold, scrambled off the boat and hastily tied it up to the pier. Olivia found herself staring at them, wondering how they could endure the cold long enough to do their work without freezing to death. Ivan could have told her, she assumed, but he was already speaking in Russian to another man. After a moment, he motioned for her to follow him towards the gangplank. Gritting her teeth, Olivia trailed after him, uncomfortably aware of the stares following her. The crew must have known they'd had a strange passenger, but just how much did they actually know about her?

That's why he wanted me to stay in my cabin, she thought, as she reached the edge of the gangplank and started down carefully. It was icy and felt dangerously unstable under her feet. *He didn't want the crew to know more than they absolutely needed to know.*

She lost her footing, suddenly, and landed on her bottom. As the horsemen laughed at her, she slipped and slid to the foot of the gangplank, silently grateful she hadn't fallen into the water. Ivan held out a hand, helped her to her feet and patted her back in a gesture she suspected was intended to be paternal – or possessive. She glared up at him, then looked over at the horses. Gwen had offered to teach her how to ride, but they'd never actually managed to get around to it. Olivia hadn't minded too much. She'd always found horses a little scary.

"These are Cossacks," Ivan said, by way of introduction. "Loyal to the Father Tsar: his most dedicated servants."

Olivia eyed the Cossacks with some interest, recalling tales she'd heard in London. They were brutal, she'd heard, utterly ruthless when it came to serving the interests of the Tsar. And they were monsters in human form ... although she knew better than to take that too seriously. The first time she'd met a Frenchman, she'd honestly expected him to look like a giant monkey. But instead he'd just looked like any other foppish nobleman.

Up close, the Cossacks were definitely hairy, with long beards and moustaches that looked straggly and uncut. Unlike the men in London, who seemed to pride themselves on neatly-trimmed facial hair, they seemed utterly unkempt. And yet there was a sense of intelligence about them that bothered her, combined with a brutality matching that of the goons she recalled from the Rookery. The Cossacks would do *anything* for their Father Tsar, she realised, including taking her to her final destination.

Ivan caught her arm and propelled her towards one of the horses. Olivia shrank back as the brute snorted at her, shuddering in fear. The Charmer laughed, picked her up and practically threw her over the horse. For a terrifying moment, she thought she was going to fall over the other side of the beast and felt absolute panic gripping at her mind. She caught hold of the saddle and managed to pull herself into the seat, her mind feeling clearer than it had in days. The panic had broken Ivan's commands!

She forced herself to remain calm as the Cossacks raised a shout and started to canter down the road, along a street crammed with people, wagons and even a handful of small carriages. The Cossacks didn't stop for anything; they just charged forward, knocking people and wagons out of the way by force. Olivia saw an elderly woman knocked over by one of the horses, then a pair of young boys jumping back to avoid a blow from a whip. The horses only picked up speed as they kept running faster and faster, as if they were being chased by the hordes of hell. Or, perhaps, as if they didn't want to get caught in a single place. It made sense, she told herself, as she saw a woman with two children being whipped across the face. Olivia had seen horsemen brought down by crowds during the Swing ...

A set of wagons was suddenly in front of them, accidentally blocking the road. Olivia saw her chance and pulled hard on the reins, bringing the horse to a sudden stop. Moments later, she jumped off the beast's back, landed as well as could be expected and started to run, silently thanking the god she didn't really believe in that the Russians had made her wear trousers. Running in a dress was damn near impossible, at least for her. She had a suspicion that the Grand Mistresses of Fashion preferred to make it harder for young women to run away from them.

She heard shouts behind her as she plunged into an alleyway, silently praying that the street was too narrow for the horses. Like any London alleyway, it was jammed with homeless people trying to get what comfort they could by huddling together. She jumped over a pair of women who looked to be around fifty years of age, but were probably a great deal younger – people aged quickly on the streets – and then turned down another alleyway. Behind her, the shouts were growing louder. She darted onwards, turning into yet another alleyway, then out onto a main street. A handful of stallholders eyed her darkly for a long moment, then looked away as she ran past them and down the street.

And then someone caught her hand. Olivia swung around, just in time to see a young boy who couldn't have been much older than she was. She threw a punch at him anyway, only to discover that he was just as experienced in dirty fighting as her; he sidestepped her punch, then slammed a haymaker into her jaw. Olivia tasted blood in her mouth as she stumbled, then heard the sound of hooves behind her. Moments later, a Cossack slipped off his horse, yanked her to her feet and slashed his whip across her back. She felt it even through the clothes she'd been ordered to wear.

She'd been beaten before, during her time on the streets. It was just one of the occupational hazards of living rough, at least for boys. Girls had it worse, which was at least partly why Olivia had worked hard to pose as a boy. She'd believed herself inured to being beaten. But six months of living in relative luxury and freedom – Gwen had never raised a hand to her and she'd forbidden the tutors to even think about corporal punishment – had weakened her more than she'd realised. The brief beating hurt far more than it should have done. She didn't want to think about what it would have felt like if he'd stripped her naked before laying into her. She found herself lying on the road, grunting in pain, as the others came up to join her captor.

"That was foolish," Ivan said. Olivia stared up at him mutely, then spat at him. "Even if you managed to get away from us, where would you go?"

He rolled her over, caught her hands and pulled them behind her back. Moments later, she felt solid metal cuffs clicking around her wrists, so tightly that she could feel the flow of blood to her hands being constricted. She wondered, briefly, why he didn't simply Charm her back into dumb obedience, then realised that he had to be having doubts about the efficiency of his powers. If he hadn't scared her so badly earlier, she would have remained his obedient servant. Or his slave. She wanted to cry as he clicked a second pair of handcuffs around her ankles, then hauled her to her feet.

Walking almost any distance would be damn near impossible.

One of the Cossacks said something in Russian. Olivia looked over at him and realised he was holding the boy who'd caught her by the arm. Ivan said something back and the boy tried to run, too late. The Cossack drew his sword – it looked like a cutlass – and sliced through the boy's throat in one smooth motion. Olivia felt sick as the boy's body tumbled to the ground, and for the first time, found herself missing the Bow Street Runners. They could be brutal and utterly unsympathetic, but they didn't kill informers out of hand. But, she realised bitterly, the Cossacks had killed him just to issue a warning to her. They would happily kill her too, if they didn't need her.

Ivan picked her up, then threw her over the horse. Olivia gasped in pain as her bruised jaw hit the side of the animal, then realised that she was going to be carried in this absurd and undignified position. Ivan slapped her bottom, hard enough to sting, then walked around and shook his head sadly at her. He didn't look a bit regretful, merely annoyed. Olivia wanted to spit at him again, but resisted the temptation. It was clear that they were quite prepared to beat her into submission if they considered it necessary.

She scowled at him, then winced as he patted her head and strode back to his own horse. If there was one thing the Rookery had taught her, it was the value of patience. There would be other opportunities to escape, she told herself firmly, and when she saw them she would take them. And next time she would be much more careful. Her next escape would be far better planned.

The horses neighed as their riders let out a shout, then started cantering forwards again. This time, thankfully, there were fewer people in the streets, but there were still some very close calls. Olivia finally closed her eyes, forcing herself to block out the sights around her. All she could do, she told herself bitterly, was wait. There would be a chance, she was sure ...

... Because the alternative was giving in to despair.

Chapter Five

wen heard the marching band long before the players – and the soldiers – came into view, parading along Pall Mall to the beat of a drum. The 5th Highland Regiment was marching to take up positions in the southeast of England, preparing for a French invasion – or to invade France itself, if that seemed possible. Hundreds of children were clapping and cheering as the Highlanders marched onwards, while young women – even some clearly of aristocratic birth – were smiling and waving at the soldiers. Gwen had to smile, despite the constant fear for her daughter in her heart. Every girl seemed to love a soldier.

But then, Britain doesn't have a large standing army, she reminded herself. The Royal Navy – the impregnable wooden walls defending the nation – made it impossible for an enemy to actually land on British soil. Or so they hoped; she knew enough about recent developments in naval technology to fear that the Royal Navy might have some rough days ahead. But the last time Britain had had a standing army, it had proved as unpopular as they now were in France, Russia and even the German states.

She smiled as she stepped inside the café and sat down, taking a seat in the window. It was a fashionable place these days, although Gwen had no idea why. A handful of middle-aged women sat in one corner, pretending not to look at the soldiers, while several young couples were chatting at private tables. They were being chaperoned, Gwen noted, just to make sure that nothing untoward happened before their weddings. It would be a major scandal if a couple was found to have anticipated their wedding night. And it would almost always be blamed on the girl. Women were often charged with being unable to control their emotions.

Gwen snorted, remembering Sir Charles. *She* had been attracted to him, she had to admit, but she hadn't allowed her emotions to blind her too far. It could easily have been a great deal worse, she knew, if she hadn't realised just how carefully he was manipulating her. And then ... she would probably have lost her position, if not her life. A husband would be in an excellent position to stick a knife in her back.

She looked over at one of the young couples – the girl younger than Gwen, the boy a couple of years older – and felt a stab of envy. They were innocent, ignorant of the responsibilities of adulthood, the responsibilities that Gwen had assumed when Master Thomas had died. She wouldn't trade her position for a return to aristocratic life, not as a young lady under her mother's thumb, but it would be nice to be able to put the burden down for a while. And yet there were no other Master Magicians ready to take her place. As far as she knew, she was the last Master Magician to be discovered.

The door opened, revealing Lord Mycroft and another man. Gwen rose to her feet and smiled at Lord Mycroft, then nodded at the newcomer. They were very different; Lord Mycroft was immensely fat, with the sharp lines of his face weakened by overeating, while the stranger was tall and thin, with short ginger hair and a neatly trimmed goatee. Gwen eyed him sharply, remembering Sir Charles. The newcomer had the same air of infinite competence around him as her would-be seducer and betrayer had had. But she'd killed him in the end.

"Lady Gwen," Lord Mycroft said. "Thank you for coming."

Gwen sat down and waved to the waiter, who bustled over with a set of menus. Lord Mycroft ordered tea and cake without bothering to actually look at the list of foods; the stranger inspected it minutely, before ordering tea and scones for himself. Gwen ordered a cup of tea for herself, then settled back in her chair. It was rare for Lord Mycroft to be seen outside his office, his apartment or the Diogenes Club. For him to come to a café, no matter how fashionable, and meet her there was extraordinary. It suggested that there was some deeper purpose to the meeting.

"Lady Gwen," Lord Mycroft said. "Allow me to introduce you to Sir Sidney Campbell, one of my special agents."

Sir Sidney stood up and bowed, then took Gwen's hand and kissed it lightly. "Charmed," he said. His voice held a faint Scottish accent, suggesting that his family came from the other side of the border, but that he'd spent enough time in England to lose the brogue. "It is always a pleasure to meet a magician."

Gwen smiled, despite herself. "You're one of the few people who would say that," she said, dryly. "Far too many people find magicians unwanted company."

The waiter returned, carrying a large teapot, a jug of milk, three cups and a plate of cakes and scones. Gwen couldn't help noticing that one of the cups was significantly smaller than the other two, suggesting that she was expected to have a feminine quantity of tea. Rolling her eyes at the casual preconceptions of a world that expected her to be dainty and ladylike, she stood and poured tea for all three of them, then settled back with the smaller cup. There was enough liquid in the teapot for her to have another, if she felt like it.

Perhaps it does make sense, she thought reluctantly, as she saw one of the older women heading toward the toilet in the rear. The lady's dress would be hard to take off, particularly if she were in a hurry. Gwen's trousers were so much more practical, but, for women, propriety almost invariably prevailed over functionality and good sense. *We aren't even expected to go to the toilet outside our homes.*

Lord Mycroft took a piece of carrot cake, then settled back in his seat. "There have been developments," he said, without preamble. "We have managed to trace Olivia's path out of England."

Gwen felt as though a knife had stabbed her heart. If the kidnappers had wanted to kill the only known Necromancer, they could have killed Olivia at any moment and made their escape. And if they'd wanted to trade her for ransom, they wouldn't have taken her too far from Cavendish Hall. But if they'd wanted to use her magic for themselves, they'd have to take her out of the country itself.

"Good," she said, keeping her voice under tight control. "Where did she go?"

"We traced her passage to the docks," Lord Mycroft said. It would have been his brother who had done the legwork, Gwen knew. "She was transferred to a steamer that was, officially, bound for Sweden. Unofficially, we have good reason to believe she was headed for Russia."

Gwen muttered a very unladylike word, just loudly enough for them to hear. Lord Mycroft showed no reaction; Sir Sidney merely smiled, as if she'd amused him in some way. Gwen eyed him suspiciously, then sat up in her seat. Russia. The only consolation was that Olivia hadn't been taken directly to France. After the French had been blamed for the necromantic outbreak in London at the height of the Swing, they'd certainly want to get their hands on a living Necromancer.

But Russia ... almost nothing was known about the Russian magical program, although everyone assumed the Russians definitely *had* a program. The French had been hampered by the Catholic Church's resistance to any form of magic, even magic in the service of the Church; the Russians, as far as she knew, would have had no such obstacles barring their path to magical research. If the Russians wanted a Necromancer ... what did they intend to do with her? No matter who was behind the kidnap, no one would have gone to so much trouble unless they had a use in mind for a Necromancer.

"We don't know," Lord Mycroft confessed. Gwen scowled. As always, he could read her expressions and use them to divine her thoughts, far more subtly than the average mind-reading Talker. "But we don't think the Russians have anything good in mind."

Gwen couldn't disagree. "We need to mount a rescue mission," she said, firmly. "Whatever the cost, we have to get her back."

Sir Sidney smiled. "Searching all of Russia for her would be tricky," he observed. "The Russians control more territory than us, most of it harsh and desolate wasteland."

Lord Mycroft gave him a sharp look, then nodded. "We don't intend to just let this pass," he said. "But finding her is going to be a challenge."

Gwen wanted to place her head in her hands. He was right, she knew; they were both right. It would be impossible to compel the Russians to return her daughter without the threat of force and she knew the global situation well enough to understand that threatening Russia wouldn't be very easy. Indeed, it would trigger the war that everyone expected to start at any moment.

"There are options, however," Lord Mycroft continued. "I do not believe that they would have taken her very far from St Petersburg, their capital. The Tsar likes to keep control of his Empire firmly in his own hands. It is quite likely that their magic-research program is based there."

He took a breath. "At the moment, it is unclear if the Russians are actually planning to join the French in war against us or not," he said. "The Russians have been giving contradictory answers to everyone who asks, British or French. On one hand, they want to wage war on the Turks; on the other, they're reluctant to risk another war after the last one turned into a disaster."

Gwen nodded. Russia's disastrous recent history had nearly brought about the collapse of its Empire. Tsar Nicolas I had considered the Ottoman Empire a prime target for violence, perhaps with the long-term aim of recovering Istanbul for the Orthodox Faith. But the Ottoman Sultan had been reforming his armies and regenerating his Empire's moribund economy and the results had surprised everyone. The Russians had been forced back, whole armies had been destroyed and dangerous tremors had run through the entire state. In the end, the Russians had conceded defeat. No one realistically expected them to accept it indefinitely.

"The Russians have agreed to accept an ambassadorial party to discuss matters," Lord Mycroft continued, breaking into her thoughts. "On the surface, this party will be intended to raise the possibility of keeping Russia out of the war, should it actually break out."

"And with a covert purpose of finding my daughter," Gwen said.

"Precisely," Lord Mycroft said.

Gwen looked down at the pile of cakes for a long moment, then looked up at him. "I will be accompanying the mission," she said. "I am the most capable magician available."

Lord Mycroft looked embarrassed. "We would prefer not to send you openly," he said, after a long pause. "You are simply far too recognisable. Besides, the Russians would be very wary of you and your powers. We don't want to spook them when war is so close."

Gwen glowered at him, rebelliously. "I'm not leaving my daughter there," she snapped. "I will go if you like it or not."

"I'm not asking you to leave her there," Lord Mycroft said. He leaned forward. "You just can't go as *yourself.*"

"You want me to go in disguise," Gwen said. She looked down at her mannish trousers and winced, inwardly. It was simple enough to pose as a man for a few short hours, but the longer she tried to maintain the deception, the more cracks would appear in the act. There was no way she could go to a male toilet – at least a public one – without revealing her true sex. "As what?"

Sir Sidney leaned forward. "As a maid," he said, flatly. "No one ever pays attention to the help."

He was right, Gwen knew. As a child, she'd thrilled to stories of brave adventurers making their way through enemy territory disguised as servants, traders or even religious figures. Sir Charles had seemed a dream come true, when they'd met, simply because he reminded her of her childhood heroes. And he'd actually dressed up as a native and walked among them, sight unseen. A servant would pass unnoticed where a noblewoman would be blindingly obvious.

"To be precise, we will insert you into the Ambassador's retinue as one of the maids," Lord Mycroft said. "He will be unaware of your true identity, as will everyone else on the mission with the exception of Sir Sidney. You will be required to play the role until you find Olivia and recover her, whereupon Sir Sidney will assume command of the mission and act as he sees fit. We have provided sealed orders for him to use if necessary."

"I see," Gwen said. "It sounds like a workable plan."

She smiled. There was no point in trying to direct events from thousands of miles away. The British Empire had expanded so far by trusting the officers on the spot to make the right decisions, without high command peering over their shoulders. Besides, even with Talkers, the situation could change remarkably before the updated orders could be sent, let alone received.

"It won't be easy," Lord Mycroft warned. "You will have to act the part of a maid until the time comes for you to reveal yourself."

Gwen swallowed as the full implications sank into her mind. Young Ladies of Quality did almost nothing for themselves, certainly nothing relating to household chores. Her mother had tried to teach her how to sew, which was seen as a ladylike occupation, but she hadn't taught Gwen how to manage a household, at least beyond issuing orders to the help. Maids, on the other hand, were expected to work from dawn to dusk for only a minimum wage. If they complained ... well, there was no shortage of young women trying to make a living from serving their social superiors. A maid could be kicked out of the house if she dared to utter a single complaint.

And there were worse things that could happen than merely being yelled at by the Lady of the House.

"I understand," she said. It was for Olivia – and for the British Empire. If Sir Charles and Sir Travis could endure torture for the sake of the nation, she could play the role of a lady's maid. "I can do it."

Lord Mycroft gave her a long considering look. Gwen couldn't read minds, but she was sure she knew what he was thinking. She'd grown up in High Society, even if they'd considered her a devil-child rather than a normal young lady to be shaped and moulded into the ideal debutante and socialite. It might have been a hard life at times, but it was nowhere near as bad as being one of the lower classes. She had been isolated and largely abandoned to a stream of tutors, yet she hadn't been kicked, beaten or forced to sell her body to survive. And her magic had ensured she was effectively unmarriageable.

"Good," Lord Mycroft said, finally. "Sidney?"

Sir Sidney smiled, tapping his fingernails as he spoke. "The mission will be headed by Lord Henry Standish, who has been appointed the Special Ambassador to Russia," he said. "Lord Standish has considerable experience in important negotiations and, more importantly, has been granted a certain amount of leeway in the hopes we can bribe the Russians to stay out of the war. I will be accompanying him as Military Attaché and his second, in the event of him needing to be overruled at some point."

He paused. "Lord Standish will be selecting the remainder of his staff from his cronies," he added. "We won't know who they are until the mission is ready to depart, although we have some good guesses. However, he will also be taking his wife, Lady Marie" – Gwen twitched at the reminder of her mother's name – "and his ward, Raechel Slater-Standish."

Gwen frowned. She paid almost no attention to the society pages, but she knew of Raechel Slater-Standish from overhearing conversations in Cavendish Hall. The young woman had been blazing a path through High Society, scandalising it and giving plenty of older women the vapours. Gwen had to admire someone like that, even though it was the sort of release she could never allow herself, not now. Anyone who managed to irritate so many of High Society's Grandes Dames deserved to be admired.

"I believe the young lady is seen as rather a trial," Lord Mycroft said. There was a faint hint of amusement on his face. "You may wish to keep an eye on her at all times."

"Because she'll try to cause trouble?" Gwen guessed. It seemed likely, but she could think of another explanation. "Or because you want to recruit her?"

"It is a possibility," Lord Mycroft agreed, neutrally. "She's smart, but totally indiscreet. We might not consider her a suitable candidate for recruitment unless she grows up."

He paused, then took another cake. "I won't say that this will be easy, Lady Gwen," he said, in an almost paternal manner. There was a grim look in his eyes that betrayed his concern. "You will find it far harder than investigating a murder or an outbreak of magical power. And there's no guarantee of success."

"I know," Gwen said. The thought of failure was terrifying. But so was the thought of staying in Cavendish Hall, waiting for news. She had to do something, anything.

Going to Russia would put her closer to her daughter. "I'll do it."

"Good luck, then," Lord Mycroft said. He rose ponderously to his feet. "Sir Sidney will fill you in on the remaining details, then make preparations to insert you into the Ambassador's household. I suggest you take a few days to learn your duties. It will not be easy to pick them up once you leave the country."

He paused. "And I would also suggest you make preparations for your death," he added. "There is a very strong chance you won't be coming back."

Gwen swallowed, nervously. "I understand," she said, through a suddenly dry mouth. "I won't let you down."

Chapter Six

livia shivered helplessly, testing her bonds to no avail. It had been four days, she thought, since they had left St Petersburg and started to gallop further to the east. Every day, it had grown colder and colder, with snow falling around the horses and making the beast carrying her as cold and miserable as Olivia herself felt. Every night, they'd stopped at a way station where she'd cuddled up to the fire while Ivan, the bastard, renewed the commands he'd put in her head. Right now, even if she'd somehow managed to break her bonds, she doubted she could make it away from the Cossacks. Her legs would simply refuse to obey her.

There were shouts from the Cossacks. Olivia allowed herself the fantasy of someone attacking the small convoy and rescuing her, but it was not to be. Instead, they cantered up towards a low dark building, barely visible through the driving snow. The horses came to a halt in what she assumed was the courtyard, and their riders dismounted. Olivia tried to glare at Ivan as he came up beside her and started to loosen the ropes binding her to the horse, but she didn't have the energy. It was all she could do to stand upright when he tugged her off the horse and down to the ground.

"I suggest you don't try anything stupid here," Ivan said, as he undid the cuffs binding her ankles together. "There is literally nowhere to run."

Olivia looked around as he half-led, half-pulled her towards the dark building. The snow was falling faster now, making it hard for her to see more than a couple of yards before her view was completely obscured. She had even less idea of where she was than she'd had at St Petersburg, where she might have been able to find help. There was no point in trying to run, even if he hadn't implanted so many commands into her head that they were giving her nasty headaches. She gritted her teeth as she saw a door yawning open in front of her, then stepped through. It banged closed behind them a moment later, leaving the Cossacks outside.

"They don't mind the weather," Ivan said, when she asked. "This is a light summer day for them."

"I don't believe you," Olivia said.

Ivan snorted, rudely. "This isn't that far to the east – or the north," he said. "There are places further to the north where winter is always dark and cold – and snow is always to be found on the ground. We send rebels, traitors and dissidents there to count trees."

He smiled, as if he'd made a joke. Olivia didn't understand. Ivan didn't seem to care. Instead, he carefully removed her cuffs, freeing her hands for the first time in four days. Olivia rubbed at her wrists frantically, remembering horror stories about criminals who had been arrested and then forgotten about for a few hours. They'd sometimes lost their hands completely, simply because the cuffs had been too tight. Ivan hadn't cuffed her that hard, but her wrists were still sore.

"Get your coat off," he ordered, as he led her into another room. The heat slapped her in the face, hot enough to make her sweaty and uncomfortable. A large bathtub, steaming furiously, was set in the middle of the room. "Get undressed completely, have a long soak, then walk into the next room. There'll be new clothes there."

Olivia nodded, cursing her treacherous fingers as they started to undo the buttons on her coat, which was dripping with melting ice and snow. Ivan gave her a sharp look, warning her against doing anything stupid, then walked out of the door, leaving her alone. Olivia immediately tested the door and discovered, not entirely to her surprise, that it was firmly locked. The Russians clearly weren't taking any chances with her. Cursing her mistake, in words that would probably have earned her a long lecture from Gwen, she finished undressing and climbed into the water.

It was gloriously warm, warm enough to make her entire body relax. She had to force herself to get out of the water after what felt like hours and stumble into the next room. Inside, there was a large bed, a robe that reminded her of a dressing gown, and a set of combs and hairbrushes. She puzzled over the robe before realising that it would provide absolutely no protection at all, if she managed to get out of the building. It was just another chain binding her to the Russians, more subtle than the others.

She pulled the robe on, then looked around. A book lay on top of a table, written in English, but she couldn't parse out the words. It was probably something religious, she decided, as there was a cross on the front. But she had never had any inclination to follow a formal religion, not when too many of their priests preferred to tut-tut at people like her rather than do anything to help. There was a knock at the door and she turned, just in time to see a thin-faced woman with long dark hair pushing a trolley into the room. Olivia's stomach rumbled as she smelt food.

The woman said something Olivia didn't understand, then removed a small bowl from the trolley and placed it on the table, along with a wooden spoon that looked absurdly small for its role. A moment later, she added a glass of brown liquid and a second glass, containing water, then bowed to Olivia and made her way out of the room. Olivia hesitated – it was easy enough to stick a drug in food – then shook her head and sat down in front of the table. If the Russians wanted to drug her, they could just have their Cossacks hold her down while they forced poisons or sedatives down her throat. They didn't need to dupe her into taking the drugs herself.

She found that she was ravenous as she devoured the bowl of dark purple soup, although she wasn't entirely sure what it actually was. It tasted faintly of beetroot, she thought, with some additional flavours she didn't recognise. But she felt human again when she had finished the bowl and decided to risk a taste of the brown liquid. It was a kind of beer, she decided, before she put it to one side. She'd never cared for alcohol on the streets and she wasn't about to start now. The water tasted oddly flat, but it was definitely safe to drink. Or so she hoped.

There was another knock on the door when she'd finished, suggesting that she was under observation. Olivia winced – she'd grown far too used to privacy in Cavendish Hall and she'd tried to stay alone on the streets – and then watched helplessly as the door opened. At least the Russians probably weren't interested in her as anything other than a Necromancer. The streets were utterly unsafe for young girls and boys.

"Good afternoon," Ivan said, as he entered. "I trust you are feeling better?"

Olivia nodded, not trusting herself to speak. The mixture of food and a hot bath had left her feeling pleasantly warm, almost completely relaxed. They might have put something in the food after all, she realised dully, or it could have just been relief at being out of the snowstorm and somewhere warm again. There was no way to know.

"I'm glad to hear it," Ivan said. He smirked, then held out a hand. "Please would you come with me?"

Her body obeyed before Olivia had quite realised what he'd said. She cursed inwardly as she took his hand and allowed him to lead her through the door, as if he was courting her like a highborn girl. Outside, there was nothing but stone walls leading into the distance. The massive, solid walls helped keep the heat in, she realised, as he led her down the corridor. She listened as hard as she could, but heard nothing apart from their footsteps. The rest of the building was as silent as the grave.

They stopped outside a heavy metal door, which opened slowly at an unseen command. A faint smell reached out towards her, one that made her recoil in sudden disgust. Ivan placed a hand on her back and pushed, forcing her into the room. There was no sign of anything that could produce the smell; the room was almost completely bare, save for a wooden table and a man standing behind it, wearing monkish robes. His beard was long, his face was pitted and scarred and his eyes glinted with a devilish insanity.

"You must be the Necromancer," he said, in cracked and broken English. His voice was curiously high-pitched, as if he wasn't quite mature. "I am Gregory. You are the answer to our prayers."

Olivia shuddered as he came around the table and advanced on her. It was all she could do to hold her ground. She hadn't felt so threatened since she'd been caught by a man who'd thought she was a young boy. Up close, Gregory smelt faintly of urine, as if he never bothered to wash. Once, she knew, the smell wouldn't have bothered her. Few people on the streets bothered to wash. Now ... it disgusted her.

"You will assist us," he said, patting her on the head. She cringed away from his touch, feeling oddly violated. "Your gift will serve the Father Tsar."

"No," Olivia said, gathering herself. "I won't help you raise the dead."

"I can make you help us," Ivan pointed out from behind her. "You would become our slave."

"Charm has its limits," Olivia countered, remembering what she'd been told by Gwen, after one Charmer had played a nasty trick on her and the other girls. "You can't push me too far."

"You'll help us," the monk said. The unshakable confidence in his voice chilled her to the bone. "If you refuse to help us of your own free will, you will be made to help us."

"You wouldn't have such a precise control over my gift," Olivia said, bracing herself for the beating she was sure would come. Gwen had forbidden her from ever using her talents without direct orders from her or Lord Mycroft. She'd heard stories of Necromancers who had practiced on dead rats and insects, but she'd never disobeyed Gwen's orders. "If you warped me into your slave, you wouldn't be able to control it."

"I imagined you would need more ... convincing," Gregory said. He grinned at her – the most disconcerting expression she'd yet seen – and then turned and led her towards the door in the far wall. "Let me show you something of what we're doing here."

Olivia hesitated, but a push from Ivan sent her forward. The smell grew stronger as Gregory opened the door and led the way into a much larger room, crammed with beds and tables. A dull moaning noise filled her ears as she saw men and women lying naked on the beds, tied down with solid chains. They were muttering endlessly in Russian, their bodies twisting and turning as they struggled against their chains. She stopped dead, feeling revolted; she'd heard stories of bedlams in Britain, but surely they weren't as horrific as the sight before her now.

"Good, good," Gregory called, addressing a pale-skinned woman wearing a white gown and a cold dead expression. "I think that last one is showing signs of improvement."

The nurse eyed him blankly, then leaned over one of the prisoners and injected her with a noxious-looking liquid. The thrashing girl started to babble in Russian, then urinated helplessly on the bed. Olivia stumbled backwards, horrified and disgusted. Only Ivan's grip on her arm kept her from running out of the door and trying to escape. Instead, she was pushed through the ward and into the next set of rooms.

"It is our task to unlock the secrets of magic," Gregory said, as he closed the door behind them. The moans, screams and endless muttering cut off abruptly. "Those who have gifts can either serve the Father Tsar or wind up here, having their gifts examined. Sometimes we learn something truly interesting."

He smiled, then waved them into the room. Instead of living victims, it held dead bodies in various stages of dissection. A handful of men in white robes moved from body to body, carefully drawing samples of blood and brain tissue from the corpses before shipping them onwards to an unknown destination. Olivia had thought herself no stranger to dead bodies – she'd seen more than her share before she'd discovered the true nature of her magic – but this was truly revolting. It reminded her of the story of the doctor who had hired footpads to waylay and kill people for him to dissect in front of his students. She had never been quite sure if there was any truth in it, but she'd seen enough horror to suspect it might be true.

"There are changes in the brain tissue when someone becomes a magician," Gregory informed her. He sounded pleased as they walked through the room and passed through a third door. "Some of the stronger magicians may actually have to adapt their brains to handle their powers – and if they fail, they are killed by their own magic."

Olivia shuddered. Some of the students at Cavendish Hall had been taken to the bedlam nearby, where they'd been shown magicians who had been driven mad by their own powers and had to be confined for their own safety. Most of them were Talkers, their powers so strong that they couldn't prevent themselves from reading every mind in range ... and were completely incapable of separating out their own thoughts from everyone else's. It would be more merciful, she suspected, to kill them outright. They had no hope of ever leading a normal life.

Gregory smiled at her. "We take samples from magicians and insert them into non-magicians, just to see what will happen," he said, as they entered a long corridor. "Sometimes, the results are quite interesting."

Olivia shuddered, again. This time, each of the patients – the victims – had their own cell, locked and barred against escape. Some of them were clearly mad, others just sat on the floor and stared at nothing. She shivered as she saw a Mover, floating in the centre of his room with his eyes firmly closed, a handful of toys orbiting his body like the Moon around the Earth.

"That one worked out surprisingly well," Gregory said. "He developed magic after the surgical infusion of brain cells from a natural-born magician."

Olivia said nothing as she glanced into the next cell. A girl sat on the bed, barely seven years old, clutching a ragged pillow as if it were a teddy bear. Her eyes were wide, staring at nothing – or, perhaps, at something only she could see. Olivia gritted her teeth as she saw the girl's bones clearly visible, despite her tattered dress. The poor thing was slowly starving to death.

"You need to feed her," she said. "She's hungry!"

"She also needs to learn to cooperate," Gregory said. "And so do you."

There was a cold evenness in his voice that made her glare at him, then look away in disgust. Beatings would have been kinder. Olivia looked back at the girl and started in shock; the child was staring directly at her, dark eyes firmly fixed on her face. She babbled something in Russian, then collapsed onto the bed. Olivia looked away, bitterly. There was nothing, she knew all too well, that she could do for the girl.

The next cell held a young boy who seemed to be in constant motion, jumping around his cell and giggling unpleasantly. He smirked at Olivia, then made a rude gesture towards the two older men, who seemed unmoved. The cell after him held a pair of middle-aged women, holding hands so tightly they seemed to have fused together. Beyond them, there was a man who was staring down at a single stone on the floor, as if it were so fascinating that it had captured all of his attention.

And the next cell held a man who seemed to be arguing with himself. Olivia stared, noting the sudden shifts in body language as his various personalities fought for dominance, then looked away as all of the personalities started hurling abuse at Gregory. It was chilling to hear how they would switch from a brave personality to one too timid to do more than mutter insults just loud enough to be heard. The personality seemed to change completely, every few seconds.

Gregory merely smiled and hurried Olivia past what seemed an endless succession of cells, each one containing a different horror. She honestly couldn't understand just what would drive someone to create such a nightmare. Even the loan sharks in the Rookery hadn't been so monstrous.

"Tell me," Gregory said. "Have you seen enough?"

Olivia wanted to scream at him. Instead, she forced herself to speak almost normally.

"What do you want from me?"

"We want you to raise the dead," Gregory said. "And help us with our research for the Father Tsar."

He turned to face her, dark eyes boring down into her own. "If you cooperate, you will be treated well," he said. "Food, drink ... even company, if you wish it. But if you refuse to cooperate ..."

Olivia glared at him. "You'll torture me?"

"No," Gregory said. "We will cut out your brain and use it to create other Necromancers."

Olivia hesitated. Despite what the monk had told her about the young Mover, she didn't know if it was possible to create a magician, certainly not through using any form of medical technique. Gwen had certainly never told her that such a thing was possible, although Doctor Norwell had been keen to remind her that they had barely scratched the surface when it came to studying magic. Maybe it was possible after all.

And if she refused, she would have no chance to escape.

"I'll cooperate," she said, promising herself that she would escape as soon as possible. "But I need to rest before I start using magic."

"Certainly," Gregory said. He patted her on the shoulder, then looked up at Ivan. "Take her back to her room."

Chapter Seven

 feel absurd," Gwen muttered, as she looked at herself in the mirror. "This isn't *me*."

"But it is what the well-dressed maid is wearing," Irene Adler said, primly. She delivered a hearty slap to Gwen's back. "The last thing you want to do is draw attention to yourself."

Gwen groaned. The last time she'd worn a dress had been at the Fairweather Ball, when Sir Charles had escorted her. It had been hideously difficult to put that ball gown on without help from her maid, something that struck her as an attempt to make it harder for the wearer to surrender their chastity. By comparison, the maid's dress was simpler, darker and designed to be donned without assistance. It would have been suitable if it hadn't been so irritating.

She looked at her reflection again. The dress was black, save for a white triangle over her breasts that drew more attention to their shape than she would have preferred. It was easy enough to hide her chest in her normal garments – the male eye rarely noticed anything out of place unless it was obvious – but the maid's outfit made it impossible to hide her femininity from roving eyes. The lower half of the dress was black, falling down to her ankles; her stockings covered the rest of her legs from male eyes.

"Consider yourself lucky," Irene said. "If you were a maid in France, you would be expected to display your charms and assets in no uncertain way."

Gwen flushed, realising that Irene was reading her thoughts. Irene's talents for disguise, mind-reading and simple powers of observation made her a formidable agent for the British Government, despite having been born female.

No one was quite sure where she'd come from, but as an Opera Singer she could get into all kinds of strange places without raising eyebrows. Gwen glowered at her friend, then erected her mental barriers. Irene shrugged, quite unabashed.

"But you managed to get the dress on," Irene said, once Gwen had spun around to make sure it *stayed* on. High Society had chatted for years about a poor noblewoman whose dress had fallen off in the midst of a dance. She'd never managed to live it down. "And now you have to work on your duties."

She led Gwen into the next room, where a pile of clothes had been dumped on the floor. "Get those packed away," she snapped, her voice becoming imperious. "And then get the floor cleaned, you lazy woman!"

Irene kept up the torrent of verbal abuse as Gwen carefully picked her way through the clothes, packing them away into the suitcase, or into the wardrobes and boxes. Some of them required special treatment, which Irene explained in-between sneering at Gwen, others could just be dropped in drawers and left alone. Gwen had never quite realised how ignorant she was about some things until Irene patiently explained how to pack a suitcase properly. She'd never had to pack a bag of clothes for herself in her life. The only thing she'd ever packed was books.

"Not too bad," Irene sneered, when Gwen had finished. She picked up the bag, opened it and dumped the clothes back onto the floor. "Do it again."

Gwen glared at her. Irene lifted a hand, as if she was about to slap her across the face. "Don't look at me like that, girl," she snapped. Her voice softened. "And believe me, showing any hint of disrespect could get you into real trouble."

"I know," Gwen muttered, as she started to repack the bag. She *knew* Irene was playing a role, just as *she* would have to play a role, and yet she didn't know how she was going to keep her calm during the mission. One snap too many from Lady Standish and she might just give in to the temptation to hurt her. "This isn't going to be easy."

Irene sat down on the bed and crossed her legs. "It never is," she said. "Most people don't pay any attention to maids, but those that do often have bad intentions. You'll probably find yourself ducking unwanted attention if you're sighted by the young bucks."

Gwen shuddered. Courtship among the nobility was a careful process, with the parents involved at every stage ... but young men had options denied to young women. They could go to brothels, find a lover on the side ... or simply mess around with the serving girls. It was, in theory, sinful, but the prospect of committing a sin had never stopped any of the young men she knew. She'd heard too much about their conduct in brothels, the brothels she wasn't supposed to know about, to take it lightly.

"And what do I do," she asked, "if they do ... try to attend upon me?"

"If they don't try to restrain you, say you have to meet your mistress," Irene said. "If they do, feel free to fight. But try to avoid using magic."

"That isn't going to be easy," Gwen muttered. Magic was part of her now, just as it had been from the very first day she'd used her powers. "I use magic instinctively."

"That's the problem," Irene said. "If you use magic, you can bet your last shilling that the victim will tell the world – and then you will be in some trouble."

"I know," Gwen said. She finished packing the bag, then passed it to Irene. "How is this?"

"Better," Irene said. She stood up in one smooth motion, then peered down at Gwen. "Why aren't you showing the proper respect?"

She went on before Gwen could answer. "You are the servant in this relationship," she snapped. "You are to curtsey whenever one of your social superiors enters the room, then keep your eyes down unless you are specifically told to meet someone's eyes. You do not have the right to even look at them without permission. Do you understand me?"

Gwen hastily bobbed a curtsey. Lady Mary had spent years trying to hammer the proper way to curtsey into her daughter, but Gwen had never really bothered to practice. Irene didn't look too displeased, she noted in some relief. A girl from the country, looking to make her fortune in the city, wouldn't be expected to have a perfect curtsey. But she would be expected to learn as quickly as possible.

"Good," Irene said. She marched over to the fireplace, then turned to smile at Gwen. "You should consider yourself lucky you're not working for Chinese John. I had to put up with him for a few days and he was a right ..."

She grinned. "You probably shouldn't learn that word," she added. "You certainly shouldn't use it anywhere near Lady Standish."

Gwen smiled back. "What was he like?"

"What was he like, *My Lady*," Irene corrected. "He spent two years in China, trying to convince the Ming to allow British traders to enter their ports and trade with the Chinese population. He took a Chinese bride and brought her back to England. And he expected his servants to perform the kowtow every time he walked past."

"The kowtow?" Gwen asked. "What's that?"

Irene knelt, then leaned forward in a deep bow until her head was touching the floor. "He liked having his servants respectful," she said, as she straightened up. "Lady Standish, thankfully, doesn't seem to be quite *that* obsessed with being treated with respect."

Gwen scowled. She'd asked her mother about Lord Standish and his family and had received, in response, a detailed report of everything High Society was saying about them. It was actually more detailed than half of the intelligence reports she'd read, which had convinced her to show it to a few of her subordinates and note that it was precisely what she wanted in a proper report. But it hadn't made encouraging reading. Lord Standish was very much a career-driven man, not unlike Gwen's father, while Lady Standish was obsessed with her social position. And their ward clearly had a sharp tongue and a desire for independence that matched Gwen's.

They could have married her off by now, she thought. As their ward, Raechel Slater-Standish could have been pushed into marrying anyone willing to take her. But if some of the rumours about her conduct were actually true, she would find it hard to marry anyone unless her uncle issued a fairly considerable bribe. *And instead they're taking her to Russia?*

"You can lay this fire," Irene said. "And then light it properly."

Gwen nodded and set to work. Laying a fire, at least, was something she could do. Some of the servants had refused to enter her room when she was a child, even though she'd promised not to try to hurt them. The young Gwen had had no choice but to learn to set up her own fires, just to keep her room warm. And when her mother had refused to allow her to keep any firelighters in her room, she'd learned how to use magic to start the fire. In hindsight, that might not have been the smartest thing to do. It would have been distressingly easy to accidentally set the entire house on fire.

"Excellent," Irene said. "And you know how to make tea and coffee?"

"Yes, My Lady," Gwen said.

"Let us see," Irene said. She nodded towards a table, where a tray of cups, a jug of milk and a kettle were waiting for them. "Heat up the water, then make us some tea."

Gwen concentrated, using magic to heat the water. Moments later, Irene slapped her bottom hard enough to sting. "Magic," she snapped, as Gwen glared at her. "You *can't* use magic!"

"I'm sorry," Gwen muttered. She rubbed her behind, then picked up the kettle, placed it over the fire and waited for it to heat up. Using magic to heat water had been one of the earliest tricks Master Thomas had taught her, using the prospect of accidentally scalding herself as a teaching tool. "I don't know if I can do this."

Irene leaned forward. "If you want to call it off, say so now," she said. "Lord Mycroft will not object to sending someone else."

Gwen winced. Part of her wanted to give up now, particularly when she still made stupid mistakes that could betray her identity. And she knew the odds against finding Olivia were terrifyingly high. But she couldn't simply abandon her daughter, no matter the odds. Olivia was her child, in everything but blood. What sort of mother would she be if she just left Olivia to her fate?

"I'll go," she said, as the kettle started to boil. She took it off the fire and poured hot water into the teapot, then stirred it carefully. Her father liked his tea strong, if she recalled correctly, while her mother preferred a weaker brew. The maids had always had to time their work carefully, just to avoid upsetting one or the other of their employers. "I'm damned if I will leave her there all alone."

She poured milk into the cups, then added the tea. Irene took one of the cups, sniffed suspiciously, then nodded and started to sip it. Gwen took her cup, then hesitated, unsure if she should sit down or remain standing. It was vanishingly rare for the servants to drink with their masters. But Irene had said they would both drink ...

"Sit down," Irene said, quietly. Gwen realised her shields had started to slip and flushed again. "You're not doing too badly, but there are other things you need to know."

She picked up a sheet of paper and made a show of reading it. "Your file states that you spent two years working for Lord Carmichael prior to his departure for the colonies," she continued. "You won't be branded as completely inexperienced, but Lord Carmichael was somewhat eccentric and no one will expect perfection. More to the point, you were also responsible for taking care of his daughter, Heather Carmichael."

"Yes, My Lady," Gwen said, remembering the file. Lord Carmichael was not only eccentric, he was one of Lord Mycroft's personal friends. If Lady Standish contacted him to ask for Gwen's references, he would provide her with a glowing account of a maid who had spent half of her time serving as a substitute mother. "Do you think that will help?"

"You spent time supervising Heather," Irene said, dryly. "Lady Standish will probably ask you to keep an eye on her ward too."

She cleared her throat. "You're nowhere near as polished as they will expect," she continued, "but that's understandable. However, you will have to answer some very uncomfortable questions. For a start, why is your hair so short?"

Gwen scowled. The truth was that she'd had it cut short to keep it from getting in the way – and to make it easier to pass as a man. But that wasn't something she could tell Lady

Standish, not if she wanted her mission to be a success. It would be far easier to simply claim that Lord Carmichael had insisted that she cut her hair, even if fashion had been in favour of long-haired girls at the time. It was unlikely that anyone would expect a maid to join the Trouser Brigade – or care much if she did – but it was probably best to avoid any mention of politics.

"Because my previous employer, Lord Carmichael, insisted I cut it short, My Lady," she said, finally. "I complied with his instructions."

"Good enough," Irene said. She paused, significantly. "There will be other questions, I'm afraid, some of them quite ... intimate. She will ask if you have a male friend, for example, and I would advise you to answer no."

Gwen coloured. The only man who had shown any real interest in her had been Sir Charles – and he'd been more interested in ensuring that no one found out that he'd murdered Sir Travis, rather than Gwen herself. She still had nightmares about the moment he'd rendered her powerless, leaving her almost at his mercy. It would be a long time before she trusted a man enough to let him get so close to her.

"Yes, My Lady," she said.

"There will be other problems," Irene warned. "She may slap you, if she feels your work is not suitable, or punish you in other ways. You will have to tolerate it until the time comes to reveal yourself."

"I know," Gwen said. She had more pain tolerance than the average women – either through magic or through constant exercise with male magicians – but she knew just how much pain a single slap could inflict. And it would be worse, she suspected, if the person slapping her thought of her servant as an object, rather than a person. "I can handle it."

"You won't be Lady Gwen, Royal Sorceress, or even Lady Gwen, daughter of Lord Crichton," Irene reminded her. "You will merely be Gwen, a humble girl from the country, someone without friends or family in London. There will be no protection for you if Lady Standish decides to take her problems out on your body. And I suspect you will not be able to use magic to stop her without revealing the truth."

"I know," Gwen repeated. Irene had mentioned the same fact time and time again. But she was right. The use of magic would be disastrous. "I won't fail."

"Be sure that you don't," Irene said. "Do you have your bag packed?"

Gwen nodded. It held a pair of dresses, a handful of underclothes and a small bag of money, enough to pass for her final wages from Lord Carmichael. There were no books, something she regretted deeply, but a maid from the country wouldn't be expected to read. Even now, after the Swing, only a small percentage of the country's population knew how to read and write. The charities that were trying to educate the poor were simply not successful, not when the poor resented being lectured to as well as being taught. After what Jack had shown her, Gwen was not particularly surprised.

She shucked off the maid's outfit and packed it away in the bag – she'd change again before she met up with Mycroft's agent – and pulled her trousers and shirt back on, taking care to cover her breasts. Irene watched without a trace of shame, something that made Gwen blush furiously, realising just how little privacy she would have while she was working as a maid. She'd had more privacy in her father's house, even though her mother had thought nothing of barging in each day to wake Gwen.

"Good luck," Irene said. "And if you run into real trouble … just remember, you asked for it."

Gwen made a face, then surprised herself by giving the older woman a hug. Irene smiled at her, then waved goodbye as Gwen walked over to the door and stepped through. Outside, she took a long breath and started to walk through Cavendish Hall, pausing outside each classroom long enough to assess progress. In one room, Susan and Jo were being taught the basics of life at the Hall, before moving on to discuss their powers and how best to improve them. They'd do well, Gwen was sure. They were both powerful and devoted young women.

She hesitated on the edge of the door, half-wondering if she should step inside and say goodbye personally, then decided against it. There was no point. When she came back, there would be time to catch up with the two girls ... and if she didn't come back, it would be better if they had fewer emotional ties to her. Shaking her head, she hurried down the stairs, picked up her bag from the office and walked out of the door. Her carriage was waiting for her there.

"Good luck," Doctor Norwell called. The dignified older man knew that Gwen was going after Olivia. He just didn't know any of the details. "Come back soon."

Gwen nodded, then clambered into the carriage. It was time to go.

Chapter Eight

ord Mycroft had warned her that Madame Hampton was strict, but Gwen hadn't realised just how strict until she'd actually *met* the woman. Madame Hampton was tall and thin, with lips that were permanently pressed together in disapproval. She clearly wasn't scared of the Royal Sorceress – or anyone, really. Gwen would have been impressed if she hadn't known that the woman ruled the lives of countless young girls with an iron hand. And that she also worked for Lord Mycroft.

"You look barely acceptable," Madame Hampton stated, her lips thinning still further. "But you must learn to fit in as quickly as possible. I will not have my reputation ruined by you."

Gwen nodded, impatiently. Madame Hampton's job was hiring young women from the country, training them to serve as everything from maids to social assistants and then hiring them out to aristocratic families. She took a share of their wages, Gwen knew, to the point where the girls found it very hard to save enough money to separate themselves from her, no matter how hard they worked. It was only borderline legal, even after the Swing, but like so much else, it wasn't precisely moral. But how else would the girls find clients for their services who didn't have unpleasant motives?

She smiled. It was clear that Lord Mycroft had used Madame Hampton to insert an agent into someone's household before, if only because of how little time it had taken to arrange the whole business. Gwen had expected it to take longer, somehow, but Madame Hampton had simply recalled Gwen's predecessor and seen to it that the girl would find another place in a different household, clearing the way for Gwen. Gwen suspected that Lady Standish would be annoyed by the timing – they were about to leave for Russia, after all – but there would be no help for it. Besides, she was getting Gwen's services practically free of charge.

But not without bed and board, Gwen thought. She was entitled to a place to lay her head, food to eat and a day of rest, although she'd been warned that the last of these might not be honoured, not when Madame Hampton was more interested in making money than taking care of her girls. *And I won't be staying for long.*

"You need to pay attention," Madame Hampton snapped. Gwen realised, guiltily, that Madame Hampton had been talking while Gwen hadn't been listening to her. "Lady Standish will not be happy if you fail to listen to her commands."

"Yes, My Lady," Gwen said, grimly. It was going to take all of her patience to endure weeks of servitude to Lady Standish. At least she'd be in a position to take revenge afterwards, if it was as bad as Irene feared. "I understand."

"Glad to hear it," Madame Hampton said, darkly.

She picked up a long dark coat and draped it over her arm, then rang the bell. When the foreman arrived, she directed him to bring the carriage around to the front entrance and make ready for departure, then she put a few more questions to Gwen as they waited. It was a shame, she mused out loud, that Gwen couldn't cook, but it was perhaps unsurprising if she claimed to have worked for someone like Lord Carmichael. He'd had a separate cook to ensure that he received meals precisely how he liked them, rather than trusting it to his daughter's maid. Gwen's fictional duties had mainly revolved around his daughter.

"Just remember to keep your eyes downcast at all times," Madame Hampton added, as she led the way out to the carriage. "And do precisely as you are told."

Gwen winced inwardly as she followed Madame Hampton into the carriage and sat down. She had never been very good at doing what she was told, something her mother had bemoaned regularly when Gwen had been a young girl. But she had obeyed Master Thomas, right up until she'd realised just how far he was prepared to go to stop the Swing. She'd been too horrified to trust or obey him any longer.

"It's harder to get good horses these days," Madame Hampton said. She lifted her eyebrows as the carriage jerked into life. "I trust you know how to ride?"

"Yes, My Lady," Gwen said. She recalled her cover story and smiled. "My Lord taught me so I could ride with his daughter."

Madame Hampton's lips thinned again as they moved out onto the street, where there were only a handful of carriages making their way down the centre of the road. Gwen wasn't too surprised. The army was calling up horses as well as men, paying bounties for every horse that was brought into the army barracks and signed over to military authority. Unsurprisingly, horse thieves were having a field day. No one was checking ownership papers too closely, no doubt in the belief that anyone stupid enough to lose a horse didn't deserve to keep it. In the long run, she suspected it would cause no end of problems, but for the moment there seemed to be nothing anyone could do about it.

She forced herself to relax as the carriage headed towards Lord Standish's residence. As an important government minister, he was entitled to a small house in Pall Mall as well as a larger mansion on the outskirts of London. Gwen remembered, suddenly, that her brother David lived in Pall Mall, when he wasn't with his wife in their own manor. If he saw her ... she shook her head. David was too straight-laced to recognise his sister in maid's clothing, even though they'd practically grown up together. Imagination had never been one of his strong points.

But he's been working for Lord Mycroft, she reminded herself, as shouts from outside suggested that the carriage had almost run over someone in the street. *He might be having his mind expanded.*

The carriage lurched again, then came to a halt in front of a large stone building. It was much smaller than any aristocratic hall, but – located at the heart of London – it would be much more expensive than almost anything smaller than a castle outside London. Gwen recalled her father's complaints about the cost of owning a home in London and smiled at the memory, recalling the time she'd asked why he wanted to live in the city. Her father had spluttered and then explained that London was the capital of the British Empire. As a businessman, even though he might try to hide his occupation, he couldn't afford to be anywhere else.

Madame Hampton stepped out of the carriage with all the dignity of her station, waited for Gwen to climb down in a ladylike manner, then strode up to the door and knocked, sharply. Gwen, who had expected her to use the tradesman's entrance, blinked in surprise, then schooled her features into respectful dispassion as the door opened, revealing a man wearing a butler's outfit. He was the blackest man Gwen had ever seen, his white teeth glittering as he smiled at them. There was a fashion for negro butlers, Gwen recalled, after the Royal Navy had brought a number of former slaves to London. It was one of the many pointless fashions that occupied her mother's time.

"Madame Hampton, here to see Lady Standish," Madame Hampton said, briskly. "I have brought the new domestic."

"Come in," the butler said. His dark eyes flashed over Gwen, missing nothing. "Her Ladyship is in the study."

Gwen kept her face impassive as they walked down a long carpeted corridor, wondering just how much the butler had seen in her. Servants were trained to read faces and body language in ways few aristocrats could match, just so they could tell when their masters and mistresses were in good moods. It was quite possible that the butler – Romulus, according to the file – had realised that something wasn't quite right about her. Or that he merely thought she wasn't up to the standards expected of anyone working for the family. Gwen had known butlers who were worse snobs than their masters.

Romulus stopped in front of a door and knocked, sharply. "Madame Hampton, My Lady," he said. There was a long pause, then he opened the door. "Please, enter."

Under other circumstances, Gwen suspected she would have rather liked the study. Three of the four walls were lined with bookshelves, while the fourth was decorated with maps and paintings of the vast domains ruled by the British Empire. Many of the books actually looked interesting, which was more than could be said of the books in her father's study. But she didn't dare look at the bookshelves when Lady Standish was in the room. Her Ladyship was already rising to her feet, her expression unreadable. Gwen hastily bobbed a curtsey, then looked down at the floor. She couldn't look up until Lady Standish wanted her to look up.

"This is Gwen," Madame Hampton said, after the two women had exchanged insincere greetings. Madame Hampton fell some way short of being Lady Standish's social equal and that rankled both of the women. "She is experienced in some matters, inexperienced in others, but you will find her suitable."

"I should hope so," Lady Standish said. Her accent was pure aristocracy, without even a trace of anything from outside London. Even Gwen's mother hadn't had so perfect an accent; hell, even the *King* didn't have such an accent! "Let me see the file."

There was a rustle of paper as she took the file and skimmed through it, then stepped forward until she was standing right in front of Gwen. "Look up, girl," she ordered. "Let me take a look at you."

Gwen looked up, careful not to meet Lady Standish's eyes. She was tall, not much older than Gwen's mother, with a thin disapproving face, dark red hair shading to grey and an air of absolute certainty that probably irritated everyone who saw her. This was not a woman, Gwen noted, who was likely to have any doubts about herself or her decisions. If she was right, it was all her own work; if she was wrong, it was someone else's fault. Gwen had met plenty of men and women who shared the same reluctance to admit they could be wrong. Almost all of them came from the aristocracy.

Lady Standish wore a long black dress, as if she were in mourning. It was loose enough to hide the shape of her body, Gwen noted, but it was surprisingly tight around the woman's neck. Fashion, Gwen recalled vaguely, fighting down the urge to roll her eyes. She'd banned fashionable outfits at Cavendish Hall, at least for the students, just to prevent it from causing arguments and bad feelings. But Lady Standish wouldn't hesitate to wear whatever she pleased, setting fashion rather than following it.

Gwen recalled Lord Mycroft's brother's lessons as she covertly scrutinised the older woman, grimly aware that Lady Standish was doing the same to her. This was not a woman used to any form of physical exertion, she deduced; there were no marks on her hands that suggested any form of work, even writing with a pen and ink. On the other hand, her dress would hardly require a maid to don, suggesting that Lady Standish was more practical than she liked to appear. Her hair was pinned up neatly, though, which *did* suggest a maid. Gwen decided that Lady Standish had once been very proud of her hair and lavished more attention on it than she did on her clothes.

"You worked for Lord Carmichael," Lady Standish said, finally.

"Yes, My Lady," Gwen said. Her heartbeat started to race. If Lady Standish was anything like her mother, she would notice any discrepancy and home in on it like sailors homed in on brothels. "I worked for him for two years."

"Unfortunate," Lady Standish observed, coldly. "He would not have taught you anything of how to act in polite society."

"No, My Lady," Gwen agreed. Irene had taught her that it was always better to agree with her mistress, at least as long as she was playing the role of a maid. "I was charged with looking after his daughter."

"And he had no wife," Lady Standish said. She sniffed, rudely. "A man with such a title should always marry again, even if he has a child. She should not have been raised by a man and a man alone."

Gwen felt an odd flicker of irritation on behalf of Heather Carmichael. It was true enough that she'd been raised by maids and tutors after her mother had died, but that was true of almost all aristocratic girls. Sons could expect their fathers to play a large role in their education, daughters were lucky if their mothers visited them more than once or twice a week. Gwen's own mother had spent more time with Gwen, but then Gwen's reputation had scared away most of the servants.

"Yes, My Lady," she said, instead.

"You looked after his daughter," Lady Standish said. "What did you do, precisely?"

Gwen took a breath. "I took care of her, My Lady," she said. The files had been very detailed on this point. "I was her companion. I escorted her to the schoolroom, accompanied her when she rode out in the countryside and supervised her meetings with other aristocratic children."

Lady Standish's eyes flared. "And did you chaperone her?"

"*My Lady*," Gwen protested. "She was *thirteen*!"

"Old enough to have a marriage arranged for her," Lady Standish observed. She didn't seem to take any offence at Gwen's tone, but it wasn't too surprising. Gwen would have been barred from going into details. "Did you chaperone her?"

"Her father did not arrange any meetings with potential suitors, My Lady," Gwen said, feeling sweat trickling down her back. It was uncommon for a girl to be married off at thirteen – the reforms following the Swing had made it illegal – but Lord Carmichael might have organised it, just so he could get back to his work without a daughter underfoot. Or, perhaps, so he could marry again without fearing the daughter's opinion of her stepmother. "If he had, I would have accompanied her, I am sure."

"No doubt," Lady Standish said. She took another step forward, and another, until she was almost close enough for her nose to press against Gwen's forehead. Gwen had to fight to avoid taking a step backwards. "Your duties will include serving as a chaperone for our ward. You will not take orders from her that would leave her alone in a compromising position. Do you understand me?"

Alone with men, Gwen thought. She understood, all right. Judging from the reports, Raechel Slater-Standish was incredibly driven to spend as much time away from her family as possible. It was an impulse Gwen understood very well. Hell, she shared it. She'd barely given her family a backwards glance when she'd moved into Cavendish Hall ... and they, too, had practically allowed Master Thomas to adopt her without even trying to fight. They'd come to regret that, afterwards.

But, without magic and with a sizeable bank account of her own, Raechel could easily get into a great deal of trouble. A young buck might manage to seduce her, then get her pregnant, just to force her to marry him. And, when he did, control over her money would pass to him. Lady Mary's extensive report had noted that Raechel's control over her own money was dependent on her remaining unmarried. Her family's will specifically stated that it was only hers for as long as she remained single.

"I understand, My Lady," Gwen said, recalling one of the more unpleasant cases Lord Mycroft's brother had told her about. A young lady had been kept unmarried by her family because, as long as she was unmarried, they controlled her money. "Your orders take precedence."

"If the situation becomes unpleasant, you are to drag her out," Lady Standish continued. "And you will report to me as soon as she is back home and safe."

Gwen winced. This time, she knew it showed on her face.

If she'd been a real maid, the orders would have been nightmarish – and trying to carry them out would have been worse. Raechel could make her life miserable in a hundred tiny ways, from leaving messes for Gwen to clear up to simply badmouthing her to Lady Standish. And, if she did manage to slip off with a young man, Gwen would get the blame. At best, she'd be in real trouble and have her pay docked. But, at worst, she would be summarily fired.

That's why they insisted on giving me a history with young girls, she thought, sourly. But Heather had been thirteen, young enough to be biddable, thanks to the age gap between her and her maid. Raechel was eighteen, a year older than Gwen herself ... and probably not inclined to listen to someone she knew would be spying on her. Gwen might not be under her direct orders, but it could still get unpleasant. Very unpleasant.

"If she refuses to cooperate," Lady Standish added, "you will take whatever steps you deem necessary."

She nodded to Romulus before Gwen could ask for specifics. "Take Gwen to the servant's quarters and introduce her to Janet," she ordered. "I shall expect them both to wait on us at suppertime."

"Yes, My Lady," Romulus said. He looked at Gwen, then gave her a half-smile. "If you will come with me ..."

Gwen curtseyed again to Lady Standish and Madame Hampton, then followed Romulus out of the room. The door closed behind the aristocratic women with an ominous thud.

"A word of warning," Romulus said, once they were safely out of earshot. "Lady Raechel is no easy person to handle. But she does have a sense of justice."

Gwen frowned. What the hell was *that* meant to mean?

"But Her Ladyship expects the very best from everyone," he added. "Don't fail her."

Chapter Nine

livia slept very poorly after her meeting with Gregory. Her dreams were full of crawling hordes of undead, the nightmare she remembered from London, but made worse by the whispering that followed her as she tried to flee. Normal people, mundanes and other magicians, heard nothing from the undead but moans. The researchers, according to Gwen, believed that the moaning was a form of communication. After all, the greater the number of undead, the greater the level of intelligence they showed.

But Olivia knew better. In her nightmares, as on the streets of London, she could hear the whispers, the endless chant of the undead. She couldn't make out any words, but the sense was unmistakable. The undead wanted to kill everyone, to build an army so large that they were utterly unstoppable. There was no way to negotiate with such creatures, no way to talk them out of their ambitions. All the living could do was destroy them all and hope they never rose again.

She jerked awake and stared around the dim room, cursing her powers under her breath. It had taken her months to get used to Cavendish Hall; she'd almost killed a maid who'd come into her room on the first day, just to light the fire. Even afterwards, when Gwen had pointed out that she was in no danger, she hadn't been able to relax for a long time. These days, the maids were always careful to knock first and go away if they received no answer. But there was no one in the room.

Gritting her teeth, she sat upright and wiped the sweat from her brow. Her body ached, both where she'd been beaten by the Cossack and where the cuffs had been wrapped around her wrists. Clearly, she'd been too frozen earlier to feel pain, she decided, as she carefully flexed her muscles. She needed another soak in hot water, she told herself, as she swung her legs over the side of the bed and stood up. Her legs almost buckled beneath her weight and she hastily sat down. The skin, when she looked, showed far too many nasty bruises that had developed overnight.

There was a knock at the door. Olivia glanced down hastily to make sure she was decent, then called out for the visitor to come in. The door opened, revealing a pale-skinned girl wearing a long dark dress and carrying a small tray of food. Her hair hung in ringlets down to her shoulders. Olivia looked at her face and recognised the signs of someone who had been beaten into submission, just like the whores she'd seen and feared on the streets. They hadn't been scary, not in and of themselves, but she'd known she was looking at her future. If Gwen hadn't adopted her, if she hadn't had any powers, she would have been forced into the brothels when she could no longer pose as a boy.

"Thank you," she said, trying to keep her voice down. "Please put it on the table."

The girl obeyed, although it was hard to tell if she really understood or was merely following someone else's orders. Olivia hesitated, then motioned for the girl to sit on the bed facing her. The girl's face seemed to pale still further, torn between two sets of orders, then she finally complied with Olivia's wishes and sat down on the bed, smoothing down her dress in one smooth movement. Olivia felt a moment of pity, followed by the angry realisation that she wasn't the only prisoner in the complex. But then, she'd seen enough of their experiments to know that it could be far worse.

"My name is Olivia," she said, remembering the days when she'd been Oliver. Now that she'd filled out, she couldn't be Oliver any longer. "Do you understand me?"

The girl hesitated, then nodded, so slightly that Olivia almost missed the motion. It was interesting, she noted, that the girl spoke English – or at least understood English – when the Cossacks had clearly not understood a word she'd said. She rubbed her stomach absently, cursing them under her breath. They hadn't needed to speak to her to get their point across.

Olivia smiled at the girl. "What is your name?"

The answer was so quiet that Olivia had to strain to hear it. "Esther."

"Pleased to meet you," Olivia said, holding out a hand. Esther ... it sounded familiar, although she wasn't sure from where. It certainly wasn't the name of anyone she knew personally. "How did you end up here?"

The girl shook her head frantically, then scrambled to her feet and practically ran towards the door. Olivia stared after her, realising that Esther had probably been given very strict orders to have as little to do with the prisoner as possible, then turned to the tray of food. It was a stew that tasted of beef and vegetables, with a hard bread that she had to soak in the stew before it became edible. When she'd finished eating, a different girl entered and removed the tray, then nodded towards the door. Ivan was standing there.

"Good morning," he said, in his unaccented English. "I trust you slept well?"

Olivia glowered at him. The Russian didn't seem too bothered by her disdain; he merely held out a hand, inviting her to come with him. Olivia hesitated, remembering the pain in her ankles, then stood up anyway. If she refused, he would simply compel her to come to him. But the pain was so overpowering that she fell to the floor, trying desperately not to scream.

"Now, that won't do," Ivan said. She felt him walking over to her, then picking her up effortlessly. "Don't worry. We will fix the pain."

"You caused it," Olivia muttered through clenched teeth.

"Yes, we did," Ivan agreed, dispassionately. He carried her towards the door, then through it and down the long stone corridor. "But we can fix it too."

They entered a smaller room that was as bare as the others, apart from a long stone table. He placed her down on it, told her to stay on the table and walked out of the door. Moments later, he returned with Gregory in tow. The monkish man smelt as bad as ever, Olivia realised, as he touched his fingers to her ankles. But she started to feel better almost at once.

"I was blessed by the Father Tsar," Gregory said, when she gave him a surprised look. A Healer. He had to be a Healer. "Where else does it hurt?"

Olivia hesitated. The last thing she wanted was him touching her, not when he smelt as if he hadn't taken a bath in his life. But her body hurt badly ... she swallowed her disgust and pointed to where her body was aching, hoping he would heal them all. One by one, he touched them and the pain faded away to nothingness. In some ways, she realised mutely, he was a more capable Healer than Lucy. And Lucy was among the best in British service.

"Thank you," she said, when he'd finished. "But it wouldn't have been necessary if your men hadn't beaten me."

Gregory laughed, unpleasantly. "And would you have done as you were told if you hadn't been tied up?"

He helped her to her feet, then headed out the door. Ivan pushed Olivia towards it, gently, then followed her down the corridor. They passed through a pair of armoured doors, each one reminding her of the ironclad she'd seen on the Thames, then deeper and deeper into the complex. Finally, they reached a room with a pair of Cossacks standing on guard, holding sabres rather than rifles. Olivia puzzled over it for a long moment – no matter how good they were with swords, a child with a pistol could kill them – and then felt her blood run cold as she realised the truth. Swords were the best weapons, short of flamethrowers, against the undead.

"Once we're inside, I suggest you obey orders," Ivan muttered, as Gregory spoke to the guards in Russian. "This is not the time to play games."

Olivia felt sick as the door opened and the stench of death wafted out at them. Inside, illuminated only by a set of torches on the walls, was a stone prison cell. No, she realised mutely; it was far more than just a prison cell. Iron bars allowed the occupant to be watched by his captors, while preventing him from reaching them without permission. Indeed, the bars were far closer together than was strictly necessary. As a child, she'd wormed her way through iron bars that would keep out grown adults, but it wouldn't be possible here. A cat would have problems getting through the bars.

But it made sense, she realised numbly. The undead had no sensitivity to pain. They wouldn't hesitate to break bones, just to fit through the bars. In the cage, they couldn't escape without crippling themselves permanently. She shuddered, remembering the undead crawling forwards, pressing themselves against the barricades. Even crippled, they were still dangerous.

A sudden flare of light made her blink and cover her eyes in surprise. When she pulled her hand away, she saw a chubby man standing in the corner, producing glowing balls of light. A Blazer, she noted, cursing once again under her breath. She might have managed to defeat a Healer, but Blazers were notoriously dangerous unless one had the advantage of surprise. And if there was one Blazer, there might be others.

She gritted her teeth as she felt despair sinking into her mind, latching on to the commands Ivan had left in her head. It was hopeless, part of her mind argued; there was no way to escape, not even into death. The very thought of suicide was somehow unthinkable. No, all she could do was obey the Russians and give them what they wanted. She knew, beyond a shadow of a doubt, that it was the result of Ivan's commands, yet it was so hard to fight. One day, she realised, she would be theirs ... and she wouldn't even know that anything had changed. She glared over at Ivan, who smiled back at her.

Damn Charmers, she thought, remembering Gwen's tales about Lord Blackburn. He'd come close to molesting *Gwen*, an aristocrat, Master Magician and Master Thomas's ward. If he'd been prepared to do that, what else had he *actually done*? *None of them are ever decent people.*

"Look inside the cage," Gregory said. There was a note of grim ... enthusiasm in his voice that chilled her to the bone. "What do you see?"

Olivia scowled as she saw the body lying on the stone floor. It had once been a young man, but someone had killed him ... judging from the marks on his throat, she deduced that he had been choked to death. Someone had just wrapped their hands around his neck and squeezed, hard. It was impossible to be sure – the room was cold enough to slow the decomposing process – but she had a feeling he'd died only a day or two ago. Perhaps even only a few hours ago ...

"So," Gregory said. "Bring the body back to life."

Olivia stared at him. "I can't bring him all the way back to life," she protested. Only Jesus had ever been able to bring a man back from the dead. Necromancers could imbue corpses with a shambling mockery of life, but it wasn't the same. "All I can do is ... make him one of the undead."

"Then do it," Ivan said. "Now."

There was an undertone of command in his voice that reminded her that Charm was always an option. Olivia hesitated, wondering if she shouldn't force him to compel her anyway, then she pushed the thought aside before it could solidify. If she let him work on her mind again, the eventual collapse into mindless surrender would come sooner, rather than later. Instead, she stepped forward, wishing she knew more about how to use her powers. But Gwen had flatly forbidden her to experiment and it was one rule she'd never even *considered* breaking.

A young girl in Edinburgh had a pet mouse that died, she recalled, bitterly. *She brought it back to life and took it to her mother, expecting to be praised. Instead, she was killed and her family transported to Australia, just to make sure no word of the affair leaked out. If the population had known that a Necromancer had been born in Edinburgh ...*

"It will take time," she hedged. In truth, she wasn't even sure where to start. The undead hordes she'd faced before might have obeyed her, but they hadn't been raised by her. God alone knew who'd turned them into the government's secret weapon. Gwen had speculated that it had been Master Thomas, but no one knew for sure. "Let me try ..."

"We are patient," Gregory assured her. There was a faintly mocking tone in his voice that suggested he knew precisely what she was feeling. "Take your time."

Olivia moved as close to the bars as she dared, then closed her eyes, recalling what little she knew about the actual necromantic process. There had been almost nothing in the books; Gwen had never tried to use the power, while the male Master Magicians had left those pages blank, preferring to pretend they didn't have the power themselves. No one had really tried to interrogate a Necromancer before killing him, Olivia knew; they'd been too scared of the possible consequences. But it had also left them alarmingly ignorant of how the power actually worked.

"Of all the magical arts," Gwen had said, months ago, "necromancy is the least understood."

Olivia tried to feel out her magic. The girls at Cavendish Hall had spoken of feeling their magic crackling through their bodies, as much a part of them as their hands or feet, but she'd never really tried to use her magic. She slowed her breathing, concentrating on her heart beating within her chest, then tried to feel for something new. For a long moment, there was nothing new or unfamiliar ... and then she heard a whisper. It echoed through her mind, as if someone was talking loud enough to be heard, but not loud enough to be understood.

But it didn't seem to reach beyond her flesh and bone.

Opening her eyes, she looked at the dead body and realised, to her horror, just how to awaken it into a semblance of life. She inched forward, reaching her hand through the bars until she was touching the body, then closed her eyes again. This time, she was aware of her living flesh ... and the dead corpse she was touching. And it was the easiest thing in the world to take some of her life energy and push it into the body. She felt it jerk under her fingers and yanked her hand back, her eyes snapping open. In the cage, the body was slowly coming to life.

Her head swam as the whispering grew louder. She toppled backwards, expecting to slam her head against the stone floor, but Ivan caught her before it was too late. Tears fell from her eyes as she clung to him, seeking comfort even in his arms. Ivan patted her back softly, his eyes never leaving the creature in the cage. Olivia forced herself to stand on her own two feet, then turned to look at what she'd done. The whispering seemed to grow even louder as she saw the undead creature slowly making its way to its feet.

It had been human once, she knew. Now, its skin was grey and its eyes were an eerie yellow colour, as if it had long lost all traces of humanity. Its hair seemed to be falling out, although she couldn't tell if that was merely a side effect of what limited decomposition had happened or something to do with necromancy. It held out one long hand and examined it, without a trace of interest or curiosity on its face, then held up its head and stared at the four humans watching it.

And then it moaned.

Olivia moaned too as the sound sliced into her head. It was a cry of hunger, a raw lust for sustenance that ran far beyond a desire for food and drink. It wanted something else, she knew; it wanted the living energy running through them all. She understood, now, why the undead had reacted the way they did. When they weren't being directed by a Necromancer, their lives were consumed by an endless desire for life energy. And, when they ran out, they just waited until they were reanimated by human contact.

She shuddered, then vomited, throwing up everything she'd eaten onto the hard stone floor. Gregory didn't even seem to hear her. He was too fascinated by the undead creature as it made its shambolic way to the bars and stood there, staring at him. It looked to have been thwarted by the bars, but Olivia knew better. The creature was waiting. She could feel the link between herself and the creature, even though they were no longer touching. It was hers to command as she saw fit ...

But the more she touched it with her mind, the louder the whispering in her head. Sooner or later, it would overcome her and then ... perhaps there was some sense in having all Necromancers executed, no matter what they were before they developed their powers. It threatened to pull her into its undead mind ...

"Take her to wash and then feed her," Gregory ordered. His voice was excited, as if he was *pleased* to see the undead creature. Olivia thought he was mad. Couldn't he understand how dangerous it was? "We will do more tests later."

Ivan helped Olivia to stumble towards the door, his hands gently holding her upright. Behind her, the creature moaned again. The further she moved from it, the weaker the link between them. But she knew it wouldn't last ...

If they let it loose, she thought grimly, *there will be hundreds of others all too soon.*

Chapter Ten

wen couldn't help feeling some relief as Romulus introduced her to the remainder of the staff. Cook, a jovial woman fat enough to make three women, was friendly enough, even though she didn't bother to share her real name with anyone. Rosie, Lady Standish's social secretary, seemed pleasant, but distant. She probably was far too aware of the gulf between herself and a simple maid. But Janet, Lady Standish's other maid, seemed friendly and quite happy to chat.

"Help her settle in," Romulus directed, with another brilliant smile. "And then prepare for dinner."

Janet smiled at Gwen. "This isn't such a bad place once you get used to it," she said, as she led Gwen into a tiny room with a pair of beds pressed against the wall. "As long as you do as you're told, Her Ladyship doesn't mind you."

Gwen nodded as she picked up the bag and carefully unpacked it, placing the clothes in the drawer under the bed. The room was tiny, too small for one person, at least for an aristocrat. Her room at home was easily five or six times as large as the room she was expected to share with Janet. She had a nasty feeling she was going to find it hard to sleep with Janet in the same room, even if her new friend didn't snore. She'd never had to share a room with anyone in her life. Even the new students at Cavendish Hall didn't have to share rooms.

"Most of the staff are at the Hall," Janet explained, as Gwen finished unpacking and straightened up, checking her appearance in the mirror. "But we're the lucky ones who get to go to Russia."

A bell echoed through the house. "That's dinner," Janet added, climbing to her feet. "We'd better go to meet Cook."

The food smelt nice, Gwen decided, although it looked as though Cook preferred to feed her family on traditional English food rather than anything foreign. It was clear that the mania for Indian or Turkish food hadn't reached the Standish Family. She picked up the plate of roast beef, already sliced into multiple pieces by Cook, and carried it through the door into the dining room. Behind her, Janet carried the potatoes and a small bowl of vegetables, then returned to bring up the rear with the gravy.

Gwen carefully kept her eyes on the meat until she put it down in front of Lord Standish, but then glanced around as she stepped to the back of the room. It was as fancy as any she'd seen, although it was too small to host more than five or six people at table. She couldn't decide if that was because of the size of the house, which was small by aristocratic standards, or if Lord Standish had deliberately designed the dining room to make it harder to invite large numbers of guests. Gwen's own father had done the same and *he* had a wife who had been reluctant to invite guests to her house. There was too great a chance of visitors seeing her devil-child.

She saw Raechel Slater-Standish sitting at one end of the table and felt an odd moment of kinship, a sense that she would have liked the young girl if they'd met before she'd gone to Cavendish Hall. Raechel was tall, wearing a dress that showed the shape of her breasts even if it didn't reveal any skin, with a strong face that gave her a ruthlessly indomitable look. She didn't have the soft features that were considered fashionable these days, but it was easy to see why she would turn heads. Long red hair – naturally red, if Gwen was any judge – drew attention to her face and hands. And she was surprisingly muscular for her sex.

She grew up in the countryside, Gwen thought, recalling Lady Mary's notes on Lord and Lady Standish and their ward. *Her parents would have taught her how to ride and take care of herself, even if she'd also had a restricted life.*

She shook her head and stood beside Janet as the Standish family slowly ate their way through a surprisingly large amount of food. Lord Standish was as tall as his wife, with a distinguished attitude that befitted a government minister, but it was clear that he was slowly losing the battle against his weight. Even sitting down, Gwen could see that he was developing a paunch that would eventually leave him as overweight as Lord Mycroft. But his eyes were sharp and there was nothing wrong with his mind. She just hoped he didn't pay close enough attention to her to realise that there was something wrong.

Janet seemed to remain perfectly still as they waited, but Gwen had to fight down the urge to fidget. She remembered all the long boring meals she'd endured with her mother and father and felt a twinge of guilt at the thought of the servants just standing there, waiting for their lords and masters to finish. It hadn't been much better at Cavendish Hall, particularly as young magicians couldn't resist showing off their powers at the expense of the servants. It had been hard to convince most of the young men that it would get them in real trouble if they did it publicly.

Finally, the dinner came to an end and the family withdrew into the drawing room. Gwen allowed herself a moment of relief, then helped Janet clear the table and carry the remains of the food to the kitchen. It seemed like a waste, she thought, until she realised that the staff would keep the food and devour it themselves. On Cook's command, she picked up a tray of three glasses and carried them into the drawing room, careful to ensure that she offered them to Lord Standish first. He was, at least in theory, the head of the household.

"Raechel," Lady Standish said. "This is Gwen, the new maid. She will be your maid. You will take her with you if you leave the house."

The younger woman looked rebellious. Gwen found it hard to blame her, even though she knew the risks of being alone and unattended in the streets of London. Rumours didn't have to be true to ruin a person's life. Hell, there were stories about the young Gwen turning people into frogs right, left and centre, when anyone with any experience of magic would know that such things were impossible. It was extremely rare for one person to be turned into an animal, let alone dozens of them.

Gwen bobbed a curtsey, trying to look attentive and obedient. Raechel stared at her for a long moment, her eyes studying Gwen's face as if she'd seen it before somewhere, then nodded sharply.

"I will be leaving at eight," she said, flatly. "Be ready."

Lord Standish coughed. "You will have your work completed by then," he said. "Or you will not be going out at all."

Raechel glowered at him. "The work isn't important," she said, in a tone Gwen knew would have earned her a slap from her mother. "I have no intention of finding a young man and settling down."

The young woman turned and stalked out before Lord Standish could say another word. Gwen found herself torn between amusement and sympathy, although she wasn't sure who she was actually sorry for. Both of them, perhaps. Lord and Lady Standish had had no children, while his younger brother had had Raechel and then died young. And Lord Standish had been away in France at the time. By the time he'd got home to take his niece into his household as his ward, she'd developed a whole series of bad habits.

But I couldn't blame her, Gwen thought, as she bobbed another curtsey and then hurried after Raechel, already feeling harassed. *What would I have done if I'd been offered the freedom of the city and plenty of money?*

She heard the sound of banging and crashing as she approached Raechel's room and hesitated, before reminding herself that she wasn't scared of anything and pushing open the door. Raechel had removed her dress and started to hunt through the vast hampers of clothing while wearing her underwear, which was revealing enough to make Gwen blush. It was funny, given how little real privacy she'd had at home, but it still bothered her. Raechel simply didn't act like a young aristocratic woman. Or any sort of woman Gwen had met.

"You," Raechel snarled. She turned to face Gwen, dark eyes flashing fire. "You will not get in my way, understand?"

Gwen knew that any normal maid would be cowering from her mistress's rage, even if she reported to Lady Standish rather than the raging girl in front of her. But she had enough pride, despite her role, to stand her ground.

"My ... *Aunt* does not control my life," Raechel grumbled, as she picked up a garment and pushed it at Gwen. "And neither do you."

That, Gwen knew, was not true. The terms of her father's will compelled Raechel to seek her Aunt and Uncle's advice in all that she did until she either married or turned thirty. On the other hand, they also prevented her Aunt and Uncle from touching her money, at least not without Raechel's willing permission. But she wouldn't inherit full control until she was too old to marry, at least by normal standards. And yet ... with so much money in her account, Gwen suspected that the rules would be rewritten for her.

She looked down at the garment and flushed. It was a dress, but one so sheer it might as well have been a nightgown, one far too indecent for her. Raechel snorted at Gwen's reaction, then picked up another dress and tossed it at her. Gwen stared at her in surprise, then lifted her eyebrows. Raechel produced another snort, then pointed one long finger at Gwen's demure dress.

"You're not coming wearing that," she snapped. "You can wear one of my older dresses and look as if you belong."

Gwen sighed, inwardly, as she took the dress and inspected it. It was marginally more decent than the others, she decided, although it revealed far too much of her breasts for her comfort, along with her ankles. She made a mental note to don a cloak too, something she could wrap around her, as Raechel pulled on another dress that was almost translucent in far too many places. Gwen stared in shock. She could practically see the girl's nipples clearly outlined by the dress.

"You ... You can't wear that," she stammered. No one, not even the most outrageous of the Trouser Brigade, wore anything so revealing. "Your Aunt will be furious."

Raechel gave her a quick, unpleasant grin. "That's the idea," she said, nastily. "She may be able to keep me in her house, but I don't have to make it pleasant for her."

"Oh," Gwen said, feeling as if she had passed beyond shock. "But ... But what if they try to stop you?"

She swallowed. Legally, Raechel was practically their property. Lord and Lady Standish would be quite within their rights to beat their niece if she kept acting like a common tart – or simply to lock her in the house until she married or turned thirty. But it looked as though they were having real problems coming to terms with their ward. Maybe they should have been more understanding from the start. But they'd never had children to teach them how to handle a teenage girl who'd suddenly been dropped on them.

"Let them try," Raechel said. She picked up a cloak, wrapped it around her body, then headed for the door. She tossed a second cloak at Gwen as she stepped past her. "Let's go."

It wasn't eight, but Gwen wasn't inclined to point it out as they strode down the stairs and out of the tradesman's exit. No one barred their way as they walked out of the alleyway and down through Pall Mall, heading towards the river. It would be a while before night fell over London, Gwen knew, but the fashionable men and women were already out, taking the breeze and chattering to one another about the forthcoming war. She gritted her teeth, wondering briefly if she shouldn't simply Charm Raechel into turning around and going back home. But someone as strong-minded as Raechel would need a great deal of Charm to convince her to give up and she could hardly fail to notice Gwen's manipulations.

Raechel stopped outside an unmarked door and knocked three times, counting five seconds between each knock. There was a long pause, then the door was opened by a man wearing a white suit and hat. He nodded to Raechel, then gave Gwen a long considering look. Raechel brushed past him, her eyes fixed on the door at the far end; Gwen followed her, wondering if the doorkeeper would try to stop her. Instead, he just closed the door behind her.

The second door revealed a large dance floor, pulsing with the sound of a band playing tunes she didn't recognise and dozens of young men and women, some of them dressed even more revealingly than Raechel. Raechel passed Gwen her cloak and sallied out onto the dance floor, capturing a young man from his partner and pulling him into the dance. Gwen sighed, stood against the wall and watched as Raechel span around the dance floor. Here, free of her aunt and uncle, she seemed almost relaxed and happy. Gwen felt a sudden stab of envy, just as a hand touched her shoulder.

"You don't have to stand here," a voice said. To her shock, Gwen recognised the speaker as one of the more scandalous aristocratic rakes. At least he'd never been formally introduced to her. "You could always dance."

Gwen shook her head, firmly. The rake eyed her, his gaze passing over her dress in a manner that made her want to pick him up with her magic and slam him against the wall, then he walked away, twitching his bottom as he moved. Gwen looked away, her eyes following Raechel; one dance had come to an end, but another had started almost at once. Raechel was still dancing with her partner. His hands, Gwen realised to her horror, were creeping down her back towards her buttocks. And he wasn't the only one groping their dance partner.

The music changed, becoming more sensuous. Gwen felt her horror rising as she realised that several of the couples were practically making love on the dance floor, their hands exploring one another as they held each other tight. One girl had opened her dress, allowing her bare breasts to bobble free; another had worn a skirt so high that it barely hid the underside of her buttocks. Gwen flushed brightly, unsure of where to look, remembering how far she'd gone with Sir Charles. But they'd been in private when they'd kissed ... here, anyone could see what happened between the couples.

She looked back at Raechel and swallowed as she realised that Raechel's partner was stroking her breasts through her dress. Raechel didn't appear to be objecting; she seemed to move like a cat, pressing her breasts into her partner's hand. That was going too far, Gwen knew, yet she found herself unsure of how to intervene. If she'd been there as the Royal Sorceress, she could have cowed Raechel into obedience, but as her maid ...

But she had to do something. She concentrated, drawing on her magic, and lashed out at the display of expensive bottles at the bar. They exploded, sending pieces of glass and alcohol everywhere. The dancers turned to stare; Gwen took advantage of their attention to knock one of the candlesticks into the alcohol. Flames spread rapidly, glowing an eerie blue colour as the alcohol caught fire.

She plunged into the panicking crowd and grabbed Raechel's arm, pulling her away from her partner. He started to object; Gwen braced herself, then yanked at his legs using magic, sending him sprawling to the floor. Raechel offered no resistance as Gwen pulled her away from the growing fire, heading out of the door as fast as possible. The doorkeeper eyed them with some surprise, then heard the sounds of panic from inside the dance room and headed to investigate. Gwen opened the door, led Raechel out onto the streets and tossed her the cloak.

"Cover yourself," she hissed. The sounds of panic behind them were growing louder. It wouldn't be long before the Bow Street Runners and the London Fire Brigade came to investigate. If she knew the government, quite a few young men and women would be very embarrassed if they were found in the hall. "And come on."

She pulled on Raechel's arm until they'd put some distance between themselves and the fire, then relaxed slightly. Raechel stared at her in shock – Gwen found herself wondering if Raechel had some sensitivity to magic – then Raechel found her voice. And then she started to complain.

"You shouldn't have dragged me away," Raechel protested. "I was having fun ..."

"And you could have been caught in the flames," Gwen snapped. Honestly! Had *her* maids seen her as a useless piece of flesh, suitable for looking good and nothing else? Raechel had a great deal of potential and she was *wasting* all of it. "If you were smaller, I'd put you over my knee and thrash you with a hairbrush."

Raechel sneered at her. "My Aunt tried that," she said. "It didn't work."

"No," Gwen sighed. "It probably didn't."

But Raechel offered no further argument as Gwen led her back to her home. As they entered the house, Gwen was relieved to hear from Romulus that Lady Standish had gone to bed with a headache. At least it would give Gwen the night to decide just how much to tell her mistress. And Raechel ...

"Go to bed," Gwen ordered, sharply. She allowed a little Charm to slip into her words, just enough to make Raechel more inclined to do as she was told. "I'll see you in the morning."

Somewhat to her surprise, Raechel obeyed without question.

Sighing, Gwen headed back into the servants quarters. She needed to eat, then sleep, and be up early. No doubt there would be an interrogation from Lady Standish about the night's events.

But what could she tell her about what her niece and ward had been doing?

Chapter Eleven

trust that you are feeling better," Gregory said, as he bounded into the room. "There is work for you to do."

Olivia shook her head, miserably. Ivan had taken her to a smaller room, allowed her to wash and then fed her bread and cheese, but she still felt awful. She could *hear* the creature she'd created, even though it was a long way from where she'd been taken. Its whispering seemed to echo in her head, taunting her with the sheer danger of its existence. One mistake, it seemed to whisper, and the undead would be unleashed upon the land. And then all hell would break loose.

Gregory muttered something in Russian to Ivan, who sighed and stood. Olivia saw the writing on the wall and followed before he could compel her, either mentally or physically, to do what he wanted her to do. Outside, there were more armed guards, wearing masks and suits of armour that seemed oddly out of place. But, against the undead, they would provide more protection than the red uniforms that British soldiers wore when they went into battle. The Russians, she realised as she was hustled down the corridor, had been planning how to make use of her for a very long time.

Or perhaps they hoped to find a Necromancer of their own, she thought, as they passed through another set of solidly armoured doors. Inside, she heard the sound of people crying further down the corridor, but saw no one apart from her two escorts. *They might have birthed one of their own, but never known it.*

She gritted her teeth. Necromancy wasn't as flashy as Blazing or Moving ... and it wasn't so easy to discover as Charming or Talking. A Necromancer might go their entire life without realising that they had magic, let alone what it actually did. *She'd* certainly had no idea what she could do until she'd come face to face with the undead, even though Jack had realised she had powers and urged her to develop them. The Russians or French might have a dozen Necromancers and simply not know what they had.

Gregory stopped in front of another armoured door, smiled at her and then opened it, allowing the stench of death to drift out into the open air. Olivia swallowed hard, trying desperately to breathe through her mouth as he led the way into the darkened room. This time, the corpse inside the cage had clearly been dead for quite some time. Even in Russia's notoriously cold weather, it had managed to decompose quite badly. Olivia shuddered, recalling bodies she'd seen in the Rookery. Few of them had ever been so bad ... but then, even the hardened denizens of the Rookery had cremated bodies, no matter how they'd died.

They wanted to avoid giving a Necromancer bodies to play with, she recalled. *And it was not enough to prevent an outbreak in the heart of London.*

"This was once a dissident who dared to speak against the Father Tsar," Gregory said, a note of heavy satisfaction in his voice. Up close, it was clear that the body had been brutally beaten and then strangled. "In death, he will serve the Father Tsar as he never did in life."

He looked down at Olivia. "Bring him back to life."

Olivia stared at him, mutely. The last thing she wanted was to touch the body in the cage. It stank, far worse than anything she'd ever experienced, and she was sure that touching the body would be very unhealthy. But she knew that, if she refused, Ivan would just compel her to do as they wanted. Gritting her teeth, trying not to throw up as she crept closer to the body, she reached out with her powers and tried to form a link. This time, nothing happened.

"It isn't working," she said. She could feel her magic, pulsing through her body like a second heartbeat, but it wasn't animating the body. It didn't seem to want to leave her warm flesh and blood. "I can't reawaken the body."

"Try again," Gregory ordered.

Olivia obeyed. Nothing happened, apart from a faint headache that flared into life and then faded away, just as quickly. She'd heard that some magicians developed headaches if they pushed their powers too far, notably Talkers and Movers, but she'd never heard of Necromancy having such limitations. But then, no one had really been interested in studying the power, merely slaughtering anyone unfortunate enough to be born with it.

Gregory muttered something in Russian. Ivan leaned forward, touching her shoulder with his hand. "Bring him back to life," he ordered, Charm flowing through his voice. "Bring him back to life."

Olivia's headache grew worse as she tried to carry out the command – and failed. The body didn't even twitch. There was a sudden burst of pain in her head, sending her stumbling backwards into Ivan's arms, then she almost blacked out. The next thing she knew was that they were outside the room, Ivan holding her and stroking her hair in an almost paternal manner. He looked almost afraid, Olivia noted, blearily. What would happen to him if he were blamed for her death?

"Most interesting," Gregory observed. "The body was simply too damaged to be brought back to life."

If you can call that life, Olivia thought, through the haze of pain. She wanted to be sick again, but she somehow managed to hold it under control. *All they do is kill and eat and spread themselves as far as possible.*

"Follow me," Gregory ordered. He turned and led the way down the corridor. "There are more experiments to try."

Olivia glared at his retreating back as Ivan helped her to her feet, then half-carried her down the corridor after Gregory. Her head felt awful, as if she'd drunk far too much in a single sitting, and yet he wanted to carry out more experiments? Of course he did, she realised grimly, remembering some of the researchers at Cavendish Hall. When they'd managed to get the bit between their teeth, they'd worked frantically to carry out experiments, even if their magician subjects had been tired and pushed beyond reason. At least one researcher had been discovered hanging from a flagpole after he'd insisted on carrying out more and more experiments on an exhausted Mover.

And he wants to experiment with Necromancy, she thought, as Gregory led her into a new cell. This time, there was no smell of death. *He has so many plans and so little time.*

She blinked in surprise as she saw the man sitting against the wall. He was short, dark-haired, with an expression of mild boredom on his face. Olivia wondered if he was drugged, then saw the bruises covering his face and realised that he'd been knocked silly. He cackled, loudly enough to make her jump, then called out something in Russian. Olivia flinched at his tone. It reminded her far too much of the whorehouse madams in the Rookery.

Gregory said something back, something Olivia didn't understand, then turned to face her. "I want you to try to take him now," he ordered. "Make him one of the undead."

Olivia stared at him in astonishment. It had honestly never occurred to her – or any of the other researchers – that it was possible for a Necromancer to turn a living human into one of the undead. But then, if the undead spread by biting their victims, it might just be possible to do it directly, rather than having to start with a dead body. She hesitated, just long enough to hear a warning grumble from Ivan, then stepped forward and touched the prisoner's forehead. It was hot and sweaty, despite the cold ... and, in its own way, as unresponsive to her power as the previous corpse. She could practically *feel* his life energy pushing her power aside as she tried to touch him.

She shuddered as the implications sank into her mind. She was Gwen's adopted daughter, heir to Master Thomas's considerable fortune, and few people knew her origins. It wouldn't be long, she knew, until she was old enough to marry ... and she knew the aristocracy had plenty of poorer members who would be willing to overlook any discrepancy in her origins just to get their hands on her money. And she wasn't entirely averse to the idea of marrying ... but what if she *couldn't* touch another living person? Gwen hugged her, from time to time, but Gwen was a magician. Could a normal human touch her without pushing her away?

Ivan cleared his throat, drawing her back to herself. Marriage was unlikely, she knew; the Russians would never give up on her. They'd want to see, eventually, if one Necromancer could give birth to others. If the British Empire had been prepared to try to farm magicians, to have lower-class girls impregnated and forced to carry magical children to term, what would the Russians be prepared to do? Gregory hadn't done anything that suggested he had any scruples about how he researched magic. Some of his experiments had taken the concept of scientific research further than anything the British Empire had ever tried.

"It doesn't work," Olivia said, relieved. "His body is completely untouchable."

She let out a sigh of relief, despite the knowledge that she might be beaten for daring to fail. She hadn't wanted to discover that she could bring death and servitude with a touch. Some of the people she'd worked for in the Rookery would have found it a useful gift, but Olivia was repelled by the very thought. Besides, they'd been able to call on Charmers to influence people if terror and beatings hadn't been sufficient. They hadn't needed a Necromancer who might easily lose control of her creations.

Gregory nodded, stepped forward and placed his hand on the prisoner's forehead. Olivia stumbled backwards and Ivan pulled her away, just as Gregory began to chant in a manner that sent chills down her spine. It didn't sound as though he was speaking in Russian, but it was impossible to tell for sure. The prisoner seemed to understand, given how he tried to shrink away from the monkish Russian. But the chains kept him firmly in place. Olivia watched in growing horror as Gregory pulled a knife from his sleeve, his chanting growing louder and louder, then pressed it into the young man's throat. Blood spurted from his wound as his body jerked, then subsided.

"Good," Gregory said. Blood pooled around his feet as he turned to face Olivia. "Bring him back to life."

Olivia couldn't move. Shock and terror held her frozen. She'd met Healers, several Healers, and none of them had been able to kill, once they knew how to use their powers. Lucy might have been violent from time to time – a woman who couldn't look after herself in the Rookery was hideously vulnerable, unless she had a strong man to serve as her protector – but she'd never actually killed anyone, even the most aggressive of johns. None of the other Healers had been able to kill either.

But Gregory had killed ... and done it as casually as a man might butcher a hog.

Life is cheap here, she realised, remembering just how many prisoners she'd seen in the complex. Men and women, boys and girls ... they'd all been taken into the building and then put to use, forgotten by the outside world. The Rookery had been bad – she knew, without a shadow of a doubt, just how long she would have lasted if she'd been forced into a brothel – but this was worse. *And how much worse will it be if they master Necromancy?*

"Bring him back to life," Gregory ordered, as he returned his knife to his sleeve. Olivia had seen concealed weapons before, but she hadn't even realised he had the knife. His robes could hide a small arsenal. "Now."

Olivia shuddered as Ivan poked her back, then took a step forward, trying to avoid the spreading pool of blood. It was funny just how fastidious she'd become in the six months since Gwen had taken her out of the Rookery; once, she'd thought nothing of working as a tanner-girl or tosh-faker. Now, the thought of doing anything of the sort made her feel sick at heart. But there was no way to escape, no way to avoid being compelled to work for Gregory ... she reached out and touched the dead man's forehead for the second time. It was still warm, but this time the resistance was gone ...

The change happened so swiftly that she was caught by surprise. One moment, it was a cooling dead body; the next, it was lunging forward, struggling desperately against the chains holding it in place. Olivia yelped, as teeth snapped at her throat, only to be saved at the last moment by Ivan, who yanked her backwards with enough force to send them both sprawling on the floor. Gregory snorted, rudely, never taking his eyes off the new creature as it pulled against the chains. There was a look on his face that reminded Olivia of some of the johns, admiring the whores. It was a mixture of lust for their bodies and the desire for power over someone smaller and weaker than themselves.

It was a long, chilling moment before the whispering began. This time, it seemed to be clearer, but it was still maddeningly impossible to make out properly. She gritted her teeth, trying to block it out, finally feeling a little sympathy for one of the Talkers she'd known at Cavendish Hall. The boy had read her mind and blurted out what she'd been thinking – and she'd punched him in the face, which was unladylike behaviour according to her tutors – but she knew now he probably didn't have any control over his abilities. To him, *everyone* was whispering.

There must be a connection, part of her mind noted. *He hears the living, I hear the dead.*

The undead creature moaned, then pulled itself forward. Olivia kept her face expressionless as she realised that the creature didn't feel pain. It was pulling at the chains, breaking its own bones, just to get free and attack the living humans. Gregory's smile grew wider as the creature pulled its hands free, then came forward with startling speed. Ivan swore, shouted a command in Russian, and yanked Olivia back towards the door. The door burst open, revealing two armoured men carrying spears. One of them charged forward, impaling the undead creature on his spear; the other hung back, drawing a sword from his belt.

Olivia watched, unable to take her eyes off the scene, as the undead creature started to pull itself along the spear, advancing on the soldier with murderous intent. The other soldier ran forward, sword in hand, and took aim at the undead creature's neck. Gregory barked a command and the soldier froze, then stumbled backwards. The creature grabbed for the spear-holding soldier, caught his arm and yanked him forward. Olivia heard the whispering grow louder as the undead creature bit the soldier, its teeth shattering against the armour protecting the man's arm. Moments later, it pulled away enough of the armour to bite the man's bare flesh. And then there were two voices whispering as the soldier sank to the ground, magic flaring through his body.

He looked up. His eyes were yellow. His skin was paling rapidly.

"Out," Ivan snapped. He caught Olivia by the scruff of her neck and shoved her out of the door, then followed her as more soldiers appeared, one of them carrying a crude flamethrower and looking grimly determined to use it if necessary. "Get up the corridor, now!"

Olivia obeyed, willingly. Behind her, she heard someone shouting in Russian – Ivan muttered a word she was *sure* was a curse – and a series of banging sounds. Ivan shoved her through the armoured doors as soon as they reached them, then sagged in relief. Olivia felt little of it. The whispering at the back of her head was growing louder. Either the undead were getting closer or they were growing more numerous. She wasn't sure which one she preferred.

She took a breath. Shaken as he was, Ivan might just give her a straight answer for once.

"This is madness," she said. "What's the *point* of it?"

"Saving the Father Tsar," Ivan said. He sounded badly shaken. "There is no other point to it."

Olivia shuddered as he caught her arm and pulled her along the corridor, through a network of passages that seemed disturbingly empty. The whispering faded slowly, but it remained as a constant presence at the back of her head. Nothing she did, even the mental disciplines they'd tried to teach her at Cavendish Hall, stilled the whispering. But then, she hadn't paid much attention to those lessons. She'd never seen the need for them.

"You can have a wash," Ivan said. "I'll have some food sent to you."

"Thank you," Olivia said, sourly. Right now, being naked and vulnerable was the last thing she wanted. But she knew she looked and smelt disgusting. "Can't you tell him to stop before it really gets out of hand?"

Ivan shrugged. "I have faith that we can control what we do here," he said. "And if we can't, we can destroy the entire complex if necessary."

Olivia hoped he was right. In vast numbers, the undead were terrifyingly fast and intelligent, capable of actually thinking and planning. It was easy to imagine the Russians losing control and being eaten, until the entire country was dead. And then the undead would come swarming westwards, eating their way through the German states and France. Could they cross small bodies of water, like rivers? She had no idea.

"Madness," she said. "It's madness."

Ivan caught her arm and turned her to face him. "Remember this," he said. "No one else here will tolerate you saying that, even if you're right. They exist to serve the Father Tsar."

His voice lowered. "And so do you."

Chapter Twelve

wen had never been one for rising late. As a young girl, she'd treasured the time she'd had alone while her parents and older brother were still abed; as the Royal Sorceress, she hadn't dared show any kind of weakness by sleeping late. But she hadn't realised just how early the servants had to rise or just how much work they had to do before their lords and masters stirred from their slumber. If Janet hadn't shaken her awake, Gwen knew she would have overslept badly, at least by their standards. As it was, she found herself wanting to go back to sleep within an hour of climbing out of bed.

But that simply wasn't an option. She swept the floors, laid the fires, washed clothes for the trip to Russia and whatever else Cook or Janet told her to do, silently promising to ensure that the servants at Cavendish Hall received a large raise as soon as she got home. Her arms and legs ached from kneeling beside the stone fire, laying out the wood, then she had to struggle to light it with a match. Eventually, she gave up and used magic to start the blaze. It grew rapidly into a fire that would start heating up the entire household.

Janet called her back into the kitchen, presented her with a tray carrying a large pot of coffee, two mugs, a jug of milk and a bowl of sugar. "Take it to the master bedroom," she ordered, softly. "And be very quiet when you enter their room."

Gwen winced, inwardly, as she carried the tray up the stairs and tapped on the door. She had never been welcome in her parents' bedroom, not even when she'd been a little girl and her magic hadn't begun to surface. But the maids had always been allowed to enter ... she pushed the door open and peered into the room, silently relieved that the curtains were already open and light was streaming into the room. Lord Standish was sitting upright in bed, reading the latest issue of *The Times*. The front cover, Gwen couldn't help noticing, warned of French spies captured near Hartlepool. She just hoped the locals hadn't caught more monkeys.

"Put it on the side," Lord Standish ordered, shortly. "I'll pour my own coffee."

"Yes, My Lord," Gwen said, feeling a flush of embarrassment as she realised that Lord Standish was naked, with only a blanket protecting his private parts from her gaze. He wouldn't care if she saw everything, she knew. It wasn't as if she was his social equal, after all, but he'd be dreadfully embarrassed if *Lady* Gwen were to see him naked. "And Lady Standish?"

Lord Standish looked over to where his wife was hidden under the blankets. "I will pour hers too," he said. "Tell Cook that I will have eggs for breakfast."

Gwen curtseyed, then placed the tray on the table and walked out of the room, closing the door behind her. Cook nodded, unsurprised, when Gwen passed on the breakfast order, then pointed to a small table with a pot of eggs sitting beside a breadbasket. Janet was already there, eating a large plate of eggs and bread for her breakfast. Gwen sighed in relief – she also needed to eat – then sat down at the table. Janet chatted happily about nothing as they ate, then returned to their duties. It seemed there was no shortage of work for them to do as maids.

I'm going to have to do something about this, Gwen thought, as she worked her way through a pile of washed clothes, placing them on the line to dry. Lord Standish, it seemed, was a firm believer in wearing dignified clothes to diplomatic meetings. *People can't be worked to death like this.*

Her own thoughts mocked her. She'd been a maid for one day, unless she counted Irene's training, and she was already tired. Janet, according to the file, had been a maid since she was twelve years old; by now, she was practically one of the family. But she wasn't, not really. If she made a serious mistake, or said the wrong thing, she could be pitched out onto the streets to die, unless she was lucky enough to find other employment in a hurry. Cook and Romulus would find it easier to get new employment ...

She shook her head, bitterly. Something would have to change.

But it won't, as long as there is a constant supply of new maids from the countryside, she thought. *There's no incentive to change at all.*

She finished her work, then walked back to the kitchen, where she found Romulus chatting to Cook about the dinner menu for the following evening, before the family's departure for Russia. Lord Standish was apparently planning a big dinner for his friends and political allies, something Gwen was privately dreading. Lord Mycroft wouldn't attend, she knew, and he would keep his mouth shut in any case, but it was quite possible that someone would attend who *could* recognise her personally. If, of course, they paid any attention to the help. Gwen had only been in the household a day, more or less, and she'd discovered that Lord and Lady Standish were quite happy to talk about almost anything in front of her. A spy wearing a maid's uniform would go almost undetected.

And that's how Augustus Howell managed to blackmail so many, she thought, grimly. *He found disgruntled maids and foot servants and paid them well for anything they sold him that could be used for blackmail.*

"Gwen," Romulus said. "A word with you."

Gwen felt her blood run cold. *What can he want?* she asked herself, as he led her into the next room. He held himself like an aristocrat, she noted, even when talking to the maids. She couldn't tell if it was just an act or if he was trying to signify a barrier between them. It was probably the latter. A butler was on a far different level from a maid, particularly when the butler was black.

"Her Ladyship informs me that she wishes to speak with you," Romulus added. "You will attend on her after she has finished her breakfast."

"Yes, sir," Gwen said, bobbing yet another curtsey. She silently ran the calculations in her head and decided that she'd curtseyed more in the last few days than she'd done in her entire life. But then, she'd never actually been presented at Court or taken from social engagement to social engagement by her mother. "Do you know what she wishes to talk about?"

Romulus's face twitched. "I believe she wishes to speak about last night," he said. There was a hint of definite amusement in his voice. "You appear to have done very well."

He turned and left, striding away with military precision. Gwen watched him go, then turned and headed back to the kitchen. It was quite likely she'd be expected to help Lady Standish dress and she knew that was one of her weaknesses. Janet could warn her of what to expect.

Somewhat to her surprise, when the bell rang to summon her, she discovered that Lady Standish was already dressed in a morning gown. It was clear she wasn't planning to leave the house, Gwen decided as she curtseyed and then waited for Lady Standish to deign to notice her. She would have worn something much more fashionable if she'd intended to call upon any of her friends. It suggested hidden depths to Lady Standish, she decided. Lady Mary had always been dressed fashionably, even when she'd had no intention of leaving the house.

But Lady Standish is older than my mother, Gwen thought. The very elderly were allowed more social leeway than the younger women – and, by their standards, even Lady Mary was a young woman, despite having two adult children of her own. *Is she old enough to care less about fashion than she seems?*

"Gwen," Lady Standish said. "What happened last night?"

Gwen thought fast. What – if anything – had Raechel told her Aunt about last night? It was hard to imagine her telling Lady Standish anything, but Lady Standish might well have heard about the fire near Pall Mall and put two and two together. Or perhaps that would be a deductive feat beyond even Lord Mycroft. It was much more likely that she wanted a general report and nothing else. And there were parts of the story Gwen knew she couldn't tell.

"I went with Lady Raechel to a ... social gathering," Gwen said, carefully. She didn't want to get Raechel into trouble –

or more trouble, if that were possible. Raechel could cause her a great many problems if she chose, even if she couldn't fire Gwen directly. "It started as a dance, but when it grew more ... excitable I pulled her out and escorted her home."

"Details," Lady Standish snapped.

Gwen cringed, making no attempt to hide the motion. If she told the full truth – or at least left out her magic and the fire – Raechel would get into real trouble. But if she tried to tone it down and Lady Standish found out later ... she would be no good to Olivia if she was fired before they even reached Russia.

"You work for me," Lady Standish said, coldly. She picked up a hairbrush and began to brush her hair, but she never took her eyes off Gwen. "I want details."

"There were young men and women, largely unescorted, in the hall," Gwen said. "Their first dances were fairly decent, but their later dances were ..."

She allowed her face to flush, reluctant to give more details unless they were dragged out of her. She'd never realised, even when there had seemed no hope of ever being anything more than a devil-child, that such parties existed, that men and women cavorted together so freely, without even a thought for their reputations. But she understood – how well she understood! – the rebellious urge, to throw away parental conventions and just *do* something outrageous.

It isn't fair, she thought, mutely. *Men can do whatever they like and it gets winked at. But if a woman loses her reputation, she has no way to recover it.*

"I can imagine," Lady Standish said, primly. "You appear to have acted well."

"Thank you, My Lady," Gwen said.

She wondered, vaguely, if one of the reasons there was a high turnover of maids in the Standish Household was that some of them found Raechel uncontrollable. Someone born to the poorer classes might not have the confidence to drag Raechel out of the dance hall ... or the magic to cause a diversion. But it wasn't something she could ask, not now. Lady Standish wouldn't answer in any case.

"I understand you were previously in charge of a young girl," Lady Standish said, as if she hadn't discussed the matter with Gwen earlier. Madame Hampton would have given Lady Standish Gwen's fake file too. "Was she ever such a problem?"

"She was too young to cause such problems," Gwen said. The thought of such a young girl getting into trouble was horrific. And Jack had shown her that some young girls *did* get into such trouble, either stolen from their families or simply bought and sold into the worst kind of servitude. If they weren't aristocrats, she knew, the government rarely gave a damn. "I would have prevented her from getting too close to anyone, if necessary."

Lady Standish smiled. "And yourself?"

Gwen blinked. "My Lady?"

Lady Standish looked up, her eyes meeting Gwen's. "Did you ever get into trouble with young men?"

"No, My Lady," Gwen lied. If Sir Charles didn't count as trouble, she didn't know what did ... but Gwen the maid had had no contact with men. "There were few men on Lord Carmichael's estate and none of them were interested in me."

"There have always been rumours about Lord Carmichael," Lady Standish said. Her eyes had never left Gwen's face. "Are they true?"

"My Lady," Gwen said carefully, "I'm sure I don't know what you're talking about."

She felt her face heat, despite her best efforts. It wasn't uncommon for odd stories to follow men who married young, lost their wives and then never attempted to remarry. And Lord Carmichael should have had no difficulty in finding a second wife. His daughter certainly needed a maternal figure in her life. But he'd kept himself aloof from women ever since he'd lost his wife, not even – according to the files – trying to tumble the serving maids. Maybe he'd just been remarkably successful in keeping it quiet – or perhaps he was more interested in men than women. Given his rank, it would be a major scandal if such a thing were ever to be made public.

"I'm sure you don't," Lady Standish said. She put the hairbrush down, a faint smile playing over her face. "You will continue to escort Raechel, wherever she goes. I will inform her that she will not be allowed to leave the house without you."

Gwen hesitated, unsure if she should point out that Raechel had left the previous evening without anyone trying to bar her way. There weren't that many servants in the household, not enough to guard all the doors – and besides, she had no doubt that someone as fearless as Raechel would simply scramble out the window if necessary.

"Yes, My Lady," she said, instead.

"And you have full authority to drag her away from any unsuitable situation," Lady Standish continued. "You can do whatever is necessary to get her out."

"Yes, My Lady," Gwen said, again.

"Good," Lady Standish said. She came to her feet and looked Gwen up and down. "I shall hope not to speak with you again. Should I do so, Raechel will have managed to get herself into real trouble and you will have failed in your duty."

The way she said it left Gwen in no doubt that *she* would be blamed if something went badly wrong. But it was common enough for the aristocracy to blame someone else for their failings. Whatever else could be said about Lady Mary, she hadn't thrown Gwen out of her house when she'd discovered her daughter had magic, even if it wasn't very ladylike. She thought, suddenly, of Susan and winced, inwardly. Susan had been very lucky. If her magic had appeared in a less public setting, who knew *what* would have happened? There was at least one report of a daughter dying at the hands of her horrified parents, when they'd discovered she had magic.

Lady Standish studied Gwen for a long moment, then made a wordless motion of dismissal. Gwen curtseyed, then hurried out the door, lifting her skirts high enough so she could move without restriction. She'd forgotten how restrictive skirts could be until she'd had to wear one for several hours, without the ability to use magic.

Janet met her at the bottom of the stairs, holding a second tray of coffee. "It's for Lady Raechel," she said. "You can take it to her."

Gwen nodded, tiredly. She would have expected Janet to be annoyed at having the new girl given so much responsibility, but Janet had probably seen several maids leave after failing to cope with Raechel. Letting Gwen handle the older girl probably worked better than trying to handle Raechel herself. Gwen smiled, took the tray and headed back towards Raechel's suite. This time, when she knocked on the door, there was an incoherent muttering from the other side.

"I said, go away," Raechel snarled, as Gwen opened the door. She looked unkempt lying in bed, her nightgown barely covering anything of importance. "You're not wanted here."

Gwen sighed. She would probably have got on well with Raechel if she hadn't been forced to play the role of a maid. Instead, she put the coffee down on the table and poured Raechel a cup of steaming black liquid, then added milk and sugar. Raechel glowered at her unpleasantly as Gwen passed her the cup, but didn't try to throw the cup at her. More relieved that she cared to admit, Gwen turned and opened the curtains as Raechel sipped from the cup. Brilliant light streamed into the room.

"You shouldn't have taken me home early," Raechel said. "How did you get me to go to bed?"

"You needed to sleep, My Lady," Gwen said, cursing mentally. Subtle Charm was harder to detect than blatant Charm, but someone with a coolly logical mind might start asking why they'd acted in a particular manner, particularly if they were used to thinking out their actions before actually *acting*. "I think you just listened to me."

Raechel eyed her, suspiciously. "There's nothing to do today," she said, as she put the empty cup of coffee down on the bedside table. "Why don't I just stay in bed?"

"Because your Aunt wishes you to attend the dinner party tonight," Gwen said. "You could spend the first part of the day doing something else."

"The dinner party will be boring," Raechel said. "You know why my Aunt is taking me to Russia?"

Gwen shook her head, genuinely curious. Raechel's rebellious nature made her look like a diplomatic incident waiting to occur. Lord Standish would be dreadfully embarrassed if his niece did something – anything – to upset negotiations. In his place, Gwen wouldn't have taken anyone apart from the core negotiation team. The ladies could remain in England, where they would be safe.

"She wants me out of London," Raechel said. "She's taking me away from all my friends and halfway around the world, just to take me out of London."

It sounded reasonable, Gwen decided. In Lady Standish's place, she would have been tempted to arrange a quick marriage for Raechel and then let someone else worry about Raechel's conduct. But Lady Standish seemed to have other ideas.

"It will be an adventure, My Lady," Gwen said, trying to sound cheerful. If Olivia hadn't been kidnapped, she would have looked forward to the trip herself. "And you might come to enjoy it."

Raechel snorted, doubtfully.

Chapter Thirteen

livia had never been particularly good at telling the time, let alone counting the days. It wasn't a prized skill among the gangs of children in the Rookery, not when few of them expected to live more than a few years before something – or someone – killed them. Life was nothing more than a constant struggle for survival, with each day being taken as it came. There was nothing to be said for mulling about the future when it was unlikely there *was* a future.

But she thought she'd been in the complex for five days, although it was impossible to be sure. Every day, she would wake up, eat breakfast and then wash, before being escorted back into the lower levels for more experiments. Gregory didn't seem to care about the accident, the one that had come far too close to getting them all bitten; if anything, it had made him more enthusiastic. He had her reanimating dozens of corpses, trying to understand the limits of her powers. Olivia would have found it fascinating if the whispering in her head didn't get louder and louder with each new corpse she animated.

It was interesting to discover what the limitations actually were. The longer a dead body had been ... well, *dead*, the harder it was to reanimate it. But only if it had decomposed. A frozen body, kept so cold that decomposition couldn't begin, could be brought back to a shambling mockery of life with relative ease. Gregory had seemed very excited by that, although Olivia had no idea why and Ivan had declined to translate his Russian babbling. And then he'd insisted on trying more and more experiments.

She winced at the memory. If a body was so badly battered that it couldn't move, she couldn't reanimate it. If someone had broken bones before being killed, it was harder to bring them back to life, although it wasn't impossible. And someone who had just died could be brought back almost at once ... Gregory seemed fascinated by that, even though he should have known about it already. It was how undead outbreaks spread.

Ivan stepped into her bedroom with a thin smile on his face. Olivia eyed him, critically; she'd tried, more than once, to tell him that the whole plan was heading for disaster, but he'd refused to listen to her. Like most Charmers, he seemed to view the rest of the world – or at least the people he could influence – as nothing more than puppets. Gregory had tried to get him to use his Charm on the undead, but they'd shown no reaction. Olivia had hoped that this failure would show him that they were making a dreadful mistake ...

"You'll be having a rest today," he said, seriously. "We might have pushed you too far."

Olivia nodded. Her headaches had only grown worse over the last few days, although she wasn't sure if it was because of the use of her power or because of Ivan's meddling with her brain. She needed to eat and drink more too, like other magicians who burned through their energy reserves regularly. It struck her, as Esther followed Ivan into the room with a large tray of food, that she'd never seen a fat magician who used his powers regularly.

"Thank you," she said. It was odd, but she felt a certain amount of liking for Ivan, even though he'd Charmed her into submission. Perhaps it was because he had also shown concern for her, while Gregory viewed her merely as a tool. "What's the special occasion?"

Ivan gave her a sharp look. "Gregory will be hosting a visit today, from the Court," he said. "You'll remain in this room until we come for you."

Olivia looked down at the fur nightdress she'd been given, after she'd complained about trying to sleep naked. "You expect me to meet them?"

"No," Ivan said. "We suggest you stay here and catch up on your sleep."

"Oh," Olivia said. It was a joke. The more undead she had whispering at the back of her head, the harder it was to sleep. Every night, she dreamed of their twisted faces as they ran riot through the streets of London. She hadn't told her captors that she could still hear the undead, not when no one had asked her if she could. It was something she might be able to use against them later. "I'll do my best."

Esther finished laying out the tray, then departed. Olivia watched her go, noted how she shied away from Ivan, then looked up at the Russian. He seemed more amused than anything else, she decided, almost as if he'd relaxed in her presence. And then she decided to ask the question that had been bothering her since she'd first laid eyes on Esther.

"That girl," she said. "What *is* she?"

"A Jew," Ivan said.

Olivia stared at him. She'd never actually *seen* a Jew, but she'd heard about them on the streets of the Rookery. No one had ever had anything good to say about the Jews. They were money-grubbing lenders, willing to squeeze the last penny out of someone in need ... which didn't make them any different from the other loan sharks infesting the poorer parts of London. Olivia had feared and dreaded the day she would have needed to take a loan for herself, knowing that she'd be killed if she couldn't keep up with the payments ...

But Esther had been normal. Just another girl, little older than Olivia herself.

"They're hated in the cities and countryside," Ivan explained, as he motioned for Olivia to start eating. "If they didn't have the Father Tsar's protection, they would be hunted down and killed by the outraged peasants if something went wrong. They are loyal because they have to be loyal."

Olivia shuddered, remembering some of the stories about Loyalist Irishmen or American Indians. They were loyal, because without their loyalty they wouldn't be protected by the King ... and without the King's protection they would be slaughtered by their enemies. If the Russian Jews were in the same boat, they'd be understandably unwilling to assist her in escaping the complex. Esther wouldn't just be killed; her entire family would be slaughtered. Olivia gritted her teeth, bitterly. She'd hoped the young girl might help her. But she knew better now.

Ivan waited for her to finish eating, then withdrew, leaving her alone. Olivia rapidly found herself bored; she climbed out of bed, tried the door – it was locked, unsurprisingly – and then went for a wash. This time, the water was alarmingly cold, but splashing her face with cold water helped to wake her up. Still, when she got back to the room, there was nothing to do with her time. No books she could read, no games to play ... not even any exercises set by her tutors. Cursing under her breath, she lay down on the bed and tried to sleep. Instead, she received a jarring series of images from the undead ...

... One of them was facing a man, his hands tied behind his back. Sheer hunger blazed through her, overwhelmingly powerful; she lunged forward, sank her teeth into his throat and sucked the glorious life from his body. Warmth ran through her as she watched her victim fall to the floor, already starting the transformation into a creature just like her. He moaned as he stumbled back to his feet, then stepped away from her. There was life just ahead of them and they intended to take it for themselves ...

Olivia snapped awake, feeling the whispering growing louder and louder until it threatened to overwhelm her. She screamed as the voices suddenly became very clear, then fell back into the darkness ...

... A woman was kneeling in front of her, banging her head on the floor as she begged for mercy. But Olivia barely noticed; she pulled the woman to her feet, bit into her arm and then dropped her to the ground. Life energy surged around her as she stumbled forward, seeing more sources of light and life ahead of her. The uniformed men would be tough, but she didn't care ...

...They stabbed at her with their weapons. She didn't feel the blows, not even when she sank to the floor and darkness overcame her ...

She screamed again as someone slapped her face. Her eyes snapped open to reveal Ivan, standing beside the bed with a concerned expression on his face. Olivia was suddenly aware that her hands were sticky and looked at them, realising – to her horror – that they were covered in blood. Behind Ivan, Gregory watched with an expression of amused interest. He made no move to heal her palms from her self-inflicted wounds.

"You started to scream," Ivan said. "What happened?"

Olivia glared at him, mutely. He was her captor, even if he'd shown more concern for her than anyone else. She had no intention of telling him anything, unless he forced it from her with his Charm. At least she would have had the satisfaction of forcing him to actually do some work. Charmers were lazy, as a general rule. They found it too easy to manipulate others into doing their work for them.

"It won't be a problem," Gregory said, in English. He meant for her to understand. "But we can leave her here for a few days ..."

"Of boredom," Olivia said. She sounded like a whiny child and didn't much care. "There's nothing to *do* here."

Gregory's eyes glittered. "You could always raise some more of the dead."

Ivan spoke to him rapidly in Russian. They had a long conversation while Olivia listened helplessly, unable to understand a single word they said. Perhaps Esther could teach her Russian ... no, she knew better than to ask the poor girl anything now. If she tried to teach Olivia or even to help her in any way, her family would suffer for it.

"We will find you some books," Ivan said, finally. "And you will have time to relax."

Olivia sighed. She knew she couldn't relax, unless they drugged her. And she didn't want to ask for drugs. They'd know that something was wrong.

"You wanted me to bring them back to life," Olivia said. "Why? What's the point?"

Gregory, surprisingly, answered her, a gleam in his eye that chilled her to the bone. "The Father Tsar is surrounded by weakness and treachery," he said. There was something about his attitude that reminded her of the doom prophets from London, the men who walked the streets clad in sackcloth and preaching that the end of the world was nigh. "He can no longer rely on anyone away from His Holy Presence."

Olivia swallowed. She had a nasty feeling she knew where this was going.

"The armies have failed him," Gregory continued. "The heathen Turks continue to advance, to threaten the sacred soil of Mother Russia. The diplomats have failed him. We are locked into an alliance with France which threatens to plunge us into another war. His people have failed him. They plot revolution in the streets and plan to take over the military. Even the weather has failed him. The population groans under a famine caused by poor weather and very bad harvests."

"So you're in trouble," Olivia sneered. She hoped – prayed desperately – that she was wrong, but she feared she wasn't. "Why do you want me to raise the dead?"

Gregory's eyes seemed to gleam brighter with the unholy glow of fanaticism. "I will give the Father Tsar an unstoppable army," he proclaimed. "The undead will march south into Turkey, crushing the Turks and their collaborators underfoot. Istanbul will return to the Orthodox Faith, while the Muslims and the Hindus are slaughtered and then made to rise again as part of our army. And then there will be France and the rest of the world. It will all belong to the Father Tsar."

Olivia stared at him. "You're mad."

His hand moved so fast that she didn't even realise he was about to hit her until his hand slammed into her face, almost knocking her off the bed. Blood trickled down her nightgown as pain surged through her jaw ... once, she would have taken it in her stride, but now ... now, it cowed her as effectively as Ivan's Charm. She touched her bruised face and stared up at him, trying to meet his eyes. He showed no hint of doubt, no fear that he might lose control of the undead. But could such a large army ever be controlled by anyone?

Master Thomas had controlled a force of undead monsters, Olivia knew. But all he'd done was give them general orders, just as she'd done – later. How long could any Necromancer maintain control over an army of thousands, of millions, of undead ... a number so large as to be utterly beyond her imagination? She suspected that no one could handle such a large army, not even the most capable Necromancer in the world. Gregory would be lucky if he got them all going in the right direction ... and God help any of his own people who got between them and their targets.

It had been years since Haiti had been depopulated by the undead, she recalled. Gwen had told her about the incident, sparing nothing. The local witch doctors had believed they could use a Necromancer and control his powers. Instead, the undead had refused to behave as predicted, broken loose and started to consume the population. French and British troops had been unable to destroy them before the entire island was rendered utterly barren. These days, no one landed on Haiti, no matter how desperate they were. There were quicker ways to commit suicide.

She tried to imagine the horror the Russians would unleash. The undead were deterred by large amounts of water, but Russia had no natural barriers between itself and the rest of Europe or the Middle East. They'd advance out in all directions, smart enough to overcome enemy defences or crush their way forward by sheer weight of numbers. There would be no stopping them until they reached the English Channel, if then. Half the world's land surface would belong to the undead.

"You have to listen to me," she pleaded. "You can't control such a large army of undead. You *can't*."

"We can," Gregory corrected. He raised his hand to slap her again, then stopped when Ivan shook his head. "The Father Tsar will get his army, young lady, and you will help us to create it."

"No," Olivia said. It was pointless defiance and she *knew* it was pointless defiance, but she couldn't just submit any longer. "I won't help."

"You will," Ivan said. He sounded absolutely confident of success – and he was right, Gwen knew. "You are ours now."

"Even I can't control so many," Olivia protested. The whispering at the back of her head seemed to be growing stronger. What were they *doing* to the undead to make them moan and whisper so loudly? The British Empire had never experimented with the undead. They believed the undead far too dangerous to play with, no matter the promise of science. "You can't control them."

Gregory leaned forward until his face was almost touching hers. "I have a plan," he said. Up close, the stench of urine was almost overpowering. "And you will play your part, as you are called upon to do."

He stepped backwards, then turned and marched out of the room. Ivan turned and watched him as he passed through the door, then turned to look at Olivia. His face was deathly pale.

"You mustn't talk to him like that," he warned, frantically. "Don't you know what he is?"

Olivia shook her head. Gregory was just another monster in human form, as far as she was concerned, like all the others she'd encountered in the Rookery. There were men who thought nothing of rape or murder, women who killed their partners or sold their children for opium or tobacco ... there were horrors that none of the children at Cavendish Hall could imagine, only a few short miles from their home. How was Gregory any different to the men who planned to slaughter their rivals in bloody street fighting?

"He's *Skoptzi*," Ivan said. "Do you know what that is?"

Olivia shook her head. The word meant nothing to her.

"They're a ... *sect*," Ivan explained. "In the past, they were misunderstood and persecuted by the State, but now they worship Father Tsar. To them, he is a *god*. He can do no wrong and they will do *anything* for him. They have nothing in their lives but him."

"Oh," Olivia said. She'd met a few nuns who had no room for anyone in their lives but Jesus Christ. Some of them had been decent enough, willing to work with the poor; others had been just as sweetly condescending as Gwen's mother. But most of the priests she'd encountered had been more interested in chasing whores than actually spreading the word of God. "And so?"

Ivan stared at her. "Have you not noticed the smell?"

Olivia's lips twitched. "Does he have problems keeping his bladder under control?"

Ivan didn't smile. "He's a eunuch," he said. "His genitals were removed when he was initiated into the *Skoptzi*. He will do *anything* for the Father Tsar because he has nothing else to live for. You have to understand that, Olivia."

He leaned forward. "You are in great danger," he added. "If you don't learn how to accommodate yourself to the *Skoptzi*, they will eventually kill you."

Olivia watched as he stood up and walked out the door, leaving her alone with her thoughts. Her jaw still hurt – she was uncomfortably aware he might have knocked out a tooth – but a cold resolve had overcome her. She was not going to stay in the complex any longer than she had to. Closing her eyes, she reached out with her mind, falling into the whispering she could hear in her head. If her magic was the only weapon she had, she'd use it, no matter what she'd promised Gwen ...

... Because the alternative, she told herself, was worse.

Chapter Fourteen

f she had met Raechel openly, Gwen told herself for what felt like the umpteenth time, she would have liked the girl. She was funny, daring and braver than Gwen would have been, without her magic. But as Raechel's servant, the whole experience was quite nightmarish, threatening social disaster on more than one occasion. Raechel disliked having a nursemaid and it showed. Given half a chance, the girl would slip out of sight and try to leave the house before Gwen could catch up with her. By the time they were finally ready to depart, Gwen was seriously considering just calling a Charmer from Cavendish Hall and having him Charm Raechel into behaving as a young girl should.

But you were never very well behaved either, her thoughts mocked her, as she packed the bags for the trip to Russia. Raechel didn't seem to have a very realistic idea of what the weather would be like in the far northern country; she'd packed several dresses that offered very little protection against the cold. Gwen was relieved that she'd managed to check the bags herself before it was time to go. Raechel offering to pack them for herself had tipped her off that something was very wrong.

"You don't need to pack those dresses," Raechel objected. "They're dreadfully unfashionable."

"They're also thick enough to provide some protection, My Lady," Gwen pointed out, feeling her temper fraying. "The weather in Russia is cold, colder than anywhere in Britain. You will freeze to death if you try to wear a summer dress in Russia."

Raechel snorted. "As if anyone would care!"

Gwen bit her lip to keep the rejoinder from coming out of her mouth. If Lady Standish didn't care about her niece, at least on some level, Raechel would have been married off by now or sent to one of the finishing schools that specialised in turning intelligent young girls into brainless young women with heads full of silly nonsense. Lady Mary had threatened Gwen with one of them, often enough, although she'd never gone through with it. She'd had some problems, Gwen suspected, finding a school that would be willing to take her. Only Cavendish Hall had been interested in recruiting magicians ... and even they had hesitated to take a girl into their employ. If Gwen hadn't been a Master ...

"You also need a thick coat," Gwen continued, pushing her thoughts aside. "Your Aunt has ordered the latest and most suitable fur coats suitable for Russia."

"Also dreadfully unfashionable," Raechel said. She picked up one of the coats and sneered down at it. "You think I can wear this to a ball?"

"I think you will have to wear it in the streets," Gwen said. "Unless, of course, you just want to wait at the Embassy while your Aunt and Uncle go to the Winter Palace."

"That's what they'll want me to do," Raechel said. She brightened, suddenly. "But there are a great many bright young men serving in our embassies."

Gwen groaned, inwardly. She could chase after Raechel in London and try to keep her from making a fool of herself – or her Aunt and Uncle – but in Russia she would be required to actually carry out her mission. And, despite herself, she was actually starting to like the girl, even though she was hellishly annoying. It didn't seem right to leave her running around on her own while Gwen did her work. Raechel was far too likely to get into trouble.

"I suppose there are," she agreed. David had spent time in an embassy, after all. "But most of them will have few prospects ..."

Raechel snorted. "Who cares about prospects?"

Gwen sighed and finished packing the bags, then stepped back to survey her work. Unlike most aristocratic women when they went travelling, Raechel only had a couple of large bags, both crammed with dresses, fashionable make-up and a handful of other items she probably couldn't get in Russia. Lady Standish, on the other hand, seemed to have packed her entire supply of clothes into a dozen large suitcases, most of which wouldn't be opened while she was in Russia. Gwen had rolled her eyes when she'd seen Janet packing the clothes, wondering if the maids were allowed a suitcase of their own. It turned out that she and Janet were expected to share a single bag between them.

Good thing I don't carry the tools of the trade around with me, Gwen thought, with droll amusement. *What would Janet make of it if I placed a gun in the bag?*

There was a sharp tapping on the door. Gwen hastily checked to make sure that they were both decent, then opened the door to reveal Romulus. The butler bowed politely to Raechel, then picked up both of the suitcases and carried them out of the door and down the stairs to where the small fleet of carriages were waiting. Gwen shook her head, impressed – despite herself – at the butler's strength. She'd seen soldiers who would have hesitated to pick up both suitcases at once.

"Well," Raechel said. "Farewell London."

Gwen said nothing as Raechel checked her appearance in the mirror – for once, she looked surprisingly decent, clad in a long red dress that matched her hair – and then led the way out of the room, descending the stairs as grandly as if she were being presented at Court. Gwen smiled at the thought, then followed her down to where Janet was waiting, their shared suitcase right next to her. Janet looked to be having problems carrying it, Gwen realised, which wasn't too surprising. She picked the suitcase up, drawing on a little magic to make it easier, and carried it out towards the carriages. The servants were expected to ride in the very last one.

"A pity Cook isn't coming," Janet said, as she scrambled into the carriage. "She would make sure we were served proper food in Russia."

Gwen had to smile. She didn't really know what sort of food was eaten in Russia, but it was typical of Londoners to eye foreign food with suspicion. Even the influx of Turkish refugees hadn't managed to change that too far, although the younger aristocrats were making a habit of patronising Turkish cafés as a way of showing their feelings for the Sultan, the man who'd given the Russians a black eye and a bloody nose. The fact that most of the refugees had fled the Sultan as he consolidated his rule seemed to have escaped them.

The door opened, revealing Raechel, who scrambled into the carriage before either of them could object. Gwen opened her mouth to say something, then dropped the thought as the coachman cracked the whip and the carriage shuddered into life. Raechel sat down next to her, folding her dress over her legs, then gave Gwen and Janet a brilliant smile.

"It was too stuffy in the carriage," she said, by way of explanation. "Uncle only wanted to talk about money matters."

Gwen didn't – quite – roll her eyes. Inheriting Master Thomas's considerable fortune had forced her to learn a great deal about managing money, one of the many useful skills that were rarely taught to young girls. If she'd married, as she would have if she hadn't been born a magician, her husband would be expected to handle her money even if it was in her name. It had been hard to learn, even with a dedicated tutor, but there'd been no choice. If someone else had handled the money, she would have been at that person's mercy.

"You are a rich young woman," she said, quietly. She could understand why someone as flighty as Raechel would find it boring, but she was only making herself vulnerable. "You need to learn how to handle your own money or someone will take it from you."

Raechel eyed her, suspiciously. "Did you teach Lady Heather how to handle money?"

"I tried," Gwen said. The file the family had received stated that Gwen had been tutor as well as maid, chaperone and confidante as well as servant. "But she had far less in her own name than you. You will be targeted by young rakes who want your money to fund their gambling habits."

"And what," Raechel demanded, "is wrong with gambling?"

"The gambling house always wins," Gwen said, remembering her visit to the Golden Turk. It had been an eye-opener in more ways than one. "You could get into debt very easily and then find yourself in the poorhouse."

"Oh, *that* would never happen," Raechel said. "Auntie would never allow it."

Gwen sighed, inwardly. The hell of it was that Raechel was probably right. An aristocrat might be sent abroad, to India or China, to escape gambling debts or scandals at home, but it was unlikely that he would go into debtors' prison. She'd never heard of a woman getting so deeply into debt that she had to flee the country, but one of her relatives could probably put her up in a country house, well away from her creditors. No aristocratic family would tolerate one of its womenfolk going to jail or being transported.

"You don't want to be in her debt," Gwen said. If Raechel did manage to gamble away all her money, she would be utterly dependent upon Lord and Lady Standish. "And you need to be careful."

Raechel gave her an odd look. She had to have realised that Gwen wasn't *quite* acting as the perfect servant, even if it was Lady Standish rather than Raechel herself who was employing Gwen. Despite her crash course in being a maid, Gwen knew her pose was very far from perfect, something she'd tried to blame on being Heather's confidante as well as her servant and chaperone. But someone as smart as Raechel might notice other discrepancies ...

It wasn't uncommon for poorer aristocratic girls to seek placement as governesses, rather than household servants. Their richer fellows saw them as being better companions and teachers than people from the lower classes. But Gwen's file included no trace of aristocracy. It had been too risky, Irene had pointed out, to risk drawing their attention. The Royal Sorceress, after all, was perhaps the best-known aristocrat of her generation.

The carriage rattled to a halt before Raechel could ask any questions. Gwen heard shouting from outside, then the coachman opened the door, allowing Raechel to lead the way down to the ground. Gwen followed her ... and stopped dead as she saw the colossal airship, hanging in the air in front of them. It was a long thin gasbag, which Gwen knew to be filled with hydrogen gas, capable of lifting a vast amount of weight into the air. Gwen's father had made his money by investing in airships, proclaiming them the wave of the future. It was certainly easier to take an airship than a sailing ship.

But it could be dangerous too, Gwen thought. She could fly – levitate, rather – under her own power, but even she had problems with airships. There had been a handful of crashes over the years and very few people had survived the explosions. Indeed, the Houses of Parliament regularly debated banning airships from overflying London, particularly after Jack had used one to storm the Tower of London. *I wonder how Lady Standish will react to the airship ...*

Her Ladyship didn't seem too worried as the small crowd made its way towards the gondola, the passenger compartment hanging down from the colossal gasbag. Instead, she spoke to Raechel in tones that suggested she would have been shouting, if she had been ill-bred and brought up to believe that shouting at her niece in public was acceptable behaviour. The younger woman, Gwen noted, didn't seem too cowed at her Aunt's words. Gwen sighed, inwardly, then watched as Romulus and a team of footmen started to pick up the bags and transfer them to the airship. She couldn't help noticing that half of the footmen were staring at him whenever they thought he wasn't watching. They'd probably never seen a black man before, at least not one dressed like a Butler.

Inside, they were greeted by a man wearing a uniform grander than any Royal Navy Admiral, an elaborate collection of navy blue and gold lace. He bowed low to Lord Standish, kissed Lady Standish's hand and didn't seem particularly put out when Raechel declined to have her hand kissed. Once the greetings were over, he allowed a pair of young women to lead them into the seating compartment, which was larger than Gwen had expected. Beyond the doors, the women explained, were the sleeping compartments, ranging from a large section for the aristocrats to a smaller set of rooms for the servants. It looked, Gwen realised numbly, as though Janet and herself would be sharing a compartment with Romulus.

A dull whine ran through the gondola as they explored the passenger section. Gwen had to admit she was impressed, even though she'd seen pictures of airships her father owned years ago. It was both spacious and compact; the staff had a cooking section, while the aristocrats had large bedrooms and a drawing room that allowed them to talk or stare out of the windows towards the ground, far below. She hastily joined Janet in unpacking the travel bags – the remainder would be stowed in the cargo compartment, out of reach – and then returned to the smoking room. Sir Sidney and several other diplomats had arrived and were clustering around Lord Standish like planets around the sun.

Sir Sidney caught her eye, then headed for the door and walked past her. Gwen followed him into his room, after checking to make sure they were unobserved. Sir Sidney was not meant to know Gwen the Maid – and if they were sighted together, she knew what sort of conclusion would be drawn. Sir Sidney, unlike Lord Standish and the rest of the mission, was young enough to feel a fire in his blood.

He looked her up and down as soon as the door was closed. "You seem to be fitting in nicely," he said, wryly. "How are you coping?"

Gwen looked down at her maid's uniform and scowled. "When we get back," she said, "I'm going to make damn sure that servants are treated better by their masters."

"A sensible desire," Sir Sidney agreed. He took a breath as he sat down on the bed. Apart from being surprisingly small, it was little different to one on the ground. "There have been worrying developments."

"Oh," Gwen said. She took a breath. "What sort of worrying developments?"

"We just picked up a message from an ... agent in Paris," Sir Sidney said. "The good news is that the Russians are clearly hesitating to join the French in war against us. That actually works in our favour right now."

Gwen nodded. The airship would be overflying French territory for part of its journey to St. Petersburg, allowing the French a chance to shoot it down if they wanted to start the war in style. But if the Russians were being baulky, the French wouldn't dare interfere with the airship for fear of convincing the Russians to join the British in war against France. They'd probably prefer to allow the British to send their envoys and then try to outbid them, if the Russians wanted to get more out of their allies before going to war.

"That's good," she said. "And the bad news?"

Sir Sidney hesitated. "We know the name of the envoy the French will be sending," he said. "It's Talleyrand."

Gwen swore an unladylike oath, just loud enough to be heard. Talleyrand was the Grand Master of French Politics, the ultimate survivor ... and the closest match France had for Lord Mycroft. Gwen had met him while he'd been in London; if there was anyone likely to recognise her under the maid's uniform and demure attitude, it was Talleyrand. And *he* wouldn't be stupid enough to ignore the help.

Sir Sidney smiled, seemingly unabashed by her oath. "It makes sense," he said. "The French have to know they don't dare lose the Russians."

"I know," Gwen said.

She ran through the situation in her head. Without the Russians, the Franco-Spanish Empire would be badly outmatched by the British-Ottoman alliance. It was unlikely that France could be defeated so completely that she could be occupied – and Gwen knew that Lord Mycroft preferred a balance of power to conquest and occupation – but the French would be foolish to start a war if they couldn't count on the Russians. They'd made huge strides forward in uniting their Latin American territories, yet there was no way to know if their work would survive the test of war.

"It can't be helped now," Sir Sidney said. "You just need to keep your head down and remain part of the background."

"I'll do my best," Gwen said. She groaned. Talleyrand had a reputation for chasing women ... and Raechel probably wouldn't run very hard if he caught sight of her. How best to shock her Aunt than by making love to a man old enough to be her grandfather? "Keep me informed if anything changes."

"I will," Sir Sidney said. "It's a minimum of five days from London to St. Petersburg. All hell could break out by then."

Gwen nodded, then motioned for him to check the corridor to be sure it was safe for her to emerge. Outside, there was nothing and no one, apart from a growing whine as the airship's engines powered up. Gwen felt the floor – the deck, she reminded herself – shudder under her feet as she left the cabin and walked back to the servants' compartment. Janet was sitting on the bunk bed, looking nervous. It was clear that the thought of flying didn't agree with her.

"Lady Raechel was looking for you," she said, as Gwen entered. "I think she's in the drawing room."

"I'll go there," Gwen said. The airship shuddered again as she turned to leave. "It never ends, does it?"

Janet gave her an odd look, but said nothing.

Chapter Fifteen

wen," Raechel said, as she entered the drawing room. "You're just in time!"

Gwen hurried over to the window and watched as the last of the ropes were pulled away from the airship. It shuddered again, then started to rise slowly into the air. Gwen vaguely remembered her father explaining to David precisely how the hydrogen was used to make the airship fly, but she couldn't recall enough of it to explain to someone else. Instead, she sat down and gripped the handles of her chair as the airship rose higher and higher into the sky.

"It's amazing," Raechel said. Below them, London was growing smaller and smaller, even though they could see all the way to the edge of the city. "I could look down on everyone from such a great height."

Gwen scowled as the airship shook, again. Flying under her own power was fun, but the airship simply didn't strike her as very safe. Quivers ran through the deck as the engines started to push the airship forward, heading towards the English Channel, while the gondola shook every time a gust of wind struck it. A single spark in the wrong place, Gwen knew, could cause an explosion that would kill them all. She knew it was unlikely, she knew her father and his designers had worked hard to eliminate risk, yet she couldn't help feeling uneasy. It would be a relief to be down on the ground once again.

"You could, My Lady," she agreed. "What are you going to do now?"

"Sit here for a while," Raechel said. She waved a hand towards London, now starting to recede into the distance. "And you?"

"I probably have work to do," Gwen said. She stood up and headed towards the door. "I can bring you a book, if you like."

"Please," Raechel said. She winked as Gwen looked back at her. "One of the more ... *interesting* books."

Gwen sighed as she walked out of the compartment and down towards Raechel's cabin, where her travelling bag had been left on her bed. It was easier, somehow, to cope with being on the airship if she wasn't actually looking out of the windows and down towards the ground, even though it was still shuddering every time the wind blew and struck the hull. She passed Lady Standish, who looked thin and pale, and paused long enough to see if her mistress needed assistance. Lady Standish waved her on impatiently and stumbled into her cabin. It wasn't going to be a pleasant trip.

In Raechel's cabin, Gwen opened the bag, removed a handful of books and looked down at them, sighing. The printing press had a great deal to answer for, she knew, starting with the publication of hundreds of crass romantic novels that ranged from coy to alarmingly explicit and crude. Some of them had actually been banned, with heavy penalties for owning them, but it didn't stop the tidal wave of filth. Gwen actually recalled attending a meeting of the Royal College where one speaker had urged using magic to destroy all such books. The fact that magic didn't actually work that way seemed to have escaped him completely.

She picked up a couple of the less unpleasant ones, wrapped a cloak around them and carried the books back to the drawing room. Raechel was still there, gazing out over south-east England as the airship's course carried it towards France. She took the books, muttered a thank you, then sat back to keep drinking in the view. Gwen nodded, then slipped out of the room and back towards the armoured smoking room. Inside, Lord Standish, Sir Sidney and the other four diplomats were playing cards and drinking port. Gwen wasn't too surprised. It wasn't as though they could actually *do* anything until they reached St. Petersburg.

The next three days went by slowly, but surprisingly well. There was relatively little work for the maids to do while they were on the airship, so Janet largely remained in her cabin, fighting the effects of airsickness, while Gwen did her best to tend to Raechel and Lady Standish. The latter, in particular, had a worse case of airsickness than Janet and was an aristocrat to boot, so the stewardesses spent a great deal of time coddling her and trying to make the older woman feel better. Gwen privately suspected that Lady Standish wouldn't feel better until she was down on the ground, even if it was Russian soil.

Gwen spent the time with a Russian phrasebook, trying to learn a handful of Russian words and how to use them. Romulus, much to her surprise, could speak Russian and taught her how to pronounce the words properly, although he also warned her that it might be a long time before she mastered the language. Gwen, who could speak both French and a surprising amount of Latin, couldn't disagree. Russian had simply not seemed a very important language to teach to English boys, let alone girls.

"You also need to be firm when you speak to them," Romulus added. "The Russians respect strength and firmness, not weakness and indecision."

Gwen wondered, as she wandered the airship's corridors, just how he would know. It was the same piece of advice, she knew, that she'd been given for handling servants by her mother, who had driven a number of maids and menservants out of the house with her incessant demands. And she was fairly sure that slave-owners made the same arguments in the American South, where negro slaves picked cotton or tried to flee southwest to French-held Mexico. But then, given how badly outnumbered the aristocracy was by the rest of the world's population, having an absolute sense of confidence would probably help them maintain their absolute control.

She peeked into the smoking room and saw Sir Sidney peering down at a chessboard, studying a problem he'd drawn from a book. It had been weeks since she'd played, Gwen recalled; part of her was tempted to sit down facing him and challenge the young man to a game. But she knew a maid couldn't be seen to sit down with an aristocrat and play, let alone win. She looked at the problem for a long moment, then walked onwards, keeping her face carefully expressionless. There was so much in her life she couldn't do as a maid. She looked into the drawing room and froze. Raechel was missing.

Gwen sucked in her breath sharply. Raechel seemed, on the journey, to have become a creature of habit; she moved between the bedroom, the dining room and the drawing room, rarely altering her pattern for anything. She was bored, Gwen knew; there were few people she could talk to as an equal on the airship. Gritting her teeth, Gwen headed down towards Raechel's cabin and looked inside. It was empty too. Gwen felt cold ice running down her back as she turned and started to search the gondola, trying to deduce where Raechel might have gone. Could she have sneaked into the engine compartment, or up towards the bridge?

She moved through the rest of the passenger compartment quickly. Raechel wasn't with her Aunt – *that* was no surprise – or trying to cadge some additional food out of the stewardesses, or even bothering her uncle. Gwen hesitated, then stepped towards the door leading to the bridge, hoping she wasn't about to made a deadly mistake. The door was locked, but picking locks through magic was now second nature to her. She stepped through into a small airlock and then opened the next door.

The sound of the engines and the wind was much louder as she saw the railing leading around the airship. There were open gaps allowing someone to look out and see the engines, even netting they could use to climb over to the engines in midflight and examine them, perhaps even repair them without having to land. She took a step forward, feeling the deck shifting as the airship shook, and walked towards the next gondola. If she hadn't known she could catch herself if she fell, she doubted she could have made it to the airlock. It clicked open on her touch and she stepped through.

She let out a sigh of relief as the airlock closed behind her, snapping off the sound of the engines. Ahead of her, she heard a moaning noise – a feminine moaning noise. Swallowing the urge to curse loudly, Gwen hurried down the corridor and peered into a small bedroom, presumably intended for the crew. Raechel was pressed against one wall, her dress pulled down to her waist, the Captain kissing and sucking at her breasts as his hand stroked between her legs.

Gwen stared in absolute shock, then cleared her throat loudly. The lovers jumped apart so quickly it was almost comical.

"Pull up your dress," Gwen snapped, forgetting her determination to be demure in all things, even if it meant risking her cover. "You can't stay here."

The Captain rounded on her. "What the hell are *you* doing here?"

"I was sent to find her," Gwen said, not entirely truthfully. She had no doubt that Lady Standish *would* have sent her after Raechel, if she'd known her niece was missing. But Gwen had been careful not to mention it to anyone. "And you left the door unlocked."

"It locks automatically," the Captain snapped. Despite being so badly shocked, his career at risk, he was still thinking clearly. "You shouldn't have been able to get here alone."

Gwen would have been impressed, if things had been different. Instead, she forced herself to cool her temper and remain calm. Raechel glowered at Gwen, her face as red as her hair, and scrambled to pull her dress back over her breasts. It was torn in several places, suggesting that their ... lovemaking had been urgent. Her underwear, a pair of satin panties from France, were ripped and torn beyond salvation. Gwen sighed, picked them up and dropped them in her pocket. They'd have to be quietly lost later, if only to ensure that Lady Standish didn't discover them and ask pointed questions.

"You didn't lock the door," she said, tartly. "How else could I have made it here?"

She waited for Raechel to finish dressing, then sighed when she saw the girl. Raechel's makeup was smeared, her dress badly damaged and her hair completely out of order, but there was nothing they could do about it, not here. They would have to sneak back to Raechel's cabin, wash her thoroughly and dress her in something that wasn't so torn. The dress, too, would probably have to be dumped.

"You just had to spoil this, didn't you?" Raechel muttered, as the Captain turned to lead them back to the passenger gondola. "I was enjoying myself."

"I'm sure you were," Gwen said, feeling her patience snap. "And what would you have told your relatives if you'd turned up pregnant?"

"He told me he was sterile," Raechel said. "I couldn't have caught a baby from him ..."

Gwen barked a harsh laugh. One of her less pleasant duties as Royal Sorceress had been forcing a magician to help take care of a woman he'd made pregnant, after telling her that he was a magician and he could make sure nothing unfortunate happened. But no magician could prevent themselves from siring a child, as far as anyone knew. Lucy had told her afterwards, that men were quite happy to tell whatever lies they had to tell just to get into bed with a girl. Gwen recalled Sir Charles and flushed at the memory.

She prayed under her breath that they wouldn't encounter anyone as they walked back through the airlocks, then into the passenger gondola. Luck was with them; they saw no one as they crept down to Raechel's cabin, then through the door. Once safely inside, Gwen locked it, then turned to face Raechel. The older girl was clearly spoiling for a fight.

"Before you start shouting," Gwen said, quickly, "you should be aware that the walls here are very thin."

Raechel glared at her, then composed herself. "Do you *have* to ruin everything?"

Gwen took a long breath. "Did you really believe him when he said he was sterile?"

Raechel's glare grew harder. "Are you saying he lied to me?"

"Men like to enjoy their masculinity," Gwen snapped. "I don't believe a man who was really sterile would advertise it to *anyone*, even a girl he was trying to deflower. It's much more likely that a virile man like the Captain has a woman in every port."

She sighed, remembering the constant stream of scandals surrounding Lord Nelson, the First Sea Lord. Most sailors had a girl in several different ports, but Lord Nelson was simply too public a figure for it to remain unnoticed indefinitely. And other sailors often found themselves charged with bigamy for actually *marrying* more than one woman at the same time. There was no reason why an airship officer would be any different.

"He wouldn't," Raechel insisted. "I *like* him!"

"Or did you just want to have fun?" Gwen asked. "He is a handsome man, isn't he?"

She didn't want to admit it, but she'd enjoyed the mild petting she'd indulged in with Sir Charles. But he'd been planning to either seduce or betray her in the end. Most doctors would swear on stacks of bibles that women knew nothing of sexual pleasure and didn't care for sex, other than as a means of reproduction, yet all such doctors were male. Lucy, who was both a woman and a Healer, said those men were deluding themselves. And Gwen knew who she preferred to believe.

Raechel eyed her. "This is *my* life," she snapped. "I can do whatever I please!"

"Of course you can," Gwen said, mildly. Her voice hardened. "If, of course, you're prepared to deal with the consequences."

She met Raechel's eyes, silently daring her to look away. "You could have wound up pregnant, giving birth to a bastard child," she warned. "You could have wound up abandoned, if he has another wife in another city. You could have been defiled, in the eyes of everyone who might have wanted to marry you. And, even if he did the decent thing and married you, you would have to endure life with him ..."

Raechel froze for a split second, then raised her hand to slap Gwen. Gwen caught it, instinctively. It was a mistake, she realised instantly. As painful as it would have been, she would have been safer to allow Raechel to slap her, rather than catch her hand and prove that she was considerably more daring than any maidservant. Raechel stared at her for a long moment, then yanked her hand out of Gwen's grasp and stepped backwards, rubbing her wrist. Gwen felt cold. She hadn't meant to hurt the older girl, but she rarely got the chance to test her own strength.

Men don't like fighting me, she reflected, morbidly. *And when they do, they hold back.*

"Your Aunt has hired me to make sure you remain reasonably safe until you are either married or come into your inheritance," Gwen snapped, going on the offensive. "And you will *not* try to slap me again."

Raechel ignored her. "Who *are* you?"

"Gwen," Gwen said, truthfully. "And I am *trying* to look after you."

She winced, inwardly, as Raechel's eyes studied her face. "*Which* Gwen?"

Gwen said nothing.

"I went to bed after the ... excitement ... at once," Raechel said. She sounded as if she were working out a puzzle, piece by piece. "Why did I do that?"

She pressed on before Gwen could formulate a response. "And how *did* you get through a locked door – a pair of locked doors?"

Her eyes brightened. "You're the Royal Sorceress!"

"That is absurd, My Lady," Gwen pointed out, knowing, even as she said it, that her denial was futile. Raechel was an admirer of the Trouser Brigade, a trend Gwen had accidentally inspired. She tugged at her dress.

"Why would the Royal Sorceress pose as a maid?"

"Because you're on a mission, just like that Scotswoman who saved Bonnie Prince Charlie from the soldiers chasing him," Raechel said. She smiled, brightly. "It's true, isn't it?"

Gwen sighed, then held out a hand. A moment later, Raechel's hairbrush flew across the room and landed in her palm. Raechel stared, then started to laugh hysterically, despite the implicit threat.

"I wish you were here as yourself," Raechel said. "We have so much to talk about."

"And we will, once we get home," Gwen said. Lord Mycroft had been right. Given some proper training, Raechel might be very useful indeed. She was clearly observant enough to notice that there were quite a few holes in Gwen's cover. "But, for the moment, I need you to behave."

"Do I have magic?" Raechel asked. "Is there a way you can test for it?"

Gwen shrugged. She'd never been very good at sensing the presence of magicians who had yet to develop their powers. It was possible Raechel had magic, but equally possible that she was simply observant and quick-witted. But that was beside the point right now.

"I need you to behave," Gwen repeated. "Your Aunt *cannot* be allowed to know who I am, nor can anyone else. Do you understand what I'm telling you?" She smacked the hairbrush into her palm to underline her words. "If you do as you're told and help me, I'll help you once we get back to London," she added. "But if you don't, I'll see to it that you regret it."

Raechel smiled. "How? My Aunt already tried beating me, you know."

"I can *make* you stay in your room," Gwen snapped. "And, when you get home, you can keep going to hell, if you like." She took a breath. "Get undressed," she added. "You need to look reasonably presentable before High Tea."

Raechel giggled. "The Royal Sorceress is going to help me dress?"

"The Royal Sorceress has to remain as your maid," Gwen said. She drew on her magic, tugging on Raechel's clothes. "And heaven help you if you betray her."

She sighed as Raechel started to undress. What would Sir Sidney have to say?

Chapter Sixteen

livia ate her way through her breakfast – she'd lost weight over the past week, despite being fed increasingly larger portions of odd-tasting food – waited for Esther to take the tray away and then lay back on her bed, closing her eyes. The whispering, which was a constant presence at the back of her mind, suddenly grew louder. This time, she tried to focus on one particular voice and bring it into her mind.

The whispering seemed to grow stronger, but she couldn't make out what it was saying to her – or if it was saying anything at all. But the cravings, on the other hand, were alarmingly strong and powerful. The undead wanted to kill, to eat, to spread themselves as far as possible and they wanted to use her to do it. She forced herself to maintain contact, as they seemed to reach for her, trying to take control of one of the undead. There was a sudden shift in her mind and she found herself looking out through a new pair of eyes.

She cringed, mentally, as the creature's desires assailed her. Its thinking seemed to be the sum of its cravings, rather than anything she might recognise as thoughts, but it also seemed to have a very strange level of intelligence. The Russians had practically crucified it, driving nails through its arms and legs to pin it in place, yet it was always testing the limits of its bonds, seeking a way to break free. Its eyesight was strange; the handful of men and women in front of her were glowing with light, while everything else was a dark shadowy grey. It was barely even able to see the walls of the prison cell.

They can't see as well as living humans, she realised, numbly. *But why don't they have any problems seeing in the dark?*

She pushed the thought aside as she watched, through the creature's eyes, as one of the Russians came up to it and started trying to extract some blood. There was no feeling, not even a hint of pain, as the Russian started to work. It was clear that the undead felt nothing when they were wounded, even though half of them shouldn't even be able to move after having their bones broken. Whatever unholy force drove them onwards was terrifyingly capable. But how did it even work?

The Russian stepped back, holding a bottle of ... something. Olivia wasn't sure if the undead even had *blood*. How could they have blood pumping through their bodies when their hearts no longer beat with life? The undead creature turned its head, just in time for the Russians to wheel in another trolley. A man was strapped to the top, stark naked. The Russian researchers surrounded him, muttering in words she couldn't understand to one another. Moments later, the researcher with the bottle of dead fluids used a needle to inject them into the living victim's body.

Olivia watched, with a kind of fascinated horror, as the victim twitched alarmingly, pulling at his metal bonds hard enough to break bones, then fell to the table, dead. For a long moment, she feared that the injection would be enough to make the corpse rise again, but it was clear that it was insufficient. Moments later, the Russians came to the same conclusion. The body was wheeled out, the researchers returned to poking and prodding at the undead creature and Olivia let go of her grip on its mind. Almost immediately, she found herself in the mind of another undead. This time, it was standing inside a cage, watching with cold intent as its guards pushed a woman into the cage. The woman had been badly beaten, blood flowing from her face, but she started to scream and fight as soon as she saw the undead. But it did her no good. The guards shoved her forward and slammed the cage door shut behind her.

The surge of sudden hunger caught Olivia by surprise. Before she could try to stop the undead creature, it was on the woman, biting into her neck. Blood flowed into its body, bringing with it a surge of life energy that sent it jumping forward to slam against the bars of the cage. The guards lifted their weapons as the undead reached through the bars, grasping for them, but they were well out of reach. Behind it, Olivia was suddenly aware of the woman joining the ranks of the undead. They moaned ...

Olivia shuddered as she snapped back to her own body. The moan wasn't just a sound, she understood now; the moan was their collective intelligence taking on shape and form. Each individual undead creature was nothing more than an animal guided by animal instincts, but collectively they were formidably intelligent. Even two of them together were smarter than the average dog. A small army of them would be smart enough to operate ships and even airships. They'd spread around the entire world.

Olivia looked down at her shaking hands, then forced herself back into the undead mindset. This time, she found herself looking up at Gregory from the perspective of yet another undead monster. She ordered the creature to lunge for him and it obeyed, her thoughts sinking into whatever passed for a mind and overriding it, but it couldn't even begin to reach him. The Russians had chained the creature so firmly that any attempt to break free would cripple it, probably destroying whatever force held it together. Gregory didn't even take a step backwards as the creature relaxed, waiting.

A minute later, a young man walked into the room, wearing nothing more than a pair of shorts, despite the cold. As Olivia watched in disbelief, he knelt down in front of Gregory, his hands touching the stone floor. Gregory touched the man's forehead, then began to speak rapidly in an unfamiliar language. Once the brief ceremony was over, the young man rose to his feet and walked up to the creature, holding one hand out for the undead creature to bite.

Olivia tried to stop it, but the undead creature's lust was too strong. It bit hard, draining the young man's life into its body. The young man screamed, looking down at his hand. This time, watching through the undead eyes, Olivia could see something black and unpleasant making its way through the man's body. Gregory stepped forward, pressed his hand against the bitten hand, then started to use his powers. Olivia stared, too transfixed to do anything, as the Healer struggled to counteract the undead bite. But it wasn't enough to save the young man from becoming one of the undead.

Gregory stepped backwards and signalled to the guards. They ran forward, swords drawn, and sliced the young man apart. Gregory watched, his face dispassionate, as the researchers picked up the remains of the body, then he rubbed his fingers together with glee. Clearly, *he* thought the experiment hadn't been a complete failure. But Olivia honestly couldn't understand why.

She jerked suddenly as a sound burst into her mind, then realised that someone was tapping the door ... no, someone was slapping her face. Her thoughts exploded back into her own body; she was suddenly very aware of Ivan leaning over her, his dark eyes worried and unaccountably nervous. Or perhaps, she thought as she realised her cheek was stinging badly, he had a very good reason to be worried. She was in his care, after all, and if something happened to her he could expect to be thrown to the undead. Or maybe, as he was a Charmer, his tongue would be pulled out of his mouth and *then* he would be thrown to the undead.

"Ouch," she said, plaintively. One hand moved to rub her cheek. "What happened?"

"I've been trying to wake you for the last ten minutes," Ivan said. He sounded worried too. "What happened to you?"

"I don't know," Olivia lied. "Perhaps I just used my powers too much and needed to rest."

"Perhaps," Ivan agreed. He helped her sit up, then passed her a glass of water. "How much practice have you *had* with your powers?"

"Almost none," Olivia said. She didn't want to go into details. "And you?"

Ivan smirked. Olivia sighed, inwardly. If he was anything like the other Charmers, he'd probably come into his powers gradually, maybe not even realising that he *had* powers until he pushed someone well over the line. From what Gwen had said about Lord Blackburn, many magicians and non-magicians had been very relieved when they discovered he'd fled to Turkey. And to think he might not even be the worst of the Charmers.

"Tell me about yourself," Olivia said. Men loved to talk about themselves, particularly to a pretty girl. It was one of the more practical pieces of man-management she'd learned at Cavendish Hall, even if most of the girls there had been silly pieces of fluff. She tried to bat her eyelashes at him as she spoke. "Where were you born?"

Ivan smiled at her, rather sardonically. It was clear she hadn't mastered how to bat her eyelashes seductively. But he answered her anyway.

"I was the youngest son of a nobleman in Russia," he said. "My father preferred being out on the farm to being anywhere near St Petersburg, so naturally I went there as soon as possible, just to get away from him. I ... disliked my father intensely."

Olivia frowned. She had no idea who her father had been and her mother had died when she was six, barely old enough to take care of herself on the streets. If she hadn't had some help from her mother's old friends, she wouldn't have survived the year. As it was, she knew she wouldn't have lasted much longer if she hadn't encountered Jack and Gwen. Gwen was her mother, legally speaking, but it wasn't the same. How could someone just discard his own father?

"You never knew him," Ivan said, correctly interpreting Olivia's expression. "My father was a very unpleasant man. He beat my mother until she died, sent my sister into an unwanted marriage, beat me ... whipped the serfs on his farm for the slightest infraction, had fun with their women ... I haven't seen him in years. And I am *much* happier without him."

"I'm sorry," Olivia said, although she wasn't sure what she was actually being sorry *for*. If she'd had a real family, she wouldn't have given it up so easily. "How did you discover your powers?"

"One of the *Skoptzi* noticed me," Ivan said. "He took me to his master, who invited me to serve the Father Tsar as his agent. I had no choice."

Olivia nodded in understanding. The Royal Sorcerers Corps conscripted powerful magicians, regardless of their social origins, or killed them if they refused to cooperate. These days, the magical underground was almost completely dormant. Between Jack's willingness to use them and Gwen's offer to take anyone who was prepared to work with her, there was no longer any need for a separate organisation. And the farms were long gone.

"You were a Charmer," she said. "What did they have you do?"

"I can't talk about it," Ivan said. He shook his head, ruefully. "You don't want to know just how much I have done for the Father Tsar."

Olivia took a breath, wondering if she was about to be slapped again. "Do you worship the Father Tsar?"

Ivan eyed her for a long moment. "I've seen him at Court," he said. "The Father Tsar is just a man."

Olivia hesitated, then pushed onwards. "Do the *Skoptzi*" – she stumbled over the Russian word – "have any real idea just how dangerous their experiments actually are?"

"I believe they think they have no choice," Ivan said, carefully. He studied her, dispassionately. "My uncle's manor was burned to the ground only four weeks ago."

"I'm sorry to hear that," Olivia lied. "What happened?"

"His serfs revolted and attacked him," Ivan said. The pain in his voice surprised her. "The revolt spread to a dozen other serf-run farms, sending hundreds of aristocrats fleeing for their lives. There were reports of women – and even men – being raped by serfs, trampled by animals, then abandoned to die on the frozen ground. Hundreds of years of work torched overnight and left as ashes."

Olivia found it hard to feel sorry for the noblemen of Russia. She'd heard similar lamentations during the Swing, when a handful of aristocratic women had been raped during the worst hours of the uprising. Such accounts rarely included the harassment of female servants or even several rapes carried out by soldiers counterattacking against the rebels. If the Duke of India hadn't been in charge, it would have been considerably worse. Somehow, she doubted whoever was in charge of the military force sent to restore order in Russia would be so considerate as to hang any rapists among his troops.

But she knew better than to say it out loud. Unlike almost anyone else at Cavendish Hall, certainly among the girls, she'd been born in the gutters. She'd lived the life of the very poor, then the life of the very wealthy ... and knew just how lucky she'd been. God alone knew how many girls, very much like her, hadn't been so fortunate. But none of the other girls at Cavendish Hall had her experience. They would weep and moan for hours over a dead horse, yet they wouldn't see the blighted lives of the very poor. It was an alien and invisible world to them.

"One revolt isn't a major problem," she said, instead. "Surely you can restore order quickly."

"It isn't just one," Ivan said. Oddly, saying as much as he already had seemed to unlock the floodgates, allowing him to talk openly. "There have been revolts over the past five years as the weather has worsened, some in the countryside and some in the cities. I saw a mutiny in a Guards Regiment outside St Petersburg herself, while several warships mutinied against their commanders and set sail for the outside world. In Court, powerful factions are gathering around the different princes, each one promising a different solution to the country's woes."

"As long as they are placed into power," Olivia guessed. She'd heard Gwen grumble about Members of Parliament who had visited Cavendish Hall, seeking the Royal Sorceress's support for their political games. The principle seemed the same. "And the factions are tearing the country apart?"

"Precisely," Ivan said. "Everyone is just waiting for the Father Tsar to die. But when he does, all hell will break loose."

Olivia stared at him, then reached out and touched his hand. "It will break loose too if the undead get free," she said. In the back of her mind, the whispering was growing louder and louder. "The more you create, the more capable they will be and the more capable they become, the easier they will find it to escape."

Ivan looked at her pale hand, then tapped it lightly. "We have you to control them, don't we?"

"I have never tried to control more than a few of the undead," Olivia said, stretching the truth a little. She'd managed to put Master Thomas's undead to sleep, but only after he'd died and the creatures had started to run amok. It could easily have been a complete disaster. "What happens if there are too many of them for me to control?"

She gritted her teeth, wishing she knew how to be more persuasive. Gregory might be a dangerously insane fanatic, but he wasn't stupid. By the time he unleashed his army of undead monsters, he'd have Olivia – his one Necromancer – Charmed to the point where she obeyed orders without question, all independent thought and feeling gone. Ivan wasn't a fanatic, she hoped; he could help her, if she managed to convince him of the looming disaster. But if he believed that Russia was doomed regardless ...

"We won't let it get out of hand," Ivan said, finally. "The undead aren't unstoppable."

Olivia remembered the horrors of London and glared at him, throwing caution to the winds. "A single undead is fast, savage and feels no pain," she snapped. "You have to cripple one completely to stop it, even though their behaviour is predicable. But a group of them will be fast, ruthless and very intelligent. You have to burn them all to stop them, yet they'll keep coming until you burn them to ash. If a few hundred of the undead forced the destruction of several miles of London, what will it do if you unleash a few hundred thousand?"

She shuddered, recalling the days after the Swing. Some undead had survived long enough to escape the first purge, popping up in London or even outside the city, where they'd started to build new swarms of undead. They'd been hunted down and destroyed, but there was always a quiet nagging doubt. Had they *really* destroyed *all* of the undead? There was no way to know for sure.

"I think you're wrong," Ivan said. "I hope you're wrong."

"So do I," Olivia said. She batted her eyelashes at him again. "Can I go for a walk?"

"I can take you through the complex," Ivan said. He gave her a reproving look. "I'm afraid I can't take you outside."

Olivia nodded, unsurprised. She needed the exercise ... and she needed a chance to try to learn more about the interior of the complex. If she managed to figure out where the doors were, she would be one step closer to escape. Ivan might join her – he clearly had his doubts – but if he didn't, she could try to make it out on her own. If worst came to worst, perhaps the guards would kill her, forcing Gregory to destroy the undead he kept in cages. They couldn't be controlled without a Necromancer.

She gritted her teeth, steeling her resolve. This time, she promised herself, she wouldn't make any mistakes. She couldn't afford them.

Chapter Seventeen

 hat was foolish and reckless," Sir Sidney said.

Gwen scowled. It was bad enough that the only way she could meet him alone was through sneaking into his cabin after the lamps had been dimmed for sleep, raising the spectre of being caught and accused of ideas above her station. She wasn't in the mood to be told off by Sir Sidney, who didn't have to pose as a maid to gain admittance to Russia.

"There wasn't much choice," she said, tartly. "Raechel already knew that something wasn't quite right about me."

"You didn't bend the knee enough," Sir Sidney growled. "You should have made her forget."

Gwen sighed. "I can't *make* someone forget anything," she said. "Charm doesn't work like that, not really. I could have tried to Charm her into obedience or merely keeping her mouth shut, but it might well not have worked. Raechel is bright, clever enough to figure out who I am; she'd have enough mental keys to undo any Charm I used on her. And then we would have a new enemy."

She sighed, again. Raechel was bright enough to be useful, but also woefully untrained for any kind of sensitive mission. Given time, Gwen was sure she'd be as useful as Irene, even without magic, yet there was no time for any proper training. She'd half-hoped that Raechel could be convinced to stay in the embassy, out of the way, while Gwen carried out her mission, but Raechel was adamant that she needed to help. At least it was a more productive use of her intelligence than allowing men to chase her, while carefully not running very fast.

"Then you should have spanked her like a schoolgirl and told her to do as she was told," Sir Sidney added. "We don't need complications."

"Raechel is old enough to understand what is going on," Gwen said. "We can use her."

"She's also desperate to find a role for herself," Sir Sidney said. "That could be dangerous."

Gwen lifted an eyebrow. "Find a role for herself?"

"It happens," Sir Sidney explained. "Someone is born to a role that doesn't suit them – like you, for instance. They start acting badly while trying to find a place where they actually belong. Raechel is too smart to fit into the life of the average young aristocratic woman, yet she's also trapped and constrained by both society and her relatives. Acting out seems to be the only solution for her."

Gwen felt her blood run cold. "But what if she'd managed to get pregnant?"

"It would certainly have changed her social standing," Sir Sidney pointed out, dryly. "Perhaps she would have been happier as a mother, even if the child was born out of wedlock."

"I doubt it," Gwen said.

She sighed, yet again. It was one of the other great social injustices of the post-Swing British Empire. Bastardy carried one hell of a social stigma, even though the bastard child was the sole innocent in the affair. Sir Charles' bastardy – well, not exactly bastardy, but close enough – had undone his life when he'd discovered the truth. Bastard children couldn't inherit or claim any ranks or titles ... most of the boys had commissions quietly purchased for them and went into the army. The girls often went into convents.

"Maybe not," Sir Sidney agreed. He looked forward, darkly. "You keep an eye on her, Lady Gwen. And make sure she doesn't say anything stupid at the wrong time."

He paused. "And there's another problem," he added. "What happens if someone reads her mind?"

Gwen muttered a curse under her breath. Talleyrand had been accompanied, in Britain, by a female magician who had passed as his daughter, a young girl called Simone. She'd been a Talker, reading the minds of everyone she encountered, until Gwen had arranged for her to be escorted by other British magicians. It wasn't technically legal to allow a Talker to accompany a diplomatic mission – as far as Gwen knew, she was the only magician attached to Lord Standish's party – but the rule had been bent more often than it had been upheld.

"I'll teach her some basic meditation techniques," Gwen said. Raechel would probably benefit from the lessons in any case. She was a bundle of energy, strong enough to overwhelm any of the older nannies and governesses Lady Standish had tried to assign to her. "But we may just have to hope that her mind remains unread."

"I don't like relying on anything of the sort," Sir Sidney growled. "And you should know better too."

Gwen shrugged, wishing she could go back to her bunk and sleep. Answering Raechel's questions, serving the family at dinner and putting the girl to bed had been exhausting. She had the distinct feeling that whoever Raechel ended up marrying was going to be bent to her will, even if he was the most unpleasant old bachelor in England. Or he'd invoke very old rights and keep his wife a prisoner, in all but name.

"They will know something's wrong if they read *my* mind," she pointed out. Irene could slip through Gwen's mental shields, at least when Gwen wasn't on the alert, but other Talkers would feel different to her. She would sense their intrusion ... and they would sense her reaction to their intrusion. There would be some hard questions when they reported it to their superiors. "I can't lower my mental shields for them."

"That's why you're a maid," Sir Sidney reminded her. "They won't bother reading your mind."

Gwen had her doubts about *that*. The aristocracy might, as a general rule, pay no attention to the help, but people as smart as Lord Mycroft or Talleyrand wouldn't allow prejudice to prevent them from employing servants as spies. She rather doubted the Russians would feel any differently. Would they understand that Lord Mycroft might have hidden an operative in with the help? It seemed quite possible. And what would they do if they realised Gwen was much more than just a Talker?

And will the Captain have anything to say to Lord Standish? She asked herself. It seemed unlikely – Lord Standish was hardly likely to thank him for making love to Raechel – but it was something she would need to watch. *If he tells him that I passed through a locked door ... and someone reads that from his mind ...*

She shook her head, running her hand through her blonde curls. Raechel had asked, partly in jest, why she didn't grow her hair out and *really* shock the stodgy old men who hated the thought of taking orders from a slip of a girl. Gwen had pointed out that it was hard to pass as a man with long hair – fashion these days insisted that men couldn't grow their hair out past their neck – and besides, long hair would simply get in the way. It was also a poke in her mother's eye, although she hadn't told Raechel *that*; Lady Mary had enjoyed combing Gwen's long hair, back before she'd gone to Cavendish Hall. Gwen had always hated being treated as a *girl*.

"You should be safe until you start poking around," Sir Sidney said, his words breaking into her thoughts. Gwen hastily replayed the conversation in her mind, then nodded. "But be careful with her, all right? If I have to take over, my first step will be to tie her up in the embassy."

"If you have to take over," Gwen said, "you'll have other things to worry about, I think."

Sir Sidney nodded, then looked concerned as she yawned. "Go get some sleep," he ordered. "And make sure you keep a sharp eye on her."

Gwen nodded, yawned again and slipped out of his cabin. At night, the interior of the airship seemed to belong to another world. Only a handful of dim lights provided illumination as she made her way back to the cabin she shared with Janet and Romulus, making it difficult for her to pick out her surroundings as she walked. It was easy to see, she decided, why so few passengers stayed in the smoking or drawing rooms after the lights were dimmed. The environment was surprisingly creepy.

She slipped into the cabin, then blinked in surprise as she saw Romulus sitting on his bunk, reading a book. It didn't surprise her that he could read – he was a butler, not a common footman – but what did surprise her was that he was reading Janet a bedtime story. Janet had never grown used to the airship, any more than Lady Standish had, and had tried to spend as much time as possible in bed. Gwen had found herself doing much of Janet's work as well as her own.

"You should have been here earlier," Romulus said, as Gwen closed the door behind her. She couldn't help feeling more than a little trapped, even though she had no sense of danger from either of them. The compartment was just too small for three people, one of them a grown man. "Where were you?"

"I was just taking a break in the drawing room," Gwen said. "It looks so dark underneath us."

"It would," Romulus said. "The German states are nowhere near as developed as England."

Gwen nodded as she removed her maid's cap, allowing her hair to spring free. The German states had been battlegrounds since time out of mind, their rulers jumping from side to side and religion to religion as it suited them, while their people bore the brunt of their decisions. It was no surprise to *her*, at least, that Germans made up one of the largest groups emigrating to the American Colonies ... and were the most enthusiastic supporters of King George. He was actually their protector, while the German Princes were more interested in their own power than their population. And the French and Russians wouldn't hesitate to turn the German states into another battleground if they went to war.

England looked surprisingly bright at night, she knew from experience. There were gas and electric lights everywhere, particularly in the centre of London. But the German states had no such developments. Even Paris, she'd been told, was dimmer than London. Looking down at the Germans from high overhead made her feel as if she was staring into another world.

"I'll go for a brisk walk," Romulus said. "But I suggest you hurry."

Gwen nodded, waited for him to leave the compartment and then undid her dress, allowing it to fall to the deck. One definite advantage of the maid's outfit was that it could be removed quickly, if necessary. Gwen still flushed at the memory of her mother advising her not to eat or drink anything before dressing and going to a ball. She honestly didn't understand why her mother and the other Grandes Dames of High Society put up with the dresses. It wasn't as if they *liked* being uncomfortable.

"Pretty," Janet said, weakly. "But you should grow out your hair."

"Maybe," Gwen said, as she reached for her nightgown. It was actually more modest and uncomfortable than anything she'd worn as a young aristocrat, but it would have to suffice. "I notice he was reading to you."

"I can't read," Janet confessed, sadly. "Can you?"

Gwen nodded. It wasn't uncommon for servants to sit with their young charges at lessons – Jo had done just that with Susan – but few of them received any formal education. Janet would never have a chance to learn, now that Raechel was too old for lessons ... and Lord and Lady Standish were unlikely to produce children. Gwen was mildly surprised they *hadn't* produced children or separated. Didn't Lord Standish know he had to produce an heir?

She changed the subject before Janet could ask more incisive questions. "Do you think he's sweet on you?"

Janet blushed, so deeply that Gwen knew she was sweet on *him*. And well she might be, Gwen knew; Romulus might have been black, but he was clearly a decent person. Besides, Janet didn't have to account for herself to the Grandes Dames. No one would really care if she married a black man. There were quite a few interracial marriages down in the Docklands, where Indians and Chinese mingled with Scots and Irish. And, if Sir Charles had been right, there were other such marriages in India.

She climbed into her bunk as Romulus returned wearing a nightshirt that looked to have seen better days. Janet winked at her, then closed her eyes and went to sleep. Romulus doused the lights, then climbed into his own bunk. Gwen allowed herself a tight smile, then closed her eyes. Morning would come all too soon.

The next thing she knew, Romulus was gently shaking her bunk. Gwen sat upright, almost banging her head against the upper bunk, then looked at the butler. The lights were back up to full brightness; Gwen scrambled for her pocket watch – a gift from Heather, officially – and glanced at the time. It was nearly seven o'clock in the morning and she felt as though she hadn't slept at all.

"They could sleep in," she muttered, as she pulled herself out of bed. "Where would they go?"

Romulus snorted, then headed for the hatch. "They need to stay in practice," he reminded her. "His Lordship cannot expect to sleep in till noon when important negotiations are underway."

Gwen nodded, then dressed rapidly as soon as he left the compartment. Janet still looked miserable in her bunk, so Gwen left her there and hurried along to the kitchen compartment, where the staff were already preparing great bowls of fish and eggs, along with sliced and buttered bread. It smelt faintly funny to Gwen – apparently, cooking at altitude did odd things to the food – but she didn't mind. Taking one of the trays of food, she carried it through the airship to the dining room, where Lord Standish, Sir Sidney and two of the other diplomats were already sitting. Romulus stood behind Lord Standish, fussing over his necktie.

"Put it on the table," Lord Standish ordered. He was reading a copy of *The Times*, but Gwen couldn't help noticing that it was outdated by several days. He'd probably already read it several times over. "And then wake my niece. Inform her I wish to speak with her."

Gwen placed the tray on the table, curtseyed and hurried along to Raechel's cabin, wondering just what Lord Standish wished to say to his niece. Inside, Raechel was sleeping in her bed, wearing nothing apart from a set of thin underclothes. Gwen sighed, cleared her throat loudly, then watched as Raechel stirred without waking. She'd probably gone to sleep very late the previous evening, even though she'd had little to do. Gwen couldn't help wondering if the Captain had sneaked into her cabin for a midnight visit.

Maybe I should start sleeping outside her cabin, she thought, then cleared her throat for the second time. "My Lady," she said, "wake up!"

Raechel jumped and sat up, looking around wildly. Gwen sighed, then reached for the bottle of water by the bedside and passed it to Raechel, who took it and sipped carefully. There were few glasses of any description on the airship and none at all in the bedrooms, just to prevent spills. Gwen rather approved. She would have had to clean up any mess caused by the occupants.

"It's far too early to get up," Raechel protested, when she looked at the clock on the bulkhead. She'd never been in the habit of rising early, even before they'd boarded the airship. "I want to go back to sleep."

"Your Uncle demands your presence," Gwen said. "And he sent me to get you."

Raechel shrugged, lay back on the bed and pulled the covers over her head. Gwen felt her temper snap; she reached out with her magic, pulled the covers away and then picked Raechel up and dropped her, none too gently, on the deck. Raechel yelped as her bottom hit the cold metal, then glowered at Gwen, shocked awake.

"You shouldn't do that," she muttered, as she pulled herself back to her feet, one hand rubbing her behind. She didn't seem intimidated, merely annoyed. "I need my sleep."

"That's why you go to bed at a civilised hour," Gwen countered. She strode over to the wardrobe, pulled out a basic dress and hovered it over to Raechel. "You can wear this, for the moment, and we will get you something else to wear after you've spoken to your Uncle."

Raechel sighed, then pulled the dress over her head and looked at herself in the mirror. She looked pretty, Gwen decided, although it was clear that Raechel didn't agree. The wild untamed look was hardly fashionable these days; Raechel was just lucky enough to look beautiful without spending any effort on her appearance at all. But as she grew older and her looks began to fade, she'd need something else to keep her going. Would she ever find someone she could marry as an equal?

"Fine," Raechel groused, after Gwen had cleared her throat twice. She stood, running her hands down the dress to try to force it to show her curves. Thankfully, it refused to cling to her body. "I should just walk in naked. Give some of those old fogies heart attacks."

"They say Tyburn is nice this time of year," Gwen said, dryly. Criminals were still hanged in Tyburn, sometimes without a trial first. Even Oliver Cromwell's body had been exhumed and hung after the Restoration, even though it seemed a pointless exercise in spite. She couldn't recall if any women had been hanged there, but it was quite possible. "And I don't think your Uncle would be amused."

"You'd better come with me," Raechel said. She headed towards the hatch, running her hands through her hair to push it into some semblance of order. "I can hide behind you if he's really angry at me."

Gwen raised her eyebrows, but said nothing.

Chapter Eighteen

he weather over St Petersburg was surprisingly clear, according to the Captain, as the airship slowly made its way over the Baltic Sea and started its descent towards the Russian capital. Gwen was relieved, as were most of the passengers; the airship had shaken so violently when they'd passed near a storm that one of the passengers had actually tried to open the door that would have sent him plummeting towards the ground from miles up in the sky and thus ensured his death.

She glanced at Raechel, then back out the window as St Petersburg came into view. Lord Standish had dismissed Gwen as soon as breakfast had finished, then taken his niece into a private cabin for a long chat. Whatever Lord Standish had said to her had been surprisingly effective, Gwen considered; Raechel had been oddly subdued all day. She hadn't even pestered Gwen for more stories about her life as the Royal Sorceress.

"It looks just like London," Raechel said, finally. She sounded oddly disappointed. "I was expecting something more."

Gwen shrugged. "Wait till you see it from the ground," she said. "You might see far more differences up close."

She watched as the airship descended slowly towards a vast airstrip outside the city. The Russians hadn't been enthusiastic about airships when they'd been invented, forcing them to catch up with both the British and French, but it was clear that they were pushing the limits as fast as possible. There were two giant airships, one larger than the largest airship in British service, and a handful of smaller airships that seemed to be more engine than gasbag. Gwen had been told that it might be possible to actually build a flying machine that *didn't* rely on hydrogen to provide lift, but she had her doubts. Unless magic was involved, somewhere ...

"That's a lot of guns," Raechel observed. "Are they planning a war?"

Gwen followed her gaze. The riverside was lined with guns, some built in solid emplacements, others positioned out in the open, as if they expected to be attacked at any second. Perhaps they *did* expect an attack, she thought. The Royal Navy liked the idea of sinking its enemy's fleet in the first battle, even if it meant charging right into the teeth of enemy fire. As far as Gwen knew, Lord Nelson had no plans to start the war by attacking Russia, but it was quite possible ... at least as long as the river was navigable. Large chunks of ice drifting out to sea suggested that forcing passage up towards the city would be hazardous as hell.

"It looks that way," she said. The river passed behind them as the airship sank lower, slowly making its way towards the docking mast ahead of them. There was a long whining sound from the engines, then the airship shook violently again as the ground rose up towards her eyes. "I think they fear the worst."

A dull thump ran through the airship, followed by a series of clunks as the ground crew attached anchors to her gondola. Gwen straightened up as she saw a line of armed soldiers running past the window, clearly readying themselves to attend upon Lord Standish and his diplomatic mission. Raechel gave her a sharp look, then followed Gwen as she walked back to Raechel's cabin and checked to make sure that everything was packed. The bags would be picked up by the Russians and transported to the embassy, no doubt after being thoroughly searched. She hadn't mentioned that to Raechel. It would only have upset her.

"Raechel," Lady Standish said. She looked much better now that the airship had touched down, a suspiciously quick recovery. "You will accompany us as we leave the airship."

"Of course, Auntie," Raechel said, lightly. "Your strongest command is my slightest wish."

"And Gwen will make sure you keep your mouth firmly shut," Lady Standish added, switching her glare to Gwen. "Do not even *think* of letting her cause a diplomatic incident."

She turned and marched down the corridor, leaving Gwen and Raechel alone. "My Uncle was much firmer about it," Raechel muttered, as soon as her Aunt was out of earshot. "He told me that if I caused any trouble, he'd sign the papers marrying me to Lord Percy."

Gwen rolled her eyes. Lord Percy was an imbecile, to put it kindly; a man so stupid that it surprised her that he could tie his own shoelaces. Gwen's mother had threatened to marry her off to Lord Percy before; she hadn't realised that it was such a prevalent threat among the aristocracy. But Raechel would run rings round him, she knew. He was too kind-hearted to do anything to restrain his wife, should he ever marry.

Which is unlikely, Gwen thought. *Who would want their daughter to marry an imbecile?*

"Don't worry about it," she muttered. "Worry instead about what I'll do to you if you mess this up."

She led the way towards the doors, where the passengers and crew were gathering. The Captain was talking to Lord Standish, carefully not looking at either Gwen or Raechel. Gwen felt Raechel tense beside her, but muttered a command for her to simply ignore the Captain's presence. Lord Standish and his wife marched forward as the doors opened, letting in a wave of cold air that made Gwen shiver and silently use magic to warm herself. The others, having only clothing for protection, looked thoroughly unhappy as they marched out into the bright sunlight.

"Stay close to me," Gwen ordered, warming the air around Raechel too. It should be undetectable, but if someone realised the air was warmer near them there might be some awkward questions. "And don't say a word."

Raechel shot her a grateful look, then watched as a uniformed Russian man, wearing so many medals on his chest it was a surprise he didn't fall over, started greeting Lord Standish in badly-accented English. Gwen listened carefully at first, realised that it was nothing more than the usual meaningless formalities and then looked away, trying to drink in as much as she could of Russia. The air was cold, but smelt faintly of industrial smoke and by-products, just like the smog of London and Manchester. She looked down and saw ice and slush on the ground, just waiting for someone to put their feet down carelessly. She had to be careful, she reminded herself, to make sure she wasn't accidentally melting the ice around them.

The Russian finished his speech, then paused, dramatically. Gwen switched her attention back to him as he spoke louder, as if he wanted to get the words out as quickly as possible. It was hard to be sure – she had never been a strong Sensitive, unlike Sir Travis – but she thought he honestly wasn't pleased about what he had to say. She narrowed her eyes as he spoke, trying to listen carefully.

"As a testament to the urgency of your mission, His Excellency the Tsar has invited you to stay in the Winter Palace," the Russian said. "Rooms have already been prepared for you."

Gwen frowned – and knew she wasn't the only one. It was rare, vanishingly rare, for a diplomatic mission to be hosted in the very heart of another country's government. There would be no room for withdrawals, no break for tempers to cool, if they were living right next to the Tsar himself. And yet, it suggested a sense of urgency she couldn't help finding encouraging. The Tsar was taking the whole matter extremely seriously.

And I would be close to the government myself, she thought. *Searching the palace would be much easier if I was already inside the walls.*

She watched as Lord Standish and Sir Sidney spoke briefly in a language she vaguely recognised as coming from India. It made sense, she knew; they'd both use something different to try to conceal their words, if they needed to speak without being overheard by their hosts. But the Russians could probably find a speaker of their own, if necessary ...

"We thank you for your offer," Lord Standish said. "We gratefully accept."

The Russian bowed, then led the way towards a line of gaudy carriages waiting for the diplomatic team. Gwen wondered if the Russians thought they were hosting visiting royalty; they'd brought out gilded carriages, fine black horses and the escorting soldiers were wearing fancy uniforms. She heard Raechel gasp as one of the men came into view and elbowed her, not gently. The man was handsome, but he was also very cold. His gaze flickered over Raechel and then Gwen, his eyes meeting hers for a split second. She shivered, despite herself, knowing that she was looking at a killer.

"Don't go anywhere with that man," she muttered, as Lord and Lady Standish were assisted into the first carriage. "I mean it."

Raechel scowled at her, but said nothing. Moments later, they were helped into the third carriage, the doors firmly closed before anyone else could join them. Gwen pulled the curtains aside, allowing her to see out of the vehicle, as the horsemen cracked whips and the carriages jolted into motion. Resting her hands in her lap, she watched grimly as they drove away from the airstrip and into St Petersburg itself. The city reminded her far too much of the Rookery, before the Swing.

"It's different," Raechel said. "I mean ... it looks different from London."

Gwen nodded. She knew little about architecture, but she had to admit that St Petersburg was definitely different. Many of the older buildings seemed topped with giant onions, some gleaming gold and silver in the sunlight, while even the newer buildings were very strange compared to what she knew. She thought she detected some French and Scottish influences in some of the newer buildings, but it was hard to be sure. One giant cathedral was so remarkable that it took her breath away when she looked at it.

But the fancy buildings were surrounded by poverty. Dark brooding buildings seemed to be crammed with families, with poor children in tattered clothes playing outside. There were few women on the streets, she noticed; hundreds of young men seemed to hang around, doing nothing apart from talking or listlessly tossing balls around in the gutter. Homeless people could be seen, sleeping against walls or in alleys; somehow, she doubted many of them would survive the coming winter. She was sure a handful of them were already dead.

"My God," Raechel breathed. "This is *awful*."

"Yes," Gwen agreed, tonelessly.

She gritted her teeth as she saw the soldiers patrolling the streets. There were no splendid uniforms, just rifles and swords. It was clear to her that the soldiers didn't dare patrol except in large numbers, for fear of being ambushed and picked off by the poor. She couldn't help remembering the early hours of the Swing, when British Redcoats had been surrounded and hacked to death by outraged crowds. St Petersburg had the same simmering tension that Jack had exploited to plan his uprising, but there was something darker and even less pleasant in the background here. It struck her, suddenly, that the crowds had no designated leader. If they ever found someone capable of uniting them, all hell would break loose.

The Tsar fears an uprising, she thought, remembering the files. *They have had poor harvests, which means less food, which means people will have far less to lose if they rise up against their masters.*

Raechel stared at her. "This wouldn't happen in England!"

"It has," Gwen said. Had it really been only a few short months since Jack had shown her the dark reality underpinning the aristocracy of England? The poor, struggling to live from day to day, while the wealthy crushed them under their boots without even noticing? "I've seen far worse, Raechel."

"Impossible," Raechel insisted. "We wouldn't let it happen in London."

Gwen snickered, rudely. "I've seen women selling their bodies for crumbs," she said, bitterly. "I've seen men thrown out on the streets after accidents at work ensured they could no longer perform. I've seen children forced to steal to live, or pushed into brothels that cater for men with truly deprived tastes. I've seen maids, like the one I'm meant to be, beaten half to death by their masters because they made a mistake ... or because their master was merely in a very bad mood. I've seen horrors you can't even begin to imagine."

Raechel stared at her. "But something has to be done," she said. "Maybe I could ..."

Gwen sighed. "Weeks ago, there was a charity – a religious charity – that tried to employ former prostitutes," she said. "It failed. Do you know why?"

Raechel shook her head.

"Two reasons," Gwen said. "First, they didn't pay the women as much as prostitution paid; the women needed the money, so they went back to selling themselves. And second ..."

She paused, wondering if Raechel would see the connection. But Raechel said nothing.

"Second, they preached to the sinners," Gwen explained. "The women didn't *want* to sell themselves, not really. They just had no choice if they wanted to survive. And the priests were going among them and telling them that they were sinners ... the priests, wearing comfortable clothes, and well-fed by donations from their parishes. The women hated them for their endless and relentless nagging."

"Just like my Aunt," Raechel said.

"Yes," Gwen said, rolling her eyes. "Your Aunt might have been involved with one or more of those well-meaning attempts to tell people how to run their lives."

She shook her head as the coach turned, rattling loudly. "The poor have lives of their own," she said, remembering Olivia. "They are not animals and they are not clay, to be moulded as you see fit. You must never forget that if you actually want to make a difference."

Raechel nodded, then stared out of the window as the Winter Palace came into view. Gwen was reluctantly impressed by the sheer size of the building; it was far larger than any building she'd visited in London, even Buckingham Palace. But it was surrounded by a thick wall and defended by armed guards; a fortress in the very heart of Russian power. Judging by the way the other buildings had been erected around it, someone expected and feared an uprising that might overthrow the Tsar. The soldiers looked grimly confident of holding the line long enough for assistance to reach them, if all hell broke loose. Gwen couldn't help fearing that they were wrong.

"It feels as if we're walking into a trap," she said, out loud. "I really don't like that sort of feeling."

Up close, the Winter Palace sat in the centre of a lawn, which was covered in snow and ice. The building practically glowed with light, each window lit up like the sun, a mocking display of power and wealth in the middle of a city of the poor and powerless. Somehow, Gwen couldn't help thinking that the Tsar was trying to display his power, either to suggest that a revolution was pointless, or in order to provoke one so that he could crush it. Lord Blackburn had argued for just that, in the days before the Swing.

"I have the same feeling," Raechel muttered back. The carriages passed through a looming arch, armed soldiers peering at them dispassionately, then drove up to the palace itself. "This place isn't safe at all."

The carriage rattled to a halt in front of a pair of large doors, which were pushed open by a team of footmen. Light spilled out, illuminating the carriages as the passengers were helped out onto the snowy ground, Lady Standish slipping and sliding as she was helped towards the doors. Inside, it was blissfully warm and bright, illuminated by countless gaslights that sparkled off the walls. Gwen sucked in her breath at the sheer finery on display as the doors closed behind them. The walls were covered with portraits of famous Russians, each one edged with gold; tables were covered with pieces of artwork she knew had to be worth thousands of pounds apiece. And the Russians were just showing off their wealth ...

There had been British aristocrats who'd done just that, in the days before the Swing. Their homes had been the first to be looted. Gwen knew that some artefacts, including family heirlooms, had never actually been recovered, even after large rewards had been pledged for their return. She couldn't help thinking that the Winter Palace would end its days in the same manner ...

"Welcome," an unaccented voice said. Gwen turned to see a very fat man, flanked by a small army of maids. "We have prepared a large suite for you, our guests. His Excellency invites you to a dance this evening, where you will be formally presented to him and his Court, so we have prepared clothes as well."

"Thank you," Lord Standish said.

Beside him, Sir Sidney looked irked. Gwen wanted to consult with him, to ask for advice, but she knew she didn't dare say a word in the Winter Palace. Walls might very well have ears. Instead, she allowed the maids to lead Raechel and her up to their rooms, after Raechel explained to Lady Standish that she needed Gwen with her to help her to freshen up. Lady Standish, clearly keen to ensure that her niece was under constant supervision, readily agreed to allow Gwen to sleep in the same room.

"That's good, isn't it?" Raechel muttered. "Isn't it?"

"I think so," Gwen said. "But you shouldn't change too much or your Aunt will start wondering why."

"My Uncle saw to that," Raechel said. She looked down at the carpeted stairwell for a long bitter moment. "I can't wait until I'm five and twenty. I'll find a place of my own and to hell with High Society."

Gwen nodded. "Do as I tell you and it will happen earlier," she promised. "But this is too important to risk damaging through errors – or personal feelings."

Chapter Nineteen

o be fair to the Russians, Gwen decided, they had gone to some trouble to make sure the British mission felt at home. Raechel's apartment was colossal, large enough to hold two or three of her rooms from Standish Hall, while the bathroom looked big enough for five or six people to wash together. There was even hot and cold running water, something that was uncommon even in most aristocratic homes in London. Raechel let out a cry of delight as soon as she saw it and hastily undressed, motioning for Gwen to run a bath. Gwen smiled to herself and obeyed. The airship bathtub had been a joke.

She waited for Raechel to enter the bathroom, stark naked, and then helped her into the bathtub. With the water still running, she leaned closer to Raechel's ear and spoke quickly, but urgently, telling her to make sure she didn't say anything sensitive out loud. Once Raechel had nodded, Gwen left her to soak and walked back into the bedroom. One wardrobe was full of dresses, all in Raechel's size; two more held several different outfits, including three fur coats and a swimming costume that concealed more than it revealed. The Russians had clearly done their homework, Gwen decided, as she pulled a long green gown out of the wardrobe and placed it on the bed. But how had they known Raechel's size?

The Russians are the most capable intelligencers in the world, Lord Mycroft had told her, once. *They have skill, they have daring and they have patience. We must assume they always know the truth.*

She shivered as the message sank in. The dresses weren't too hard to obtain, she suspected, not when there were plenty of young girls in the Winter Palace. But the message behind them was alarmingly clear. If the Russians knew Raechel's sizes well enough to provide clothes and boots for her – there was a pair of heavy fur boots under the dresses – what else did they know? Lord Standish might go into talks knowing that the Russians already knew what he was permitted to offer, which would put him at a serious disadvantage.

Carefully, she closed the wardrobe and searched the rest of the room, looking for secret panels and eavesdropping stations. There was a large bookcase with English books – most of them basic novels, nothing too exciting – and a handful of paintings, each one showing a young girl from childhood to adulthood. It took Gwen a moment to realise that it was the same girl in each separate picture, her dress and hairstyle changing so radically between pictures that only the shape of her chin was recognisable. The words under the paintings were written in Russian, which had a different alphabet. There was no way she could read them.

She paused, then looked through the set of books. One of them turned out to be a guide to the Winter Palace, as if it were nothing more than a tourist attraction. Gwen found a map, glanced at it, and noted that large parts of the building were marked as being off-limits to unauthorised personnel. Other parts seemed to be designed for the Russian Royals and their families, including a swimming pool and a sauna. Their sense of entitlement was evidently greater than that of the British aristocracy. Gwen would have sworn that was impossible. Bracing herself, she tore the floor plans out of the book and dropped them on the bed, then turned her attention to the paintings.

One painting proved to be fixed to the wall; the others were clearly intended to be moved, if necessary. Gwen studied the painting for a long moment, recognising the telltale signs that someone had established a watching post behind the wall, shielded by the painting. She briefly considered trying to cover it with something else, but knew it would betray her awareness that they were being watched. Closing her eyes, she concentrated and tried to feel for the presence of someone on the other side of the painting. But she sensed nothing.

Hopefully they don't consider Lord Standish's niece a major priority, Gwen thought, as she picked up a pair of towels and dressing gowns, then walked back into the bathroom. *And I don't dare tell her that she's being watched.*

Raechel was half-sleep in the bathtub, red hair soaking wet. Gwen wasn't surprised – none of them had been able to wash their hair on the airship – so she helped Raechel to sit upright, then used the showerhead to wash her hair thoroughly with soap and shampoo. Raechel giggled as she stood, then took the towel and dried herself before stepping out of the bathtub.

"Get a wash yourself," she muttered, as she pulled on her gown and strode into the bedroom. "You smell almost as bad as I did."

"I was trying not to mention it," Gwen said. She rather doubted that any of the diplomatic mission smelt very good. Normally, there would have been a day at the embassy to freshen up after the flight. But that plan had gone by the wayside. "I'll be as quick as I can."

She climbed into the bathtub after removing her dress and underclothes, then washed herself as quickly as possible. She'd always enjoyed soaking herself in the bathroom, but there was no time to relax, not when she was pretending to be a maid. Instead, she washed her hair quickly, used magic to dry herself and then pulled the dressing gown over her body, wrapping it tightly to make sure that it stayed in place. She didn't want to take any risks if the room was under observation.

"They've left some food here," Raechel called, as she entered the bedroom. She was looking at the floor plans while eating something that smelt of chocolate. "Come and try one of these."

Gwen frowned as she realised she hadn't checked the drawers. One of them had held a large box of chocolates, which Raechel had taken out and placed on the bed. Gwen took one, decided she didn't really like it, then reached for the dress. Raechel sighed, but shrugged off the dressing gown and stood upright, allowing Gwen to lower the dress over her head. It was surprisingly simple to don.

"I think I might ask if I can keep this," Raechel said, admiring herself in the mirror. "Do you think they'd let me?"

"I'm sure they would," Gwen said. Now the airship flight was over, she was starting to worry about Olivia again. Who knew what was happening to her? "And what am I meant to wear, do you think?"

"Take one of the other dresses," Raechel said. She looked Gwen up and down. "We're not that different in size, are we?"

Gwen snorted, but found a relatively simple dress and examined it, carefully. It was designed for someone of imprecise size, she realised; a good seamstress could fit it to suit just about anyone, unless they were excessively fat. She pulled it out, decided it would suit her, then hesitated. What if they were being watched? Silently cursing herself, she dropped the dressing gown on the floor and pulled the dress over her head. She looked respectable, she decided, as she peered at herself in the mirror, but not aristocratic. If she had, she just *knew* that Lady Standish would have shouted at her for being uppity.

"You look plain," Raechel said, darkly. "Why not wear something more spectacular?"

"I don't want to be noticed," Gwen said.

"Pity, really," Raechel said. "Those eyes! And that hair!"

Gwen glowered at her, just as there was a loud knock on the door. When she opened it, after schooling her features back into place, she saw a handsome young Russian officer standing there, smiling at her. His gaze moved to Raechel and his smile grew brighter, much to Gwen's private amusement. Clearly, he had no doubt which of them was the aristocrat.

"My Lady Raechel," he said. He bowed deeply, his sword almost touching the carpeted floor. "It is my sworn duty to escort you down to the ballroom."

Raechel coloured. "Thank you," she said, rising to her feet. "Gwen will accompany us, I'm afraid. My Auntie insists that I go nowhere alone."

"My sympathies," the Russian said. He smiled at Gwen, then held out his arm to Raechel, who took it. "But we will survive, I am sure."

Gwen rolled her eyes at his back as he led them through a network of twisting corridors and stairwells, each one making it harder for her to find her way back to their room. Large parts of the Winter Palace seemed empty, other parts seemed to be bustling with life as people chatted in corners or handed out official orders from the Tsar. If it was anything like London, Gwen suspected, some of the orders would actually come from the staff, rather than the Tsar personally. But just being close to the Tsar would give the staff enormous clout.

And patronage, she thought, remembering the struggles between King George and Parliament over just how much Royal Patronage the King was allowed to distribute. *Someone in a position to influence the Tsar could distribute a lot of patronage and build up a power base of his own.*

They came to the top of a colossal open stairway, leading down into a ballroom that was larger than any Gwen had seen in London. Her eye was drawn immediately to the Tsar himself, perched on a throne that seemed designed for someone considerably larger. He was thinner than Gwen had expected, a neat little moustache on his face, his dark hair trimmed close to the scalp. But it was his eyes that caught her attention, sunk deep into his gaunt face; they were dim and grey, almost manic. She couldn't help thinking that he looked like a man who wanted to put down a colossal burden and relax, perhaps even sleep until death came for him. He might have ordered the kidnapping of her daughter, but she couldn't help feeling a flicker of sympathy for him.

He's the sole power in Russia, she thought, remembering Lord Mycroft's briefings. *There's no parliament, not even a House of Lords. He has to handle everything for himself and woe betide him if he misses something, because someone will use it to put a knife in his back.*

There were a handful of men in black robes standing just behind the Tsar. Gwen studied them with some interest, trying to determine if they were bodyguards, advisors or something else. They looked odd among the finery of the courtiers, like hens or ducks among peacocks, something that bothered her. In her experience, anything that stuck out like a sore thumb was almost certainly going to be trouble. And then Raechel's companion broke into her thoughts.

"You are not permitted on to the dance floor," he said. "Servants are only permitted down there with the permission of the Tsar."

Gwen nodded and took a place on the balcony, alongside Romulus and a handful of other servants that she didn't recognise. The butler nodded at her as she leant on the railing and watched Raechel descending to the dance floor, arm in arm with her companion, who led her into the dance as soon as they reached the bottom of the stairs. It looked like a slow waltz, rather than one of the faster dances Gwen enjoyed; she hoped – prayed – that Raechel would be more sensible, now she knew she had something to hope for in life. And then she turned her attention back to the Tsar.

Lord Standish was standing in front of the Tsar, speaking to him, although Gwen couldn't make out the words. He ended his speech by passing the Tsar an envelope, then bowing and withdrawing back to the dance floor, where his wife was waiting for him. Gwen felt cold ice running down her spine at the shunning of all known diplomatic protocol, then felt her heart skip a beat as someone new walked down the stairway without paying attention to her. Lord Talleyrand had entered the room.

He looked older than she recalled, his wig greyer than it had been when they'd first met, but there was no mistaking France's diplomatic mastermind. Talleyrand strode down the stairs as if he owned the building and marched over to the Tsar with an attitude that warned everyone else to get out of his way. Beside him, a young girl – no older than Gwen herself – captured eyes with her floral yellow dress, long dark brown hair and winsome expression. Gwen swore under her breath as she recognised Simone. She was beautiful, far better than Gwen at flirting with men ... and a Talker. Gwen knew just how many minds she'd read during her stay in London. But did the Russians?

I may have to ask Sir Sidney to warn the Tsar, she thought, as both Talleyrand and his companion dropped to one knee in front of the Tsar. They might have stolen a march on the

British, Gwen realised grimly. It was a point of pride that British statesmen and diplomats never knelt to anyone, but their own monarchs. *And then work much harder on helping Raechel build mental shields of her own.*

She carefully checked and rechecked her shields as the Tsar leaned forward, speaking to Talleyrand slowly and distinctly. It was impossible for her to read the Tsar's lips, but Talleyrand seemed surprised by his words. Simone took a step forward and curtseyed to the Tsar, who laughed and patted her on the head. Looking a little put out, Simone stepped backwards and behind Talleyrand, who kept speaking to the Tsar. Moments later, he took his pretend daughter's hand and led her on to the dance floor.

"Odd," Romulus commented. "What was all *that* about?"

Gwen looked over at him, interested. "You can read lips?"

Romulus nodded. "The Tsar was saying no to whatever the frog wanted," he said, one dark lip curving in a magnificent sneer. "And then he made a suggestion that Simone should find a nice young man to marry and stay in Russia."

"Oh," Gwen said. Perhaps it was lucky that Raechel hadn't been presented to the Tsar. There were all sorts of stories about shady diplomatic dealings that had included the wife or daughter of the ambassador sharing a foreign monarch's bed. Gwen would have preferred to believe that such things didn't happen in Britain, but she'd heard too much to doubt it was at least possible. "Maybe he wanted her for himself."

She returned her attention to the dance floor, her eyes silently tracking Raechel as she made her way from partner to partner. The dance seemed to be completely unstructured, with men and women entering or leaving the dance as the whim struck them, but the more she stared at their movements the more she realised there *was* a pattern. Certain groups of men – and a handful of young women – were refusing to dance with anyone outside their groups, let alone mingle along the sidelines. It looked very much as though there were four separate groups of young noblemen and women, steadfastly refusing to dance together. Five, if one counted the men in black.

Bracing herself, she closed her eyes and opened her mind, despite the risk of Simone realising who and what she was.

The torrent of impressions crashed into her mind at once, mingled thoughts and feelings she could barely read; she staggered under the sudden impact, frantically trying to raise her shields again. But, as her shields grew stronger, she realised that there were far darker feelings in the ballroom than she'd expected. The groups she'd counted hated and feared each other, some nervously expecting trouble and others plotting it ... and it was all centred around the Tsar himself. He was a maelstrom of dark and twisted emotional energy, as if he were the centre of his country.

A hand touched her back. "Gwen? Gwen? Are you all right?"

Romulus, Gwen realised. "Sorry," she stammered. "I must have eaten something bad earlier."

"You should have joined Janet and I," Romulus said, although there was no real reproof in his words. He knew Gwen hadn't really been offered a choice. "Do you want me to escort you back to your room?"

Gwen pulled herself together slowly, leaning on the railing for stability. The sensations were still fading away, but the impressions persisted. For a long moment, she thought she hallucinated men carrying knives in the middle of the dance floor and almost shouted out a warning, before she gathered herself and pushed the hallucinations out of her mind. Down below, Talleyrand was making his stately way through the room, greeting all of the Russians equally. It was easy to see, even without her magic, that some of the groups liked him while others hated him so completely that they would have killed him in seconds, if he hadn't had the protection of the Tsar.

"I'll walk back myself," she said, as soon as she was sure she could stand upright without problems. "You need to keep an eye on Their Lordships."

"Janet is in her bedroom," Romulus said. "Go and see her if you need anything, understand?"

"Yes, sir," Gwen said. As Butler, Romulus was effectively the head servant. She had to follow his orders as long as they didn't conflict with anything she'd been told by Lady Standish. But she knew she couldn't go straight back to her bedroom. It was the perfect opportunity to explore the palace and she intended to make use of it. "I'll see you tomorrow, sir."

Bracing herself, she walked out of the door and into the curiously empty corridor, opening her mind as soon as the door was closed behind her. No one moved to block her way; the corridor seemed to be completely empty. Puzzled, and disturbed in a way she couldn't articulate, Gwen hesitated, then started up the stairs towards the government offices.

It was, she decided, the best place to start.

Chapter Twenty

he sense of unreality grew stronger as Gwen made her way up the stairs, every sense alert for guardsmen or even passing servants. If a manor the size of her parents' house had at least a dozen servants, ranging from butlers to footmen and maids, a palace the size of the Winter Palace should have hundreds of servants. But she saw no one as she crept forward, heading towards the centre of Russian government. There should be guards or servants everywhere, if only because there were two foreign missions hosted within the palace. Instead, there was no one.

She paused outside a set of locked doors, then carefully touched them with her bare fingers, trying to peer beyond them with her senses. There was no one on the far side, as far as she could tell, but she cloaked herself as best as she could before she unlocked the doors using magic. The doors clicked open, revealing another passage as ornate as the previous corridors, but completely devoid of portraits of famous Russians. Gwen hesitated, knowing that she would be committed the moment she stepped through the doors, then walked forward, pulling her magic around her like a protective shroud. As long as she was very careful, it would be extremely hard for any guards or servants to see her.

Inside, the complex was almost disappointing. There was an endless series of offices, some locked and sealed, others left open, all barren and empty. Gwen slipped inside one of them and glanced around, only to discover that the tables and drawers had been emptied by a previous occupant. It was impossible to be sure, but she couldn't help thinking that the Russians had transferred most of the bureaucrats and civil servants who actually ran their government elsewhere. Maybe, given the constant state of ferment outside the Winter Palace, they'd been transported somewhere more secure.

The British Government did that during the Swing, she thought, as she left the office and continued to creep down the corridor. *But Jack managed to catch or kill many of the civil servants anyway.*

She froze as she heard someone muttering in Russian ahead of her, then sneaked down the corridor and peered through the door. Nine men in hooded robes were kneeling on the floor, their backs to Gwen, their eyes locked on a portrait of the Tsar. It was an idealised portrait, Gwen couldn't help noticing; it showed none of the weaknesses of the *real* Tsar. And the men – the monks, she guessed – were practically worshipping the image. Gwen had never been very religious, not when practically everyone had called her a devil-child in her youth, but the thought of praying to a living man was disconcerting. The Tsar was hardly Jesus Christ.

Carefully, she walked past the prayer room and into a much larger office, dominated by a throne and a gilded table. Gwen guessed that it belonged to the Tsar; the room was not only more ornate than any of the previous rooms, but there were no other chairs in the compartment. Everyone else would have to stand or kneel in the presence of their lord and master. Gritting her teeth, she slipped over to the Throne and frowned as she saw a set of maps on the table. She couldn't read the writing on the sheets of paper, but it was clear that they showed Russia, Central Asia and the Ottoman Empire.

She sucked in her breath sharply as she saw large arrows gliding down from Moscow towards the Turks, passing through the mountains as if there were no natural barriers. It looked odd; Gwen knew little about military logistics, but she did know that supplying armies in Central Asia was an ongoing problem for both British and Russian officers. They'd agreed to leave Afghanistan as a buffer zone because neither side wanted to expend effort bringing the state into their sphere of influence. But the lines on the map seemed to defy any kind of military logic. The armies it showed didn't seem to have to eat or sleep or take notice of natural barriers.

Cold ice ran down her spine as she realised what it portended. An army of the undead could march endlessly, walking over mountains or through rivers ... and expand along the way, as they overran villages and towns, bringing their inhabitants into their ranks. It wouldn't even need to be controlled, she suspected; the Russians could just point them in the right direction and let them march all the way to Istanbul. God knew the Russians had never given up hope of capturing the city – and, with it, control over the passage from the Black Sea to the Mediterranean. An army of the undead would allow them to overrun the Turks, no matter how tactically competent the Turks had become. And then they could just go onwards.

She swore under her breath as she looked at the other maps. Red lines, giant arrows showing unrealistic troop movements, struck south into Persia and east into India. Gwen had never been to India, but she knew from Sir Charles just how many souls were under British rule in the subcontinent. They'd be killed, only to rise again as part of the undead, an unstoppable tidal wave making its way ever eastwards until it reached China and the very Far East. And by then ...

Feeling sick, Gwen glanced through the remaining documents, hoping they'd show her how the Russians intended to *control* such a large force. She couldn't doubt that they had Olivia, not now, but so many undead would be an intelligent and uncontrollable force in their own right. How could they raise so many without risking their own destruction? They had to be insane ... Gwen shuddered as she recalled what she'd seen of the Tsar, remembering his manic expression. He was mad, she realised, and willing to do whatever it took to preserve his power ...

She froze as she heard someone outside, walking along the corridor. Quickly, she glanced around, then darted behind the curtains. The temperature dropped rapidly, revealing that one of the windows was open. Gwen shivered, despite herself, wondering why the Russians had left one window open in the darkness. And then she heard someone come into the office and cursed mentally. If her senses weren't playing tricks on her, the Russian was suspicious. Had she made a noise someone had heard? Or did the Russians have their own magicians monitoring the complex? Gritting her teeth, knowing she didn't dare let herself be discovered, she sneaked over to the window, levitated herself up and out into the cold night air. Behind her, she heard a rustle as someone pulled the curtains aside.

It was bitterly cold outside, Gwen realised, as she rose upwards as quickly as possible. In her experience, no one ever looked up, particularly when they didn't know they were chasing a magician. She heard a thumping sound as the man closed the window firmly, then pulled herself all the way up to the rooftop. Oddly, it was unguarded; she settled down onto the roof and caught her breath, then looked out over the city. St Petersburg was as dark and cold as the grave.

It was nothing like London, she realised, as she drew on her magic to warm herself. London had plenty of gaslights, even in the most deprived areas. The Swing had encouraged the Privy Council to do *something* for the poor, after all, although Gwen suspected it was mainly cosmetic. St Petersburg, on the other hand, was dark. She hesitated, then levitated herself high up into the air. There were some lights on the fortresses, she saw, but almost all of the city was dark, a silent brooding mass. But, below her, the soldiers continued their patrols of the palace grounds.

She dropped back down again, pulling her magic around her protectively. In the darkness, she would be almost completely invisible, unless the Russians got very lucky. She lowered herself down past the government complexes on the highest floor, then found a window she could unlock with magic. Inside, it was almost blissfully warm. Gwen sagged in relief, then froze as she heard someone stepping into the room. She looked up to see a Russian guardsman, staring at her. He barked at her in Russian, then reached for her arm.

Gwen hesitated. Killing the guard, or stunning him, would be easy, but his superiors would notice someone was missing. And yet she didn't dare let him take her prisoner. At the very least, Lord Standish would have some hard questions to answer ... and he might simply decide to hand her over to the Russians, if he thought she had acted badly. She reached for her Charm, then spoke a single order, over and over again.

"You have to drink," she said, in badly-accented Russian. Romulus had helped her learn a few phrases, but he hadn't taught her anything like enough. "You have to drink."

The guard swayed under the impact of her Charm. Gwen swore under her breath as she realised it wasn't working properly, then tried to use both Charm and Talking at the same time, pushing the command into his mind. Master Thomas had used it once to influence – to *control* – Gwen herself at a distance, but it was a power she had steadfastly refused to try to develop. Feeling her own body turned into a puppet still gave her nightmares. The guard swayed again, then turned and left the room, his thoughts set on drinking himself into a stupor. Gwen had heard enough to know that there was alcohol everywhere in Russia and that everyone, from the highest to the lowest, drank every day. The guard wouldn't remember her ... or his superiors would dismiss it as a drunken hallucination.

She looked down at her pale hands, wondering if she'd crossed a line. Charm was one thing, but Charm could be resisted, its influence detected and neutralised. *This* ... was something new, a power born of combining two separate aspects of magic. If she worked with it, played with it, learned how to use it ... what could she not do? The power to control people at will ... it sounded like a dream, but it would become a nightmare. And there was no one she could ask for advice. Master Thomas was dead and everyone else who heard the truth would see her as a potential threat. And to think they thought Charmers were bad!

Gwen hesitated, then walked to the door and slipped outside, glancing around to try to locate herself. If she was right, the ballroom was down the corridor and her rooms were some distance upwards. She turned and started to walk, wondering if Raechel had made it back to the room already. It took nearly twenty minutes for her to find the right room and slip inside, only to discover that it was empty. Raechel's bags had been placed neatly on the floor, ready for Gwen to open and empty. A quick check revealed that someone had searched the bags, pawing through Raechel's clothes, while trying to find anything incriminating. Gwen had to smile.

Unless they saw her using her powers, they wouldn't be able to tell who she was ... and she'd brought nothing with her.

She ducked into the bathroom and turned on the taps, then recovered a new towel from the railing along with the dressing gown. Her body still felt cold, despite her magic; she climbed into the bathtub as soon as there was enough water and allowed it to heat her body thoroughly, leaving her feeling tired and drained. The Russians had put a second bed in the room, one barely large enough for her; she climbed into it and closed her eyes. It was morning when she awoke.

"You snore," Raechel called over from the giant bed. "I couldn't sleep because of the rumbling thunder."

Gwen glowered at her. "I do not snore," she said, as someone knocked on the door for the second time. "And what time did you get in?"

She pulled herself out of bed, wrapped the gown around herself and opened the door. A pair of very pale maids stood there, each one carrying a large silver tray of food. Gwen watched as the two girls, both thinner than Olivia had been when they'd first met, placed the trays on the table, then withdrew. She couldn't help being reminded of one of her father's friends, a money-lender who specialised in loans to the aristocracy.

"That smells good," Raechel said. "Do you think we're meant to eat it all ourselves?"

Gwen frowned. It was vanishingly rare for a maid to eat with her mistress ... but even if she was, there was enough food for at least four people in front of them. Raechel wasn't *that* big an eater, one of the few points she had in common with other girls of her age. Gwen ate more than her, but Gwen needed to eat to power her magic. She hadn't realised, last night, just how hungry she'd become.

"Eat what you can," she said, placing bacon and eggs – and something she didn't recognise – onto a plate and passing it to Raechel. "You never know when you will be able to eat again."

Raechel eyed her. "Your experience talking?"

Gwen nodded, then started to eat herself. The food tasted good, although there were odd flavours that suggested the cooks weren't entirely used to cooking English food. She ate enough bacon and eggs to make Raechel give her another look, then stood upright and checked to make sure they weren't being watched. When she was sure, she leaned forward to whisper in Raechel's ear.

"I have to go speak to someone," she said. "If anyone asks, say you got sick of the sight of me and told me to get lost for a few hours."

"That's not much for me to do," Raechel complained.

"But it's important," Gwen said. She leaned forward and surprised herself by giving the older girl a hug. "I need an excuse to be out and about."

She dressed rapidly, then checked her watch. It was nearly twelve o'clock; she'd overslept quite badly. If she'd been with Janet and Romulus ... shaking her head, she slipped out of Raechel's room and headed down towards the rest of the diplomatic suite. Lady Standish was chatting to a Russian woman who seemed to speak perfect English, while Janet was sorting out her clothes and Romulus was nowhere to be seen. The remaining diplomats, apart from Sir Sidney, were gathered in the smoking room. Gwen left them before they could start demanding food and drink, then headed into the next room. Sir Sidney was standing there, a glass of brandy in his hand.

"Gwen," he greeted her. One hand tapped an ear. "How is the Young Mistress?"

Gwen took the hint and reached out with her senses, trying to determine if they were unobserved. It certainly seemed that way, so she relaxed as best as she could without letting go of her enhanced awareness. This wasn't the airship, where they could be assured of relative privacy. There were any number of people who might overhear their words.

"She's fine," she said, shortly. It was suddenly hard to concentrate; her awareness told her, all too clearly, that Sir Sidney was male. "And you?"

"Lord Standish met with the Tsar this morning," Sir Sidney said. "The Tsar had an offer for him. In exchange for a free hand against Persia – not the Ottomans: Persia – the Tsar will stay out of the war between Britain and France."

Gwen considered it, recalling the maps she'd seen. "That would put the Ottomans in a bind," she said. "If the Russians controlled Persia as well as their holdings in the Balkans, they'd be able to attack the Turks on two fronts."

"I'm glad you can see that," Sir Sidney said. "Because Lord Standish is very tempted."

"It's a looming disaster," Gwen said, and rapidly explained the maps she'd found during her exploration of the uppermost levels of the palace. "They've definitely got plans to use the undead."

Sir Sidney frowned. "Are you sure? It wouldn't be the first time some civilian drew up completely impractical operational plans."

"The Tsar was a soldier," Gwen pointed out. "He'd know better."

Sir Sidney sighed, loudly. "There are some very stupid officers out there," he said. "Men who purchased their commissions, then left their regiments in the hands of their juniors while they partied all night." He shook his head. "The Tsar is planning to go to Moscow," he added, "and we're invited."

Gwen rubbed her tired eyes. "Why?"

"Good question," Sir Sidney said. "He may feel safer there."

"Try to keep Lord Standish from making any stupid agreements," Gwen said, recalling how much trouble the Airship Treaty had caused Lord Mycroft. If Lord Standish made an agreement that compromised Turkey so badly, Parliament would have no choice but to reject it ... thus compromising the authority of other diplomats. "The lines on the map came from Moscow ..."

She froze as she sensed someone – Lady Standish – making her way towards the drawing room. For a moment, she found herself utterly unsure of what to do. Gwen the Maid should not be talking to Sir Sidney, certainly not alone. She couldn't afford to be caught, yet she was too tired to hide herself ... and she had to let the woman draw a reasonable explanation for why Gwen was there.

"Lady Standish is coming," she said, and grabbed Sir Sidney before she could think better of her mad idea. His eyes went very wide as she pulled him close. "I'm sorry."

She kissed his lips, firmly. It felt odd to start a kiss, something she'd never done in her life ... hell, it wasn't ladylike. And yet, it brought a strange sense of freedom, a sense that she might have enjoyed it if things were different. She felt him respond, his arms going around her ...

And then Lady Standish burst into the room.

Chapter Twenty-One

wen!" Lady Standish snapped. "What is the *meaning* of *this*?"

Gwen jumped back from Sir Sidney, schooling her features into fear. If she'd been a normal maid in London, she would have been blamed for everything, even if Sir Sidney had forced himself on her. It was yet another problem she knew she would have to try to fix, somehow, even though she wasn't sure where to begin. The upper classes found it so much easier to blame everything from wanton behaviour to outright rape on the lower classes.

"Get away from him," Lady Standish snapped. "You utter ..."

"You will have to excuse her," Sir Sidney drawled, in his best aristocratic manner. "The fault was mine."

Lady Standish rounded on him. "My husband will be hearing about this," she thundered, angrily. "Luring young ladies into lives of sin!"

She caught Gwen's arm and swung her round. "You represent *my* household," she added, then lifted a hand and slapped Gwen across the face. "Your actions bring shame upon me!"

Gwen glared at her, feeling magic pulsing under her skin. It would be easy, so easy, to kill the woman right there and then. A tiny pinch in Lady Standish's brain and she'd collapse, leaving no traces of anything to suggest it hadn't been a natural death. Or she could Charm her into complete and total submission. Or ... she controlled her temper with an effort, running through meditative tricks to make the pain fade away. She couldn't afford to blow her cover, not yet. But when she did ...

"Come now," Sir Sidney drawled. "The fault was not hers."

"Be quiet," Lady Standish snapped. "You should not lead young women into sin!"

Gwen stayed quiet as Lady Standish told Sir Sidney off in no uncertain manner. It almost seemed comical; Lady Standish was in no position to blight either of their careers, no matter what she reported to High Society when they got home. But if Gwen had been a real maid ... a shiver ran down her body as Lady Standish turned and practically dragged her out of the room. If they'd been in London, a real maid could expect to be turned out onto the streets for disgracing her mistress. Even here ... would Lady Standish try to abandon her, thousands of miles from home?

If she does, Gwen thought, as she was pulled down the corridor towards the rooms that had been assigned to Romulus and Janet, *I'll have to Charm her and take the risk of discovery.*

"You spent most of your time in the countryside," Lady Standish said. She sounded calmer, but the rage had been replaced by cold anger. "You are unaware of the true dangers of the world, particularly those posed by young men. That man would have used you, then discarded you, once you had served your purpose. Do you understand what I am saying to you?"

The hell of it, Gwen realised, was that Lady Standish had a point. If Gwen had been a real maid, pulled into a relationship with a man from the upper classes, it might well have ended badly. No, it *would* have ended badly. In her own way, Lady Standish was actually trying to help. But it wasn't really any help at all.

"You are not to be alone with him ever again," Lady Standish hissed. "I expect you to spend all of your time, after today, with my niece. If I catch you without her or near him, you will be dismissed on the spot."

She pushed the door open without bothering to knock. Romulus was bending over an ironing board, carefully ironing his butler's jacket. Gwen flushed as she realised the butler was topless, wearing nothing above the waist, but Lady

Standish showed no reaction. He was, after all, of a very different social class to herself.

"Gwen requires discipline," Lady Standish said, as Romulus turned and bowed. "You will handle it, then send her to my niece."

"Yes, My Lady," Romulus said. He nodded to Gwen, then pointed to a chair. "Wait there. I will see to you shortly."

Lady Standish threw one last disgusted look at Gwen, then strode out of the door, slamming it shut behind her. Gwen looked over at Romulus, wondering just what Lady Standish had had in mind when she'd ordered him to discipline her. She couldn't mean she wanted Gwen *beaten*, did she? But Gwen knew, all too well, that servants were often beaten. And she'd have to lie there and take it ...

Romulus finished ironing his jacket, then pulled on his white shirt and carefully buttoned it up. Gwen couldn't help admiring the sheer precision of his movements – they reminded her of the sergeants who supervised the male trainees at Cavendish Hall – as he turned and inspected himself in the mirror, then pulled his jacket on over his shirt. He might be in Russia, where his duties were really nothing more than a manservant's, but he saw no reason to allow standards to slip. Gwen felt her heart sinking as he turned to face her, wondering if she dared try to Charm him. But he was self-aware enough to make that a very dangerous prospect.

"I'm surprised to see you," he said, his dark eyes meeting hers. "What happened?"

"Lady Standish caught me kissing Sir Sidney," Gwen said, bitterly. Her mission had just become much more complicated ... in hindsight, they could probably have sneaked back to his room to chat, rather than staying in the open. "She was ... not happy."

"She wouldn't have been," Romulus said. He frowned, thoughtfully. "Her Ladyship likes to be in control and yet she knows she isn't really in control of anything."

Gwen nodded. Lady Standish might come from impeccable breeding, a bloodline that dated all the way back to the Norman Conquest, but she was as helpless as any other wife in the face of her husband. She had no money, no land

and no rights of her own, save what her husband chose to give her. No wonder she was so obsessed with making everything perfect; it gave her a sense of power, of control, her life denied her. Not for the first time, Gwen wondered what would have happened to the Grandes Dames of High Society if they'd been allowed to shape their own lives.

But none of them had the chance, she thought. *Only the very lucky women get to choose their own paths through life.*

Romulus leaned forward. "That was careless of you," he added, warningly. "Her Ladyship will be watching you like a hawk from now on."

"Yes, sir," Gwen said. It was true. Lady Standish would be looking for other signs of wanton behaviour. Even if she was with Raechel, Lady Standish would be watching. "I know."

"You could have lost your position," Romulus warned. "Stand up."

Gwen obeyed, then braced herself as he swung her around and delivered a sharp slap to her bottom. It stung, but the pain faded quickly. She couldn't help thinking that Lady Standish had meant something worse when she'd ordered Romulus to provide discipline. But she wasn't about to complain.

"I suggest you wait here for a while, then I will escort you to Lady Raechel," Romulus said, coldly. His face was curiously impassive. "You should make an attempt at looking miserable."

"Yes, sir," Gwen said.

"And try not to sit down anywhere," Romulus added. "Lady Standish *will* be watching."

Gwen nodded. "Do you have an onion?"

Romulus surprised her by laughing. "I think you need more than just an onion," he said. "But you can do whatever else you need to do here before I take you to Lady Raechel."

Gwen sat back and tried to think about what she'd learned, both about the Tsar's plans and the offer he'd made Lord Standish. On the face of it, she had to admit, the offer seemed tempting. Britain had no alliance with Persia, no reason to go to war on the state's behalf ... except, of course, for the fact that whoever controlled Persia could attack the

Ottoman Empire or British India. Or Russia, of course. It had been why all three powers had seemed content to leave Persia as a buffer like Afghanistan, carefully coordinating their political influence to ensure that the state remained neutral. But the Russians had clearly decided to change their minds ...

But what did they really want?

Perhaps the Tsar wanted to avoid joining the French in war against Britain. Judging from the problems beyond the Palace's walls, the Russian population was restive and the Russian military might be needed at home. She doubted that the Russians actually *wanted* the war, they just feared being abandoned by the French or left to fight the Ottomans on their own. If they came to a deal with Lord Standish, they could abandon the French at will and leave them to fight alone.

And yet ... the plans she'd seen had called for the use of vast numbers of undead. She was sure of it, even though she knew Sir Sidney had had a point; it *was* possible that the plans had been drawn up by ignorant idiots more interested in impressing the Tsar than actually doing genuine staff work. But her instincts – and Olivia's kidnapping – told her otherwise. The Russians wouldn't have kidnapped a Necromancer if they hadn't had some use in mind for her.

She looked over at Romulus, who was carefully sorting out the contents of his suitcase. Why had he spared her? And she was sure that he *had* spared her. Lady Standish, if Janet was to be believed, was another firm believer that sparing the rod spoiled the servants. If she was prepared to beat Raechel, she was certainly prepared to beat her maids. But Romulus had spared her ...

Bracing herself, she opened her mouth. "Why didn't you thrash me?"

"Her Ladyship can go too far," Romulus said. He gave her an odd little smile. "I would suggest, however, that you stay well away from Sir Sidney. It will only end in tears."

He turned. "Wash your face," he added, "and then I will walk you back to Lady Raechel."

There was no one in the corridor between Romulus' room and Raechel's suite, much to Gwen's relief. Inside, Raechel looked up as soon as they entered, her face pale and worried. Gwen wondered, suddenly, just what Lady Standish had said to her niece, perhaps a stern warning against contaminating the maids or even just an order to keep Gwen with her in future. At least Raechel didn't look to have been beaten herself. She just looked worried.

"Your Aunt wasn't happy with me," she said, as soon as she'd checked that they were unobserved. "And I have to stay with you, for the moment."

"Then we will have to wander the palace together," Raechel said. She paused, looking down at Gwen. "Are you alright?"

"Magic makes it easier to recover," Gwen said. It was true enough – and she had a feeling she didn't want to call Romulus' mercy to anyone's attention. "What about you?"

"She just told me off for not keeping an eye on you," Raechel said. She stood and looked at Gwen. "What do you want to do now?"

"I have to teach you some techniques that might help you keep your thoughts under control," Gwen said. Someone without magic couldn't hope to shield their thoughts completely, but they could detect an intrusion and force the spy out. "You never know who might be listening to your thoughts."

Raechel paled. "I always thought my Aunt knew what I was thinking."

"I doubt it," Gwen said. If Raechel's thoughts were no cleaner than her actions, her Aunt would probably have sent her to a convent by now. There had been one case of a mother reading her children's minds, one that had ended very badly. "But there are others here who might take a peek into your mind."

"No," Raechel said. She paused. "Can *you* do that?"

"Not very well," Gwen admitted. "I can read emotions, but not thoughts."

Raechel eyed her, nervously. "You could be lying," she said. "Or trying to reassure me."

"I'm not lying," Gwen said, defensively. She understood precisely how the girl felt, but it was annoying to be accused of something she considered immoral. "Besides, Talkers often have problems coping with more than one or two people close to them at any one time."

She pulled Raechel over to the carpeted floor, then sat down and crossed her legs. "The key to detecting someone trying to intrude upon your thoughts," she explained as Raechel sat down, "is to monitor your own thoughts carefully. One must be completely aware of one's self to detect thoughts and feelings that are not yours. You must become aware of your own mind."

"I think, therefore I am," Raechel said. "Or is that the wrong way to go about it."

Gwen took Raechel's hands in hers, then smiled. "Close your eyes," she ordered, "and start breathing regularly, in and out, in and out."

Raechel giggled. "This feels silly," she said. "And how will I know if it works?"

"It takes practice," Gwen agreed. "And it takes more practice to monitor your shields in the midst of a distraction. If someone is talking to you, your mind will be on them, rather than on yourself."

She paused. "Breathe in ... and breathe out. Breathe in ... and breathe out."

Irene had told her, back when she'd started more advanced lessons, that there were people who never truly mastered any form of mental discipline. The extroverts like Raechel – and Gwen herself, to some degree – had too many problems maintaining their thoughts in order when thcy were constantly responding and reacting to the world around them. But Raechel seemed to be managing just fine. Maybe all she needed was a little encouragement.

Gwen squeezed her hand lightly, then opened her mouth. "I'm going to try to touch your mind very lightly," she warned. "When you feel me, I want you to squeeze my hand. Don't open your eyes and don't try to speak. Just concentrate on monitoring your own thoughts."

She frowned as she saw Raechel stiffen. It wasn't a surprise – few people liked the thought of having their mind read – but it ensured that Raechel would have to start meditating again from the beginning. Gwen sighed, then carefully talked her back into the semi-trance and then reached out with her mind. Raechel was a glowing ball of emotions and thoughts, all seemingly jumbled together. It would take time and practice for her to school her mind long enough to detect an intrusion.

Gwen let out a gasp as she sensed a sudden wave of emotions, followed by garbled thoughts that refused to resolve in her mind. Raechel's grip tightened suddenly – Gwen winced in pain – then relaxed; there was a sudden flood of triumph in her mind. Gwen managed to refrain from pointing out that a skilled Talker would already have been monitoring her thoughts for information before she noticed his presence. Irene would probably have learned whatever she wanted to learn and then withdrawn without being detected.

"Not bad, for a first try," she said, instead. "But we are going to have to do this again and again until you have mastered it completely."

Raechel leaned forward. "Who's the mind-reader?"

Gwen lifted her eyebrows. "I beg your pardon?"

"You wouldn't be doing this if there wasn't some reason to worry," Raechel said. Her voice hardened with anger and a kind of bitter helplessness. "Who might be poking into my thoughts?"

"You remember those dark-clad men around the Tsar?" Gwen asked. She didn't want to mention Simone, not now. "At least two of them were magicians. I suspect they were doing more than just broadcasting mental static to ensure that no one read the Tsar's mind."

She shuddered at the memory of watching the monks praying to the picture of the Tsar, wondering just what that portended. Talkers made everyone uncomfortable, even British Ministers. The strongest laws on the books were intended to deal with Talkers as well as Necromancers, although Talkers were far more useful. Did the Tsar make the monks so faithful to him in the hopes of ensuring they didn't abuse their positions?

"I asked Adam about them," Raechel said. She looked oddly embarrassed. "You know what he told me?"

Gwen shook her head, impatiently.

"He said they castrated themselves," Raechel said. She flushed, then giggled. "Can you imagine? They cut off their own manhoods just to serve the Tsar!"

"I've seen stupider things," Gwen said. She frowned. "And *Adam*?"

"I thought I should try to see what he could tell me," Raechel said. "And I didn't give him anything more than a smile."

"Good thinking," Gwen said, hoping that no one tried to read Raechel's mind. She knew far too much. "And ..."

There was a sharp tap at the door. Gwen hesitated, then hurried over to her bed and lay down on it, face down. Raechel frowned after her, then opened the door. Her Aunt stood outside, glaring around the palace as if she owned it. For a dreadful moment, Gwen was convinced she wanted to see the scars. But instead she just looked at Raechel.

"Your Uncle and his staff have been invited to Moscow," she said. "We will be leaving tomorrow morning. You will be woken early in the morning and you will be ready to leave on time. I will not have you embarrassing me any further."

"Yes, Auntie," Raechel said.

"And Gwen can get back to work," Lady Standish added. "She's had long enough to recover."

"*Yes*, Auntie," Raechel said. "Bye, Auntie."

She closed the door in her Aunt's face and turned around. "I hate her, sometimes," she said, to Gwen. "She's such a ... a bore!"

"It could be worse," Gwen said, as she sat upright. If Lord Standish was going to Moscow, it suggested he hadn't rejected the Russian proposal out of hand. "Believe me, it could be a great deal worse."

Chapter Twenty-Two

e have something quite special for you today," Gregory said, as Ivan led Olivia down into the experimental chambers. "I want you to watch and be ready to assist us, if necessary."

Olivia scowled at him, bitterly. She'd spent the last few days trying to convince Ivan that the experiments would end in disaster, but the Russian had been reluctant to abandon his loyalty to the Tsar, even if he did think the *Skoptzi* monks were making a dreadful mistake. He'd taken care of her, played chess and cards with her, yet he hadn't *listened* to her. It was utterly frustrating and the growing whispering in her head only made matters worse.

"And what," she asked finally, "are you trying to do?"

The Russian smiled at her, the gleam of madness clearly visible in his eyes. She'd seen enough of his experiments through the eyes of the undead to understand just how far he was prepared to go, but the ultimate objective of his research defeated her. He'd injected undead tissue into living subjects, attempted to torture one of the undead, which had been a pointless waste of time, and hundreds of other experiments. And, throughout them all, he'd kept smiling. He genuinely believed they were moving closer and closer to a breakthrough.

"The undead will have a new member today," Gregory said, finally. "We will see if they can use a magician's powers, if that magician becomes one of the undead."

Ivan saw her flinch and looked at her, oddly. "Do you already know the answer?"

Olivia shook her head. As far as she knew, the undead in London hadn't bitten or consumed any magicians, although it was quite likely that they had. But there had been no evidence of the undead using any powers, apart from their natural aggression and growing levels of intelligence. They didn't seem to have access to the powers their victims had once possessed ... or so she thought. It was quite possible that they'd never worked out how to use the powers.

"Then we shall see," Gregory said. He turned and opened a door that led down to the cells, then plucked an oil lamp from the walls and walked down the stairs. Olivia followed him, picking her way down the stone stairs carefully. She'd already slipped once and the Russians had laughed at her. "Let us see what we have here."

He'd stopped outside one of the cells. Olivia followed his gaze and saw a young girl with dirty-blonde hair, lying on the bed with a drugged expression on her face. Merely *looking* at the girl made her feel queasy, as if she was staring at something fundamentally *wrong*. There was a gasp behind her, followed by one of the guards turning and running back up the stairs, fleeing for his life. The girl turned her head to look at Olivia and smiled, very slowly. There was something about the smile that made Olivia want to run too.

"She's quite a curious specimen," Gregory said. "We found her on the streets, running her own gang of youths. They were all terrified of her, not without reason. It took fifty men to exterminate them and take her alive."

He barked a command in Russian. The cell door was opened and the girl dragged out by two of the guards. She made no attempt at resistance. All she did was smile at them, as if her mind was gone. The guards still seemed nervous even to touch her, as if they were handling a poisonous snake or something that might explode at any second. Up close, she smelt of blood and shit and piss, just like someone from the streets of London. Olivia shuddered, remembering that she too had smelt like that, once upon a time.

"Her powers are odd," Gregory continued. "When we had her here, she actually started to influence the guards. Some of them were made to commit embarrassing acts for her amusement, others were forced to wound themselves or even attack their fellows. Even drugged, she has an influence on the world around her. We don't understand why."

Olivia shivered, remembering one of the few times she'd seen Gwen genuinely angry. Two of the boys from Cavendish Hall had been caught in one of the local opium dens, drugged to the eyeballs and their powers spinning out of control. Doctor Norwell had speculated, afterwards, that perhaps they could unlock deeper magic through using drugs to decouple a person's mind from reality, but Gwen had forbidden all such experiments. Perhaps, she wondered as the girl was hustled down the corridor, she was seeing the result of something similar.

The whispering at the back of her head suddenly grew louder as they stepped into a room holding one of the undead, locked in a cage. Olivia's vision seemed to blur for a long moment, giving her the odd sense that she was looking at herself through the eyes of one of the undead; she staggered and almost hit the floor. Ivan caught her, then looked over at Gregory and the guards. The girl was being pushed into the cage.

Olivia saw her chance and reached out with her mind, trying to trigger the undead into action. It lunged forward with terrifying speed, ignoring the girl in its desperate haste to get at the guards. Two of them were ripped apart within seconds, but the remaining guards ran forward and used prods to shove the undead back into the cage. Olivia moaned in pain as the beast howled in rage, then fell on the girl. There was a long moment when the girl seemed to be trying to hold it back, before the undead lunged at her. The girl's neck was rapidly bitten and she sank to the floor, dying.

"Take control of her," Gregory ordered. He knew that she *could* control the undead, at least to some extent. "Take control of her and use her powers."

Olivia hesitated, then forced her mind into the girl's body. The dark power that lay behind Necromancy was already spreading through her, an infection that drew on her remaining life force and used it to convert her into one of the undead. There was a sudden surge of thoughts and feelings – the girl had flown once, Olivia realised – and then there was nothing, but the darkness of death ... and the feelings of the undead. The girl pulled herself to her feet and stared at her captors, now on the other side of the bars. Olivia saw herself looking at her and felt her head swimming.

"Use her powers," Gregory ordered. "Make her do something."

Olivia tried, but she honestly wasn't sure what she was doing. And what *was* the girl, anyway? Influencing people suggested a Charmer – there were Charmers in many criminal gangs, pulling the strings from behind the scenes – but the way she'd used her powers was nothing like Ivan or any of the other Charmers she had met. And if she'd flown ... it suggested multiple powers. And multiple powers meant a Master Magician.

She couldn't help herself. She started to laugh.

"And what," Gregory demanded, "is so funny?"

He pulled at her, yanking her around to face him. "Why are you laughing?"

"It tickles when I try to use her powers," Olivia lied. She was tempted to throw their own failure in their face – if they'd had a female Master Magician, they could have kept her drugged while they impregnated her and took the children away to be indoctrinated – but she suspected it would merely result in another beating. "I can't handle them properly."

"Try again," Gregory said. There was a desperate note in his voice that surprised her as he looked over at Ivan, "Make her try again."

Ivan stepped forward, his face reluctant. "Try again," he ordered. Charm ran through his voice, but it wasn't as strong as Olivia had feared. He could have made her do anything, yet he seemed curiously reluctant to push her as hard as he could. "Please. Try again."

Olivia tried to resist, but she was tired, so tired. She closed her eyes and peered through the girl's eyes, distressed at just how easy it had become to possess one of the undead and even influence it. The younger the corpse, part of her noted, the easier it was to take control. But, no matter how she tried, it seemed impossible to use the girl's magic. And yet there was an odd hint it should be possible.

"It won't work," she said, as she opened the eyes. She could feel the remains of the compulsion pulsing around her. "I can't use her powers."

"There are other ways," Gregory said. He looked over at her, then nodded to the guards. Two of them came forward and grabbed Ivan by the arms, while a third clamped a hand over his mouth. "And this unbeliever will help us find them."

Olivia backed away, hastily, as two more guards reached for her. But there was no room to dodge them, no way to escape and run. She brought her knee up, trying to hit the first guard in the groin, only to discover that he was wearing protection. The guard grabbed her, wrestled her hands behind her back, then held her there. His companion held a knife to her throat. Olivia froze, wondering if she had finally reached the limits of her usefulness. They didn't need her to create more of the undead.

But they need me to control them, her thoughts howled through her mind. *Without me, the undead will go for anyone living, no matter which side they're on.*

"We are aware that not everyone venerates the Father Tsar like we do," Gregory said, addressing Ivan. "It is of no consequence to us if they believe in him or not, provided that they obey. But this one was not planning to obey."

He looked over at Olivia. "This one was planning to steal you away from us and take you to his faction," he added. "A plan years in the making, a plan to save the Father Tsar from the failings of his slaves, would have broken because of this one's failure to have faith in the Father Tsar. And Holy Mother Russia would have been lost before the invaders from the West and the South and the East. His failing demands the harshest of punishment."

Olivia stared at him. Ivan had planned to save her? But he hadn't said anything to her ... and he'd acted as though he had no intention of doing anything to help her escape or even save his country from the doom waiting in the cage. She jerked her head over towards the two undead and shivered. The girl was waiting patiently, as if she knew, sooner or later, there would be a mistake and she would be free. She had all the time in the world.

Gregory walked over until he was standing right in front of Olivia. "You belong to us now," he hissed. "And you will serve your purpose in the assigned plan."

Olivia shuddered at his touch as his hand stroked her chin. His hand felt disgusting; up close, the stench was appalling, worse than the dead girl. But no matter how she struggled, she couldn't get away. The guards held her tightly.

"It never occurred to this one that the true faithful read minds," Gregory continued, as he turned and walked back towards Ivan. "We have no secrets from one another; we stand naked in front of one another, as we stand naked when a newcomer joins our sacred band of believers. Those who do not believe are weeded out before they are permitted to learn the mysteries of our order. And those who work with us have their thoughts scrutinised for signs of disbelief and treachery."

Olivia shuddered. Charmers were feared and hated, but Talkers were not far behind. What privacy was there if a person's thoughts could be read, memories extracted from their minds for careful scrutiny. Even the most liberal Englishman, the men who opposed torture and slavery, had qualms about allowing Talkers to roam free. It hadn't even been settled if Talkers could be used to give evidence in court.

"We found this one preparing to commit a daring act of treachery," Gregory said. His voice was soft, but there was infinite malice behind it. "His plans would have impeded the arrival of the Father Tsar and destroyed everything we had worked to build."

"This is madness," Olivia said. The guard holding the knife moved it away and clamped his hand over her mouth instead. Olivia bit it, forcing him to yank it back from her face. "You have to understand you can't control these creatures ..."

"But we know, now, how to control them," Gregory said. "And why are you arguing in his defence?"

His voice became silky. "Do you believe him to be right? Or has he Charmed you into caring about him, even loving him? And would you know if your feelings are true or not?"

He turned back to Ivan and muttered a command in Russian. The guard removed the hand over Ivan's mouth, then forced his mouth open by pinching his nose hard. Olivia tried to look away as Gregory removed a knife from his belt, but the guard holding her held her head firmly in place, forcing her to watch. Gregory reached into Ivan's mouth, caught hold of his tongue and yanked hard. Moments later, the knife flashed once and the tongue fell to the ground, trailing blood behind it.

He's taken Ivan's magic, Olivia thought, too shocked to move or try to speak. *He can't Charm if he can't speak.*

"You will be taken back to your quarters," Gregory said. "You will be prepared for transport. If you fail to obey in any way, you will be chained and dragged to your destination. Do you understand me?"

"Yes, sir," Olivia said, staring at Ivan. He was choking. Blood was pouring out of his mouth and pooling on the ground. "Sir ..."

"So you do care about him," Gregory said. "But are your feelings *real?*"

He pushed his fingers into Ivan's mouth, using his powers to staunch the bleeding. But he made no attempt to replace the tongue. Ivan lunged forward, but the two guards caught him and held him effortlessly in place. Olivia stared at him, then felt herself shoved forward as the guards pushed her out of the cell. Behind her, she heard the undead starting to moan ... had Gregory thrown Ivan to them? But she had no time to concentrate on reaching their minds as the guards half-carried her back to her room. Inside, Esther and two other girls were waiting for her, their faces pale and wan. Olivia couldn't help wondering if their minds were read regularly too, just for signs of disloyalty.

How horrible it must be to know that a random thought could get you killed, she thought, as the guards pushed her inside and closed the door behind her. *And they couldn't even hope to escape.*

She gritted her teeth as Esther came forward and started to pull Olivia's clothes off, leaving them on the floor, until she was stark naked. Olivia tried to pull away, but the other two girls caught her arms and frogmarched her into the bathroom, where they picked her up and dropped her in the bathtub. Olivia shouted in pain and kicked out as the hot water scalded her body, but the girls ignored her. Instead, one of them washed Olivia's hair thoroughly while the other two scrubbed down her body until she felt cleaner than she'd ever been in her entire life. As soon as the soap was rinsed out of her hair, she was hauled back into the bedroom, where Esther was waiting for her.

"I'm not wearing that," she said, as Esther held up the dress. It looked ridiculous, as if it was designed for a girl five or six years old, not someone who had started her cycles. Whoever had designed it had thought more highly of frilly ruffs than anyone else since the time of Queen Elizabeth. "It looks absurd."

Esther looked up, meeting Olivia's eyes for the first time. "We have orders to dress you," she said, flatly. Her voice was cold and dead. "If you do not help us to dress you, we will hold you down and dress you by force. We have been offered no choice."

Olivia sighed, then allowed the girls to help her pull on sheer undergarments, followed by the dress itself. When she looked in the mirror, she almost laughed at herself, but the girls showed no reaction. They were too badly scared, she realised grimly. Whatever had been said to them, while she'd watched Ivan's tongue being removed, had clearly pushed any thoughts of disobedience right out of their heads.

"Now," she said, wondering if she could talk them into actually telling her something useful. "What happens now?"

There was a tap on the door. Two guards stepped inside, their dark eyes glancing everywhere before alighting on the girls. They shrank back as the guards stepped forward, pulled Olivia's hands behind her back and cuffed them firmly together. Olivia glowered at them, but they ignored her. Instead, they pulled her out of the bedroom and down towards a large open room, where a carriage and a set of horses waited. Ivan was standing next to the carriage, his hands and feet in chains. His face was set in utter misery.

"I'm sorry," Olivia said, as she was helped into the carriage and chained to the seat. The guards carefully wrapped blankets around her, then pushed Ivan in after her. "I'm sorry."

Ivan made a face at her, then opened his mouth. There was a stub at the back of his mouth where his tongue should have been. Revolted, Olivia looked away.

Moments later, the carriage rattled into life.

Chapter Twenty-Three

hey really hate us, don't they?"

Gwen looked over at Raechel and tried not to roll her eyes. The girl had attended another evening dance – this time, Gwen had stayed on the balcony under Romulus's watchful eye – and then gone to bed late. But the Russians had insisted on waking Raechel up early in the morning, even though she normally slept until at least ten in the morning. Gwen found it rather hard to be sympathetic. After all, the Russians had brought breakfast too.

"It's a long journey from St Petersburg to Moscow," Gwen commented, as she walked into the bathroom and started to run a hot bath. "They're probably determined to ensure we leave early."

Raechel glowered at her as she followed Gwen into the bathroom, dropping her nightclothes in a basket for the maids to pick up and wash. Gwen smirked, then helped Raechel into the bath and scrubbed her thoroughly, before helping her out again and drying her with a towel. She took the opportunity to wash and dry herself, then pulled on one of the heavier outfits the Russians had sent for her. It was clear that the Russians expected the trip to be bitterly cold.

"You'd think they'd install railways," Raechel grumbled, as she struggled with her woollen trousers. "Or something warm."

"They're backwards," Gwen said, recalling Lord Mycroft's notes. "And railways can be threats as well as opportunities."

She sighed. The Russians were notably behind even the Ottomans when it came to constructing railways binding their territories together. She was surprised they hadn't made use of French expertise in producing railways. The French had surpassed the British when it came to laying down rails within their territory. But, in England at least, the railways had made it easier for people to move from place to place, making the country smaller. The last thing the Tsar and his aristocracy would want was something that allowed peasants and serfs to flee to the cities or ally themselves with urban revolutionary groups.

Raechel looked over at her. "Do they have good reason to feel threatened?"

Gwen nodded, recalling the feel of St Petersburg ... and the looming spectre of violence in the Winter Palace itself. Tsar Nicolas wasn't *that* old, but he'd looked as though he could die at any moment ... and then there would be an almighty struggle over the succession. His heirs were minor children and whoever got into position to control them would be in place to set Russia's course for years to come. Their enemies wouldn't leave them in peace, knowing they would only be killed as the power-brokers consolidated their power ...

And a civil war would risk breaking the Russian Empire into dozens of fragmented states.

She shivered at the thought. If Russia collapsed into anarchy, the French and Ottomans ... perhaps even the Chinese ... would seek to make gains at Russia's expense. The balance of power that so suited the British Empire would be shattered beyond repair. Hell, somehow she doubted that British statesmen would leave Alaska alone when they could take the territory from a weakened Russia and add it to the British Empire. There was no shortage of voices in British North America crying out to annex Alaska.

Raechel coughed. "Are you all right?"

"Just thinking," Gwen said. She smiled, rather wanly. "A terrible habit."

"That's what my Aunt used to say," Raechel said. "She always tried to discourage me from actually thinking for myself."

Gwen wasn't surprised. Lady Standish would want a niece who did as she was told, not one who risked dragging her into scandal after scandal. But at least she hadn't locked

Raechel away in her room, forbidding her to do anything apart from read the bible and pray. There were mothers and aunts in London who'd done just that to their charges. Gwen sometimes wondered why her own mother hadn't abandoned her, years ago.

She was my mother, she thought, shaking her head. *She wouldn't let go of me, no matter what I was.*

There was a knock on the door. Gwen checked that Raechel was decent, glanced down at her own clothes, then strode over and opened the door, revealing a handsome young Russian officer. The Tsar seemed intent on introducing Raechel to as many of his younger courtiers as possible, although Gwen wasn't sure why. Perhaps the young officers themselves had asked for the honour. Raechel had to look quite exotic to their eyes.

"The coaches are ready," the officer said, with a deep bow. His English, oddly, was tinged with a French accent. "If you would care to come with us ...?"

Raechel stood up, then nodded. "We will come," she said. "What about our bags?"

"They will be brought," the officer assured her. "The staff will see to that, My Lady."

Gwen followed Raechel down the stairs and out into the lobby, which was heaving with Russian servants and a handful of foreign representatives. She caught sight of Lord and Lady Standish being escorted out of the room by an older Russian officer, then saw Sir Sidney on the other side of the room. She cursed under her breath, wishing she had a moment to talk to the older man, but she knew it was impossible. They couldn't talk privately in the midst of a Russian crowd.

She winced, inwardly, as she caught sight of Talleyrand. The Frenchman's face was as impassive as ever, but Gwen suspected he was annoyed at the need to move from a comfortable and cosmopolitan city – insofar as there was one in Russia – to Moscow, which was reputed to be far more insular. Beside him, Simone looked pretty and winsome in her fur coat, attracting the attention of several Russian officers. Gwen hoped, with a touch of malice, that they were thinking impure thoughts. A mind could be a terrible thing to read at times.

The Russian officer smiled at Raechel, then led them through a pair of solid doors. Cold air slapped at Gwen's face as they passed through the second door; she almost slipped on ice below her feet. Raechel muttered a *very* unladylike word, just loud enough for Gwen to hear, as they walked through a final door and out into the open air. The palace grounds were covered with snow, either lying flat on the lawn or pushed into piles away from the road. It was bitterly cold, despite the fur coats they'd been given. Gwen drew on magic to warm herself as they were escorted towards a large golden carriage. Beyond it, there were dozens of other such carriages. A handful were already making their way towards the gates, escorted by Cossacks.

"I feel like a queen," Raechel said, and giggled.

"Or a target," Gwen muttered back. If she'd wanted to advertise someone's wealth and power, she would have used a carriage like the one the Russians had prepared for them. It looked to have been made of real gold. "And let us hope it will be warm inside."

She shook her head in disbelief as the Russian opened the door, allowing them to scramble into the carriage. Inside, there was a small heater, with a fire burning merrily inside the grate. Raechel sat down next to it, then looked over at Gwen expectantly. Gwen sighed and expanded her magic, warming the small compartment quickly and efficiently. Raechel settled down on the seat and looked over at Gwen.

"So," she said. "What do we do now?"

"It depends," Gwen said. The carriage looked large enough to seat more than two people, but it was quite possible the Russians intended to leave them alone. "If we're alone, you can work on your meditation."

She waited until the carriage lurched into life, then leaned forward and stared out the window as the massive convoy started to move. There was a small army of Cossacks escorting them, she noticed, many of them blocking her view of the city. The locals didn't seem too happy to see them, she did manage to see; their sullen hatred followed her until the royal procession was finally out of St Petersburg. Gwen silently prayed that they managed to complete their mission and leave Russia before the powder keg finally exploded. The Russians, it seemed, were on the verge of a revolt that would make the Swing look like a minor disturbance.

Closing the curtains, she turned to face Raechel. "You can work on your meditation," she ordered. "And I *will* be poking at your mind from time to time."

Raechel sighed. "I wish I had never come," she said. "There's *nothing* to do here."

Gwen laughed. "Next time we go somewhere, you can be the maid and I will be the spoiled brat," she said. She'd had the Russian servants doing most of the work in St Petersburg, but there had still been a great deal for her to do. And Janet, she suspected, had had the same problem, with the added issue of Lady Standish finding work for idle hands. "See how much *you* like it."

"I wanted to be in dramatics," Raechel muttered. "But my parents would never allow it."

"Of course not," Gwen said. "You *do* know what they say about women who go on the stage?"

Raechel sighed again, then closed her eyes and started to meditate. Gwen concealed a smile, remembering when she too had wanted to be an actress. But acting was no profession for an aristocratic young woman. Everyone knew that women who went on the stage were whores ... and if they didn't have a lover when they started, they would have one soon enough. King Charles II had formed a relationship with an actress. He was far from the only one.

She tested Raechel's mental shields carefully, but provoked no response. Gwen wasn't too surprised; it could take weeks or months to build up a working shield, particularly without magic of one's own. But it posed a security risk ... briefly, Gwen considered arranging for Simone to have an accident. It would be relatively easy to kill the girl without arousing suspicion, yet she was hardly the only Talker in the country. The Russians had Talkers of their own guarding the Tsar. She would just have to hope that none of them considered Raechel worthy of their attention.

Bracing herself, she pulled the curtain aside and peered out into the Russian countryside. It was prettier than she'd expected, with long tracts of untamed wilderness reaching out for miles around the royal road. But the impression of pristine countryside vanished as they passed through a small village, barely larger than an English hamlet. She sucked in her breath in horror as she saw the peasants making their way through the fields. They looked so ... so *inhuman*, compared to the glittering creatures who made up the Russian nobility. It was easy to see why so many aristocrats considered the peasants to be animals.

"Disgusting," she muttered.

Pity – and an odd kind of shame – ran through her heart as she saw how the peasants lived. Their village was practically swimming in mud. She saw pigs and a handful of other animals waddling through the sludge, while children worked with their parents in the fields. It was impossible to tell which children were male and which were female; they were dressed the same, their hair cropped close to their skulls. They were so thin that even the older girls, the ones who should have been developing breasts, were hard to separate from the men. And the older men and women looked beaten down by life.

"This is disgusting," Raechel agreed. "Why doesn't someone do something about this?"

"They don't care," Gwen said. She saw a legless man sitting beside his house, drinking from a large glass bottle. "The aristocrats simply don't care."

They paused at a large guesthouse as the night started to fall. No one seemed in the mood for dinner and dancing, or for anything more than sleep. They resumed their journey over the following days, passing through five more guesthouses before they reached their destination. Even with a change of horses every twenty miles or so, Russia was *vast*. It took days to travel from St Petersburg to Moscow.

There were more horrors as the carriages raced onwards. Gwen saw a field where chained men worked, picking what they could from the harvest, supervised by armed soldiers wearing fancy uniforms. A large house, larger than Cavendish Hall, had been badly damaged by fire and seemingly abandoned, along with most of the hovels nearby. The fields looked to have been left untended, although it was hard to be certain. She was sure she caught glimpses of men hiding in the forests as the coaches passed through them, stopping for nothing. The armed escort, she realised grimly, might be the only thing between them and bandits in the countryside.

Raechel caught her arm, pulling her back to the seat. "Is there anywhere in England like this?"

Gwen hesitated. "Not in England," she said, recalling what she'd heard of the slave plantations in America. "But there are places just as bad as this in the British Empire."

Something would have to be done, she told herself, as she settled into her seat and closed her eyes. She had power and influence, both as the Royal Sorceress and as the person who had brought Howell's reign of blackmail and terror to an end. There were people who owed her favours. She could use that power to try to change things for the better, to ensure that servants were treated decently and slavery was finally abolished ... but how could she tackle the economic underpinnings? If there was a surfeit of cheap labour, what was the incentive to treat maids and menservants better? And if slavery was profitable, why would slaveholders free their slaves?

"That can't be right," Raechel said, breaking into Gwen's thoughts. "I would have seen ..."

Gwen laughed, without opening her eyes. "How much of the world have you seen?"

But she'd been just as big an ignorant fool, she knew. If Jack hadn't shown her the dark underside of London, the horrors that had been completely out of her sight, what choice would she have made during the Swing? Would she have thrown herself completely behind Master Thomas?

"Not enough," Raechel muttered. "Clearly, not enough."

Gwen tried to sleep, only to be woken – what felt like only moments later – by the carriage swaying to a halt. The Russian servants moved from carriage to carriage, handing out sandwiches and bottles of juice, before the carriages rattled back into life. Gwen was silently relieved she wasn't anywhere near Lord Standish or Talleyrand, although she was privately certain the latter wasn't showing any reaction. Diplomats should have calm and peaceful journeys through the countryside, not pell-mell rides to a far from welcoming city. And they should have nine-course banquets too ...

"Your uncle isn't going to be very happy," she warned, as she picked her way through one of the sandwiches. The meat inside seemed to be chicken, but it was basted in so many sauces that it was hard to be sure. "This isn't how most countries treat diplomats."

"He never has any time for me in any case," Raechel assured her, chewing through her sandwich with obvious enthusiasm. "I think there are days when he simply forgets he has a ward."

"I'm sorry," Gwen said, and meant it. "My father did that too, sometimes."

She must have fallen asleep again, because the next thing she was aware of was Raechel poking her and waving to the window. Gwen opened her eyes and looked out, just in time to see the line of carriages passing through a set of gates and into the city. Moscow looked darker and grimmer than St Petersburg, even though there was less snow on the ground. The buildings at the edge of the city were brooding monstrosities, without any of the strange charm of St Petersburg. Even the older structures towards the centre of the city seemed to lack charm.

The population, though, looked as battered and weary as the population of St Petersburg. It was easy to see the hatred in their eyes, despite their constant exhaustion and the watching soldiers patrolling the city. Gwen had never seen so many soldiers in one place, even in St Petersburg, or London after the Swing. They looked weary too, but also alert ... and they never went anywhere alone. The smallest group of soldiers she saw was of no fewer than nine.

"Nice building," Raechel commented, as the carriages drove up to a large building that seemed a cross between a castle and a mansion. It might be defendable, Gwen noted, if it wasn't attacked with artillery. "Is this where they want us to stay?"

"It looks that way," Gwen said. The carriages slowly rattled to a halt. "I suggest you keep your head down."

Raechel looked at her. "You have a bad feeling about this too?"

The door was opened before Gwen could answer, allowing them both to scramble outside, into the cold. She heard someone talking loudly and angrily and looked over towards the door, where Lord Standish was talking to one of the Russians, gesturing angrily. The diplomat didn't sound very diplomatic, she decided, but it was hard to blame him. *She* felt tired and crabby after the nightmarish ride down nightmarish roads through nightmarish scenery. And Lord Standish was a professional diplomat. He wasn't used to being treated in such a manner.

A Russian officer bowed deeply to Raechel, then invited her to enter the building and walk up to her suite. Gwen followed, looking from side to side as they passed through another maze of corridors. The walls were lined with bladed weapons, she couldn't help noticing, ranging from standard swords to oddly-shaped examples from China or Japan. Notes written underneath in the Russian alphabet, she presumed, told the stories of those weapons. But she couldn't read them.

"Spoils of war," the Russian officer said, when Raechel asked. "Taken from our enemies in glorious combat."

Gwen sighed, inwardly. She would have bet half her inheritance that the Russian officer had seen no serious combat. Beating up unarmed peasants was very different from fighting armed men – or magicians – intent on killing you.

"There will be a dinner tonight, hosted by the Tsar," the officer said. He bowed again as he opened the door to Raechel's suite. "You will be welcome."

"Thank you," Raechel said. She sounded tired, but willing to carry on. "I will be there."

Chapter Twenty-Four

f there was one advantage to being considered a devil-child, Gwen had come to realise slowly, it was that she wasn't invited to very many balls. Normal aristocratic girls were taken to balls as soon as they could curtsey properly, and taught their place in society, particularly the deference due to the Grandes Dames. But Gwen hadn't been taken to many of them, not when the aristocracy thought that woman shouldn't have magic – or if they did have it, they should keep it to themselves. Her social isolation was very definitely a relief.

She peered down from the balcony at what had to be one of the least welcoming balls she'd ever seen, worse even than those that had been held in the midst of family feuds and other unpleasantness. The different Russian factions were starkly clear, men cleaving to their allies, the women gathered around them, while the foreigners sat together and watched their hosts with growing concern. Lord Standish and Talleyrand seemed to have reached an unspoken agreement not to bicker, despite the approaching war. Gwen would have been impressed if the meal hadn't been sending chills down her spine.

Beside them, Sir Sidney ate his food, his face set in an unreadable mask. He had to be using mental discipline, Gwen realised, knowing that both Simone and Russian Talkers were in the room. She wanted, desperately, to talk to the older man, to ask his advice, but she knew that was impossible. Lady Standish would react badly if Gwen was caught with Sir Sidney a second time, particularly after Gwen had been 'disciplined' by Romulus. The last thing she needed, right now, was to be caught doing something indecent. Gritting her teeth, she looked away from Sir Sidney towards the head of the table.

The Tsar himself lounged on his throne, staring down at his food with a curiously deranged expression on his face. Gwen couldn't help wondering if he were drugged, or under some form of magical influence; he seemed to verge between the deepest depression and an oddly childlike enthusiasm, as if he were waiting for Christmas Day. His bodyguard of dark-clad men had been reinforced with a pair of men in monkish robes, one of whom whispered to the Tsar from time to time. Were they his bodyguards, Gwen wondered, or his masters? But when she reached out with her senses, all she picked up was mental distortion aimed at Simone and the other Talkers. The Russians were determined to ensure that no one learned anything through magic.

Romulus poked her arm, making her jump. "I've never seen His Lordship so concerned," he muttered. "And Her Ladyship is picking up on it too."

Gwen followed his gaze. Lady Standish was talking – too loudly – to Simone, who looked torn between boredom and amusement. Gwen had no idea of Simone's social standing, but she had managed to woo the London rakes before Talleyrand had been told to go home and take his fake daughter with him. Lady Standish either hadn't heard about that experience, Gwen guessed, or she'd simply decided it couldn't possibly have happened. She was chatting to Simone as if the girl was a new ward. Judging from Raechel's expression, she was being compared – unfavourably – to the French girl.

But it was clear that Lady Standish was nervous. Gwen had to admit that that was more than a little frightening. Women like Lady Standish walked through life protected by an invisible bubble, an overwhelming confidence that no one would so much as *try* to hurt them. They rarely even considered the possibility that they could be torn down from their pedestals and made to suffer like ordinary mortals. For someone like her to be nervous was worrying. It meant that the mood pervading the palace was even seeping into her.

"I see," she muttered back, as a line of Russian servants brought out the next course. "What do you think they're doing?"

"I don't know," Romulus said. "But it looks as though the Tsar is waiting for something."

Gwen nodded as she scrutinised the Tsar and his bodyguards. The Tsar was definitely waiting for something and not, she noted, doing a very good job of hiding his anticipation. But someone like him wouldn't have to wait for anything, not normally. He was an absolute ruler, after all. What was he waiting *for*?

"I'm going back to our rooms," she said. Janet would still be there, helping to unpack the clothes she'd packed into bags only yesterday. "I don't think Her Ladyship will need me for a while."

"Probably not," Romulus agreed. "Watch yourself."

Gwen smiled as she stepped through the door, then headed up the stairs towards the topmost floor. If this building was anything like the Winter Palace, the important offices would be on the uppermost floor. But as she reached the top of the stairs and looked around, it became alarmingly clear that, just like the Winter Palace, the building was almost completely empty. She peered into a handful of rooms and saw nothing, apart from lines on the floor where tables and chairs had once stood. It looked as though the building had been stripped before the British – and French – representatives had been moved into their rooms. There weren't even any guards on the uppermost floors.

She went down a flight of stairs and searched the next floor, only to find little more than a smoking room, a handful of meeting rooms and a large room crammed full of yet more bladed weapons. She checked, carefully, but found no firearms or anything more advanced than a bow and arrow. Puzzled, she crept into the next room and discovered that it was crammed full of furniture. They'd moved everything down one flight of stairs and then abandoned it.

This doesn't make sense, Gwen thought, sourly. *What are they doing?*

Down below, she heard the band start to play. The tune was unfamiliar, but the beat was recognisable as one of the diplomatic waltzes. Rolling her eyes, Gwen crept back down the stairs and back into the balcony. The tables had been pushed to one side, the diplomats and noblemen had moved onto the dance floor and a number of women had appeared from nowhere, making up the numbers. A nobleman was calling the dance, his voice echoing through the entire room ...

... And there was no sign of the Tsar. Gwen felt ice shivering down her spine. Where had he gone?

"He told them all to relax and enjoy themselves," Romulus said, when she asked. "And then he went out of the room, escorted by his bodyguards."

Gwen had never really believed in precognition. It was theoretically possible, she knew, but few of the Seers at Cavendish Hall – or the local bedlam – had produced anything that was actually usable. And yet, the sense of impending doom running down her spine made it impossible to believe that something bad *wasn't* about to happen. She hesitated, wishing – again – that she could talk to Sir Sidney. But he was somewhere within the mass of people on the dance floor, utterly untouchable.

"Keep an eye on Raechel," she said, heedless of the fact she was giving orders to her superior. "Take care of her."

She slipped back out of the door before Romulus could argue, then pulled her magic around herself like a shield, concealing her presence as best she could. It would work against normal guards, she knew from experience, but it was anyone's guess how well it would work against the magician-monks protecting the Tsar. They might overlook her too or they might recognise that something was wrong and start hunting for her. And, she also knew from experience, if someone had a good reason to look, they found it easier to see through her magic. But there was no other way to hide.

It grew colder as she made her way towards the lower levels, concealing herself in the shadows as she passed a handful of armed guards, who seemed more intent on keeping people *in* the building rather than keeping people out. There were more guards outside, she discovered, as she entered the reception hall in time to see a line of monks filing out of the building, chanting quietly in unison. The words sounded like Formal Latin, but Gwen couldn't understand them. There was no sign of the Tsar.

Outside, she sensed pulsing waves of magic emanating from a second group of monks, probing the minds of their fellows. If the magic touched her, Gwen knew, she would be detected. She drew on her own magic and leapt into the air, floating high above the monks and peering down as they swept through the newcomers. Two were pushed to one side, then beheaded on the spot, their heads falling on the driven snow. Sickened, Gwen looked away as the monks resumed their march out of the grounds and onto the streets. Carefully, she drifted after them, praying that she remained unseen. It was clear the monks would happily kill all intruders.

Moscow was no brighter than St Petersburg, she realised, as the moon rose higher, casting an eerie shimmering light over the whole affair. The soldiers and monks had driven people indoors or out of sight; they moved, unseen, through the city, heading towards a large cathedral that looked new, lacking the grime that covered most Russian buildings. Gwen felt another chill running down her spine as she saw lines of monks entering the building, magic sweeping around them in a manner that was new to her. There was something odd about their magic, something that bothered her. A new form of magic?

And something else was wrong. There were thousands of monks and soldiers entering the building, yet the building didn't seem to be growing any fuller. She puzzled over it for a long moment, then blinked in surprise as she saw a large golden carriage rattling down the street and come to a halt in front of the cathedral. Moments later, the Tsar stepped out of the carriage and smiled at his worshippers. The monks promptly fell to their knees and prostrated themselves in front of the Tsar. Gwen felt sick – and chilled – as she realised the monks truly did worship their Tsar. No one, as far as she knew, worshipped King George.

The Tsar walked into the building, looking neither left nor right. His monks waited until he was inside the building, then rose to their feet and followed him, the sound of their chanting growing louder as they entered the building. The soldiers brought up the rear, weapons in hand, leaving the grounds completely empty. Gwen hesitated, then dropped down, looking for a way into the building. The doors gaped open invitingly, but there were two monks standing just inside, watching for latecomers. Gwen gathered her magic and banged their heads together, hard. They collapsed to the ground, looking stunned.

Smiling, Gwen checked them both, then pulled the bodies into the shadows and removed the robe and cowl from one of the monks. It smelt of urine, she discovered; underneath, he wore something that looked like a nappy and little else. She remembered one of Sir Charles's stories and shuddered, forcing herself to breathe through her mouth as she pulled the robe over her head. The eunuchs of India and China were often called the Foul Fraternity because they couldn't control their bladders after they had their testicles removed. No wonder they stank!

You've smelt worse, she told herself, as she stepped into the building. The traces of magic she'd sensed earlier were gone. *And you've seen worse too.*

The cathedral was empty. Gwen stared in disbelief as she looked around the giant hall, seeing nothing and no one, apart from a giant statue of the Tsar at the head of the room. She knew she'd seen thousands of monks and soldiers enter the building, yet there was no sign of them. For a crazy moment, she wondered if she'd hallucinated the whole affair before she caught sight of marks on the ground leading towards a door set into the far wall. Inside, there was a stone staircase heading down into the darkness. Bracing herself, altering her magic so she would look like a monk if anyone saw her, Gwen started to make her way down the steps.

There was a faint glowing light at the bottom, revealing a stone passageway deep under Moscow, leading back towards the centre of town. She paused as she heard the sound of chanting, then froze as she heard something else, a faint whispering right at the edge of her mind. It was chillingly familiar, a noise that had haunted her nightmares since the Battle of London. There were undead somewhere within the complex, far too close for comfort.

She kept moving down the corridor until she saw a door set within the stone passageway. Inside, a number of soldiers sat on the floor, playing cards or rolling dice, clearly bored and unaware of why they were in the complex. Gwen didn't know either, as she walked past them, but she was starting to have a very nasty idea. The sound of whispering was growing louder and louder as she kept moving forward, telling her that she was moving towards the undead. And if she found them ...?

The thought made her shudder. If there was one thing that Britain and France agreed on, it was that necromancy was incredibly dangerous. But Master Thomas had unleashed the undead in the hope of putting an end to the Swing ... the Tsar might be just as prepared to use the undead as the British Government. Maybe the Tsar was mad enough to consider unleashing the undead because no one dared to tell him no. No one had dared tell Master Thomas and the Privy Council that their scheme was madness either.

I should have, Gwen thought, feeling a flicker of the old guilt. But she hadn't known what they'd been planning, not in time to stop them. *All I could do was go to Jack and beg for help.*

The sound of chanting suddenly grew louder. Gwen pushed herself into the wall, wrapping magic around her, as a line of monks marched past her, chanting in deep tones despite their mutilation. Several of them had their hoods down, revealing unkempt beards and wild eyes that reminded her of the Cossacks who'd escorted the diplomatic party to Moscow. Others had their hoods up so high it was impossible to make out anything, apart from pale white chins. They looked thoroughly sinister.

Gwen followed them as they made their way down the corridor, hoping to blend in at the rear of the group. The chanting grew louder and louder as they paused outside a large door, then passed into an even larger chamber. It had been carved out of the earth, with a large statue of the Tsar dominating the room; hundreds of monks were kneeling in front of the statue, praying heavily in thick voices. A line of men stood against the far wall, wearing nothing but loincloths; it took Gwen a moment to realise that their hands were cuffed to the railing. Their expressions suggested they were drugged.

They don't normally drug and cuff people to get them into church, she thought, with wry amusement. *Unless they're really short on worshippers.*

She sighed, remembering. There had been a preacher outside Cavendish Hall every day for a few weeks, screaming that magicians had been touched by the devil and their mere presence would bring God's judgement down upon Britain. Gwen would have ignored him if he hadn't started harassing trainee magicians, some of whom would have retaliated, given half a chance. She'd had to arrange for his transportation to Australia as part of a chain gang. No doubt he was now preaching to the other convicts.

The monks she'd been following sat down at the rear of the room and joined the chant. Gwen followed, hoping they didn't ask her to take off the hood. If they did ... they'd see a girl, rather than a monk. She'd have to fight her way out and vanish, knowing that the Russians would have no trouble recognising her and then claiming that the party's diplomatic immunity was no longer in effect. But instead, the monks just sat and waited. Gwen felt herself starting to get bored rapidly, wondering just what they were doing here. And then a low rustle ran through the room as a man wearing golden robes entered from a side door.

One by one, the monks fell into prostration, banging their heads on the ground. Gwen hesitated, then forced herself to kowtow too, knowing that the danger of being discovered outweighed the blow to her pride. She hoped the robe stayed in place as she touched her head against the stone floor, then straightened up with the rest of the monks. The man in golden robes took a place between the statue's legs and started to speak in Russian. His listeners muttered a few words of their own between sentences.

A prayer, Gwen guessed. *But for what?*

The formality sounded like something from the Catholic Church, at least from what she'd been told about the Split with Rome, the Civil War and Reformation. With the Pope a French mouthpiece, England had largely barred Catholics from its shores. Gwen had never met one, as far as she knew.

The ones who remained in England tended to keep their heads down and not make waves. They knew how easy it was to be blamed for every little thing that went wrong.

And then another rustle ran through the room. The Tsar had arrived. He wore black robes, decorated with gold braid and studded with medals. It couldn't conceal his thin frame, Gwen thought nastily, even though the tailor had clearly tried his best. The Tsar showed no sign of respect or appreciation for the monks, even the ones hastily prostrating themselves in front of him. And, behind him, escorted by a pair of monks ...

Gwen started. *Olivia*!

Chapter Twenty-Five

livia ached all over as they pulled her from the carriage after a long and uncomfortable ride, her wrists hurting so much that she doubted she could pick up a pencil, let alone pick a lock like she'd learned to do on the streets. The Russians half-carried her through a large door, down a set of steps and into yet another prison cell. Behind her, Ivan was dragged away in a different direction, causing her to lose sight of him almost at once. Losing him gave her an odd wrench, even though she knew he deserved death or worse. He'd started the whole affair by taking her from Cavendish Hall.

"Smelly," a voice said. Olivia looked up to see a woman wearing noblewoman's clothing, standing in the cell. Her snooty tone could give Lady Mary a run for her money. "And to think you're supposed to be presented to the Tsar."

Olivia glared at her, wishing she had her hands free. One good punch and that aristocratic nose would shatter like an egg. The woman gave her an amused smile, then reached out and touched Olivia's forehead. Instantly, she felt a strange tingle running through her body, followed by a burst of energy. She felt almost completely refreshed.

"Magic," the woman said. She reached for Olivia's cuffed hands, then slotted a key into the cuffs and undid them. "I suggest you cooperate. It will make this go so much easier."

Olivia rubbed her wrists, frantically. "For whom?"

"I can call the guards and have them strip you by force," the woman pointed out. She eyed Olivia's rumpled dress with some amusement. "You'd think they'd know by now that long carriage rides aren't good for dresses."

She leaned backwards, then sighed. "Undress," she ordered. "You should have time for a wash before the Tsar arrives."

Olivia hesitated, then realised she had very little choice. She tore the dress away from her body, taking a crude delight in seeing the noblewoman wince at torn stitches and damaged silks, then walked over to the bathtub. The water was warm, but not scalding hot. Relieved, she climbed in and splashed around, trying to get clean. Her entire body felt mucky after hours in the carriage.

"Hurry," the woman said. "You don't want to be presented to the Tsar naked and dripping wet."

"As if they would," Olivia muttered, but she pulled herself out of the bath anyway. The woman had already found a new dress, just as frilly and ridiculous as the last one; Olivia groaned when she saw it, then started to pull it on. "Why can't I have trousers and a shirt?"

"Because you are going to be presented to the Tsar," the woman said, patiently. "And because I have to make you look nice."

"Oh," Olivia said. "Another prisoner?"

The brief haunted look in the woman's eye answered *that* question. Olivia cursed under her breath, remembering Esther and her sisters, then finished pulling on the dress. Like so many other such dresses, it was remarkably fiddly, almost impossible for one person to don on their own. One of the Trouser Brigade she'd met had called dresses the signs of female enslavement, worse than handcuffs. Having been handcuffed as well as forced to wear a dress, Olivia disagreed, but she had to admit that the dresses came a close second.

"I'm sorry," she said, as she struggled with the laces. "Where are we?"

"Moscow," the woman said. "I used to live here."

Olivia tried to be kind. "What happened?"

"My husband was caught plotting against the Tsar," the woman said. Her voice was dead, filled with utter hopelessness. "He was burned alive in front of the Kremlin. My brothers were sent to count trees in Siberia. My children were taken from me, held hostage for my good behaviour.

And now I am a maidservant for the Tsar, forced to serve him until the day I die."

Olivia shivered. The Russians, it seemed, believed in collective punishment. She wondered, suddenly, what would happen – might have already happened – to Ivan's relatives. If the Charmer had lost his tongue, who knew what might have been done to his family? They could have been killed or exiled or forced into servitude or ...

"I'm sorry," she muttered again.

"You are to be presented to the Tsar," the woman said. "You could speak on my behalf."

"I don't think he would listen to me," Olivia said. If she'd had a chance to integrate herself with Gregory and his monks, she would probably have lost it the first time they read her mind. And they *would* have read her mind, if she'd claimed to accept the Father Tsar as God. "I'm sorry."

She had only just started tying up the bows when there was a sharp knock on the door, which opened moments later to reveal two black-clad men. Behind them, there was another man in a dark suit covered in gold braid. Olivia fancied she would have recognised him as the Tsar even if her assistant hadn't immediately flung herself to the ground and started banging her head against the cold floor. It didn't take an expert to realise that the woman was completely terrified.

"The Necromancer," the Tsar said. His English was almost completely unaccented. "It is a great pleasure to meet the one responsible for my immortality."

It took Olivia a moment to parse out the grammar. "I haven't done anything yet," she protested. Those lessons at Cavendish Hall might have been worthwhile after all. "And I won't do *anything* for you."

The Tsar looked amused, rather than annoyed. "Of course you will," he said. "I have Charmers to *make* you do as I wish."

Olivia gritted her teeth, feeling hopelessness slide its way into her heart. The Tsar had Charmers; of *course* the Tsar had Charmers. And no doubt an entire staff practiced at inflicting pain on unwilling victims without causing serious damage. If she defied him, she would simply be forced into compliance.

"And you might wish to take notice," the Tsar added. He stepped over to the noblewoman, still prostrating herself on the floor, and placed his boot on the back of her neck. "I can kill anyone, if I have to."

"I grew up on the streets," Olivia sneered. Cold fury drove her onwards. "You think I haven't seen *death* before?"

The Tsar smiled. "You will make me one of the living dead," he said. "And then the country will be united under my rule."

Olivia stared at him. "It won't work," she said. "You'll die."

"Then you will have the pleasure of watching me die," the Tsar said. He looked down at the woman under his boot, then pushed down, hard. There was a snap and a gasp, then the woman lay still. "But you will not deny me, not now."

"The only person I care about is thousands of miles from here," Olivia said. The streets didn't encourage long-term friendships, not among boys when one of them was a girl pretending to be a boy. Gwen was about the only person she cared for, even at Cavendish Hall. What did *she* have in common with the rest of the girls? "You can't threaten to kill me."

"But you can be Charmed," the Tsar said. "And you will be, if you refuse to serve."

He paused. "But I give you my word," he added. "If you do as you are told, one final time, you will be sent home."

Olivia stared at him, hope warring with experience inside her breast. She knew the Tsar would never let her go, not when she knew far too much, but part of her wanted to believe him, wanted to believe that there was a way out. She tried to resist the sudden burst of homesickness, yet it was too strong.

I'm sorry, Gwen, she thought. *I'm sorry.*

She bowed her head.

"Excellent," the Tsar said, smiling like a little boy. A dull gong echoed through the complex, then faded away to nothingness. He held out his hand to her, for all the world as if he were inviting her to a dance. "Shall we go?"

The monks closed in on them as they walked out of the cell and headed down the corridor, the cold stone unpleasant against her bare feet. Olivia looked around frantically, searching for a way out of the trap, but found nothing. If she'd managed to break free of the Tsar's hand, they would have caught her before she managed to get out of the crowd and flee. They stopped outside a large door, where a man in golden robes waited for them, then the Tsar let go of her hand and spoke briefly to the man. He stepped through the door, leaving them alone. Long moments passed before the door opened again, allowing the Tsar to lead her into the large chamber.

She cringed as she realised just how many monks there were in the chamber, several of them banging their heads on the floor. The Tsar could have killed half of them and the remainder would have hailed him for it, she thought, bitterly. He might have sounded affable, but he'd been prepared to kill one of his own noblewomen just to make a point. She wanted to glare at his back, yet she didn't quite dare. The entire room might rise up against her if she showed him the slightest hint of disrespect.

"Welcome," a voice said. She looked up to see Gregory, standing under a large statue of the Tsar. It was all she could do not to snicker when she realised just which part of the Tsar's anatomy he was standing under. "You will serve your purpose now, My Lady Olivia."

Olivia looked away. A line of cuffed men were attached to the far wall, staring wildly at her and the monks. One of them was Ivan, she realised; she tried to send him a look of reassurance, even though they both knew there was no way out. Whatever Gregory intended to do, whatever form the Tsar's madness took, neither of them was going to survive.

"Let us begin," Gregory said. "Father Tsar?"

The Tsar stepped forward, rolling up his sleeve to reveal bare flesh. Olivia watched, surprised, as Gregory held out a large syringe of reddish liquid – *blood*? – and injected it into the Tsar's veins. She vaguely recalled being told that some forms of blood were poisonous if injected into the wrong person, but Lucy hadn't been very clear at the time and rarely needed to use blood transfusion in any case. It didn't matter, she realised grimly; the Tsar didn't even look uncomfortable as the blood flowed into his body.

"He has survived," Gregory said. "He is truly our Father Tsar!"

That was it? Olivia thought, as the monks started to chant in their thick tongue. *They injected him with blood?*

"Let us proceed," Gregory said. The monks quietened; silence fell over the room. "My Father Tsar, the path lies open before you."

The Tsar reached into his pocket and removed a long silver knife. Olivia stared in disbelief as he pushed the tip of the blade against his chest, then slowly moved it up to his lung. Was he planning to *kill* himself? She couldn't tear her eyes away as he braced himself, his eyes glowing with an unholy gleam, and plunged the knife into his lungs. He didn't even cry out as he slumped to the floor, his breath coming in great rasping gasps. It didn't look quite right.

There must have been something on the blade, Olivia thought. *Something to make his death easier.*

A monk grabbed her arm. "Use your magic," he ordered. "Make him one of the undead."

Olivia hesitated. If she did nothing, the Tsar would die ... and, if Ivan had been telling the truth, all of Russia would collapse into civil war. It would be worth her death to see the scheme collapse for want of a country – and a Necromancer.

"Use your magic," he repeated, lacing his voice with Charm. "Make him one of the undead.

Olivia jerked as the commands thundered into her mind. She knelt beside the Tsar, trying desperately to resist, but it was futile. Her magic slipped into his body, seeking to bring him back to a shambling parody of life. Gregory knelt beside her, allowing his magic to merge with hers. Olivia tried to flinch back – melding the best and brightest of magic with the darkest felt like blasphemy – but the Charmer's commands were inescapable. Her magic flowed from her, interacted with Gregory's and shimmered into the Tsar's body. And then there was a shock that threw her backwards, away from the Tsar.

He moaned, then started to climb to his feet. His face was already paling, his eyes slowly becoming a dull yellow colour, but something was dreadfully wrong. She'd expected him to go for her throat, or at least the throat of Gregory or one of the others in the chamber, yet he seemed to be almost *considering*. A thought struck her and she reached out with her powers, trying to guide his body, only to discover that she couldn't get in. It felt almost as if he still possessed a soul.

The Tsar turned to face her, moving slowly and deliberately. His mouth opened, revealing sharp teeth; he smiled, widely. Olivia backed away slowly until she walked right into the Charmer, who held her upright in a grip of steel. His touch brought her back to herself, revealing what was missing. She'd grown used to the whispering in her head, but now it was gone. The chamber was silent.

"Brethren," Gregory said. His voice was quiet, but carried immense force. "It is time to serve the Father Tsar one last time."

He's still in there, Olivia thought, with growing horror. Gregory's experiments had *worked*! The Tsar had become a healthy mind in an undead body ... her thoughts gibbered inside her brain as she tried to think of a way out, or a way to stop the Tsar before it was too late. *We saved his mind even as his body became one of the undead.*

The first row of monks climbed to their feet and stepped towards the Tsar, who smiled at them in welcome. They tilted their heads, allowing him to bite their necks ... and then fell to the floor, already beginning the change. There was a sudden burst of whispering, terrifyingly loud in her head, then nothing. One by one, the new undead rose to their feet and walked towards the door, blocking all escape. No matter how fanatical the monks were, Olivia realised grimly, they were unlikely to care for the idea of becoming undead. The Tsar seemed to be in control.

"The blood," she said, remembering what Gregory had told her. They'd had some success with creating new magicians by transplanting blood and body cells from a magician to a mundane. "You injected him with my blood, didn't you?"

"Of course," Gregory said. He seemed more amused than horrified at what he'd done. "You were drugged, one night, and blood was taken from you."

The Tsar's body seemed to shake as it absorbed more and more life energy from the monks, shudders running through the undead as they responded to their master's feelings.

Olivia stumbled as another burst of whispering echoed through her head – the Charmer held her upright, or she would have fallen to the ground – and she sagged against him. The Tsar wasn't in full control, she realised, but he could fall back on the instincts the undead possessed, then regain control when it suited him. There was going to be an unholy slaughter, she thought, as the undead started leaving the room. They were in the heart of a city. And somehow she doubted the Russian population was armed to fight anyone, least of all the undead.

"I think you have outlived your usefulness," Gregory said. "But the Father Tsar will claim you personally."

The Tsar turned and advanced towards Olivia, blood dripping from his fangs. And they'd become fangs, part of Olivia's mind noted, as she struggled against the Charmer's grip. The life energy he'd absorbed from his victims was warping his body, shaping him into a vampire-like being. She stamped her foot down on the Charmer's foot, only to discover that her bare feet simply didn't hurt him enough to force him to let her go ...

And then the Charmer's head exploded. Bloody chunks flew everywhere, scattering debris over Gregory and the Tsar. Neither of them looked upset to be suddenly showered in blood.

Olivia stared – had she done that? – then she felt a force tugging her away from him and yanking her out over the monks. Some of them tried to grab her, but seemed too scared of falling out of line to make a proper grab for her. Olivia felt her head spinning – she hated it when someone levitated her into the air – and nearly threw up. If she hadn't been so hungry ...

One of the monks was rising to his feet; no, *her* feet. Olivia had seen enough women disguised as men to know the subtle clues that revealed her true nature. Her hood was thrown back to reveal blonde hair and bright blue eyes ... *Gwen?*

There was no time to wonder what her adopted mother was doing here. There was no time to embrace the warm feeling running through her heart, no time to come to terms with the awareness that someone had cared enough to track her down and come to the rescue. All she could do was scream a warning.

"Burn them," she shouted, as she landed in Gwen's arms. There was no other cure for an undead epidemic. If they were lucky, they could stop it right here, right now. "Burn them all!"

Flames flared around Gwen, sending dozens of monks falling backwards, screaming in pain, then lunged towards the Tsar.

Chapter Twenty-Six

t had been all Gwen could do not to snatch her daughter at once and then fight her way out of the chamber. She knew there were other magicians in the room, but they wouldn't have her training or her ability to use multiple powers. And yet, she also needed to know what the Russians were planning to do. She had forced herself to watch, in growing horror and disbelief, as the Tsar killed himself, and then was reanimated by Olivia and the bearded monk with mad eyes.

The Tsar seemed to defy all the normal laws of Necromancy. Everyone *knew* the undead could not resist the siren call of living human flesh, or the urge to spread the infection as widely as possible. But the Tsar was holding still, summoning his devout followers and biting them ... and, somehow, he was directing the undead. By the time he reached for Olivia, Gwen had gone beyond horror. The Russians had to be mad. Either the undead Tsar would lose control of his creations or he would grow and grow until there was no room for any intelligence, but himself.

The State is Me, King Louis of France had said, years ago. Gwen had the awful feeling that the Tsar was taking it to its logical conclusion.

She threw a burst of magic at the Charmer, blowing his head into little pieces, then caught Olivia with her magic and yanked her over to where she was standing. Olivia stared at her, her face for once utterly unguarded, then started screaming for Gwen to burn the undead nest before they started to spread out of the chamber. Gwen summoned fire, knowing that Olivia was right. If they could immolate the Tsar and his creations right here, right now, the outbreak would be halted before it had even started. Flames roared towards the Tsar, burning countless monks along the way, and stopped just short of his position. Gwen barely sensed the wave of magic before it expanded and blew Olivia and her into the back wall.

Movers, she realised, as she saw the monks clustering round the undead Tsar. They'd protected him from the flames – and struck back at her. They were clearly used to working together, which made them a major problem. Collectively, they'd be able to smash her into paste.

"I am the Father Tsar," the Tsar said. His voice was hoarse, as if he'd forgotten how to speak and was slowly relearning the ropes. "I will rule eternal as the Lord and Master of Mother Russia."

Gwen stared as she pulled herself to her feet, one hand clutching Olivia protectively. No one had ever heard one of the undead speak before. Even when controlled by a Necromancer they weren't much good for anything, apart from terror tactics and as shock troops. She'd always assumed they lost the ability to speak along with their minds. They certainly didn't need to breathe. But the Tsar was far from a normal undead. His mind had somehow survived the transition from a living being to undead.

"The country is racked with traitors," the Tsar continued. He made a grasping motion with his hand, then stepped forward, slowly relearning how to walk as well as talk. "They seek my death so they can tear the country apart over their competing ... ideologies." He spoke the word as though it were a curse. "But I shall rule forever as the Father Tsar," he warned. "I shall not be defied. I shall be one with my people."

Gwen glanced at the undead. They were standing there, just waiting. She could sense, somehow, the pulsing intelligence binding them to the Tsar. His mind had expanded, she realised, in ways no Talker had ever dreamed of matching. The undead were more than just his servants; they were *part* of him, an intelligence slowly spreading itself out over multiple bodies. He might be completely indestructible, even if she destroyed his original body. Or would he still need his brain?

She thought, frantically. There was so *little* research into necromancy. The only way to stop the undead was to behead them or make it impossible for them to walk, which made it hard to collect samples for analysis. Even when samples were recovered, few people would take the risk of experimenting with necromantic tissue. There were just too many dangers involved in such research. But it left her blind now ... could she win by destroying the Tsar or would she have to burn the entire city to the ground?

"You're mad," Olivia said. She held Gwen's arm, sweat running down her face despite the rapidly cooling temperature. Someone, high overhead, had opened the doors to the cathedral, allowing the first of the undead to walk out into the streets. "You're not even *human*."

The Tsar laughed. "I am the Father Tsar," he said. "The country is mine. My people are my servants, to do with as I will. The world will bow before me and know peace."

Olivia was right, Gwen realised. The Tsar was mad. Either he'd been slowly going mad while sitting on his throne, watching his courtiers planning for life after his death, or the experience of committing suicide had unhinged him. Maybe he'd started the whole mad plan as a desperate gamble to save his country, but it was clear now that he would do nothing but destroy Russia. The country was already on the brink of anarchy. It couldn't survive a tidal wave of the undead.

"I shall march out with my armies and bring all into my fold," the Tsar said. Four of the undead turned their attention to the prisoners. One by one, they were bitten and started the transformation into more undead. "The Turks will bend the knee before me when I walk over mountains and through rivers, stopping for nothing until I have the Sultan in my grip. And then I shall go onwards until I am master of an empire greater than any the world has ever seen."

"An empire of the dead," Gwen said. How long could the undead live, if *live* was the right word? They needed living flesh to survive. Was the Tsar too far gone to realise that his new army would need the living to serve as livestock? The thought was horrific, but the Tsar wouldn't hesitate, she suspected. He already viewed commoners as little better than animals. "It won't last forever."

"I shall rule eternal," the Tsar repeated. There was a sudden surge of whispering, so loud that it almost sent Gwen to her knees. Beside her, Olivia shuddered helplessly. "And you will become part of me."

The undead lunged forward, claws extended. Gwen summoned more fire, despite her growing tiredness, and reduced them to ash. The Movers lashed out at her, their power sending her back into the rocky wall ... and crumbling it under the blow. Gwen hastily shielded both Olivia and herself as they smashed through the wall, then picked herself up and started to run. Behind her, the undead surged forward, moaning in unison. Gwen kept a tight hold on Olivia as they headed for the stairs, then stopped long enough to infuse some energy into the stone. It exploded, moments later, as the undead ran over the magic, blowing some of them into pieces. But the remainder just kept coming.

Gwen gritted her teeth, then blasted the ceiling. Chunks of rock rained down on the undead, blocking their path ... although she knew it wouldn't stop them indefinitely. The Movers would have no problem clearing the rocks, allowing the Tsar to walk out into Moscow. She reached the top of the stairs, then froze as she heard more whispering – and screaming. Ahead of her, there was a large stone door ... inside, the undead were infecting dozens of soldiers, some of whom were trying to fight. But, unarmed, they didn't have a chance.

"Burn them," Olivia said.

Gwen nodded, despite the growing pain in her temple. Flames burst into existence and raged through the ranks of undead and infected soldiers, giving the uninfected men a chance to flee. One of them paused long enough to stare at Gwen in absolute disbelief – she was so strange to his eyes she suspected he didn't believe what he was seeing – and then joined his comrades in flight. Gwen wanted to warn them of what was going to come, of the undead raging through the streets of Moscow, but she knew it was impossible. Her Russian was far too rudimentary to do anything more than ask for directions and order food.

"I can hear him," Olivia said, suddenly. She shivered. The dress she'd been given, the dress she had to have been Charmed into wearing, was far too thin for the Moscow night. "He's coming."

Gwen reached for one of the bodies, removed the man's heavy leather coat and passed it to Olivia. Her daughter took it gratefully, but kept shivering. A Necromancer would be far more sensitive to the undead than any other magician, even one who shared all the talents. If she could hear the Tsar, Gwen told herself, it meant he was on the way.

The ground shook as the Movers removed the obstruction, sending pieces of debris flying into the sky. Gwen grabbed Olivia and pulled her out of the cathedral as the swarm of undead burst out of the stairwell and started heading out onto the streets. Their yellow eyes reflected a dark purpose, something lacking in the last set of undead she'd seen. Behind their eyes, she fancied she saw the Tsar looking back at her. Olivia moaned, then fainted as the whispering grew louder. It had to be a form of Talking, Gwen noted, as she threw her daughter over her shoulder, but one that only worked for the undead or those who had a special connection to them.

They used to think that Talkers had larger brains, she thought, remembering the Darwinists from London. They'd believed that magicians were superior to non-magicians, with the precise degree of superiority among magicians determined by whoever was doing the talking at the time. Lord Blackburn, a curse on the man, had believed Charmers were superior to everyone else. *Does something happen to the undead to make them Talkers?*

There was a crash as two magicians landed in front of Gwen, hands already lifted to direct magic towards her. She braced herself, knowing she was in no state for a fight, then blasted magic directly towards them. As she had expected, they used their magic to shield themselves, but the light show blinded them for a few crucial seconds. Gwen used the time to infuse more magic into the ground, detonating an explosion right underneath their feet, blowing them into pieces. Neither of them had bothered to form a protective bubble, knowing that few threats could get around their normal protections. But they hadn't realised who Gwen actually was.

She hesitated, then reached for her magic and hurled herself into the air, carrying Olivia with her. It was risky – there was at least one Mover left in the cathedral – but she needed to put some distance between herself and the undead. She looked down as she climbed higher and saw a steady stream of the undead making their way out of the cathedral and heading into the streets. She could hear screams in the still night air as the undead encountered homeless people hiding in alleyways and bit them, adding to their growing numbers. Bangs and crashes suggested that the undead were breaking into homes and infecting the owners.

A disarmed population, Gwen recalled. It was unlikely Russian civilians could offer any real resistance to the undead, even if they hadn't been sleeping. But then, regular weapons weren't too effective against the undead either. Shotguns and machine guns were the only firearms that made a real impression, unless the shooter was an excellent shot. It was far better to fight them with flamethrowers or even swords and axes. *They don't stand a chance.*

She dropped down to a rooftop and carefully put Olivia down. The young girl was sweating, as if she was feverish, despite the temperature, reminding Gwen of their first encounter, months ago. Olivia had reacted badly to the undead that Master Thomas had unleashed, providing the first clue to her powers. She'd been able to stop those undead, but somehow Gwen doubted it would be so easy this time. There was a malign intelligence infesting the undead of Moscow.

Gwen sighed. "I haven't been the best of mothers, have I?"

Olivia showed no reaction. It had only been seven months, more or less, since Gwen had adopted her. High Society had been stunned; they knew nothing about Olivia's powers, so they'd assumed it was a joke. They would have implied that Olivia was Gwen's bastard daughter if it hadn't been alarmingly obvious that Gwen would have had to give birth at nine or ten. It hadn't stopped some of them hinting that Olivia was actually *Lady Mary's* daughter, but that hadn't lasted long. There were other ways to introduce a bastard daughter into High Society without doing something that had been bound to cause comment.

But Gwen had wanted to protect Olivia. It was the only way, she had known, to ensure that the Demonic Powers Act wasn't invoked to justify Olivia's execution. Necromancers had to die, according to the law. They were just too dangerous to keep around. Now ... she shivered as she heard screams echoing out over the city. It was quite likely that others would insist that Olivia be executed anyway, no matter what Gwen or King George said. And it would be very difficult to convince them otherwise.

We could run, Gwen thought. She had assumed an obligation, one she would have honoured even if she hadn't come to love the girl. *There are plenty of places we could hide.*

She shook her head and carefully picked Olivia up and slung her back over her shoulder, then reached for her magic. The throbbing in her temple suggested that she might have pushed herself too far, but there was no other way to get back to the palace. As tempted as she might have been to leave Lady Standish to the tender mercies of the undead, she wasn't about to leave Sir Sidney and Raechel to be eaten, then rise again as monsters. Or Romulus, Janet and even Lord Standish. Besides, she had the feeling she'd need their help to get out of the city.

Moscow looked darker than before as she rose high over the city, although she knew it might just have been her imagination. There were shouts and screams, but she couldn't *see* much of anything, apart from darkness. She peered down into the shadows, then turned and forced herself to fly towards the palace. Something warm dripped from her nose as she flew, touching the edge of her lips. When she tested it, she tasted blood.

A light flared up below her. Gwen looked down, just in time to see a line of soldiers running towards the disturbance. There was probably a curfew in Moscow, she guessed, with anyone caught outside after hours being summarily arrested. London had endured curfews too, once upon a time, although only rarely. It had impeded commercial activity, the city councillors had argued, and won the case. Unfortunately, it had also made it easier for criminals to go out and about unimpeded.

She shivered, again. This time, it was nothing to do with the cold. Those young men had no idea what they were about to encounter – or just how badly they had been betrayed by their own leaders. She wanted to shout a warning, but she just didn't have the words. And besides, they might shoot at a strange girl floating in the sky. She watched them run towards the screams, silently praying that they would see the undead in time to fall back and summon help, then turned and kept powering her way towards the palace. Her head started to spin as she got closer, a faint light shining up from the palace rooftop. In her dazed state, it took several moments to realise that it was a skylight and that she was about to crash right through it.

Desperately, she wrapped magic around herself and Olivia as she touched down and felt the glass shatter under her weight. It was all she could do to keep from losing her grip and allowing gravity to reassert itself. Dimly, she heard screams as she plummeted to the floor and landed hard enough to hurt, somehow shielding Olivia from the worst of it. Her legs buckled – it didn't feel like she'd broken anything, but it was hard to be sure – and she had to draw on magic to remain upright. The trickle of blood from her nose had become a flood.

"Gwen," an aghast voice said. Lady Standish sounded shocked, as if she didn't quite believe her eyes. "What is the meaning of this?"

Gwen fought down the urge to giggle inanely as she carefully lowered Olivia to the floor and straightened up. Her vision had blurred, but now she was no longer drawing on her magic to fly it was clearing up rapidly. Magic seemed to heal her automatically when she wasn't using it for anything else, which was lucky. She'd never really managed to master the healing powers she knew she should have.

"This ... this means war," she said. Her head was still throbbing. "This building is about to be attacked."

She felt Lady Standish grabbing her by the collar. "Make sense, girl," she snapped. "What have you done?"

Raechel came up behind her Aunt. "She's not a maid, Auntie," she said. "Let go of her!"

Gwen wanted to roll her eyes as Lady Standish, perhaps for the first time, really *looked* at Gwen. Her dress was covered in blood and gore, more blood was dripping from her nose and she'd lowered a young girl to the ground. It was astonishing just how much the aristocracy could miss when it didn't suit their preconceptions.

"Let go of me," she ordered. She pushed the aristocratic tone her mother had taught her into her voice as she met Lady Standish's eyes. "I am the Royal Sorceress."

Chapter Twenty-Seven

mpossible," Lady Standish said. "I refuse to believe ..."

"It is true," Sir Sidney said. He seemed to be taking everything in his stride. "Lady Gwen?"

"The Tsar has unleashed a horde of undead," Gwen said. More detailed explanations could wait, she decided. "They'll infect all of Moscow, then come for us."

"I see," Sir Sidney said. He turned to face Lord Standish, who had been staring at Gwen, his mouth opening and closing soundlessly. "Henry, I am assuming command of the mission, under authority vested in me by the Privy Council. I do trust you're not going to be tiresome about this?"

"Now hold on, wait a minute," one of the other representatives said. Gwen hadn't even bothered to learn his name. "You can't just claim authority ..."

Sir Sidney reached into his jacket and removed a cream envelope, which he opened and passed to the representative. The representative read it, then paled. Gwen had seen emergency orders before and knew they tended to warn that anyone who tried to object would face a full investigation when they returned to London. Maybe an aristocrat couldn't be stripped of rank or station, but Lord Mycroft and the Duke of India could ensure that they never served the British Empire again, in any capacity.

"Sidney," Lord Standish said, finally. "What about the mission?"

Gwen wiped blood from her nose and glared at him. "The mission has failed," she snapped, furiously. "I don't even know why the Tsar was so keen to bring us all to Moscow!

But right now, he's gone mad and has turned on his own people. He'll come for us soon enough!"

She caught sight of Talleyrand and smiled as she realised the Frenchman, for the first time, looked to have been caught completely off-guard by events. The last time they'd met, Talleyrand had seemed to take everything with Gallic sangfroid, even his exposure and forced removal from Britain. Now ... he had to have missed her completely, Gwen thought, with a moment of vindictive amusement. Finding Gwen among the maids had to have shocked him.

Good thing I was never alone with him, she thought. She knew Talleyrand's reputation for chasing skirts. *He might have noticed something if he'd removed my cap.*

"He'll come for you too," she added, looking over at Talleyrand. "He's gone completely mad."

"I understand," Sir Sidney said.

He turned to face one of the Russian officers and started a long conversation in Russian, clearly trying to get the Russians to work with the foreigners to defend the palace against the undead. They wouldn't discriminate, Gwen knew, but the Russians didn't seem so keen in getting involved. The Tsar might spare them ... Gwen shook her head at the thought. He was completely insane – and besides, he loathed the aristocracy as much as the peasants and serfs in the field. They'd plotted his death often enough, after all. Now, he could make them his undead slaves.

"But you can't be the Royal Sorceress," Lady Standish said. Horror was written over her face – horror, and a kind of wilful disbelief. "You just can't ..."

Gwen felt her temper snap. She'd endured the woman's behaviour for what felt like years, even though she knew it had only been two weeks. Raechel might have been a brat at times, but she was nowhere near as bad as her Aunt. And Raechel hadn't ordered Gwen beaten by the Butler. Magic rose up within her, demanding an outlet ... it would be so easy to lash out at Lady Standish, to humiliate her in front of the entire room. And yet ...

She threw caution to the winds, then levitated Lady Standish up into the air and flipped her over, allowing her dress to fall down to cover her face. "I don't have time to deal with you any longer," she said, as Lady Standish started to wave her legs desperately. Gwen wasn't sure why she bothered. Her undergarments were almost as modest as her dress. "You will find a quiet place to wait for us to deal with the undead – or be eaten, if we fail. Or I will do something to you to make sure you do nothing else."

It was hard to put the woman down on the ground gently, but somehow she managed it. Lady Standish seemed to be in shock, utterly astounded that someone had managed to humiliate her – and that no one had come to her aid, not even her husband. Gwen forced herself to remain stable, then waved to Romulus. The Butler strode over and bowed, his dark eyes glittering with suppressed amusement. Gwen hadn't been the only person to find Lady Standish unbearable.

"Take her to her bedroom, put her inside and lock the door," Gwen ordered. The last thing she needed was Lady Standish whining to her husband, trying to convince him to defy Lord Mycroft's orders. "Then come down and assist Sir Sidney."

She turned to Raechel as Romulus half-carried Lady Standish towards the door. "Help me with Olivia," she said. She felt too tired to levitate anything, even someone as slight as Olivia. "We need to get her to bed."

"I'll take care of matters down here," Sir Sidney said. He seemed to have managed to convince some of the Russians to join the foreigners, although others had started to make their way out of the ballroom. "Come back down when you're ready."

Gwen nodded, then lifted Olivia and – with Raechel's help – carried her out of the door and up the stairs. Raechel looked as if she had a thousand things she wanted to ask, but she held her tongue until they reached her bedroom, whereupon she burst out with a series of increasingly hysterical questions. Gwen smiled inwardly, then carefully placed Olivia on the bed and picked up some food from the table. After everything she'd done, she was ravenous.

"Wait," Raechel said. "Shouldn't we be saving food?"

"It probably won't matter," Gwen said, with the added thought that she needed to build up her reserves as quickly as possible. "This building isn't really designed to serve as a fortress."

"Oh," Raechel said. Her face was suddenly very pale. "What's going to happen next?"

Gwen sighed, stuffing a piece of bread and cheese into her mouth. "I don't know," she said, as she washed it down with a glass of water; alcohol and magic didn't mix, even if she hadn't needed to keep a clear head. "We should be looking for a way to get out of the city."

Raechel looked over at her. "Can't you fly us out of the city?"

"I couldn't carry everyone," Gwen answered. She thought about it, briefly. Maybe if she carried two people at a time, she could get them out ... but it was far too likely the Tsar and his magicians would intercept them *en route*. "We might have to fight our way through hordes of undead."

She finished the food, cursing herself for still feeling hungry, then started to undress, leaving the bloodstained dress on the floor. "I need to wash," she said, as she strode naked into the bathroom. The water in the tub was cold, but a little magic fixed that problem. "See if you can keep an eye on Olivia."

Raechel followed her, then stopped at the door. "Who is she?"

"My daughter," Gwen said. She wanted to close her eyes and sleep in the warm water, but she didn't quite dare. "It's a long story."

"I see," Raechel said. "And just what happened tonight?"

Gwen sighed and started to explain, wondering – grimly – just what the Tsar was doing. The infection pattern, if nothing else, was alarmingly well-understood. And it wasn't as if the Tsar was short on victims. Judging by what they'd seen as they drove into the city, Moscow had been attracting immigrants from the countryside for years. The Tsar might even have been covertly encouraging the trend, just to make sure he had thousands upon thousands of warm bodies for his mad plan. But there was no way to know precisely what he'd had in mind at the time.

"If one undead bites a living person," she concluded, "there will be two undead. If they then bite two more living people, there will be *four* undead. And then sixteen, two hundred and fifty-six, and then ...”

She shook her head, wishing she had time to sleep. “The figure of undead within the city will rise rather sharply,” she said instead, standing up and allowing the water to drip from her body. Raechel was seeing more of her than anyone ever had, her tired mind noted, apart from her maid. Even Sir Charles had never seen her naked. “We will be in deep trouble by the time the undead come for us.”

Raechel frowned. “Then why did the Tsar bring us here?”

Gwen shrugged. “Perhaps he intends to issue demands,” she said, although it sounded unlikely. Simone was the only Talker in the building and Gwen suspected she didn’t have the range to contact the other Talkers in Paris, not if she’d been reading minds. The Tsar could make whatever demands he liked of Lord Standish or Talleyrand, but they would have no way to communicate them to their respective governments. “Or perhaps he just wanted to make sure we didn’t go talking to his aristocrats until the plan was unstoppable.”

She used a towel to dry herself, then walked back into the bedroom and glanced at Olivia. “I need you to keep an eye on her,” she said, as she poked through the wardrobe for something suitable to wear. She eventually settled on a riding outfit that looked rather odd, but at least was less constraining than a dress. “When she wakes up, offer her food and then a bath. But don’t try to undress her.”

Raechel looked surprised. “Why would I try to undress her?”

“One of the maids tried,” Gwen said, recalling Olivia’s first days in Cavendish Hall. “Olivia panicked and kicked her in the throat. I don’t think she liked the thought of being undressed by someone else.”

She kept the rest of her thoughts to herself. There were things she had never dared ask her adopted daughter, mainly for fear of the answers. A young girl on the streets would certainly be angry if someone tried to undress her, but Olivia had reacted very badly and almost killed an innocent maid. Was there some further trauma buried in her mind or was she simply unused to the army of servants in noble households?

"I won't, then," Raechel said. She paused. "Should I look for a weapon?"

"I'll bring you something," Gwen said, with the private thought that Lady Standish would have a heart attack if she knew Raechel was planning to fight. Lady Mary hadn't reacted much better to Gwen's career. But the undead wouldn't discriminate between male and female victims when the time came to start infecting the living. "Just remember – cut off their heads or make sure they can't move. They're very resilient to other forms of damage."

She took one last look at Olivia, then stepped out of the door and walked back down to the ballroom. Sir Sidney had taken command and put everyone to work, including a number of soldiers from outside the palace. The Russian noblemen had talked them into helping, Gwen guessed, perhaps encouraged by the screams echoing out over the city. So far, the undead hadn't entered the centre of Moscow, but that breathing space surely wouldn't last long. The Tsar seemed to be concentrating on building up his army before turning and dealing with the foreigners.

"Lady Gwen," Sir Sidney said. Beside him, Romulus seemed to be serving as an aide. "How is she?"

"Asleep," Gwen said. She looked from one to the other, a thought striking her as she met Romulus's dark eyes. "You're working for Lord Mycroft too, aren't you?"

The Butler smiled and bowed. "Being underestimated comes in handy," he said. "But I never actually had to do anything ... *special* until now."

"Be grateful," Gwen said, dryly. She looked back at Sir Sidney. "What's the situation?"

Sir Sidney, at least, didn't seem to have any qualms about reporting to a girl. "We have fifty-seven able-bodied men and thirty-one women," he reported. He pulled himself up to attention as he spoke. "Some of our ... allies ... believe that others will come in from the city as the undead plague spreads, but I'm not hopeful. Right now, we're setting up barricades and doing our best to secure the building. Fortunately, we have an ample supply of swords and other such weapons."

He paused. "I've put spotters out to watch for any signs of the undead, but so far we've seen nothing approaching the building," he continued. "The Russians want to extend our defensive line until we can protect the entire complex, but I have my doubts. There just aren't enough of us to hold the line."

Gwen nodded in agreement. They had *her*, true, but she knew there were limits to her magic, even without the Russian magicians becoming involved. They were fanatical enough to keep serving the Tsar, even though he was an undead monster. Or perhaps they were already bitten, but the same technique had allowed them to keep their minds. There was no way to know. Gwen made a face at the thought. Just how far had the Russians carried their experiments and what was the planned end result?

A world of the dead, she thought, sourly. *Is that what they have in mind?*

She looked over at Romulus. "And Lady Standish?"

"Locked in her room," Romulus said. "I dare say Her Ladyship will insist I be fired when we get home."

Gwen snorted. "You and Janet can come and work for me," she said. Romulus clearly had hidden depths – and besides, she'd started collecting people no one else wanted. "How is Janet, by the way?"

"Scared, but helping with the medical supplies," Romulus said. He paused, looking from Gwen to Sir Standish and then back again. "*Can* we get out of here?"

Gwen hesitated. If it had been just her, she would have made a run for the edge of the city by now, flying over the heads of the undead. But with over a hundred dependents she couldn't see how they could make it to the edge of the city without being overwhelmed ... and even if they did, it was roughly four hundred miles to St Petersburg and the Baltic Sea. They'd never make it before the undead caught up with them. And then they'd die.

"I don't know," she said. Maybe she should take Olivia and run. But she couldn't leave everyone else in the lurch. "The Tsar didn't strike me as being willing to negotiate."

"I'll speak to the aristocrats," Sir Standish said. He didn't sound optimistic. "Perhaps they can suggest a plan."

"Good," Gwen said. She staggered, slightly. It had been over a day since she'd slept and her body was telling her that she urgently needed rest. "Maybe there's somewhere closer we can go than St Petersburg."

Sir Sidney nodded and walked away from her, followed by Romulus. Gwen watched them go, then settled down on a chair, trying to focus her mind. The next thing she felt was someone *touching* her mind. She jerked awake and saw Simone kneeling in front of her.

"It *is* you," the French girl said. She sounded impressed. "I never even sensed your presence."

"I hid," Gwen said, darkly. She hated to admit it, but looking at Simone made her feel uncomfortably dowdy. The French girl was staggeringly beautiful, with a winsome air that called boys to her like moths to a flame. Whatever the truth of her origins, she looked far more aristocratic than many who had been born to the purple. "What do you want?"

"Just to say thank you," Simone said. Her voice was soft and sweet, suggesting someone in desperate need of protection. It was no doubt very appealing to young aristocratic men who liked to think of themselves as protectors. "The undead could have killed us all if you hadn't come to warn us."

"You're welcome," Gwen muttered. She yawned. The temptation to just push the girl away was becoming overwhelming. Magic seemed to shimmer through her mind, responding to her desire. But she was too tired to focus. "Just do whatever you can to help the defenders."

"I will," Simone promised. She paused, then pasted a concerned expression on her face. "Would you like a hand getting back upstairs?"

Gwen glared at her. Her mental shields were starting to crack because she was completely exhausted. Having help to get back upstairs was tempting, but it would allow Simone too much opportunity to poke around in Gwen's mind. Instead, she pulled herself to her feet, shook her head and walked towards the door. Somehow, she managed to stay awake until she reached Raechel's room and sank down on the small bed the Russians had provided for her.

"You didn't bring a weapon," Raechel observed, from where she was sitting next to Olivia and pretending to read a book. "I ..."

"Keep an eye on Olivia," Gwen ordered, and closed her eyes. She was too tired to snap at Raechel, even though Gwen *had* forgotten to bring her a weapon. "She's the most important person in the room."

But she wasn't sure she knew what to do with her adopted daughter, she realised. The Tsar had done something that isolated his undead, largely severing their connections to other Necromancers and Gwen herself. Maybe, if the Tsar died, Olivia could take control of the undead, if they hadn't developed an intelligence of their own. There were so many potential undead in Moscow that it was easy to imagine them crossing the threshold and developing intelligence if their Lord and Master died. Olivia wouldn't be able to issue orders if they could think for themselves.

"I'm sorry," she muttered. "Goodnight."

Sleep overcame her and she knew no more.

Chapter Twenty-Eight

livia snapped awake.

There was a strange girl in the room, sitting on the bed reading a book. Olivia stared at her, then looked around the room. It wasn't another prison cell or her rooms at Cavendish Hall, although there was no shortage of gilt and paintings of dead men on the walls. It looked almost welcoming. The strange girl tapped her lips, then pointed to a bed in the corner of the room. Olivia saw Gwen lying on the bed, snoring loudly.

"You can tell her she snores," the stranger said. "She didn't believe me."

Olivia studied the girl for a long moment. She was tall, stronger than she looked at a guess, with long red hair and an angular face that made her look sharp, rather than conventionally beautiful. The dress she wore looked odd on her, as if she would have preferred a set of trousers or even a simpler dress. Olivia's instincts told her that the stranger was a good person, but that didn't mean much. She'd met far too many well-meaning aristocrats who'd caused more trouble through good intentions than through outright malice.

"I will," she said, darkly. "Who *are* you?"

"Raechel," the girl said. "Welcome to ... some unpronounceable Russian palace."

Olivia rubbed her head as her memories surged back into her mind. The Tsar had injected himself with her blood, then killed himself, somehow maintaining his conscious mind while becoming one of the undead. Gregory's Healing had probably helped with that, she decided, although she had no idea how the Russians had even decided it was possible in the first place. Maybe they'd just kept pushing the limits of magic until they'd decided there were *no* limits.

"Thank you," she said, as she swung her legs over the side of the bed and stood. Her legs felt wobbly, but nowhere near as bad as she'd feared. "Is there a place to wash?"

"In there," Raechel said, pointing towards a door. "Do you require assistance?"

Olivia shook her head, hastily. She'd never been comfortable with the idea of being naked in front of anyone, but the Russian girls hadn't given her a choice. Now, she entered the bathroom, closed the door firmly behind her and undressed hastily. The absurd Russian dress was so pitifully thin that it had been practically falling apart even before she tore it off and dropped it on the floor. Once she was naked, she looked at herself in the mirror and froze. Her body was badly bruised, her eyes were haunted ... and she looked so thin that she could see her bones through her skin. Clearly, the Russians hadn't fed her anything like enough to power her magic.

Somehow, she managed to wash herself in the warm water, then pull a bathrobe over her body before she walked outside. Raechel was sorting out a plate of food; Olivia felt her stomach rumble as soon as she saw it. She took the proffered plate and tore into it, forgetting six months' worth of etiquette training in her desperate need to fill her stomach. There was a faint cough from where Gwen was lying and Olivia looked up, just in time to see her adopted mother sitting upright. The sight sent an odd burst of warmth through her body.

"You came," she said, wonderingly. No one had ever given a damn about her before, not even Jack. "I ..."

Gwen smiled at her. "Did you think I wouldn't?"

Olivia lowered her eyes. A life on the streets had convinced her that no one, absolutely no one, put themselves out for someone else unless there was something in it for them. If she'd been adopted by an older man, she would have expected to be forced into his bed or made to serve him in some other way. And there were even women who liked women ... but Gwen hadn't asked for anything from her. She'd even come all the way to Russia to save her life.

She didn't want to cry. It had been years since she'd let herself admit to any form of weakness. But she found herself crying now.

"It's all right," Gwen said, as she stood up and walked over to Olivia. "You're safe now."

"But only for a given value of safe," Raechel said. "Have you looked out of the window?"

Olivia stood up and walked to the window, then pulled the heavy curtains aside. Outside, a line of undead stood on the streets, staring up at the building with unblinking eyes. She sucked her breath in sharply, wondering why she couldn't hear any whispering. Their presence had been completely unsuspected until she'd actually laid eyes on them. She cast her eyes down the line of undead, noticing that some were wearing uniforms, some were wearing rags and some were completely naked. But they were all united under the Father Tsar.

Gwen walked up behind her, then swore. Olivia giggled, remembering Tanya's threat to wash her mistress's mouth out with soap, then looked back at the undead. There were more of the bastards beyond the watching line, some crawling over buildings and hunting for living victims, others performing ritualistic marches, as if they were toy soldiers. Was the Tsar testing the limits of his control, Olivia wondered, or was he up to something else? There was no way to know.

She started as Gwen touched her shoulder. "Can you hear them?"

Olivia shook her head. "No whispering," she said. "I can't even sense their presence."

"Nor can I," Gwen said. "They're completely silent."

Raechel coughed. They both looked back at her. "Why would you expect to hear them?"

Olivia looked up at Gwen, wondering how she was going to answer that question. One rule Gwen had hammered into her head, time and time again, was never to tell anyone what she actually was. The last thing either of them needed was for someone to try to invoke the Demonic Powers Act – or, for that matter, use the failure to invoke it to bring down the government. With Britain on the verge of war, a political catfight could be disastrous.

"Olivia is a rather unusual Sensitive," Gwen said, smoothly. "But not much else, I'm afraid."

Raechel didn't look convinced, but she held her tongue. Olivia eyed her for a long moment, then turned to look back at the undead. It was impossible to escape the feeling that they were clustering there to keep the foreigners penned into the building – and that they were just waiting for the order before attacking. The Tsar might come to supervise the deaths of the foreigners in person.

"You should have woken me," Gwen said. She sounded irked. "I needed to see this earlier."

"You were completely exhausted," Raechel countered. "And there was nothing you could do."

Gwen sighed loudly, then walked over and out of the door, still clad in her rumpled dress. A moment later, she returned, carrying two short swords with her. Olivia eyed them with some surprise – she'd never seen Gwen carrying anything other than a pair of pistols – then took the sword Gwen offered her. She'd taken fencing lessons at Cavendish Hall, once the tutor had been convinced that a young woman needed them, but the sword felt heavier than the ones she'd used for practice. Raechel seemed to have no idea what she was doing with the sword at all.

"Remember what I said," Gwen warned. "Go for the neck and behead them, or make it impossible for them to move."

She paused, eying Raechel. "Perhaps you should go and ask one of the Russians for fencing lessons," she said. "I'm sure the one who was waltzing you round the dance hall would be happy to teach you."

Raechel nodded and left the room, sword in hand.

Olivia eyed her adopted mother accusingly. "You *Charmed* her."

"I did," Gwen agreed, looking guilty. "But Raechel would have insisted on staying, if I'd let her, and there are things I want to talk about without someone listening to us."

She leant forward. "What – precisely – happened to you?"

Olivia frowned, conflicted. Part of her wanted to object, to tell Gwen off for Charming a girl she clearly thought of as a friend ... and Charming her so casually too. The rest of her understood Gwen's point. Raechel could not be allowed to know everything that had happened since Olivia had been taken from Cavendish Hall. There were details that shouldn't go any further than Gwen herself.

"They were running tests," she explained. The whole story came out of her slowly, aided by Gwen asking pointed questions whenever she didn't understand what she was being told. "I think they were hoping to unlock some of the secrets of magic."

"Blood transfusions," Gwen mused. "I don't believe that anyone has tried that in England."

"It worked, sometimes," Olivia said. She smiled, suddenly. "Do you know they found a Master?"

Gwen looked at her, sharply. "How?"

"They killed her," Olivia said. She grinned, wondering just what the Tsar would say when he found out that a Master Magician had been in the complex ... and never identified. "I don't think they ever realised she was combining powers."

"I never did," Gwen mused. She'd been a holy terror, according to Lady Mary. "But the Russians should have known that talents run in sets, with only a handful of people combining the powers."

"Maybe they just thought she was an unusual Charmer," Olivia said, shivering as she recalled the strange girl and her fate. "They wanted to try to get her to use her powers even once she became undead."

"Odd," Gwen said. She shook her head. "But they clearly succeeded in making the Tsar into ... what? An undead Necromancer?"

Olivia looked up at her. "Would I still have my powers if I became undead?"

"I don't think so," Gwen said. "Would you even have your *mind?*"

Olivia shivered, but said nothing.

"This is just too unprecedented," Gwen said. She stood. "When Raechel comes back, the two of you can practice with your swords. You'll probably have a chance to use them, sooner or later."

"The fencing master liked teaching me," Olivia said. "Do you think he'll like teaching her too?"

Gwen smiled, clearly remembering the master's praise of Olivia, once he'd managed to get used to the idea of tutoring a girl. Olivia, he'd said, had had much less to unlearn than the boys he tried to teach ... and didn't have their attitude, their automatic assumption that they already knew all there was to know about swordfighting.

"I can see her having a ball," Gwen said. She looked up as Raechel re-entered the room. "No Russians to teach you?"

"They're all busy with the defences," Raechel said. "Sir Sidney wants to see you downstairs, if you're decent."

Gwen smoothed down her outfit, then sighed. "See if you can find something suitable for Olivia to wear," she said. "I'll go speak to Sir Sidney."

Raechel eyed her back as she left, then turned to Olivia. "What would you like to wear?"

"Something I can move in," Olivia said, relieved that Raechel wasn't going to ask any awkward questions. "Trousers, for preference."

She watched Raechel leave, then walked back to the window and stared out at the undead waiting patiently for their master to arrive. There were no reinforcements constantly arriving, she saw, just row upon row of the undead. Did the Tsar hope they'd try to sally out and fight the undead they could see, allowing him to ambush them with undead hiding in nearby buildings, or did he have something else in mind? Perhaps his armies were already heading to the south, marching towards the Ottoman Empire. It would take weeks, perhaps months, for them to reach Turkey, but they'd be gathering strength all the while.

"It turned out that the footman has a young son," Raechel said, coming into the room. "He was convinced to donate a couple of pairs of trousers and shirts. But I suggest you bind up your breasts."

Olivia turned to see Raechel holding a pair of dark trousers and two white shirts, then glanced down at her chest. On the streets, she had dreaded the day when her breasts first started to appear, knowing that it would mean the end of her life. There was no way she could pass for a boy now. But now, part of her didn't mind any longer. She would never have to go back to the streets.

"I can try," she said, as she pulled on the trousers. They felt rough and uncomfortable against her bare skin, but at least they weren't a silly dress. She struggled with her breasts for a few moments, binding them up with the remains of one of the dresses, before pulling the shirt over her chest. "How do I look?"

"Pretty," Raechel said. "Adopted?"

Olivia *looked* at her. "Do I look young enough to be her daughter?"

"No," Raechel said, dryly. "But how did you two meet?"

"Long story," Olivia said. She stood and picked up one of the swords, hefting it in her hand. "Let me show you how to handle this properly."

"I think I need a bigger sword," Raechel said, as she picked up her own blade. "How am I meant to slice off their heads without being grabbed and bitten?"

"You're not strong enough to carry a heavier blade," Olivia said, firmly. She still recalled the first time she'd picked up a heavy blade in Cavendish Hall. It had been so heavy that she had almost dropped it seconds later. "And you need to hold the weapon upright at all times, rather than lean on it or put it down when you're not fighting."

She gave Raechel a cautionary look, then started to demonstrate the correct way to handle the blade. It felt odd, compared to the fencing blades she was used to using at Cavendish Hall, very clearly a dangerous weapon. There were no Healers in the building, she reminded herself, and the closest Healer she knew was Gregory. It was unlikely he would do anything to heal a foreigner, particularly someone who might fight the army of undead.

Olivia sighed. Normally, she would have fenced lightly with her partner, but now she merely concentrated on how to thrust, parry and defend oneself. The undead weren't likely to come at them with swords. She'd certainly never seen them using anything more than hands and teeth as they charged their enemies.

"Go for the neck," she said, again and again. "I've seen the undead take blows to the chest that leave them torn in half and yet they keep coming forward, crawling on their hands until they are smashed flat."

Raechel gave her an odd look. "You were in London?"

"Yes," Olivia said, flatly. She found it hard to like Raechel, even though she understood what Gwen saw in her. They were very alike, in many ways. "I was at the barricades during the Swing." She watched Raechel's expression furrow and sighed, inwardly. "Where were you during the Swing?"

"At my father's estate," Raechel said. There was a bitter tone in her voice. "My parents died shortly afterwards, leaving me in the care of my Aunt and Uncle. But they weren't back in London until recently."

Olivia shrugged. At least Raechel had known her parents. Olivia hadn't known her father at all, while her mother had died while she was very young. Raechel looked slightly put out by her reaction, but it wasn't something Olivia wanted to explain. Raechel was dangerously smart, smart enough to wonder why a mere Sensitive would be considered a suitable adopted daughter for the Royal Sorceress.

"My arm aches," Raechel said, changing the subject. "Why?"

Olivia smirked. "Are you used to waving a sword about the room?"

Raechel shook her head. Olivia smiled, remembering how much she'd ached after the first few sessions, despite her tolerance for pain and discomfort. Raechel might be a fun person, but Olivia would have bet good money she'd never suffered any real discomfort in her life, even after her parents had died. The young aristocrats might feel the weight of their father's hand from time to time – or the Sergeant's cane, if they lived in Cavendish Hall – yet they'd never been starved almost to death. Nor had they had to struggle to find enough money to get a place to stay for the night, or sell their bodies just to stay alive. The little bastards didn't know discomfort.

"You'll be fine," Olivia promised. She'd healed quickly, even without Lucy's help, but Raechel didn't seem to have any magic. There was no way to know just how quickly she would recover from anything. "You just need to build up the tolerance to handle the sword."

Raechel looked oddly hopeful. "Can I pretend they have the face of my Aunt?"

"If you want," Olivia said. She'd never thought of any of her fencing partners as her tormentors at Cavendish Hall; indeed, her tutor had strongly discouraged it. But now ... she could think of the undead as having Gregory's face. It would help her behead them before they got to her. "Or think of them as having the face of your least favourite society butterfly, if you wish."

"Still my Aunt," Raechel said. She grinned at Olivia, then picked up the sword again, wincing slightly. "More practice?"

Olivia smiled. "Pain is how you know you're stretching your muscles," she said, remembering one of her tutor's sayings. He'd never held back, once he'd finally grasped the idea that he was meant to be training a girl how to fence. "But you have to be careful not to take it too far."

She paused as a banging sound echoed down the corridor. "What was that?"

Raechel smirked. It wasn't a pleasant expression. "Oh, just my Aunt," she said, airily. "She's locked in her bedroom. I don't think she likes it very much."

She shrugged, her face hardening. "She's locked me in once or twice too," she added, nastily. "Serves her right."

Olivia had to laugh. Somehow, she discovered that she quite liked Raechel after all.

Chapter Twenty-Nine

In the sunlight, Gwen couldn't help realising that Moscow was almost beautiful. It didn't have the elegance of St Petersburg, but it had a style all of its own, particularly the core of the city. The reddish-brown buildings, some glittering with gold paint in the sunlight, were strikingly different from London. But the screams – and the hordes of undead moving through the streets – painted a very different picture. Moscow was fast becoming a city of the dead.

A Necropolis, Gwen thought, recalling just how many plays had been set in infested cities and towns after the first outbreaks of undead creatures. *But there's no one here to save the day.*

She floated in the air, looking down at the dying city below. There were no signs of any humans in view, just the endlessly marching undead, breaking into houses, searching for any traces of the living and then moving on to the next house. It was almost hypnotic; they searched one house, then they searched it again and again, as if they didn't quite realise that they'd searched the house already. Gwen hoped that meant that the Tsar, wherever he was, was having problems coordinating so many undead at once, no matter how far his mind had expanded. Or maybe he was just thinking of something else.

The undead paid her no heed as they moved about their deadly work. Her blood ran cold as she saw newcomers joining their ranks; men, women and children, some barely old enough to walk. Most of them were dressed in nightclothes, but others were naked, not that it mattered any longer. Their faces were twisted into savage masks, each one displaying a desperate hunger; their eyes burned with eerie yellow light. The only consolation, as far as she could see, was that none of them were carrying weapons. It looked impossible for the Tsar to coordinate an infantry unit made up of undead.

Unless he is just learning how to use his new abilities, Gwen thought. *He may master it soon enough.*

She shook her head. There was no precedent for someone to become a magician at such an advanced age ... but the Tsar wasn't really *that* old, was he? He'd merely been worn down by trying to rule his ungrateful country during a series of natural and not-so-natural disasters. Gwen could understand the frustration that came from struggling against entrenched interests and determined opposition, but *she'd* never killed her political enemies. The Tsar might have been justified in purging his noblemen, yet now he'd sentenced his entire country to death – and then a hellish non-life. He'd gone completely mad.

She wanted to summon fire and rain death on the undead from above. It would be so easy, after she'd had a chance to sleep and regain her strength. But she couldn't incinerate them all, while using her magic so blatantly would tell the Russian magicians precisely where she was. All she could do was watch and wait and hope to hell they found a way out of the necropolis before the undead came for them. But she wasn't hopeful.

A dull rumbling sound caught her ear and she turned to look, just as a small palace collapsed into rubble. The undead swarms walked through the debris, tearing through the rocks and brick, looking for traces of human life. Gwen's eyes narrowed as she puzzled over why the building had just collapsed. A building designed to survive Moscow's winters would be strong enough to survive a horde of the undead, surely?

Magic, she thought, and drifted away from the building. Now she saw more clearly, she realised that the undead were swarming through *all* of the palaces, palaces that had to have belonged to some of the more treacherous noblemen. The Tsar, not content with killing his noblemen and watching them rise again to join his army, was wiping out all traces of their existence. She recalled some of the burned buildings from the Swing and shivered, despite the magic keeping her warm. The Tsar would have reshaped the continent completely by the time he was done.

She wanted to cry in frustration. She'd been too late to stop the Tsar, despite everything she'd done to sneak into Moscow, and now all she could do was watch as swarms of undead made their way through Moscow's streets, looking for the living. There had been hundreds of thousands of poor refugees in the outskirts of the city, she knew; now, they would all be part of the undead army. And there was nothing she could do to stop the nightmare unfolding right in front of her. There was no magic that could burn an entire city to ash.

A scream split the air, a young girl's scream. Gwen turned and saw a pair of girls and their parents, standing on a roof as the undead slowly climbed up towards them. Their father was holding a sword in one hand and a gun in the other, but Gwen had no illusions. One man, no matter how capable a swordsman, couldn't stop a horde of charging undead. She acted before her mind quite caught up with her intentions, swooping down towards the rooftop and summoning fire. The undead fell backwards as her flames washed through them, burning them to ash. But there were countless more where they had come from, advancing towards the building.

Gwen landed on the rooftop, praying that at least one of the Russians spoke English. The father reminded her of the nobleman who had taken Raechel to the first dance in St Petersburg, although he was clearly older and wiser. He gaped at her as if he didn't quite believe his eyes. Behind him, his wife and daughters stared openly, the younger daughter muttering a word under her breath time and time again. Gwen smiled at them, suddenly aware of her appearance. They had to find her more frightening than the undead.

"I don't speak Russian," she said, as a low moaning rose up from the undead below. "Can you understand me?"

The Russian stared at her, then nodded. "I understand you," he said. His voice was low and raspy, while his accent made his words almost impossible to understand. "Who are you?"

"A friend," Gwen said. She'd seen some of the French propaganda about the Royal Sorcerers Corps and the Royal Sorceress in particular and she had no wish to make them baulk at accepting her assistance. "I can take you somewhere safe."

"Yes, please," the Russian said. "But how?"

Gwen turned. The moaning from below was getting louder, attracting hordes of undead towards their position. Gwen watched them flowing out from buildings, summoned by a call that seemed incomprehensible. But if dogs could communicate a great deal of information through barking, she thought, why couldn't the undead do the same? And the Tsar might be watching through their eyes, just as Olivia had done during her captivity.

She swore under her breath as the undead started scrambling up the scorched walls, climbing over one another to get to the top. They weren't showing the cold intelligence of large swarms of undead, unlike the ones in Haiti, which suggested the Tsar was still controlling them, if indirectly. But piling themselves up against the walls would eventually allow them to reach the humans on the top. Gwen summoned fire and launched it down towards the undead, then turned to smile at the Russians.

"This is going to be disconcerting," she warned. Doctor Norwell had once asked her to take him for a flight, an odd request for the normally staid theoretical magician. But he hadn't enjoyed the experience as much as he might have thought. "Brace yourself."

She caught hold of them with magic, then launched all five of them into the air, flying away from the burning building. It had caught fire, she saw, hopefully incinerating more of the undead before they could escape the flames and regroup. The moaning grew louder, hundreds of undead looking up from the streets towards the flying humans, before slowly fading away. Somehow, Gwen and her charges had passed beyond their awareness.

The Russians looked panicked, she saw, as she angled their course back towards the palace – and the ranks of waiting undead. She tried to shoot the mother a reassuring glance, but it came off as more of a grimace. Her two daughters were staring down at the ground, their hands stroking the air as if they expected to feel something transparent holding them up and protecting them from the undead. Gwen felt a moment of sympathy – despite her powers, she had never liked flying under someone else's control – which she ruthlessly pushed aside. She had no time to let pity distract her.

Romulus was standing on the roof, supervising several of the older diplomats, when Gwen landed, dropping the Russians to the floor. They looked surprised to see Romulus – they'd probably been raised on horror stories about dark-skinned Mongols – but they were clearly too relieved to make any trouble. Romulus chatted briefly to the father, then directed the mother and her two daughters inside the building. Gwen settled down on the rooftop, feeling sick at heart. The girls couldn't have been older than eight or nine and yet the Tsar would have turned them into the undead, if they'd survived the first bite. None of the undead were particularly gentle when they bit their victims.

"Lady Gwen," Sir Sidney said. Gwen looked up to see him coming out of the rooftop entrance. "Did you see anything interesting?"

"Just hordes of undead," Gwen said, and recounted her observations. "We're going to have to barricade the windows, just to stop them climbing up and breaking in."

Sir Sidney looked irked. Gwen didn't blame him. The building was stronger than any comparable building in London, but it had far too many glass windows – a sign of status in Russia – and all of them could be broken down by the undead. Barricading them all could take time, time they didn't have. The ranks of undead outside the palace wouldn't stay still forever.

"We need more people," Sir Sidney said, finally. "Did you see many others?"

Gwen shook her head. The Tsar had launched his first strikes in the night, when most people would have been tucked up in bed. They would have been overwhelmed before they knew what was going on, let alone had a chance to defend themselves. The family she'd saved had been lucky, she suspected. But their luck had finally run out.

"By now, he could have the entire city," she said. "Do we have any way to get a message out?"

"Not that we've found," Sir Sidney said. He took her arm and led her towards the edge of the roof, some distance from the handful of guards. "How far can you fly?"

Gwen looked at him, sharply. She'd once flown from Cambridge to London, back during the Swing, but the effort had almost killed her. If it hadn't been for Master Thomas, it *would* have killed her. And that was around sixty miles. It was over four *hundred* miles from Moscow to St Petersburg.

"Maybe around fifty miles," she estimated. "Why?"

"If worst comes to worst," Sir Sidney said, "I want you to leave us and fly home."

"No," Gwen said. Even if she had been willing to abandon Olivia, Raechel and everyone else, she couldn't have flown all the way back to London. Even reaching the German states would be difficult. She'd have to stop along the way and hunt for food ... in the middle of the Russian countryside, where finding food was far from easy. "I won't leave you."

Sir Sidney rested his arm on her shoulder, an oddly intimate gesture. "There are thousands upon thousands of the undead in this city," he said. "I don't know why we have been spared so far, but when they come for us – and they will – we will be overwhelmed. Even your powers aren't enough to hold back thousands of undead indefinitely."

Gwen didn't want to admit it, but he was right.

"And then the Tsar will start attacking other Russian cities, then advance down south to Turkey or west into France," Sir Sidney continued. "They have to be warned and we have no other way to get a message out."

He squeezed her shoulder lightly. "Talleyrand can give you letters of introduction, should you reach French territory," he added. "Hell, some of the noblemen here can give you letters for other Russian officers. You can get the word out."

"And leave you all to die," Gwen said.

There was a Talker at the embassy in St Petersburg, she knew, one with the reach to contact London. But getting there would be difficult, even for her. She'd need to find a great deal of food along the way or die in the Russian countryside, but where could she find the food? It was unlikely that the peasants would be interested in helping her. They'd be more likely, if some of the horror stories she'd heard were true, to chop her up for the stew pot.

But even if she did make it to St Petersburg, there was no way anyone from Britain – or France – could reach Moscow in time to help. And God alone knew what the Russian nobility would do. They might side with the Tsar, despite his madness, or start a civil war, while the undead advanced in all directions. It seemed unlikely that they would join the outsiders in stopping the undead while there was still time.

If there is still time, she thought, morbidly. The Tsar's undead empire was already snowballing rapidly. Who knew where it would end?

Her own words came back to haunt her. If one undead bit a living person, there would be two undead; if both undead bit a living person, there would be four undead; if all four undead found a new victim each, there would be eight undead ... then sixteen, then thirty-two, then ... it would just keep going until they ran out of victims. But Russia was a heavily populated country. By the time they ran out, there would be an unstoppable army heading towards the German states or the Ottoman Empire.

Sir Sidney coughed. Gwen looked up at him, apologetically. She hadn't realised her thoughts had slipped away from him.

"I wish there was another way," he said, softly. "But if the end is nigh anyway, use your magic and escape. Get out and warn the rest of the world about the Tsar."

"Understood," Gwen said, bitterly. Cold logic told her he was right. But cold logic was no consolation. How could she abandon Olivia, knowing that she would be killed ... or forced to serve the Tsar again? But if she tried to carry someone with her, there was no way she could get as far as she could on her own. "If that's what I will have to do, that is what I will have to do."

Sir Sidney tugged on her arm. "Council of war," he said. "Come on."

Gwen followed him back across the roof, down the stairwell and into a large room that had been hastily converted into a command centre. She had her doubts about the value of any coordination; the sheer mass of undead would ensure that they would break through the defences in multiple locations, but there was no choice. A handful of men drilled with swords, serving as a reserve to be rushed to any threatened breakthrough. But there weren't enough of them to hold the line.

A nasty thought occurred to her and she frowned. "We need to check for tunnels," she said, remembering the catacombs under the cathedral. "Can they bypass our defences by sneaking in underground?"

"We looked," Sir Sidney said. "But we found nothing."

Gwen resisted the temptation to roll her eyes as the Council of War slowly gathered. There were procedures for the Royal Sorcerer – and then the Royal Sorceress – to call Councils of War, but as far as she could tell Master Thomas had never bothered. But then, few had doubted his competence and none had doubted that he knew where a great many bodies were buried. If the Royal Sorcerers Corps did wind up going to war, Gwen knew, she would be expected to work with her senior magicians, rather than issuing orders.

Talleyrand gave her a sidelong look, then a wink, as he entered the room. He carried a sword by his side, although Gwen had no idea if he knew how to use it. Talleyrand's great skills lay in diplomatic manipulation, according to Lord Mycroft, rather than swordplay or military operations. But life at the French Court was sometimes touchy. It was quite possible that Talleyrand knew how to use the blade.

Behind him, Lord Standish stepped into the room. He looked tired, tired enough merely to nod to Gwen rather than say a word. Gwen suspected the older man was looking at the end of his career, even if they did manage to make it out of Moscow successfully. His reputation would not survive losing command of the mission to Sir Sidney, no matter what their sealed orders said. Gwen felt a moment of pity, which she ruthlessly suppressed. Lord Standish had done absolutely nothing to control his wife.

The Russian aristocrat she'd rescued followed Lord Standish in, escorted by one of the other diplomatic representatives. Gwen gave him a surprised look, only to see him bow deeply to her. At least he recognised he owed her a debt of gratitude. She'd met noblemen and women in England who would happily have complained if Gwen had carried out the rescue, as if she'd saved their lives just to spite them. Some people were never satisfied.

"We are all here," Sir Sidney said. "We shall begin."

He looked over at Gwen. "I think it is time to discuss everything," he added. "Tell us how this crisis began."

Gwen kept her face expressionless with an effort. He could have warned her what he was planning to ask. But that would have given her time to think of a reason not to tell them anything.

Gritting her teeth, she started to explain.

Chapter Thirty

our daughter is a *Necromancer*?" Lord Standish said, when Gwen had finished. "Why is she still alive?"

Gwen kept her voice as firmly under control as possible. "It was decided, in the wake of the Swing, that it would be better to have a Necromancer under our control," she said. There were other considerations, but she kept them to herself. "Olivia's life was spared and she was allowed to study at Cavendish Hall."

Talleyrand cleared his throat. "This is a breach of the Treaty of 1810, barring the use of necromancy," he said. There was a faintly mocking tone to his voice. "I will have to inform my government."

"Go inform the Tsar," Gwen snapped, tartly. "I'm sure he'd be very impressed."

"That would not have happened," Talleyrand pointed out, "if you'd killed Olivia when you discovered what she was."

"You used Necromancy in London," Lord Standish snapped. "How dare you blame us for keeping a pet Necromancer when you did the same?"

Gwen shifted, uncomfortably. The French might have been blamed for the necromantic outbreak in London, but Gwen knew better ... and she suspected Sir Sidney knew better too, if Lord Mycroft had briefed him thoroughly. It had been Master Thomas who had unleashed the undead, allowing them to roam freely and hopefully put an end to the Swing; it had taken Gwen, Jack and Olivia to stop him and bring the undead back under control. The French had been blamed for the crisis afterwards, just to conceal the truth. If it ever got out, Gwen knew, there would be outrage, perhaps even civil war. The secret had to remain buried.

Sir Sidney cleared his throat. "That is beside the point," he said. "If we don't get out of Moscow soon, we won't be reporting anything to anyone."

He looked from face to face. "We have around four days worth of food, assuming we don't take in any extra mouths," he said. "Some of us" – he carefully did *not* look at Gwen – "require extra food to be effective. However, we can expect to be attacked before we run out of food to eat. Once the Tsar has secured Moscow, he will turn his attention to us and we will be overrun. Our defences are insufficient to stop him."

His face twitched into a ghoulish smile. "So ... what do we do?"

"We could speak to him," Lord Standish said. "Remind him that we have diplomatic immunity ..."

Gwen snorted, rudely. "The Tsar is mad," she said. She had to smile at his shocked reaction. Being contradicted publicly by a slip of a girl had to be a blow to his pride. "He is unlikely to care about diplomatic niceties. Besides, he has good reason to want us all dead. We know too much."

"Aye, about what he did to himself," Sir Sidney said. "Lady Gwen – do you think we could fight our way out of the city?"

"I doubt it," Gwen said. "He can pour undead on us like raindrops. We wouldn't even have the protection of these walls. He'd kill us, easily."

Sir Sidney looked down at the table. "Stay; we die. Go; we die. We need to consider desperate measures."

"There is a possibility," the Russian nobleman said. "The Tsar might not yet have claimed control of the garrisons outside the city – or the airship landing strip."

Lord Standish stared at him. "We could have flown here on an airship?"

"The Tsar dislikes flying," the Russian explained. "But yes, there are airships near the city."

"That's an interesting possibility," Sir Sidney said. "Alexander, would the crews work for us?"

"You'd have me with you," the Russian said. "They'd do as they were told."

Gwen shook her head. "Any Mover or Blazer worthy of the name could bring down an airship," she said. It would be almost pathetically easy to use magic to cause an airship to explode in midair. "We'd just make ourselves an easy target."

"If we could get to the airstrip, we could get out, heading away from the Russians," Sir Sidney mused. "And then make a run for French territory."

"That would be acceptable," Talleyrand said. "I'd be happy to hand out safe conduct passes to you and your fellows."

"We'd still have to get out of the city," Gwen pointed out. "And we would have no idea what reception awaited us."

Sir Sidney nodded. "Desperate measures," he said. He looked up at Gwen, meeting her eyes. "Can your daughter take control of the Tsar's undead?"

"Apparently not," Gwen said. "His intellect seems to be directing them – occupying their minds – in a manner no normal Necromancer can match. He's one of them, to all intents and purposes, as if their shared intelligence resides in one body."

"Kill the Tsar and the rest of the undead would revert to their normal patterns," Sir Sidney mused. "But there really are too many of them, aren't there?"

Gwen nodded. If a few hundred undead could form a hive mind that was terrifyingly intelligent and cunning, a few hundred thousand would be almost unstoppable. Kill the Tsar and the undead would become far more dangerous. But leaving the Tsar alive was almost as risky. His madness would make it impossible to talk sense into his head.

"Then we give them another centre," Sir Sidney said. "You said an injection of Olivia's blood was enough to turn the Tsar into an ... undead Necromancer. What if we made a second undead Necromancer of our own."

Talleyrand jerked. "Are you mad?"

Sir Sidney glowered at the Frenchman. "Do you have another idea?"

"There's no guarantee that we would be able to repeat their success," Gwen said, hastily. She really didn't like the idea, not least because there were just too many unknowns. "And even if we did succeed, whoever we choose to serve as the test subject might collapse into madness too. We'd be swapping one problem for another."

"We might be able to get enough soldiers from the garrisons to retake the city," Alexander said, quickly. "There would be no need for extreme measures."

Gwen and Sir Sidney exchanged glances. The Russians would be unprepared for the undead, no matter how heavily armed they were. It was unlikely the Tsar would have doubted his own success enough to have his men armed with weapons designed for killing undead. And fighting through an urban environment was always difficult. They might be better off advising the Russians to burn Moscow to the ground, keeping the undead penned up until they were consumed by the flames.

"It would be tricky," Sir Sidney said, diplomatically. "But Lady Gwen can fly you to the garrisons. You can speak to the soldiers and try to convince them to help us."

Gwen nodded. That, at least, she could do.

There was a sharp tap on the door. Romulus opened it, looking grim. "Sir," he said, "we have a visitor. He wishes to speak with you."

Sir Sidney looked puzzled. "A visitor?"

Moments later, a man with a long unkempt beard and a manic look in his eye was shown into the room.

"Greetings in the name of the Father Tsar," he said. "My name is Gregory."

***

If there was one advantage to being trapped by a wall of undead, Olivia had decided, it was that most social convention seemed to have gone by the wayside. The Russian girls had thrown themselves into helping to prepare the defences, clutching swords in one hand while rigging up barricades with the other. Olivia had a feeling that they would probably be more dangerous to themselves than the enemy, but at least it would delay the undead, winning the defenders a few more seconds. Or so she hoped.

"There's someone coming towards us," Raechel said. She had refused to leave Olivia's side, even after Olivia had insisted on leaving the bedroom. Now, she spent half of her time staring out of the windows, looking towards the undead. "Just one person."

Olivia scrambled up beside her and peered through the crack in the boarded-up window. She had warned the defenders that the boards wouldn't stop the undead for long, but they'd ignored her. Raechel had pointed out that they had to do something, so Olivia had let it slide ... now, she peered through the crack and stared in horror as she saw Gregory walking, as calmly as if he were going to dinner, towards the main doors. It didn't look as though he was undead, but it hardly mattered. He was a slave of the Tsar.

"Come on," she said, turning away from the window and picking up one of the throwing knives. "We have to get down there to see him."

It took nearly five minutes of arguing to get past the guard on the stairwell, who seemed bound and determined to make sure that none of the womenfolk went down to the ground floor. Olivia felt her patience nearly snap before she finally managed to talk their way past him, eventually pointing out that the upper levels were a trap. She was just in time to see the black butler usher Gregory into the room Sir Sidney had turned into a command post. One hand played with the knife as she followed him, knowing that Gwen would understand. And the others simply didn't matter to her.

"The Father Tsar intends to unite all of Russia under his rule," Gregory said. "You will not be permitted to interfere."

Olivia winced at the sound of his voice. It was just as hateful as she remembered, while the smell – if anything – had grown worse. His robes were stained with blood, as if he hadn't bothered to wash himself since the brief and violent encounter in the catacombs. Perhaps he simply didn't care, she told herself. It had only been a few short hours – it felt like days – since the Tsar had killed himself, only to rise from the dead.

Gregory swung round to look at one of the Russian noblemen. "The Tsar has the best interests of Russia at heart," he added. "Why do you oppose him?"

"The Tsar is killing his own people," the nobleman said. "He's gone mad."

"The Tsar is bringing them all into a glorious new union," Gregory said. "As you too will be brought in, when the time comes."

"Never," the nobleman said.

Gregory turned his attention back to Sir Sidney and Talleyrand. "Your nations have engaged in plots against the Father Tsar and his country. You have armed the enemies of the Tsar – and the enemies of God Himself. You have allowed foreign ideas to waft into the Russian Empire and contaminate its people. You have threatened to destroy a stability that has lasted for hundreds of years and replace it with chaos. You cannot be forgiven for your crimes."

"We cannot be blamed for the spread of liberal ideas into your country," Sir Sidney said. "If your people saw fit to consider them ..."

"Your claims of innocence are ill-founded," Gregory said. "Your people exist as servants of your monarchs. Whatever they do is done with the consent of their rulers. We know you saw fit to weaken Russia" – his gaze fell on Talleyrand – "even in the guise of allies."

He was mad, Olivia knew. The Father Tsar *had* to know that monarchs weren't absolute rulers, able to dictate the thoughts and actions of their subordinates. His own experience should have taught him the dangers of assuming so, even before Ivan had tried to sneak Olivia out of the complex to safety. Or maybe he was just trying to build up a justification for attacking the palace.

She shook her head. But why would he *bother*?

Gregory's gaze swept the room. "But the Father Tsar is merciful," he continued. His voice became a sneer. "In exchange for one little concession, he will allow you and your families to leave the country, alive and well. You will be escorted back to St Petersburg and put on a ship bound for your homelands. But we will demand the concession first."

"And what," Talleyrand said, "do you want in exchange?"

Gregory swung all the way around until he was staring at Olivia. "We want the Necromancer," he said, his face twisting into a leer. "Give her to us and we will allow the rest of you to leave."

"No," Gwen said, flatly.

Talleyrand looked over at her. "Can we hope to escape?"

Gregory took a step towards Olivia. "I will take her from this place," he said. "And you and yours may leave in peace."

Cold hatred, rage and fear burned through Olivia's mind. She clutched the knife in her hand, then threw it with lethal force. Gregory staggered as the knife landed in his throat, his face becoming a shocked mask, then fell to the ground, blood pooling around his body. Olivia watched, fearful that he would rise again, but instead his body merely twitched and went still. Behind her, she heard Raechel being noisily sick.

"That ... that could have cost us our lives, you stupid girl," one of the older men snapped, angrily. "They could have let us go!"

"They wouldn't have let us go," Gwen said. She rose to her feet and hurried over to Olivia, holding out her arms, tossing her look over her shoulder at the older man. "Do you really believe he meant a word of his offer?"

"But now we don't have a chance," the man objected. "Lady Gwen ..."

Gwen hugged Olivia tightly, then turned to face her accuser. "Lord Standish," she said, "the Tsar has every reason to want us dead, if not undead. *We know too much.* They will come to the building and kill us, if they can't lure us out into the open."

"Then we take action now," Sir Sidney said. He stood. "Lady Gwen, can you fly Alexander to the nearest garrison – if the undead haven't got there first."

"Perhaps we should start with the airstrip," Alexander said. His voice was alarmingly like Ivan's, although with a much thicker accent. "It will be easy to tell if the undead have reached the airships."

"Good thinking," Sir Sidney said. "Ah ... Lady Olivia, we need to talk about what the Russians did to you. I need all the details."

Olivia looked up at Gwen. "You may as well tell him everything," her adopted mother said, finally. "Don't leave out a single detail."

"I'll stay with her," Raechel said. "Someone has to make sure she eats, if nothing else."

Gwen and Olivia shared a smile.

"Thank you," Gwen said, finally. "But remember – you can't talk about what you hear to anyone."

"Perhaps Simone can also be of assistance," Talleyrand said. Olivia looked up to see him standing near, his sharp eyes fixed on her face. "She could probe the memories dragged up by the discussion."

"No," Gwen said, flatly.

"Be reasonable," Talleyrand said. "Olivia may not think to recount a detail that exists in her mind."

Olivia understood Gwen's concern. The British Empire had always enjoyed an advantage in raw numbers, at least when it came to magic. If the French developed a way to turn the blood transfusion technique into a reliable process, it would change the balance of power, perhaps giving them an advantage that would allow them to win the war. But, at the same time, she knew she didn't have any gift with words. She might well miss something that should be pointed out to the listeners.

And yet ... did she want someone crawling around in her mind?

No, she thought, but she knew the odds against them.

"It'll be fine," she said. She looked up at Gwen, reassuringly. "I'll be fine."

"I'll expect you to make sure of that," Gwen said, addressing Sir Sidney. She turned and started to walk towards the Russian officer. "And you'd better look after his family too."

Olivia watched Gwen go, then allowed Raechel and Sir Sidney to lead her back to the bedroom, where she sat down on the bed. Sir Sidney looked suddenly awkward, clearly realising that he was alone with two girls of marriageable age. Olivia and Raechel shared a glance, then started to giggle. His offended expression only made them giggle harder.

"I understand I am needed," a soft voice said. Simone was entering the room. "How might I be of service?"

Olivia clenched her teeth. The French girl was pretty – too pretty. Long dark hair, a sweet face and a perfect figure ... part of Olivia hated her on sight. But the rest of her knew just how long Simone would last on the streets, Talker or no. Hell, as a Talker, she could expect to be sold to a very special brothel. The thought, unpleasant as it was, made her smile.

"Right," Sir Sidney said. The look he gave Simone was a mixture of interest and apprehension. "Olivia ... just what happened when the Tsar became an undead ... *thing.*"

Olivia hesitated and started to go through the entire story from the beginning. Sir Sidney would have made an excellent interrogator for the Bow Street Runners, she decided, as he seemed to have a knack for zeroing in on the important details. But there were still so many questions she couldn't even *begin* to answer. Had the Russians done anything to her blood before injecting it into the Tsar? She didn't know. Hell, she wasn't even sure when they'd *taken* her blood.

They drugged me, she thought, with a hint of bitter vulnerability. *And then ...*

The memory brought back other memories from the streets. She recalled the man who had tried to jump her, then forced the thought aside. But it was too late to stop Simone seeing the memory in Olivia's mind. Moments later, the French girl fled the room in horror. Just like Raechel, Olivia reflected, she'd probably never experienced real discomfort in her life, let alone seen some of the darkness in the world. But she'd seen it now.

Outside, she heard shouts ... and then whispering rang through her head, so loud it almost sent her to her knees.

"They're coming," Sir Sidney said. "We're too late."

Chapter Thirty-One

hy did you save my life?"

Gwen considered it as she flew over the city, carrying Alexander with her magic. The screams seemed to have stilled, but plumes of smoke rose up from several of the poorer areas, where the living might have set fires to try to keep away the dead. She carefully steered them away from any such scenes, knowing she wouldn't be able to resist the urge to jump in again and perhaps get them both killed. The Tsar would know that they were both still alive.

"Because it was the right thing to do," she said, finally. "I could at least save one person."

Alexander twisted so he could look up at her. "But you could have saved many more if you'd killed the girl," he said. "Why did you let her live?"

Gwen scowled at him. "Because it was the right thing to do," she said, again. Olivia hadn't deserved to die, just because her powers had been declared illegal. "And because we might have needed her in the future."

"Like the Tsar needed her?" Alexander asked. There was a bitter tone in his voice. "Would this have ended better if she'd died in London?"

"You can't blame Olivia for the Tsar's madness," Gwen snapped. Cold ice ran down her spine as she considered the likely reaction in England. It could bring the government down if the truth came out. "He made his own decisions." She sighed. "He used Olivia as a weapon. A weapon isn't to blame if someone misuses it, is it?"

"Some weapons shouldn't be built at all," the Russian pointed out. "And this one shouldn't have been allowed to live."

Objectively, Gwen knew, he was right. If Olivia had been executed, under the terms of the Demonic Powers Act, there would have been no Necromancer for the Tsar to kidnap and put to work. But there would have been no guarantee that the Tsar wouldn't have found another Necromancer from among the Russian population ... or that he wouldn't have come up with something else, perhaps even something worse. And even if he hadn't ...

She shook his head. There was no way to escape the simple fact that executing Olivia would have been executing a young girl, solely for an accident of birth. Gwen knew that children had been hanged before, sometimes for crimes of a very adult nature, but there was no way she could condone executing someone for being born a magician. Perhaps she would have felt differently about it if she hadn't been a magician herself, but she was. And besides, she had come to care deeply for Olivia.

"She cannot be blamed for existing," she said, firmly. "And if Sir Sidney's mad plan is necessary, she will be our only hope."

"Follow the river," Alexander said, changing the subject. "The airstrip is two miles away from the city."

Gwen looked down at the countryside as they turned and followed the river to the west. There were signs that hundreds, perhaps thousands, of people had fled the city, probably followed by the undead. She couldn't see any signs of organised resistance, however; it was quite possible that the soldiers had fled or simply already been overwhelmed. But the Tsar's plans had to have been badly damaged by Gwen's arrival, she told herself. He couldn't have been expecting her.

"There it is," Alexander said. "I suggest you put us down outside the gate."

The Russian airstrip looked primitive, Gwen decided, but it hardly mattered. A large airship, somehow cruder than the ones she'd seen at St Petersburg, floated at anchor, while another was perched inside a hanger, ground crews working desperately to prepare her for flight. Gwen dropped down, casting a wary eye around as they touched the ground, then followed Alexander towards the gate. The guards on duty pointed rifles at them as they came into view, shouting orders in Russian. Gwen sighed and kept her hands in view, but prepared herself to shield them both if necessary. The undead had a habit of making everyone paranoid.

Alexander shouted at the guards in Russian and a brief discussion occurred, before the guards waved them forward and into the complex. A handful of soldiers sat on the hard earth, their weapons close at hand, playing cards; behind them, a squadron of Cossacks sat next to their horses, eying the newcomers suspiciously. Alexander ignored them all magnificently as he strode towards the nearest building, which was guarded by yet more soldiers. Inside, Gwen could hear the sound of shouting. When they strode inside, they saw a dozen officers perched around a table, arguing over who was in command.

She watched, impatiently, as Alexander introduced himself, then explained to the officers what had happened. Gwen didn't understand a word, but she had the very definite impression that the Russians had lost contact with Moscow and didn't know what to do, while they'd seen enough refugees to give them the idea that something had gone badly wrong. It seemed to take hours – a glance at her watch told her that it had been twenty minutes – before Alexander assumed command of the airstrip.

"We'll send messengers to the garrisons," he said. "Assuming the undead haven't reached them first, we should be able to get them to work with us."

Gwen nodded. The Russian officers kept sending her glances, as if they couldn't quite believe their eyes. "And the airships?" she asked.

"Should be able to reach St Petersburg," Alexander said. "How do you plan to get your people from the palace to here?"

"I don't know yet," Gwen said. "What sort of supplies do you have here?"

There was a long discussion between Alexander and his new subordinates, then he turned back to her. "Not much," he said, regretfully. "Just gas and fuel for the airships and not much else."

"The fuel might come in handy," Gwen said. She'd used fire to burn undead, but it drained her badly. With a little ingenuity they might be able to build a primitive flamethrower. "Can you have them make up a barrel for me to take back to the palace?"

"Of course," Alexander said. "And when you come back, please will you bring my family?"

"I will certainly try," Gwen said.

She knew it wouldn't be easy. Sir Sidney would almost certainly worry that Alexander might take the airships and flee, leaving the foreigners to the mercy of the undead. He'd be very tempted to keep his family until the rest of the foreigners were out of the palace, ensuring that Alexander would stay at the airstrip. But even if he did treat them as hostages, the rest of the Russian crew might take the airships anyway ...

"Thank you," Alexander said. He took her hand and kissed it. "And thank you for saving our lives."

Gwen nodded, waited for the Russians to come back with a large barrel of fuel, then carried it back into the sky. It would be needed, desperately, at the palace.

∗∗∗

"My Aunt is screaming," Raechel said. "Will she be safe in her bedroom?"

Olivia barely heard her. The sound of whispering was growing louder and louder in her head, no matter what she did. She jammed her hands over her ears, even though she knew it was futile. The whispering was a mental attack, rather than a normal sound. Somehow, she managed to stagger over to the window, just in time to see the first wave of undead charge towards the palace. Behind them, a second set of undead waited, with cold inhuman patience. It was out of character for them, Olivia noted. They were normally not particularly subtle.

"The Tsar must be directing the attack personally," she said. "But where is he?"

She cast her eyes towards the buildings that might have served as vantage points, then realised it was a waste of time. The Tsar could be studying them through a thousand undead eyes. She wondered, briefly, just how many undead could host his thoughts before his mind snapped completely, then decided it didn't matter. They would either face the Tsar or a swarm of undead large enough to have their own intelligence.

A moaning sound echoed through the undead as the first wave piled into the barricaded door, pushing the defenders back by sheer weight of numbers. Olivia cursed out loud – Raechel looked shocked, then amused, and finally horrified as she saw the danger – as she realised that the undead could just keep pushing until the defences shattered. The defenders could kill hundreds of the undead, yet there would still be thousands more behind them. And even dead bodies could be used to shield the newcomers as they pushed through the defences.

"Keep your sword in your hand," Olivia said, as the moaning came closer. A line of undead were massing below the window, as if they knew where to find her. The thought chilled her to the bone. Did the undead know where she was because the Tsar had used her blood to make himself a Necromancer? Or were the undead simply threatening every window and she merely *thought* she was being targeted? "They're climbing up the walls."

She shuddered as the whispering grew louder, a mocking counterpart to the moaning. The undead were forming a human chain, scrambling up onto their fellows' backs, just to get higher and higher. They felt no pain, nor were they scared of falling to their deaths; moments later, the window shattered as the undead shoved their way through the glass.

Raechel ran forward, sword in hand, and beheaded the first undead to start climbing into the room. It fell backwards, but there was another and another; Raechel waved her sword like a demon, slicing through them one by one. Olivia gathered herself, summoned all her magic and broadcast a single command to the undead. GO AWAY. They seemed to hesitate, just long enough for Raechel to behead several more of them, before a tidal wave of whispering drove Olivia backwards. The undead gathered themselves and resumed the advance.

There was a thunderous crash as ... *something* fell from high overhead, squashing the undead as it landed on them. Olivia had a brief glimpse of something that looked like a piano, then shook her head in awe as the undead fell away. For a moment, they had a chance to catch their breath. Raechel was breathing heavily, sweat pouring down her face and staining her dress, but she was grinning from ear to ear. Her dress was ripped and torn where the undead had clawed at it before she'd killed them.

"I've met more grabby men," she said, looking down at her bodice. "And ones who did more damage."

Olivia had to smile, despite the whispering in her head. Raechel's Aunt would probably have a fit of a vapours when she saw her niece, although she *had* saved Olivia's life. No matter what she'd tried to do, the whispering had made it so hard to do anything, but stand there and watch. She found it hard to even *think* clearly.

There was a crash from outside as something hit the wall. Olivia frowned, turning her attention back to the window, just as an undead came rocketing through the shattered window and landed on the floor. The creature was barely halfway to its feet when Raechel sliced its head off with a blow from her sword, then kicked the head back out of the window. But the next creature was already on its way.

"We need to block the window," Olivia said. She tried to think of something they could use, but there was nothing left in the room, apart from the bed and wardrobes. "Do you think we can move the wardrobes?"

"They're bolted to the walls," Raechel said. "We looked at them while you were asleep."

"Shit," Olivia muttered. They were pushed to the limits guarding one window. It was far too likely that someone else would lose, allowing the undead a chance to get into the building and start attacking from behind. Once that happened, it was all over. "What else can we do?"

Another undead hit the side of the window and broke its skull. Olivia watched him fall, an oddly peaceful expression on his grey face, feeling sick. The undead didn't care how many of their own were killed, as long as they got to the living inside. Raechel stared at it, then shook her head in disbelief. The excitement was wearing off, leaving terror in its wake.

"Olivia," she said slowly, "how long is this going to go on for?"

Olivia shuddered as another undead caught hold of the window. Raechel shoved her sword into its throat, then pushed hard. The undead toppled backwards, taking her sword with it as it fell. Olivia swore, then passed Raechel her sword. It wasn't as if there was any other choice.

"It will go on until we die," she said, hoping and praying that Gwen would get back before the defenders collapsed. "Just keep killing them as long as you can."

***

Gwen let out a breath as she saw the ranks of the undead surrounding the palace, some pushing at the main doors while others were either climbing the walls or trying to throw their comrades through the window. It looked as if the defenders were holding out, but there were too many holes in the defences for them to resist indefinitely. Gritting her teeth, she hovered above the horde, struggling to open the barrel. The Russians had screwed the lid on far too tight.

Finally, she used magic to open it and started to pour the contents on the undead below. They didn't seem to notice as she washed fuel over their bodies, even though it was falling down from high overhead. But then, they had almost no sensitivity in their bodies left, according to Olivia. It made sense. If they couldn't be distracted by knife wounds and bullet shots, they were unlikely to notice a little light rain.

As soon as the barrel was empty, Gwen dropped it on their heads, then summoned fire. The sudden wave of flame surprised even her, the wave of heat sending her upwards at speed. It was impossible to hurt herself directly using magic, but the side-effects could still be lethal – and she'd used fuel to cause the blaze, rather than more than a spark from her own magic. But the flames were magnificent, burning through the undead at terrifying speed. She used magic to push them here and there, trying to sweep up as many undead as possible, then added flames of her own to burn the undead away from the building. Flames spread through the Moscow streets as the undead seemed to waver, then pulled back from the building.

Gwen hesitated – *that* wasn't normal behaviour – then threw extra bursts of fire after the retreating undead. Several nearby buildings caught fire, flushing out the undead who'd been hiding in the shadows. A number of burning undead hurled themselves towards the defenders, then stopped as Gwen picked them off from high overhead. She dropped lower, low enough to allow the defenders to see her clearly, then felt an odd tickle at her mind.

Lady Gwen? Is that you?

Simone, Gwen thought. Clearly, she did have some broadcasting talent, although not as much as might have been useful. *Yes, it's me.*

Sir Sidney greeted her as she stepped through what remained of the main doors. The undead had caused havoc, tearing through wooden barricades as if they were made of paper. She sucked in a breath as she saw one of the elderly diplomats, his body lying on the ground without its head. The pang of guilt almost sent her to her knees. She'd never bothered to learn the man's name before he died. Now, she felt as if she should at least have *known*.

"We almost lost before you arrived," he said. Outside, the flames were licking higher, despite the cold weather. It would be a miracle if they didn't spread to the palace, creating yet another hazard for the defenders. "We can't stay here for long."

"I know," Gwen said. She ran through it in her head. There were nearly two hundred people in the palace; British, French and Russians. She knew, all too well, that she couldn't carry them all to the airships before the Tsar intervened. It wouldn't take more than a handful of undead to destroy the airstrip and kill the guards. "Simone – just how far can you broadcast?"

The French girl hesitated. She looked tired, her yellow dress stained with blood, and yet she still managed to look striking. Gwen wondered, nastily, why she didn't wear something more suitable. She had no idea what fashion was like in France these days, but wearing trousers could make the difference between escape and certain death. Simone wouldn't look half so pretty as one of the undead.

"Several miles, if I have someone to hear," Simone said. If she'd heard Gwen's unguarded thoughts, she gave no sign of it. "*You* heard me."

"I'll fly you to the airships," Gwen said. Simone could communicate with her at a distance, she hoped. "And then we have to start thinking about what to do next."

She hesitated. An idea – in its own way as insane as Sir Sidney's idea – had just struck her. If she made her presence very obvious, she could attract the attention of the Russian magicians ... and then kill them, allowing the airship to fly over the city. But it was far too risky. The Russians might have enough magicians left to kill her and bring down the airship ...

"We *know* what we have to do next," Sir Sidney said. His voice was calm, but he spoke in deadly earnest. "One of us has to become a rival controller of the undead."

Gwen swallowed, her throat suddenly dry. "And who is going to volunteer for this ... madness?"

"Me," Sir Sidney said. He looked down at the bloodstained floor. "It was my idea."

Chapter Thirty-Two

wen felt almost dazed as they made their way towards Olivia's room, as if she were asleep and having a nightmare. She felt as if she was looking at disaster – predicable disaster – and yet she could do nothing to stop it. Sir Sidney would, at the very least, become one of the undead, even if he would be under Olivia's control rather than the Tsar's. And even if the mad scheme succeeded entirely, he would still be an undead monster.

The thought hurt, more than she cared to admit, and she wasn't entirely sure why. She *liked* Sir Sidney; he was one of the very few people who'd treated her as an equal from the start, rather than just another weak, feeble and foolish woman. To watch him plan, coldly and calmly, to throw away his life on a mad gamble was horrifying. And yet, for all her power, she knew there was no other choice. She couldn't burn the entire city to the ground, nor could she carry everyone from the palace to the airstrip before the Tsar caught up with them.

And the next assault will finish us, Gwen thought. It puzzled her why the Tsar hadn't launched the next attack already. It wasn't as if he didn't have a suitable supply of cannon fodder. Had her incineration of hundreds of the undead caused some kind of psychic feedback that had harmed the Tsar? It seemed unlikely. None of the other known Necromancers had shown any reaction to losing dozens or even hundreds of the undead.

She had to smile, despite the darkness pervading her mood, when she stepped into Olivia's room. Raechel stood there, sword in hand, her dress liberally spattered with blood and undead brain matter. She was grinning from ear to ear, despite her appearance, enjoying the exhilaration of winning the fight and coming out alive. Gwen smiled back at her, remembering her first real fight and how good it had felt to win. She didn't have the heart to point out that the next assault would definitely finish them.

Sir Sidney frowned as he looked at the bodies and gore on the floor. "Are those safe?"

"They should be," Olivia said. Her voice was weak, but firm. "The only way the infection spreads is through a bite."

That made no sense, Gwen knew, but so much about Necromancy made no sense. Even during the worst of the British experiments into magic, no one had touched on Necromancy, apart from gathering reports from outbreaks around the world. They'd concluded that a necromantic infection wasn't a disease, at least in the conventional sense. Eating necromantic flesh wouldn't turn someone into one of the undead. It took a bite from an undead to start the transformation. But no one knew why.

She pushed the thought aside and knelt down beside Olivia. Her daughter was shivering, only partly through cold. Sweat stood out on her forehead, making her look feverish; her eyes were bright, yet cold. Gwen looked towards the broken window, wishing they could seal the gap completely. But if they pulled back into the interior of the palace, they'd only cut their line of retreat. There was nowhere to go that wouldn't make their situation worse.

"Sir Sidney has a proposal," she said, carefully.

Olivia produced a weak chuckle. "Shouldn't he be asking you for my hand in marriage?"

Gwen smiled; Raechel giggled, outright.

"It isn't that sort of proposal," she said, as Sir Sidney blushed. "It's something rather different."

"I want you to give me some of your blood and turn me into a creature like the Tsar," Sir Sidney said, talking rapidly to overcome his embarrassment. "You can do that, can't you?"

Olivia hesitated, nervously. Gwen didn't blame her. If they made it home, there would be an inquest into the whole affair – and with so many high-ranking diplomats involved, to say nothing of Talleyrand, it would be impossible to cover it up. There would be questions asked about Olivia's continued survival, then urgent suggestions put forward to invoke the Demonic Powers Act and execute her. If Olivia used her powers again, without compulsion, it would only give her enemies ammunition once they realised the truth.

"I don't know," Olivia said, finally. "We don't have a Healer."

Sir Sidney looked at Gwen. "You can Heal, can't you?"

Gwen winced. Healing was *not* one of her skills. Lucy could put a badly wounded person back together easily, Gwen could barely heal herself – and *that* was largely instinctive, given food and drink. In theory, she should have the power; in practice, even months of effort hadn't taught her how to use it. But there was no other Healer in the palace ...

"I shouldn't have killed Gregory," Olivia said, bleakly. "I'm sorry."

"We couldn't have made him cooperate in any case," Gwen said. A fanatic would have been largely immune to Charm. She looked over at Sir Sidney. "I can try, but ... but it would be incredibly dangerous. You might wind up dead – or a soulless monster, Olivia's puppet."

Sir Sidney looked at Olivia for a long moment. "Do you have a better idea?"

"I did manage to influence the creatures slightly," Olivia said. "If the Tsar died ..."

"They'd form a new hive mind of their own," Gwen said. She took a long breath. "I won't force you to do this ..."

She swallowed as her voice trailed away. It would be worse for Sir Sidney, she knew; the experiment might fail completely, leaving him a shambling monster. But it wouldn't end there, not when he'd killed himself. His soul would go to Hell for suicide, even though he was sacrificing himself for the good of the entire mission. It didn't seem fair, somehow.

Perhaps there's an exception for someone who kills himself for the good of others, she thought, bitterly. Religion had never been a large part of her life, not since David had driven away one tutor by demanding to know why Caesar and

Cicero were in a hell they'd never heard of, as they'd both lived and died before Jesus Christ. *Or perhaps he simply doesn't believe in God.*

"I can't think of anything else," Olivia said. She looked up at Sir Sidney's pale face "If we do this ..."

She shook her head. "*When* do you want to do this?"

"Lady Gwen has to fly Simone to the airstrip," Sir Sidney said. "I can wait until she gets back."

"I bet you can," Raechel muttered.

She glared at all three of them, angrily. "This is crazy! This is ... obscene! You're talking about killing yourself and you don't even know it will work!"

"There's no alternative," Sir Sidney said. "We don't have any other means of fighting our way out of this. Or can you suggest something?"

Raechel glared at him, but said nothing.

"Take Simone to the airstrip," Sir Sidney ordered Gwen. "We will ... we will do it when you get back."

Gwen nodded, then left the room. Simone was waiting for her, carrying a small bag in one hand and a pistol in the other. Gwen wondered, absently, just how well the French woman could shoot, then decided it was probably immaterial. The undead were unlikely to be deterred by the small feminine pistol, even if she shot them in the head. They'd just keep going until she managed to cripple them.

"My father wanted me to take a handful of papers with me," Simone said, lifting the bag. "Is that all right?"

"As long as they include safe conducts," Gwen said. "We're going to need them."

She sighed. With war between Britain and France so close, travelling over French territory would be very dangerous without formal permission from a French representative. But she suspected the French would be very tempted to shoot down the airship if they knew she was on it, no matter what Talleyrand said. Her death would ensure a power struggle in Cavendish Hall.

"They do," Simone assured her. "When do we go?"

"Now," Gwen said, as she turned to lead the other girl up to the roof. "And you'd better work on charming the Russians at the far end."

Janet was waiting for them on the roof, her eyes downcast. Gwen sighed, inwardly; she hadn't had a chance to talk privately with Janet since she'd been forced to reveal herself, but it was clear that the maid had taken the news badly. To know she'd shared a room with a noblewoman powerful enough to overrule Lady Standish on a whim ... Janet had to have been replaying her actions in her mind, looking for something – anything – that Gwen might hold against her. But she hadn't done anything even remotely objectionable.

"I'll take you too," Gwen said. She could carry two people without straining herself – and besides, Janet was an innocent. "Get ready to fly."

Simone gave her a sharp look, but Gwen refused to rise to the bait. Instead, she concentrated on keeping her mental shields in place and waited for Janet to finish saying goodbye to Romulus. She looked away hastily when Janet and Romulus shared a kiss, then smiled at Simone's reaction. The French girl scowled at her, then looked nervous, clearly remembering that Gwen could simply drop her over the city and swear blind that it had been a terrible accident.

"We'll be there in no time," Gwen said, remembering how badly Janet had reacted to the airship. "And don't worry about a thing."

"Apart from the horde of undead below us," Simone said. "And the difficulty in navigating all the way to Paris. And the Russians deciding they don't want to help us. And the undead coming after us ..."

"Shut up!" Gwen ordered. She caught hold of them both with her magic, then leapt into the air. Below, the ranks of the undead were slowly reforming, as the Tsar directed reinforcements towards the palace. "We need to hurry."

She forced herself to fly faster. The next attack would be far more serious and it would fall on already weakened defences. It might just be enough to crush the defenders ... and condemn them all to join the ranks of the undead.

***

Olivia sucked in her breath as Sir Sidney left the room after making her promise not to hesitate when the time came to use her powers. The thought was horrifying, worse – somehow – than raising bodies from the dead and making them her slaves. She knew that the Tsar had become an abomination, an offence against nature ... and Sir Sidney wanted to become something comparable. Maybe inserting another mind into the undead gestalt would work, Olivia told herself, or maybe it would simply create a controller without anything to control. How *did* the Tsar control his slaves anyway?

It wasn't easy to direct the undead, Olivia knew. The more complex the command, the harder it was to get them to do what the Necromancer wanted. It was quite possible that the Tsar had real trouble controlling so many of the undead, no matter his intentions and expanded mentality. *That*, more than anything else, might explain why the undead had fallen back in the wake of Gwen's return to the palace. The Tsar was regrouping, re-establishing his control and preparing for another attack.

But where *was* he? The whispering had faded as the undead fell back, but it was still present, an uneasy feeling at the back of her mind that threatened to overwhelm her the moment she lost control. She'd wondered if the Tsar had claimed exclusive control of his undead – she hadn't tried to control the undead in London before Master Thomas's death – but it seemed that the Tsar's control wasn't exclusive, merely very powerful. And then a thought struck her and she blinked in surprise. Could the Tsar have overlooked something?

She looked over at Raechel. "I need to try something," she said, as she lay down on the bed, taking deep breaths. "Can you watch me for a while?"

"Of course," Raechel said, although she looked nervous. She had no magic. If something went badly wrong, there was nothing she could do to help. "What do you want me to do?"

Olivia hesitated. Confessing any form of weakness still struck her as a very bad idea, even though she *liked* Raechel. Liking anyone on the streets was a form of weakness in and of itself, not least because a friend could turn on you with terrifying speed. But she knew she needed someone, even if it was just a comforting presence. The undead would find it harder to get into her mind if she had someone helping her.

"Just hold my hand," she said. "And squeeze every few minutes."

She allowed Raechel to take her hand, then closed her eyes and concentrated on the whispering. It grew louder within seconds, suggesting she was growing more practiced with her powers, no matter how unpleasant she found the thought. The undead were suddenly all around her, great sweeping flickers of emotion and a powerful drive to feed, all firmly fettered by the Tsar's giant thoughts. Olivia realised, suddenly, that the Tsar was definitely having problems controlling so many undead at once. His mind hadn't expanded far enough to control them all.

Their minds died the moment they were infected, she thought, recalling Gregory's desperate struggle to preserve the Tsar's brain. His body had been allowed to transform, but his brain had been left alive. *He can't expand his mind into them easily.*

Another thought struck her and she winced. *Is that why they wanted me?*

She felt a sudden sensation in her hand, which puzzled her until she remembered that Raechel was holding it. Bracing herself, she threw her mind deeper into the undead gestalt, looking for the undead she'd raised at Gregory's command. She'd *heard* them in the underground complex, before she'd helped turn the Tsar into a monster; they hadn't been destroyed. Gregory had wanted to continue his experiments, after all. And even though the Tsar might be able to direct them, they were *hers*. If there was any justice in the universe ...

Olivia almost laughed as she found herself staring out of the undead creature's eyes. It was in a cage, surrounded by a dozen others, all part of the same gestalt. The Tsar, it seemed, had forgotten about them, as had the other undead. But then, why not? They were hardly living creatures, nor were they openly hostile. They'd just been left in a cage to rot.

She contemplated the cage for a long moment. It was almost childishly simple; it wouldn't have kept a living breathing human inside for more than a few seconds. A prison cell required proper locks, all on the right side of the door. Instead, she directed the undead to approach the lock and start pushing at it with its hands. Human intelligence, combined with undead resiliency, could simply pick the lock. She allowed herself a smile as the cage opened, then directed the undead out of the cage and into the passageway. And then she muttered a curse as they came face to face with another group of undead.

Walk past them, she directed. It was odd to realise that her undead barely *saw* the others – and, she assumed, vice versa. The undead were simply uninterested in other undead, even if they weren't part of the same gestalt. *And then up the stairs.*

She smiled as she felt another squeeze on her hand, then felt a sudden flash of panic as she realised just how closely she'd mingled herself with the undead. It gave her strength as she pulled herself free, then fell back into her own body, unable to escape the impression that she'd just fallen onto the bed from a great height. Her head span as she looked up – for a long moment, she thought she saw undead features pasted over Raechel's face – then realised just how dry her mouth was. Pain flared through her head and she winced in pain.

"Water," she croaked.

Raechel passed her a glass, her eyes deeply worried. Olivia struggled to sit upright – her strength seemed to have deserted her completely – and finally had to allow Raechel to dribble water into her mouth. It was hard to swallow, but she forced herself to drink – and then accept assistance to sit upright. Raechel kept a worried eye on her even as Olivia regained some of her strength, as if she could hear the whispering herself. Now she'd reformed her links with her own undead, the whispering seemed to be so omnipresent that Olivia couldn't help wondering if it was more than just an echo in her head.

"I need to speak to Gwen," she said, when she could speak properly again. "Is she back?"

"Not yet," Raechel said. She looked down at Olivia. "Are you sure you want to do this?"

Olivia shrugged. There were too many unknowns to take it lightly. If they failed to turn Sir Sidney into another controller, they'd have thrown away his life for nothing. But if it worked ... at the very least, the Tsar would have to struggle to maintain control of his undead, fighting Sir Sidney for their servitude. It would provide a distraction that might, perhaps, allow the rest of the party a chance to make it out of the city. But it could also drive Sir Sidney mad.

"I don't think I have a choice," she said. *Gwen* wouldn't use Charm to compel her to obey, Olivia knew, and Sir Sidney had no magic. But he would probably try to guilt her into it if she baulked. "If this works, we would have a fighting chance to get out."

"Sure," Raechel snarled. "And if it failed, he'd be dead and we'd still be trapped."

Olivia smiled at her. "Are you sweet on him?"

Raechel coloured. "No," she said. "But I don't want to see him die."

"Me neither," Olivia said. "But if there's one lesson I've learnt in my life, it's that everyone dies."

Chapter Thirty-Three

ir Sidney was waiting for Gwen on the roof when she returned, carrying another barrel of fuel and a large crate of explosives with her. There hadn't been a second attack, she noted to her relief, but it was clear that the Tsar was gathering his forces. Sir Sidney smiled at her as she put the crate down on the rooftop, then nodded towards the way down into the palace. Gwen briefly explained what she'd brought to Romulus, then followed Sir Sidney, feeling an odd mixture of emotions. He was walking to his death and there was nothing she could do to stop him.

He turned to face her as soon as they were alone, completely out of earshot. "If this doesn't work, if I go mad, I want you to kill me," he said. "Burn my body to ash."

Gwen eyed him, darkly. "There's still time to change your mind," she said, unsure why she was feeling so conflicted. She liked Sir Sidney, but she was also pragmatic enough to understand that they had no choice, even if she didn't *like* it. "You could think of something else."

He scowled. "Like what?"

"I wish I knew," Gwen said. She considered, briefly, but came up with nothing. "I wish there was a better way."

Sir Sidney sighed. It struck her, suddenly, that she was feeling *attraction*, the feeling she hadn't let herself feel since Sir Charles had betrayed her so deeply. She'd realised, in hindsight, that he was manipulating her, yet at the time she'd felt flattered by his attentions – and angry at her mother for her hypocrisy. He'd taken advantage of her feelings and wormed his way into her heart. Sir Sidney had done none of those things. He'd just treated her as a person in her own right.

But so did Sir Charles, she thought, dejectedly.

"I can't think of one," Sir Sidney said. "We go through the sewers; the undead can see or sense in the dark, allowing them to hunt us down. We go through the streets; we get overwhelmed by weight of numbers. You can't fly us all to safety – and besides, they'd attack the airstrip. Our only hope is to try to dislodge his control of the undead."

"I know," Gwen said, bitterly. "I'm sorry."

Alexander had, at least, managed to rally the garrisons outside the city. It was clear that Gwen had *definitely* managed to upset the Tsar's plans; his attempts to infect the garrisons had failed, once some of the refugees had alerted the soldiers to the threat. The Russian soldiers seemed torn between wanting to try to liberate the city and merely sealing the undead inside the city, although Gwen knew *that* wouldn't last. There was no way they could hold back the undead indefinitely, once the Tsar decided he was ready to start expanding his control.

But the soldiers couldn't help the foreigners. There truly was no other choice.

She braced herself – acting in such a forward manner went against everything her mother had taught her, at least when it came to dealing with men – and leaned forward, bringing her lips to touch his. He started in surprise, even though it was the second time she'd kissed him, then kissed her back. Gwen felt her heartbeat starting to race, suddenly understanding why Raechel had allowed herself to make love to so many men, then she forced the feeling to the back of her mind. There was no time to explore her emotions any longer.

"For luck," she said, pulling back and breaking contact. "And I'm sorry."

"Don't worry," Sir Sidney said. "There are worse ways to go."

Gwen followed him into Olivia's bedroom, remembering some of the more morbid stories from India and China. It had seemed a mark of British superiority that English criminals were merely hanged, rather than chopped to pieces or tortured to death. What sort of state killed minor criminals by slowly bleeding them until they died? But she couldn't imagine anything worse than becoming one of the undead.

"I need to talk to you," Olivia said. "I managed to make contact with some of my undead."

Gwen frowned as Olivia explained. "Where are they now?"

"Making their way onto the streets," Olivia said, after a moment. "I don't think they're noticeable as long as they don't do anything to attract the Tsar's attention."

"Then keep them out of sight," Gwen ordered. She had no idea how they could use this new tool, but she wanted to hold it in reserve until she came up with a plan. "Sidney?"

Sir Sidney pulled a knife from his belt. "I am ready," he said. His voice didn't waver. "And you, Lady Olivia?"

Olivia looked nervous. "This could go badly wrong," she warned. "And ..."

"I know," Sir Sidney said. "Lady Gwen?"

"I'll do my best," Gwen promised. She reached for her magic, feeling it sparkling around her fingers. Why was it, she asked herself silently, that destructive magic was so much easier than constructive magic? Healing was *definitely* not an easy magic to master, but pure Healers seemed to be able to acquire far greater levels of skill than Master Magicians. "But ..."

She shook her head, fighting down the urge to cry – or to kiss him, again. It had been years since she'd cried; she'd never even broken down after Sir Charles had betrayed her, fearful of confirming the thoughts and prejudices of those who saw her as a weak and feeble woman. But now ... now she wanted to cry. Instead, she gathered herself, drew on her mental disciplines, and stood upright.

"I am ready," she said. She pushed her doubts to one side and took up position beside Sir Sidney, who lay down on the bed, looking for all the world like a human sacrifice.

"Do it."

Blood transfusion was not an exact science, Gwen knew, as Raechel picked up the needle and carefully inserted it into Olivia. Sometimes, it worked; sometimes, the patient had an allergic reaction that killed them, for reasons modern science had yet to explain. It was quite possible that Olivia's blood alone would kill Sir Sidney, even though it hadn't killed the Tsar. Gwen couldn't help feeling queasy as Raechel removed the needle from Olivia, then injected her blood into Sir Sidney. And if there should have been more preparations involved, Gwen knew, they had no idea what they might be.

There was a long pause. Sir Sidney's breathing grew ragged and harsh, then he recovered. Gwen watched him nervously, then nodded to Raechel to move to the other side of the room. If she had to act quickly to burn Sir Sidney, it was better not to have Raechel anywhere nearby. And then she nodded to the man. It was time.

Sir Sidney raised the knife until it was level with his eyes, hesitated a moment, then stabbed down into his chest. Gwen had seen more horror and violence in the last year than any other noble-born woman in Britain, but the sight of his suicide still shocked her. Blood bubbled up from the wound, then started to run down his chest and soak the bed. Olivia let out an odd sound and took a step forward, pressing her hand against Sir Charles's chest. Gwen felt her head twist suddenly as she sensed her adopted daughter draw on her powers.

"Heal him," Olivia snapped at her. "Now!"

Gwen forced her reaction aside, placed her hands on Sir Sidney's head and concentrated, trying to focus her magic through his body. It felt *vile*, utterly unlike any other magic she'd tried to use, as if there was something fundamentally *wrong* with what she was doing. Her hands felt as if she'd buried them in a cesspit. The reaction was so strong that it was all she could do not to throw up on the spot, despite her experience. And the touch of Olivia's magic was almost worse.

Life energy, she thought, suddenly. Olivia's power was drawing on the remains of Sir Sidney's life, rather than her own magic. *If the prospective undead is dying, there's more energy already in place to tap and convert. But if the undead is dead already, it needs to draw life energy from the Necromancer.*

She forced herself to concentrate as Olivia's magic surged towards Sir Sidney's brain, threatening to convert him into one of the undead. The sheer surge of power shocked her; she forced herself to hang on grimly, trying to keep Sir Sidney alive and reasonably well. But there was a long moment when she felt as though she'd failed completely, before she sensed a spark of energy flowing through Sir Sidney's mind. And then there was a much larger surge and she felt herself flung back from his corpse.

"Gwen," Raechel called. "What happened?"

Gwen shook her head as she picked herself off the floor. On the other side of the room, Olivia was doing the same. It had been a physical reaction, of that she was sure, but where had it come from? Sir Sidney was no Mover. Had the magic somehow triggered *her* magic, she asked herself; had she thrown *herself* away from Sir Sidney? Or had something else happened? Perhaps God Himself had interceded to prevent them committing a dreadful sin ...

She looked over at Sir Sidney, just in time to see his face take on the grey tone of the undead. His eyes were tightly closed, but by the way they were twitching she was sure that they too were transforming into something else. She watched as his fists trembled, then his entire body jerked violently. It was impossible to tell if they'd succeeded or not. Sir Sidney just wasn't reacting like the Tsar.

"Stay back," she ordered sharply, as Raechel started to move towards the convulsing corpse. "Do *not* go anywhere near him."

She summoned fire, ready to burn Sir Sidney to ash if necessary. His body jerked again, then his eyes snapped open, revealing – as she'd suspected – a dull yellowish glow. He sat upright slowly, moving with a cold deliberateness that chilled her to the bone. But at least it wasn't the fast movements of the undead. He looked more as if he were relearning to move his body.

His mouth opened, slowly. "I ..."

Gwen shuddered at the sound. He sounded *dead*, as if his soul was gone completely, and yet he was *talking*. No other undead, apart from the Tsar, had been able to *talk*. All they'd been able to do was moan. Sir Sidney paused, opening and closing his mouth a few times as his lips worked soundlessly, then started to speak again.

"Gwen," he said. His voice was so harsh it took Gwen several seconds to understand that he'd spoken her name. "It ... worked."

"Good," Gwen said, keeping the flames crackling around her fingertips. It was easier to increase the strength of her fires than restart them, if necessary. "How are you feeling?"

"Dead," Sir Sidney said. His voice sounded better this time, as if practice was making it easier to talk. "I feel ... strange. My body is heavy. Yet my mind is bound to it."

Olivia walked around Sir Sidney until she was standing near Gwen. "Can you hear the whispering?"

"I can hear more than whispering," Sir Sidney said. "I can hear the Tsar's great thoughts thundering in my head. I can sense his mind struggling for control. The undead are ... odd."

Gwen watched grimly as Sir Sidney rose to his feet. His movements were deliberate, as if he could no longer rely on his body. She couldn't help remembering some of the young magicians who went out drinking and came back to Cavendish Hall struggling to walk in a straight line. Was Sir Sidney effectively drunk or had the link between his mind and his body been badly damaged? She would have bet on the latter.

"I know," Olivia whispered. "But can you control them?"

"I don't know," Sir Sidney said. "I feel so ... heavy."

Olivia looked over at Gwen. "We'll take him down and test his powers on some of the dead," she said. "If we have succeeded ..."

Gwen nodded, then turned to Raechel. "You go first and tell them what to expect," she said. The last thing they needed was one of the guards beheading Sir Sidney when they saw his face. "I want to stay behind him."

Raechel nodded and slipped out of the room. Gwen hesitated, then motioned for Sir Sidney to start walking. He obeyed, staggering slightly as he moved, as if he didn't quite know how to walk properly. It was odd, given how fast some of the undead could move, but perhaps unsurprising. His body had been effectively crippled. Gwen had seen stroke victims struggling to relearn how to use their bodies, even after a Healer had mended the damage, but this was worse. His body was literally dead.

What does this mean, she asked herself, *for the Tsar*?

She shuddered at the thought as they slowly walked down the stairs. If the Tsar was really nothing more than a healthy mind in a dead body, just how long could his mind last? But Gregory had to have done more to the Tsar than she'd realised, even if she'd done something comparable. Could his body be caught permanently between living and undead? Her head hurt when she tried to reason it out. If the Tsar's heart was no longer pumping, how was he getting the oxygen to his brain? And if he wasn't getting oxygen, why wasn't he dead – or deader?

"I need to walk faster," Sir Sidney said. "But my body will not obey."

"Perhaps that is for the best," Gwen said. If the Tsar was mad now, Sir Sidney might well go the same way. "Let them see you can't chase them."

They came off the stairwell and through what had once been the ballroom. Defenders – British, French and Russian – stared at them in disbelief. Gwen allowed them to see the flames dancing over her hand, hoping it would provide some reassurance. Lord Standish looked torn between horror and a strange kind of delight, knowing that Sir Sidney's new status meant that he was back in command of the mission. Gwen silently promised herself that she would slap him down if he tried to assert himself too much. There was no time for a power struggle in the ranks.

The handful of dead defenders had been placed in a side room. Gwen cursed out loud as she saw shapes moving in the darkness, then generated a light globe and cursed again as she saw the rats near the bodies. A thought struck her and she reached out with her magic, catching one of the rats and yanking it through the air until it dangled in front of Sir Sidney. The rat squeaked and struggled helplessly against the invisible force holding it in place.

Behind her, Olivia let out an odd sound. "It might be better to let me use the rat," Olivia said, quickly. "We don't want to split his mind too far."

Gwen nodded and hastily pulled the rat away from Sir Sidney. A handful of young Necromancers had discovered their powers by accidentally bringing a beloved family pet back to life – or, rather, to a shambling mockery of life.

Using undead rats was risky, she knew, but there were few other weapons at their disposal. Besides, there were so many rats in Moscow that they would never run out of them.

"You want to bring a rat back to life," Raechel said. "Is that *wise*?"

"I wish I knew," Gwen said. Could the undead infection spread from a rat to a human? There were no reports of it, but she knew that meant nothing. Most undead infections tended to come from murky origins. "What else do we have to use?"

She snapped the rat's neck, then dropped it in front of Olivia and returned her attention to Sir Sidney. He was kneeling in front of the body of one of the defenders, almost as if he were at prayer. Moments later, the body twitched and jerked to life, shambling madly around the room. Gwen watched, grimly, as two other bodies rose, before Sir Sidney almost collapsed from exhaustion. The Tsar had had an advantage, she realised grimly. He'd picked on live victims for his first display of power.

"I am ready," Sir Sidney said. He looked at Gwen, then staggered back to his feet. His undead followed him, shambling forwards like dogs. "Let us go to confront the Tsar."

"With three undead?" Raechel demanded. "Are you sure?"

"It will be enough," Sir Sidney insisted. His voice sounded stronger now, despite his obvious weakness. "I can try to force my way into his gestalt, to take control of his creatures, to fight it out with him and win you time to evacuate the palace. But it will not last for long."

He started to walk towards the door, followed by the undead. Gwen shuddered, looked over at the gathering crowd of undead rats, then nodded for Olivia and Raechel to stay back as she followed Sir Sidney out towards the main door. She shuddered again as a line of rats streaked past her, gambolling around Sir Sidney even though they were under Olivia's control. They didn't moan, but there was something eerie about their silence.

She gritted her teeth as the defenders stared in horror at the undead, their hands clutching their weapons tightly. Gwen hoped and prayed that no one would take a shot at Sir Sidney. A bullet might not impede one of the undead, but God alone knew what it would do to him.

Outside, the smell of burned flesh was almost overpowering. Gwen gagged, but managed to stay on her feet. Sir Sidney showed no sign of noticing as he stopped, just outside the barricades. Perhaps that wasn't surprising, Gwen thought; the undead, if Olivia was right, had no sense of smell. She heard, faintly, the sound of whispering as the undead registered their presence ...

... And then swarmed forward, moaning with rage.

Chapter Thirty-Four

he rats, Olivia rapidly discovered, were much – much – easier to reanimate and control than human beings. Perhaps there was less of a gap between living or dead rats than there was between living or dead humans, or perhaps it was their far simpler minds, but she found herself almost taking pleasure in bringing more and more dead rats under her control. The rats she touched originally bit others, who in turn brought others into the gestalt. By the time Olivia directed the rats to swarm outside and join Sir Sidney, she had over seven hundred under her control and more on the way.

They'd be a major problem for a living army, she knew, but the undead would largely ignore them unless they worked together. She directed them to mass behind Sir Sidney, trying to see through hundreds of ratty eyes. It was harder to see through their eyes than control them, but she could still direct them to prepare to attack. A swarm of fifty rats, chewing at dead flesh, would bring down an undead within seconds, then leave it crippled and helpless on the ground. And then she saw the horde of undead thundering forward, moaning with rage ...

... And then she felt Sir Sidney's mental commands reaching out to grab the undead, screaming his orders into their gestalt. There was a long pause, then the first row of undead stopped, only to be pushed over and trodden on by the second or third row. Olivia staggered under the impact as Sir Sidney's command – a simple STOP – slammed into her head, even though it wasn't directed at her. The undead seemed completely confused; some stopping, others still lunging towards Sir Sidney, right into his influence. For a long moment, Olivia thought they'd won.

Olivia shuddered as she felt the Tsar, suddenly aware of what was happening, reach out his mind towards the undead. His orders washed through the gestalt, driving out Sir Sidney's orders, but they were weaker, somehow. It took Olivia a long moment to realise that he was trying to issue orders that were simply too complex, given the situation. The undead were torn between a simple command to stop and the more complex commands to ignore Sir Sidney and charge.

But they can't ignore him, she realised, as she understood – finally – the link between her blood and the undead. *They appear to be speaking with the same voice. Neither of them are actually superior, so one set of orders cancels another, only to be cancelled in turn.*

She hesitated, then directed the rats into the fray. The more undead to be wiped out while they were confused, the better, if only because there were millions of rats in the city. Indeed, she could feel others joining the gestalt at the corner of her mind, killed and yanked back to life by undead rats under her control. The ranks of undead staggered, then started to fight one another. It was clear the Tsar was grimly aware of the danger of leaving too many undead too close to Sir Sidney, even though the Tsar hadn't bothered to show himself. He was trying to obliterate the undead who might have followed Sir Sidney before it was too late.

But it's too late for him, Olivia thought, grimly. *We can drive them away from the palace.*

Sir Sidney started to shamble forwards, growing in power with every step. More and more undead were falling under his influence, allowing him to start directing them to attack other undead themselves. It looked like one of the brawls in the Rookery that had so terrified her as a child, ones where there were no rules and no sides. It was every man for himself; Sir Sidney might hold a particular undead under his control, then lose it seconds later to the Tsar. Both controllers were trying desperately to maintain control over as many undead as possible, but Sir Sidney had an unfair advantage. He was simply closer to his undead than was the Tsar.

Gwen walked over to her and frowned. "Are you all right?"

"I feel sick," Olivia confessed, as she pulled her mind away from the rats. The swarms were still spreading, attacking the undead wherever they found them. But it wouldn't be long before the Tsar tried to take control of the rats for himself. Olivia was speaking with the same voice too. "What about you?"

"I've felt better," Gwen confessed. "Can you locate the Tsar?"

Olivia closed her eyes, reaching out towards the undead she'd created. Three of them seemed to be trapped in swarms of undead, as if they were being dragged along by sheer weight of numbers; the remainder were wandering the city. It seemed impossible to locate the Tsar, at least directly. But they could still sense his pulsing thoughts.

"I've sent them after him," Olivia said. "But I don't know where he is now."

Gwen nodded. "Don't worry about it," she said. She looked up, sharply. "I think I have company coming. You and Raechel can get everyone ready to make a run for it."

"I will," Olivia said. "But how should we get out?"

"The river seems the best bet," Gwen said. "Just make damn sure you check the boat thoroughly before everyone gets inside."

Olivia nodded as Gwen turned and threw herself back into the air.

****

Gwen sensed the four magicians as they flew through the air towards her, driven by madness and the Tsar's growing desperation. Two Movers, she decided, and two other magicians with unknown powers. She was fairly sure the Russians didn't have any Masters – they wouldn't have overlooked the one they'd caught if they'd known anything about Master-level magic – but the others could be anything from Blazers to Charmers. They would be dangerous.

She dropped to a rooftop and looked up as the magicians landed around her, their eyes gleaming with power. The two Movers were obvious – Gwen could sense the magic billowing around them – but the remaining two were harder to identify. There was a long pause as they sized her up, hopefully underestimating her. Russia was even less kind to women than England and she hadn't seen any female magicians among the strange monks. It was just possible that they'd take one look at her chest and refuse to take her seriously.

One of the magicians spoke, in Russian. Gwen felt the Charm – powerful Charm – echoing through his words, but did nothing. There was no way to obey when she honestly didn't understand the orders being hurled at her. She gritted her teeth as the Charm grew stronger, then lifted her hand and sent a pulse of magic directly at the Charmer. One of the Movers shielded him, then threw magic back at her. Gwen jumped upwards, then threw another pulse of magic towards the rooftop. It shuddered, forcing the Charmer and the fourth magician to their knees. Moments later, the second Mover caught her with a wave of power, sending her falling back towards the streets. It was useless to resist, so she concentrated on cushioning her landing. The impact took her breath away, but she survived without serious injury.

A pair of undead lunged towards her. Gwen picked them both up with magic and hurled them towards the Charmer, knowing that his Charm would be useless on the undead. He let out a sound like a rat – Gwen's lips twitched; she'd never met a Charmer who wasn't a physical coward – and he called to one of the other magicians. The Mover shredded both of the undead seconds later.

The other Mover landed in front of Gwen. She smiled, charged the street with magic and jumped straight up, relying on her magic to carry her out of the blast range. The Mover had clearly seen the trick from the last time she'd used it, because he shielded himself in time to avoid the worst of the blast, but he still staggered backwards. Gwen recalled the Russian for *sleep* and shouted it as loudly as she could, pushing Charm into her voice. The Russian staggered, long enough to drop the wall of magic protecting him. Gwen drove a burst of magic into his skull and watched as it exploded into chunks of blood and gore.

There was no time to congratulate herself. The other Mover started to throw pieces of debris at her, bombarding her with bricks, stone and pieces of wood. Gwen gritted her teeth, concentrating on shielding herself, then created a dozen separate illusions, each one showing her walking in a different direction. The Mover was distracted long enough for Gwen to blast the lower floors of the building he was standing on, causing the whole structure to begin to collapse into debris. He jumped up into the air and dropped down towards her, wrapped in a haze of magic. Gwen braced herself, then summoned fire and hurled it back at him. Even if he could shield himself, it wouldn't be enough to prevent the fire sucking away the oxygen and suffocating him.

And then Gwen felt an arm wrapped around her neck. She gasped in shock, feeling her magic draining away, as she realised the fourth magician was a Leech, a power-drainer, someone impossible to sense or track through magic. A professional too, part of her mind noted dully, as he started to make it harder for her to breathe. He wasn't trying to grope her, merely to put her to sleep as quickly as possible. And it was clear they wanted her alive. He could have put a knife in her back if he'd wanted to kill her outright.

Bracing herself, she threw her head backwards and slammed it into his chin. His grip loosened and she pulled herself free, reaching for the knife she'd hidden in her sleeve. But he caught her again before she could draw it fully and struggled to hold her in place. Gwen twisted, trying to bring up her knee to strike him in the groin, then felt someone else behind her, too late. The Charmer held her while the Leech returned his grip to her neck. There was a moment of blurriness, then Gwen plunged down into darkness.

***

Olivia was grimly aware of the stares following her and Raechel as she ran into the council room and saw Lord Standish, Romulus and Talleyrand standing there, staring down at a map of Moscow. The shortest route to the river was marked clearly, but no one was sure if there were any boats available – or if the undead could swim. Olivia rather suspected they couldn't, yet they could probably survive underwater. They didn't need to breathe, after all.

She checked on the rats as she caught her breath, trying to see through their eyes. The battle for control between Sir Sidney and the Tsar was only intensifying, both men struggling for dominance. She tried to see Gwen through the ratty eyes, but saw nothing. The rats didn't seem to be capable of recognising individual humans, any more than most undead saw anything more than the life energy in a living human. The rats just kept attacking the undead wherever they saw them.

"We need to start moving," Raechel said, urgently. Her uncle eyed her in surprise. "Lady Gwen and Sir Sidney are distracting the Tsar, but that won't last."

"Then we had better move now," Romulus said. "We won't have much time, whoever wins."

Lord Standish glanced at him, then looked away. "Get everyone together," he ordered one of the Russians. "Hand out the weapons. And then we'll make a rush for the boats."

He looked up at Raechel. "You can go and recover your Aunt," he ordered. "And bring her down here."

Raechel smiled, although the smile didn't quite touch her eyes. "Yes, Uncle," she said. "I'll bring her down, right now."

Olivia followed her as she led the way upstairs to the bedroom they were using as a makeshift prison. The banging Olivia had heard earlier had faded away, leaving the corridor eerily silent. Raechel looked oddly worried as she reached for the key at her belt, then slotted it into the lock. Moments later, the door burst open, revealing a noblewoman who looked to be on the brink of madness. Her face was so horrific that Olivia couldn't help wondering if an undead had got into her room and bitten her. But she was definitely human.

"Raechel!" she shouted, her voice cracking with fury. "You ... you ..."

Raechel drew the sword from her belt and held it out, point first, towards her Aunt. "No, Auntie," she said. "Today you listen to me."

Lady Standish stared at the blade with mad eyes. Olivia smirked, inwardly. No doubt Lady Standish had never anticipated being at her niece's mercy. Judging from what little Raechel had said, Lady Standish hadn't been a very kind Aunt, although it was quite possible that she'd meant well. Most aristocrats did, Olivia had noted; it was just their judgement of what was doing good that was at fault. At least Gwen was smart enough not to assume that her birth automatically made her better than everyone else.

"We are surrounded by millions of undead monsters," Raechel continued. "You are going to walk with us to the boats, where we will get on the river and escape. You are going to keep your mouth firmly shut, do as you are told and help us to escape without screaming, fainting or having a fit of the vapours. And, when we get home, you will surrender control of my inheritance without any further ado."

"But ..." Lady Standish managed to say. "I ..."

Raechel leaned forward, her eyes glinting with near madness herself. She had to be exhausted, Olivia realised suddenly. She'd only been able to catch a few hours of sleep overnight, before the attack had begun. And she'd fought as valiantly as anyone else during the attack itself. No wonder she was tired and cranky.

"You will do as I say, or I will tie you up and carry you," Raechel hissed. "I've had enough of you trying to direct my life. Do as I say or you'll be carried out of here or left to the undead."

Lady Standish glared at her furiously, then nodded slowly, tears dripping from her face. Olivia couldn't tell if it was an attempt to influence her niece or genuine shock, but it hardly mattered. Raechel tore her aunt's dress, making it easier for her to run, then pushed her towards the stairs. Olivia smiled at her, tiredly, then followed Raechel and her aunt as they walked down towards the ground floor. Romulus was handing out weapons as the remaining defenders and women, including Alexander's little girls, gathered in the dance hall.

"Romulus," Lady Standish's strident voice thundered, "I am most displeased with my niece's conduct!"

Romulus turned to face her. Lady Standish stepped backwards in shock. Olivia understood; a society queen, someone so used to reading body language, would be shocked to see the change in her butler. Romulus had moved from someone who obeyed orders to someone who was very different, perhaps issuing orders himself. And Lord Standish wasn't trying to gainsay him. To someone as sensitive as Lady Standish clearly was, that was as good as an advertisement in the newspapers that there had been a shift in power.

"Your niece has been doing very well," Romulus said mildly, although there was an icy edge under his voice. "And I would suggest you keep your voice down. You never know what it might attract."

Olivia caught his eye as Lady Standish staggered away. "What do you want me to do?"

"Lady Gwen hasn't returned," Romulus said. "Do you know where she is?"

Olivia looked up, alarmed. Gwen had said she had company ... and then, what? Other magicians? Gwen was powerful, combining all of the known talents, but she wasn't all-powerful. It was quite possible that Gwen could be overwhelmed by two or three magicians working together, particularly if they were each masters of their own talent. But if so ... was she dead?

"I don't know," she said. She wanted to sit down and start peering through undead eyes until she found her adopted mother, but there was no time. "I'll tell Sir Sidney to start clearing the way for us."

"If he's still sane," Romulus said. He sounded as worried as Olivia felt. "Does he still need to sleep?"

Olivia shrugged. Was *that* why the Tsar hadn't mounted an attack before Gwen had had time to fly to the airstrip and back? If a natural-born Necromancer like herself needed to sleep, what about a created Necromancer? But the Tsar was undead. No one had ever recorded any of the undead needing to sleep. It had never happened before, as far as anyone knew. They sucked on life energy and just kept going.

"I don't know," she said, again. What would *Gwen* want her to do? She knew the answer – Gwen would want her to get everyone out first – but she didn't want to leave Gwen behind, even if she was dead. The thought of Gwen rising again as part of the Tsar's army was horrific. "I'll speak to Sir Sidney."

"We'll be ready in ten minutes, I think," Romulus said. He looked over at Lady Standish, who had sat down in a corner, looking lost. "Some of us excluded, of course."

"You won't be working for her any longer," Olivia noted. "Does it matter?"

"Not really," Romulus said. "But it was important to me to maintain my cover."

Olivia shrugged, then headed outside to find Sir Sidney. The whispering grew louder as she approached him, his commands echoing through the mental atmosphere. She tried to shield her mind as he turned to face her, then forced herself to smile. He looked ghastly, his entire body twitching with the stress of maintaining control of so many undead.

"We're almost ready to run," Olivia said. "Are you ready to support us?"

"Yes," Sir Sidney said. He groaned, as if a moan was trying to escape his lips. "But you should hurry."

Olivia took one last look at him and nodded.

Chapter Thirty-Five

he whispering grew louder as Olivia stepped outside, following Raechel and the rest of the womenfolk. Despite Raechel's protestations, the women were put in the centre of the formation, walking right down the road towards the river. There was no attempt to sneak through the shadows; the undead lurked in nearby buildings, waiting for anyone unwary enough to get too close. Instead, they moved as quickly as they could, right out in the open.

"We'll see them coming," Raechel had muttered, when she'd been told where they would be walking. "But is that a good thing?"

Olivia walked beside her, her eyes half-closed as she reached out towards her army of undead rats. The Tsar didn't seem to be trying to control them – it looked as though he could only maintain control of his army of undead humans, not an army of rats – but his undead were striking out at the rats whenever and wherever they found them. Olivia sensed dozens of rats dying, their undead magic snapping out of existence, as they were crushed below human undead or kicked hard enough to shatter their bodies. At least the Tsar was still having problems keeping his undead away from Sir Sidney's influence.

But that won't last, she thought, grimly. *Sir Sidney simply has far less practice in controlling the undead.*

Sir Sidney stood at the edge of the group, keeping his distance from the living humans. His face had grown slack, almost completely emotionless, yet his body shivered, rocking backwards and forwards with the effort he was expending to control the undead. Olivia saw several of the diplomats, including Talleyrand, looking at Sir Sidney, as if he was a monster that might turn on them, given enough time. They might well be right, Olivia knew, as much as she hated to admit it. Almost all stories about Necromancers concluded with them eventually going insane, if they weren't killed first.

Raechel placed a hand on her shoulder as Olivia shivered, hearing the sound of whispering growing louder. Both the Tsar and Sir Sidney shouted into the ether, their commands so loud it was impossible for the undead to disobey, yet the whispering was also growing louder. It was hard to be sure, but Olivia rather suspected the undead were forming a mental gestalt of their own anyway, even though they had two semi-Necromancers trying to control them. And who knew what *that* would mean for the future?

"They're coming," Olivia whispered, sensing the cold dead thoughts flowing around her. "He knows we're trying to move away from the palace."

She opened her eyes fully and glanced around, trying to locate the undead she knew had to be watching. They could be anywhere in any of the nearby buildings, looking down at the living humans through eerie yellow eyes. But she saw nothing, apart from dead bodies on the ground, many of them badly charred. Gwen's flames had wiped out dozens of the undead, she noted, but there were hundreds of thousands more in the city. How many people had lived in Moscow before they became the Tsar's undead slaves?

Romulus muttered a sharp command as the first of the undead jumped out of a window and landed on the stone road, then hurled himself towards the humans. More followed, a strange combination of men and women, boys and girls; Olivia shuddered as she saw a young girl wearing a tattered noblewoman's dress, her face as gray and cold as the rest of the undead. Beside her, she felt Raechel brace herself, lifting her sword ... and then the ranks of the undead simply halted. Olivia cringed as she felt Sir Sidney's mental commands booming in her head, ordering the undead to stop and submit themselves to his orders. But more and more undead were on the way.

Sir Sidney reacted, sending his undead back to fight the newcomers. Olivia watched in growing horror as the subverted undead tore through the loyalists, both sides ripping each other apart with superhuman strength. Grey flesh flew everywhere, but there was surprisingly little blood. What happened to blood anyway, if someone became one of the undead? No one knew for sure. If they ever made it home, Olivia promised herself, it was time to end the taboo on research into Necromancy. The Tsar's experiments would be duplicated, sooner or later, even if he died today. And then all hell would break loose again.

A new line of undead appeared, charging forward. Olivia waited for them to fall under Sir Sidney's influence, then recoiled in horror as she realised he was too occupied with his first undead to even notice they were there. Gritting her teeth, she tried to send mental commands herself, but the roaring from both controllers drowned out her instructions. The undead seemed to stumble for several seconds, yet they never fell under her control. Romulus and several of the Russians, carrying swords, struck out at the undead, trying to behead them before it was too late. But one of them made it through and leapt at Olivia ...

Raechel sliced out with her sword, beheading the creature. Olivia looked up at her, then looked at Lord and Lady Standish, both of whom looked absolutely stunned. Lord Standish, at least, seemed to be taking it in his stride; Lady Standish's mouth worked silently for a long moment, before she looked away, as if she refused to believe what had just happened. Olivia wondered, spitefully, just how long she could choose to deny reality, before remembering just how many aristocrats could deny reality indefinitely, if they so chose. There were quite a few girls, she'd been told by Lady Mary, who kept spending despite their fathers and husbands running into money problems. They needed to keep up appearances, after all.

She was shocked out of her thoughts by a sudden wave of magic. For a moment she thought Gwen had returned, then she realised the magic taking hold of her and yanking her up into the air was nowhere near as gentle as Gwen's touch. She glanced around, hearing Raechel's helpless shouting below her, and saw the Russian magician standing on a rooftop, smiling unpleasantly at her. The Mover was powerful, she noted, maybe more powerful than some of the others at Cavendish Hall. Or perhaps, she wondered, he was merely being rough with her to terrify her into submission.

He dropped her on the rooftop, then pressed down on her with magic, keeping her pinned firmly in place. A bullet cracked out and struck the magic surrounding him, ricocheting away into the distance. Olivia winced as he turned to smile at her, then gathered his magic to lash out at Sir Sidney. He could just tear the controller apart and then let the undead have the remaining humans. But there were undead rats everywhere, even in the building ... Olivia reached out with her mind, summoning all the rats she could reach, ordering them to reach the roof by any means necessary.

"Don't," she said, hoping to distract him long enough for the rats to arrive. "This is madness."

The Russian turned back to her. "This is for the Father Tsar," he said. "It has to be done."

Olivia saw madness in his eyes and wondered, grimly, why she was surprised. The Russians wouldn't have tolerated a Mover so powerful unless he was loyal ... and they had the tools to ensure that he would always be loyal. Perhaps a Charmer like Ivan had been assigned to work on her captor, pressing away on his mind until he couldn't even recognise the *concept* of disloyalty. He would obey orders from the Tsar, even if it was clear the Tsar had become an undead monster bent on destroying his people and absorbing them all into one undead mass.

"This is madness," she repeated, desperately. Maybe, just maybe, she could get him to listen to her. "What does it profit anyone if the entire population becomes undead?"

The Mover glared at her. She winced as the pressure holding her down grew stronger; her bones ached, as if they were on the verge of shattering into dust. Perhaps the Tsar had only intended to convert his noblemen and soldiers into undead, she thought, wondering how otherwise intelligent men could support such a mad scheme. Or maybe they'd thought the Tsar only intended to convert the peasants.

Either way, the Tsar's madness had driven him to absorb everyone his undead encountered ...

She smiled as the rats burst out of the hatch, the drain and even over the walls. The Mover stared, too shocked to react, as thousands of rats swarmed over him, nibbling at his flesh with sharp teeth. Olivia heard him yelp once, then fall silent, his body collapsing to the ground and lying still. The force holding her down vanished at the same moment, allowing her to stand up, despite the aches and pains running through her body. She pulled back her shirt to glance at her bare flesh and swore. It looked as though she had been beaten black and blue by experts.

The sound of ratty whispering grew louder as the rats surrounded her, chilling her to the bone. She forced herself to remain calm, then directed the rats to search the building for any traces of the undead. They found nothing, apart from a handful of bodies that hadn't risen again, as far as they could tell. Olivia forced herself down the stairs and through the darkened corridors until she found the bodies, lying in one of the side rooms. It looked, she realised numbly, as though the family had seen death coming for them and committed suicide, rather than allow themselves to rise again. The Tsar had clearly decided it wasn't worth the energy to reanimate the bodies after their deaths.

Olivia considered reanimating them herself, then decided she didn't have the energy. Instead, she staggered out of the building, back towards the human party. Raechel waved to her as soon as she stepped into view, but her uncle and Talleyrand insisted on asking Olivia several questions at a distance before they let her into the circle. Olivia couldn't blame them, not really. They had to fear an undead who looked close enough to human to pass muster, if only for a few seconds. But, somehow, she was fairly sure a normal undead couldn't fool anyone, even for a second.

She cringed as she heard moaning in the distance, echoing from thousands of undead throats. Romulus hurried the group along, sticking to the main road as it headed down towards the Tsar's private docks. According to the Russians, the Tsar maintained a small fleet of river craft, each one surprisingly luxurious and capable of navigating through canals and locks that linked Russia's rivers together. The Russians had seemed incredibly proud of the canals, stating that they would bring Russia into the modern world. But the Tsar seemed to have brought Russia into the land of the dead.

"That noise," Raechel said. "What are they *doing*?"

"Summoning the troops," Olivia said. Part of her *recognised* the moaning; part of her wanted to throw back her head and moan too. She shuddered, remembering some of the more unpleasant suggestions about Necromancy. Did her powers come from a mental link with the dead? "The undead will home in on their fellows, the ones moaning, then take up the cry themselves, attracting more and more of the undead."

"Sounds like a way to trap them," Raechel said. She smiled. "Stand at the top of a cliff, moan loudly, then let them plummet to their deaths."

Olivia considered it, briefly, as they reached the docking complex. It was smaller than she'd expected, after growing up in London's docklands, but at least it was largely intact, if abandoned. Two middle-sized boats were clearly missing, yet three more remained, all fairly simple. She reached out with her mind as they paused on the edge of the water, searching for any traces of the undead. There was nothing, apart from the growing sense of the Tsar's influence pervading the city. When she turned to look at Sir Sidney, she was badly shocked by just how far he had fallen towards madness. Somehow, she doubted he would remain safe much longer.

We need Gwen, she thought, wondering if she could control Sir Sidney. *But where is she?*

"Get everyone on the boat," Romulus directed. Lady Standish staggered aboard with a dazed expression on her face, as if she no longer knew where she was or what she was doing. Her husband and his men gathered around the boat, swords in hand, while the Russians started to untie the boat from the dock. "Lady Olivia?"

Olivia smirked – Romulus clearly had no idea of her origins – but nodded, allowing him to lead her to one side. "Yes, My Lord?"

Romulus gave her a sharp look, then frowned, indicating Sir Sidney. "Is he safe?"

Olivia swallowed, nervously. In truth, she had her doubts. Sir Sidney was clearly cracking up under the combined pressure of tiredness and his mental contact with the undead. Unlike the Tsar, he had no constant source of life energy to sustain him, nor – unlike Olivia herself – was he truly *alive*. Sooner or later, he would fall to the undead and become one of them. It boded ill, Olivia suspected, for the Tsar's own future. Did he have the self-control to realise he needed to keep large numbers of humans alive, just to provide himself with livestock? Or was he too far gone to see how destructive his activities had become?

"I don't know," she said. She understood what Romulus was *really* asking. Should they leave Sir Sidney behind? "I think we need him."

She watched as Sir Sidney staggered again, then stumbled towards the gangplank as the boat prepared itself for departure. Romulus eyed his former superior's back, one hand twitching over his sword, then nodded reluctantly and nudged Olivia towards the boat. Olivia winced, then obeyed. The boat shivered uncomfortably as she boarded it, then took up a place on the deck. Raechel joined her, the only other woman to do so. The others went into the cabin and hid there.

Idiots, Olivia thought, as the boat slipped away from the dock. *If we go over, the people on the deck will be the only ones to have a chance to survive.*

She hadn't been on many boats in her life; she'd been on one riverboat with Jack and a pair of ironclads with Gwen, but the Tsar's boat was definitely the oddest she'd seen. On one hand, it was staggeringly luxurious, complete with gilt controls; on the other, it bobbled around as if it were in a storm, even on the relatively calm river. She couldn't help wondering if the Tsar had designed the boat to convince himself that he was having an adventure, complete with unstable boat. Or maybe he'd just wanted to annoy his older aristocrats by forcing them to join him on a boat that practically guaranteed seasickness. But there was no way to know.

Moscow looked oddly ... darkened, even in the bright sunlight. There was a haze hanging over the city, a haze of darkness and shadow, and a stench of death that she knew would linger for years, even if the Tsar were defeated. The undead swarmed over the buildings, bringing out any remaining living and biting them, adding to their growing ranks. None of them seemed to pay any attention to the boat, something that relieved and worried her at the same time. They were in no position to survive if the boat was swarmed, but at the same time the Tsar was clearly occupied somewhere else. What was he doing?

She heard a moan behind her and turned to see Sir Sidney, standing on the edge of the deck as if he were considering plunging into the icy water. Olivia exchanged a glance with Raechel, then walked over to him. Up close, Sir Sidney was starting to decompose, his flesh flaking off his body. Olivia shuddered at the reminder of what she'd helped do to him, then braced herself and touched his back. He turned to look at her, his eyes glinting with grim light. Olivia found herself wondering if she shouldn't kill him – or try to control him – now, before it was too late. How long could he hold out against the undead?

"We need your mother," Sir Sidney said. There was no amusement or mockery in his tone, just a curious deadness that worried her more than anything else. She would almost sooner be laughed at, if it meant Sir Sidney was normal. "Where is she?"

"I don't know," Olivia confessed. Gwen was tough, but not unbeatable. Where *was* she? "I wish I knew."

"When we make contact with the garrison, we will see if Simone can reach her," Sir Sidney said, flatly. "And then we will decide what to do next."

Olivia nodded, then tried to think of something else to say, something to talk about, something that would keep his thoughts engaged. But nothing came to mind. They had next to nothing in common, even if it was rare for men and women to just talk. Raechel, thankfully, came to the rescue, asking Sir Sidney about the work he did for Lord Mycroft. Olivia listened, relieved, as Sir Sidney started to sound more human. But she knew it wouldn't last indefinitely.

They slipped out of the city and linked up with a Russian patrol, which guided them to the airstrip. Simone was waiting for them, looking relieved to see Talleyrand again, but when she tried to find Gwen nothing happened. Olivia gritted her teeth, found somewhere to sit down, and started to reach out with her mind. Her undead were still in the city and it was time to use them. She was damned if she was leaving Gwen behind, not after everything Gwen had done for her. And God help anyone who stood in her way.

Chapter Thirty-Six

wen slowly, very slowly, staggered back towards wakefulness. Her head hurt, a throbbing pain that threatened to drive her back into the darkness, while her entire body ached, as if she'd been beaten to the very edge of her endurance. Whispering echoed through her mind, right on the brink of her awareness. Something seemed to be clamped to her right wrist. It took several long minutes – they felt like hours – to pull herself together to the point she dared open her eyes. She was lying on a straw pallet inside a metal cell, right next to a living breathing man. Her hand, she discovered, was cuffed to his wrist.

He leered at her, unpleasantly. Gwen reached for her powers in shock, only to feel them slithering and sliding away from her. He had to be the Leech, she realised dully; she hadn't had a good look at him during the battle, but there was no one else who would serve as her gaoler. As long as his powers were active, hers were useless. But she wasn't helpless, she reminded herself, savagely. The first Leech she had met, Sir Charles, had made the same mistake. She was *not* a weak and feeble woman.

She sat upright, feeling sparks of pain as she moved. Her legs were shackled together, suggesting that the Russians didn't have as much confidence in their Leech as they should have done. She could probably pick her way out of the shackles even without magic, she noted; Olivia's lessons on lock-picking had been surprisingly useful before, once or twice. It was why people were normally handcuffed behind the back. But the Russians had left her hands free, if cuffed to a Leech.

Outside, there was darkness ... and things moving in the darkness. She caught a flash of yellow right before the undead creature stepped up to the bars and peered through at her, his dead gaze passing across her face with no interest. Her guards, she realised, held back by the Tsar's will. If she somehow knocked the Leech out or killed him, the undead would swarm into the cell and kill her, before she recovered control of her powers. And he was probably looking at her right now, through the eyes of his undead servants.

"Lie still," the Leech advised. "It takes time to recover."

Gwen scowled at him. The real question was why they'd let her wake up at all? It wasn't as if they could get her to help them, no matter how much Charm they applied – and she knew very little the Russians might find interesting. Lord Mycroft had encouraged her to attend Privy Council meetings, but Gwen had never really bothered. She had enough trouble battling the senior magicians in Cavendish Hall. And the Russians probably knew far too much about the Hall and how it worked without having to force Gwen to talk.

It was hard, so very hard, to form words, but she managed it. "Why am I here?"

"The Father Tsar wishes you to be kept alive," the Leech said. "I believe he wishes to speak with you."

Gwen closed her eyes, thinking fast. What did the Tsar *want* from her? Magic? It wasn't something she could *give* him and, as far as they knew, magic didn't survive the transition from living to undead. Olivia had told her that the Russian experiments to create undead magicians hadn't succeeded ... but they *had* succeeded, to some extent. The Tsar had become a Necromancer, of sorts. Did they hope to use her to produce additional magicians?

Her blood ran cold as she considered another possibility. No one really knew how magic was transmitted, but they did know that the children of magicians were almost always magicians themselves. The farms had been based around using common-born female magicians as mothers of new magicians, fathered by men from Cavendish Hall. If Gwen hadn't been born to a noble family, she knew she would have ended up in the farms, drugged while her body brought forth an endless supply of children. Did the Tsar intend to use her as a brood mare?

"The Father Tsar is mad," Gwen said, flatly. Outside, the undead whispered angrily amongst themselves. "How long will it be until he absorbs you too?"

The Leech smiled at her, apparently taking no offense. "We are his most loyal servants," he said, calmly. "He will not make us undead."

Gwen sighed. "Are you *sure* of that?" She pushed forward before the Leech could say a word. "He needs life force to keep himself going," she added. "Sooner or later, he's going to run out of life force. And then he will turn on you."

She wondered, vaguely, if the Leech would even *listen* to her. The poor bastard had grown up in an environment where even the slightly disloyal thought could be read and used against him. Gwen suspected she would have gone mad very quickly if Master Thomas had intruded on her thoughts whenever it suited him, reading her deepest darkest secrets while searching for traces of disloyalty. If someone was brought up with the certain knowledge their thoughts could be read at any point, they'd have a very strong incentive to condition themselves against any form of disloyalty.

"We are his servants," the Leech said. "We will be part of his elect once he rules the world."

Gwen sighed and started to study the Leech, trying to conceal her interest as best as possible. Irene had taught her a few things about fighting men, warning her that while most men tended to underestimate women as combatants, they also tended to be stronger and faster when push came to shove. The Leech looked strong and healthy, too strong for her to overcome without her powers. And, as long as he was cuffed to her, it was unlikely she would be able to get out of his range.

"You should listen to me," she said. She wondered, vaguely, what Irene would do in such a situation. Try to seduce the Leech, she suspected, which wouldn't be easy. The undead were watching them, after all. "He's going mad."

"He's woken up for the first time," a new voice said. "And you are his slave."

Gwen turned to see the Tsar as he stepped into the room, on the other side of the bars. His face was almost unrecognisable. Pieces of flesh were slowly dropping from his exposed skin, as if his body was decomposing inhumanly quickly. The cell didn't smell very nice – Gwen hadn't wanted to think about what else might have been held captive in the cell – but the Tsar *stank*, so badly that Gwen had to fight down a wave of nausea. And to think she hadn't been sick since Jack had shown her the dark underpinnings of London ...

She pulled herself to her feet, feeling the Leech rising behind her. Not that he had a choice, thanks to the cuffs. She wondered, absently, what they would do when one of them needed to use the toilet, then pushed the thought aside hastily. By then, she would have to be out of the complex or dead. Up close, she saw, the Tsar was becoming more and more like one of the undead. His moustache, which had seemed so prominent, was coming out of his skin, as if it was no longer part of him. She had a sudden mad impulse to reach out and tug at the hair, expecting it to come out without a struggle. But she pushed that aside too.

"You're dying," she said, wondering if *dying* could really be said to apply to one of the undead. And she was sure the Tsar counted as undead, even though his mind was still in control. "Why did you do this to yourself?"

The Tsar's hand snapped through the bars and clenched around Gwen's throat, squeezing tightly enough to hurt. "Silence," he snapped. He said a handful of words in Russian that didn't sound remotely pleasant. "You will do as you are told."

He let go of her and shoved her back, hard. Gwen stumbled backwards, one hand touching her bruised throat. He'd almost lost control, she realised dully, almost killed her even though he wanted to keep her alive. The darkness – the whispering – was howling at the back of his mind, dragging him down into the undead gestalt. Sooner or later, she suspected, he would lose control completely and that would be the end. But a great many innocent people would die before the whole affair finally concluded.

If it ever does, she thought. Moscow had a population numbered in the millions, if the Russians were to be believed. That was easily enough to form a gestalt that would be terrifyingly intelligent. The Tsar might be dead, but the nightmare he'd created would live on. *Can we destroy a million undead formed into one mind?*

"I'm not very good at doing what I'm told," she said, when she managed to gather herself. "I used to object to everything my mother wanted me to do."

"I have no doubt of it," the Tsar said. He looked as if he wanted to smile, but he had forgotten how. "You will *heal* for me."

Gwen eyed him, sharply. If his body had been living, it might have been possible for a Healer to put him back together. Gwen had seen a young aristocrat with several broken bones and massive trauma saved by a Healer, after taking a fall off a horse while trying to combine fox hunting and heavy drinking. But the Tsar was undead, his body rotting away at a terrifying rate, far faster than any of the normal undead. She rather doubted she could do anything to salvage his undead life, even if she'd been a full Healer.

The Leech yanked at the cuff on her wrist. "Give him what he wants," he ordered. "The Father Tsar requires your services."

Gwen gritted her teeth, then had to fight to hide her smile. "Give me my powers back," she said. "How else am I meant to heal him?"

The Leech smiled with genuine amusement. "You will have to be prepared first," he said, dryly. "We wouldn't want you doing something else with your powers."

Gwen made a show of rolling her eyes in a manner that had once driven her mother to distraction, followed by fits of rage. "If you refuse to let me use my powers," she said, in the sweetest tone she could muster, "I won't be able to do anything for your Father Tsar."

She paused. "I suppose I could provide him with a light snack," she added. She was fairly sure that no undead version of her would have her powers. "Would *that* be helpful?"

The Tsar stared at her for a long chilling moment. He didn't blink, she saw, nor did his body move normally. His face was utterly inhuman, as though he could no longer muster the energy or incentive to pretend to be somewhat normal. A piece of skin peeled off his body as she watched, dropping down to the floor. Did he have the intellect, she asked herself, to realise the potential danger in allowing her access to her powers? Or was he desperate enough to take the risk?

"You will be prepared," he said. He turned and moved away, his every step careful and deliberate. It wasn't an act. He had genuine difficulty in remembering how to walk. "And then you will save me."

Gwen watched him go, realising that Olivia might well have done far more than just extract a little revenge when she'd killed Gregory. The Healer should never have been so badly exposed, not when he was clearly the only one the Tsar had on hand. Gwen was no Healer and no one with access to her files would have doubted it. If there had been any other candidate, she knew, they would simply have killed her out of hand, then forced her body to rise again.

She looked over at the Leech. "Do you not see it? He's mad!"

"But he is still the Tsar," the Leech said. "We will begin soon."

Gwen sighed, inwardly. The upper classes in England had worked hard to convince everyone, including themselves, that their rule was divinely mandated, but it was clear that the Russians had taken the concept a great deal further. Lacking any tradition of organised dissent, even of loyal opposition, the Russians found it hard to rise up against the Tsar. But the unrest simmering in the streets of Moscow and St Petersburg would eventually have exploded into the light. When society broke down completely, who knew where the pieces would fall?

She lay back on the straw, thinking hard. If there was an opportunity to escape, or to kill herself, she would have to take it. There had been at least three Charmers working for the Russians. One of them *might* be able to reprogram her to do as the Tsar wanted, no matter how strongly she was opposed to his desires. And then she would no longer be herself.

But there seemed no way out of the cell.

She struggled to draw on just one spark of magic, just enough to kill the Leech by moving cells in his brain. But nothing worked. She was trapped.

***

Olivia found herself struggling to maintain mental contact with her undead as they approached the source of the Tsar's waves of power. The sheer level of power he was tossing around so casually was terrifying, even to a born Necromancer. Olivia had the uneasy suspicion that she would have fallen under his sway if she'd been there in person, despite not being one of the undead. As it was, she had to struggle to keep her undead under her control.

The other undead ignored them as they walked into the complex. Olivia looked around, through the eyes of her puppets, and saw no trace of anyone living. A handful of the undead wore monkish robes, like Gregory and his servants, but none of them were alive. The Tsar seemed to be surrounding himself with more and more slaves, all undead. If there was anyone living left in the complex, she couldn't see them.

Deeper underground, she found a set of cells. She felt her head spinning as she peered into them, one by one, only to discover that most of the cells were empty. Her undead puppet staggered under the growing waves of power, but somehow kept moving. The fifth cell was occupied, she discovered; three undead stood on guard, while Gwen sat in a cell, handcuffed to a man.

Olivia frowned, wondering why Gwen hadn't broken free. Cuffing her to someone would hardly deprive her of her powers. But she understood, a moment later; the Russian cuffed to her had to be another magician, a Leech. She couldn't help wondering what would happen if a Leech was allowed to step too close to one of the undead. Would a Leech drain away the magic holding the undead together? Or would the undead simply rip off his head or bite him, starting the transformation into yet another undead?

She thought hard, trying to decide how best to proceed. It would be easy to deal with the undead guards; as always, they seemed to have problems even *seeing* her undead puppet. But the Leech might be a far more dangerous prospect. She considered several options, then decided to deal with the undead first. If nothing else, Gwen would have a chance to break free. Bracing herself, she lashed out at the first undead, sending its head flying from its shoulders to crash against the far wall. The other undead appeared to be surprised – from their point of view, the attack seemed to have come out of nowhere – but the Leech let out a cry of shock.

Olivia took out the second undead, then the third. And then she felt the Tsar's mental influence growing stronger and stronger ... hastily, she dropped out of the undead puppet before he could overwhelm her completely. She'd done the best she could, she knew. She just hoped Gwen could take advantage of it.

***

Gwen saw the fourth undead enter the prison cell, but thought little of it. The Tsar would be trying to intimidate her with the sheer scale of his power and control before his Charmers started to work. If she was halfway to being convinced that resistance was futile, she knew, it would be much easier to bring her completely over to his side. And then the undead creature's hand lashed out and beheaded one of its fellows.

Olivia, she thought, as the Leech started to his feet, dragging Gwen along with him. The thought made her smile, giving her renewed energy. *She's alive!*

The Leech stared in disbelief as the undead kept slaughtering its fellows. Gwen saw her chance and took it, throwing herself at his back. They crashed forward, his head cracking into one of the bars with a sickening thud. Gwen felt her magic flaring through her body once again as the Leech shuddered, clearly badly stunned rather than dead. The remaining undead advanced towards her; Gwen summoned fire, blasted both of them to ash, then sliced through the Leech's hand and the chains around her ankles. There would be time to unpick the cuffs later.

A terrible moaning echoed through the complex as she broke out of the cell and rushed for the door. Four undead were already running towards her; oddly, they were holding weapons in their hands. Gwen blasted all four of them, then almost collapsed as everything caught up with her at once. Whispering – terrible whispering – echoed through her mind, reminding her that the Tsar was somewhere within the complex. But she didn't have the energy to go after him, not now. All she could do was try to make her escape.

Another swarm of undead greeted her as she reached the stairwell and threw herself up it, their arms reaching for her with deadly intent. Gwen knocked them down, feeling her head starting to pound again, then ran past them and out of the building. Whatever happened, she told herself, she would die free.

Behind her, the Tsar's whispering grew louder, echoing through her mind.

Chapter Thirty-Seven

t took Olivia several moments to gather herself after escaping the Tsar's increasingly harsh mental commands. The certain knowledge that he'd almost taken *her* as well as her undead had shocked her to the bone. And yet, she knew she couldn't just lie there and wait to see what happened. She had to try to muster help for Gwen before it was too late.

She snapped open her eyes and stared across the airstrip. One airship was already being loaded with passengers – foreign diplomats and Russian aristocrats – while the other was being prepared for flight. Hundreds of soldiers stood around the airstrip, several carrying makeshift swords, while others were assembling barricades around the complex. Olivia had few illusions as to their effectiveness. If the Tsar chose to throw thousands of his undead at the barricades, they would collapse into rubble within seconds.

"Olivia?" Racchel asked. "Are you all right?"

"Gwen isn't," Olivia said. She stumbled to her feet, looking for Sir Sidney. "Where's Sidney?"

"At the edge of the airstrip," Simone said. She sounded concerned; her powers, Olivia realised, would let her hear the whispering through Olivia. "What's happening?"

Olivia ignored her as she walked frantically towards Sir Sidney. He was definitely coming apart at the seams, she realised, but there was nothing they could do about it. The only solution she could think of was to allow him to bite someone and that would just give him a taste for it. When she reached him, she saw that someone had tried to feed him bread, cheese and dried meat. It was clear that he hadn't been able to eat any of it.

Which isn't surprising, she thought, morbidly. *He doesn't have a real digestive system any more.*

Sir Sidney looked up at her, his face slack. His voice, when he spoke, was raspy, as if he had forgotten how to speak for the second time. "What ... has ... happened?"

"The Tsar took Gwen prisoner," Olivia said. She had no idea why the Tsar hadn't simply slit Gwen's throat, but she was glad of the oversight. "I helped her, I think, but we need to get after her. The Tsar won't want her to escape."

Sir Sidney looked down at the ground. "I can hear him," he said. "And I can hear the whispering."

"It's getting louder," Olivia agreed. "We have to help Gwen."

"The soldiers will be useless," Sir Sidney said. "In the streets, they will be overwhelmed and destroyed."

"I know," Olivia said. The Russian troops might have surrounded the city, but Moscow was a huge place. It would take more troops than they had to keep the undead confined indefinitely – or to destroy Moscow, burning it to the ground. She had no illusions about what would happen when the Tsar tried to break out of the city. "Just you and I."

Sir Sidney looked back at her. "I don't think I'm *me* any longer," he said. "My thoughts keep fading in and out of existence."

Olivia shuddered, remembering one of the most terrifying men she'd ever met, long before she'd known Jack or Gwen. He'd had no conscience; indeed, he'd had no emotions at all, as far as anyone knew. The streets had whispered that he killed, tortured and raped, yet felt nothing, not even sadistic pleasure in his acts. Some of the nastiest gang lords had used him as an enforcer, paying him hundreds of pounds to send a very clear message to their debtors of what would happen if they failed to pay. He had never failed to get results.

And what would happen, she asked herself, if Sir Sidney went the same way?

"Then we can fight now," she said, flatly. If nothing else, going into the city would keep Sir Sidney away from the living. "And we really have to go after Gwen."

Sir Sidney nodded, then rose to his feet. "See if Simone can call Gwen," he ordered, as he started to walk towards the city. "And then run after me."

He paused. "And get some food too," he added. "Gwen will need to eat if she's been kept prisoner."

***

Gwen burst out into the bright sunlight and swore as she saw hordes of undead turning to face her, the Tsar's thoughts yammering them into action. Blood trickled from her nose as she hesitated, gathering herself, then clawed for as much height as she could muster. The undead seethed below her, their hands reaching up into the air, as she tried to fly towards the airstrip in the distance. But the pain in her head was making it far harder to fly levelly.

Gwen, a thought said, exploding into her mind. The impact almost made her fall out of the sky. *Where are you?*

She had to think hard to focus her mind enough to reply. *On my way to the airstrip*, she thought, knowing that Simone would pick up on her growing pain and desperation. *But I don't know if I can make it.*

There was a sudden stab of pain from her nose, followed by a gout of blood that splashed down towards the ground. Gwen felt herself lose her grip on the air, falling down, then somehow she managed to pull her magic back together long enough to get aloft. She honestly had no idea what to do next. It was unlikely that anyone could help her in time, nor could she make it out of the city before she fell out of the air. She really needed a rest and something to eat, but she knew it was unlikely she would get either.

Olivia and Sir Sidney are on their way, Simone sent. *Can you find a place to hole up until they arrive?*

Gwen gritted her teeth. The pain in her head was making it harder to think clearly, but she still found it hard to imagine that Sir Sidney and Olivia could make a difference. But maybe they could control enough of the undead to give the Tsar a fight. She felt herself falling again and desperately fought to hold herself in the air. Below her, the undead were climbing on rooftops and leaping up towards her, as if they thought they could grab her and pull her out of the air. If she fell much lower, she realised, they might be right.

She sensed the sudden surge in power moments before the cathedral exploded behind her, sending pieces of debris flying through the air. Gwen turned, despite the effort, and saw a wave of power shimmering through the air, as a thousand Movers were working together. But, instead of Movers, she saw the Tsar striding out of the remains of his base of operations, followed by a horde of undead. His gaze was firmly fixed on her.

Is he a Mover too now, she wondered, *or am I seeing things*?

It was impossible to be sure, she realised, as she turned away and forced herself to keep going, despite the commands pounding their way into the ether. If Olivia's blood could be used to make a new Necromancer, why couldn't a Mover's blood help make a new Mover? Or could the Tsar have finally mastered the art of using the magic that had belonged to an undead when it had been alive? Or was there a Mover or two following the Tsar and she simply couldn't see them? She had no way to know.

The Tsar's commands grew stronger and stronger as he walked after her, hammering them into her head. She gritted her teeth, even though her weak Necromancy gave her some protection; if she fell asleep or even fell into his hands, she might well be broken completely. And to think that Olivia was walking into the madness ... she tried to call Simone, to tell her that Olivia should stay well away from the city, but there was no response. She was too badly battered to tell if her powers were actually working. It was quite possible, she knew, that she was too tired to send any message to the Talker.

And then she felt the other commands, slashing into her brain. They felt ... *better* than the Tsar's commands, even if they weren't specifically directed at her. Down below, hundreds of undead looked confused, then started attacking their fellows. The sudden surge in commands, oddly, brought her some relief from the Tsar's endless shouting. She looked down and saw Sir Sidney, walking right down the middle of the street. And Olivia was sitting on his shoulders ...

Gwen stared. The undead seemed to be completely confused, once again, as the two controllers fought it out for dominance. A line of undead surrounded Sir Sidney, acting as bodyguards; beyond them, the undead struggled with one another, tearing each other apart. The Tsar seemed to be pouring undead into the struggle, with little regard for numbers, as he advanced slowly towards Sir Sidney, as if he was attempting to overwhelm him by sheer force. And he was probably more powerful, Gwen realised, as she dropped down and landed behind Sir Sidney. It was clear, up close, that Sir Sidney was decomposing faster than the Tsar.

Olivia scrambled off Sir Sidney's back and ran over to Gwen, thrusting a bag into her hand. Gwen opened it and sighed in relief when she realised it contained a large number of cheese sandwiches and even a handful of apples. She practically swallowed the first sandwich whole, despite the odd taste of the cheese, then consumed the next few almost as quickly, using the food to recoup her power. The trickle of blood from her nose faded along with the pounding headache, although that refused to clear completely. She was still hearing the Tsar's commands in her head.

"He's pressing closer," she said, as she stood upright. "And he's using magic."

"I know," Olivia said. Her voice was strained. "I can feel him too."

***

Getting into Moscow had been easy, surprisingly so. Sir Sidney had simply carried her, noting that his body no longer needed to rest; he'd run faster than anyone Olivia had ever encountered, without ever losing his breath. Once they'd entered the city, the undead had swarmed towards them ... and he'd simply taken control, with a little help from her. They'd built up a sizeable army by the time the Tsar noticed and came after them, his thoughts reaching out to snatch back his undead slaves. And then the battle had truly begun.

Olivia felt herself caught between two mighty forces, between two separate minds that wanted to enslave her, to make her their puppet. The Tsar was cold and powerful, his thoughts raging through the ether and trying to sneak into her mind, while Sir Sidney was grimly determined to hold himself together long enough to destroy his opponent. Olivia knew she was the Necromancer, that she was responsible – directly or indirectly – for bringing both of them into existence, yet she had the eerie feeling that both of them would control her, given a chance.

But neither of them have human limits any longer, she thought, as the Tsar came into sight for the first time since the ceremony. *And they're not even thinking like humans now.*

Hordes of undead swarmed around them, raging backwards and forwards as first one controller, then the other, managed to take control of the undead. The undead almost seemed to be dancing, but it was a dance with a deadly purpose. Every time one of them fell to Sir Sidney, he lashed out at his comrades, while the ones held by the Tsar kept pressing forward, trying to force their way closer and closer. And they were slowly winning. There was no way to avoid noticing that Sir Sidney was slowly crumbling under the pressure exerted on him by the Tsar.

She tried to think of something she could do, but nothing came to mind. If she tried to help, all she would do was expose her mind to the Tsar – and lose herself. Living or not, she would be overwhelmed and enslaved, her talents turned against her adopted mother and the entire world. Hell, Gwen might be overwhelmed too, given her limited access to necromancy. And then the Tsar would have a Master Magician under his control.

"You have to go," Sir Sidney said, desperately. "I cannot hold him forever."

There was a sudden surge forward as a wave of undead made it through Sir Sidney's influence and lunged towards Sir Sidney. Gwen caught them with her powers, setting them ablaze and then hurling them back towards the Tsar, but it was only delaying the inevitable. Both sides knew that Sir Sidney was losing. His undead were slowly being reabsorbed into the Tsar's gestalt. Olivia couldn't even think of a way to get Sir Sidney out without being overwhelmed herself ...

She caught sight of his face and knew it wouldn't matter. His flesh was melting from his bones, revealing the dull white skull beneath his skin. It was a wonder that he wasn't dead already – or deader, part of her mind noted – but it was only a matter of time. He sank down, his legs becoming puddles of melted flesh, his mind slowly cracking completely. There was a howl of triumph from the Tsar, so loud that Olivia was sure that the entire world had heard it, then his thoughts refocused on her with terrifying speed. The impact was so irresistible that it forced her to her knees, his thoughts boring through her mind as though he had become a strange combination of Talker and Charmer. She found herself grovelling in front of him, prostrating herself ...

There was a brilliant flash of light. The Tsar howled and reared backwards.

***

Gwen had watched, in growing horror, as Sir Sidney's mind finally snapped into nothingness, his body joining the Tsar's slaves. And then she staggered backwards under the impact of his thoughts, only her limited connection to Necromancy saving her from instant enslavement. But it was clear that Olivia hadn't been so lucky. She was kneeling in front of the Tsar, as if she was acknowledging him as her lord and master ...

Bracing herself, Gwen summoned light and blasted the Tsar. It wasn't a physical attack, but it was bright enough to send him staggering backwards, long enough for her to grab Olivia and yank her up into the air. The Tsar howled in rage, his magic crackling around him, then he lunged after her, but it was too late. Gwen forced herself to keep flying, despite Olivia's increasingly desperate struggles, until she was well out of reach. Behind her, the Tsar and his forces turned and followed her along the ground. They knew very well that she would have to come down sometime and then they would have her.

Olivia kept struggling until Gwen, desperately, drew back her hand and slapped her face. Her adopted daughter stared at her, awareness slowly flowing back into her eyes, then she started to cry. Gwen winced, wishing she had time to do more than give Olivia a sympathetic look; she'd seen too many people who had been Charmed into obedience and then broken down under the realisation that someone else had turned them into a puppet. And it would be worse for Olivia, she knew. Her own talent had been used as a weapon against her.

"I'm sorry," Gwen said, as she dropped down towards the airstrip. One of the airships was already ready to go, the other still being prepped. "But we don't have time."

She changed her mind as she touched down, wrapping Olivia in a tight hug. Olivia clung to her desperately, as if she never wanted to let go. Gwen understood; she'd felt dreadful too once or twice, particularly after she'd first used her powers. No wonder they'd called her a devil-child. What she had done had been partly an accident, partly deliberate malice ... and, either way, it was unforgivable.

Romulus ran over to her, followed by Raechel. "We have one of the airships loaded," he said, "and the Russians are working on the second one ..."

Gwen shook her head. "Get everyone onto the first one and then start heading away from Moscow," she said. An idea had occurred to her. "The Tsar is on his way here."

Raechel paled. "Are you sure?"

"Yes," Gwen said, flatly.

She looked at Romulus. "Take Olivia with you – take everyone, apart from me. I want the airstrip completely evacuated, but leave the other airship here."

"Yes, My Lady," Romulus said. He reached out for Olivia. "What should I do with her?"

"If I don't make it out," Gwen said, "head for St Petersburg and use the Talker at the Embassy to report home. Then do as you're told."

She carefully disengaged Olivia from her grip, then passed her to Romulus, who hefted her into his arms.

"You have to go too," Gwen said, to Raechel. "And I hope your career goes well."

Raechel stared at her, then gave her a tight hug. "Thank you," she murmured in Gwen's ear. "Thank you for *everything*. But please make it back."

Gwen sighed. Raechel was definitely someone worth knowing, if she was given half a chance to show what she could do. Lord Mycroft would definitely find a use for her, she was sure, perhaps as Irene's apprentice. Or, perhaps, as an intelligence agent undercover in France. There was never any shortage of work for skilled agents. All Raechel needed was some training and she would be perfect.

And, if nothing else, Raechel had managed to break free of her Aunt and Uncle without turning into a monster or a degenerate. There were worse things to do with one's life than serve as an intelligence operative. And many of them were grossly immoral.

"I'll do my best," Gwen promised. She felt a sudden surge of affection and hugged Raechel back. "But nothing is certain in war."

Chapter Thirty-Eight

he sound of moaning was alarmingly loud in the distance by the time the airship finally spluttered into the air and headed westwards, towards Europe. Gwen sighed; it had taken far too much arguing, first with Talleyrand and then with the Russians, before they had consented to her plan. But there really was no alternative, she told herself, as she drifted up into the air. If the Tsar remained master of the undead, the entire world was in serious trouble. He had to go.

She watched, grimly, as the Russian soldiers harassed the undead, but failed to do more than slow them down. They simply didn't have the right weapons to take out vast numbers of undead, unsurprisingly. Rifles and pistols weren't enough to do real damage to the undead swarms. If the undead hadn't been so focused on the airstrip, she knew, they could have wiped out the remaining soldiers or bitten them, adding hundreds of newcomers to their ranks. Instead, the Russians fired their shots and then fled, all discipline broken. It was very hard to blame them.

Gwen drifted higher as the Tsar came into view, surrounded by a handful of his monks and several undead wearing aristocratic clothing. In his madness, Gwen decided, he had to think he was issuing orders to his nobility – who, for once, were being completely obedient. She passed her gaze over them slowly preferring to study the monks. One of them, at least, was a Mover. The others might be magicians in their own right.

We took magic and made it part of our system, she thought, *but the Pope did no end of damage to French attempts to use magicians for themselves. The Russians seem to have wrapped it in religious trappings and killed those who refused to comply. And it worked for them. They controlled magic rather than being controlled by magicians.*

She dropped down to the ground as the Tsar's advancing horde reached the first line of defence, a ditch dug by Russian soldiers and filled with barbed wire, sharp objects and other deterrents. It *would* have posed a barrier to an army of living soldiers, particularly if a handful of infantry were assigned to cover it, shelling anyone trying to pick their way through the trap, but it was no barrier to the undead. They just marched into the ditch. The leaders ended up stuck in the wire or impaled on the sharp objects, but their successors kept marching over their bodies and towards the second line of defence. Gwen watched, feeling curiously dispassionate, as the undead swarmed over the barricade and finally broke into the airstrip. The whispering – and the Tsar's commands – grew louder as they advanced towards her.

There was a crash as the Tsar's guards knocked down a chunk of the barricade, allowing him to walk forward, onto the airstrip. Gwen noted it absently, unsure if the Tsar was still clinging desperately to the remains of his humanity or if he was genuinely afraid of what would happen if his undead body was to be badly damaged. There was no way to know, so she filed the datum away at the back of her mind for later consideration. Instead, she clenched her fists and waited as the hordes of undead slowed to a halt. The Tsar stepped forward and stared at her.

He was now almost unrecognisable. If he hadn't been the source of the whispering, Gwen suspected, she wouldn't have recognised him at all. His flesh had melted from his face, leaving his skull completely exposed, while the rest of his body was rotting away at an accelerated rate. If he hadn't been wearing his aristocratic uniform, his entire body might have collapsed by now, just like Sir Sidney. His hands dripped flesh, revealing white bone underneath, as he pointed at her. Gwen honestly wasn't sure what was keeping him alive, or even in his undead state, apart from magic. He'd become something utterly monstrous.

And utterly unsustainable, she thought, as the Tsar stared at her. The thought brought her some comfort. If the Tsar won, if he managed to capture or kill her, then continue to spread through Russia, he wouldn't survive for long. He would need more and more life energy to maintain his body and, sooner or later, he would run out completely. *And that will be the end.*

One of the monks stepped forward, eyes flashing with madness and a curious desperation, and held up a hand. Gwen felt a tickle at the back of her mind and raised her mental shields, noting the monk's desperation with some amusement. Clearly, *someone* had had second thoughts, far too late to do any good. Even the most fanatical fanatic would have noticed that *something* had gone badly wrong by now. And, if he was one of the Talkers, he might be able to hide his change of heart from his fellows.

Not that it will do him any good, Gwen thought. The monks would be surrounded by hordes of undead. Any noticeable backsliding would result in immediate death. *They can't escape their Tsar now.*

The Talker spoke in heavily-accented English. "The Father Tsar demands your surrender and your willing servitude," he said. "If you surrender, if you open your mind, the Father Tsar will allow the rest of your party to go free."

Gwen smirked. The Tsar clearly wanted a Healer, even though she was fairly sure that no Healer ever born could have mended his dying body. It made him hostage to Gwen's continued existence, which meant he couldn't simply kill her. But there were ways, she knew, to reprogram someone to obey. He might have a surviving Charmer ... or he might simply drug her into obedience.

"Tell me," she said, as hundreds of undead advanced onto the airstrip, "why I should believe a word the Father Tsar had to say?"

A low rustle of anger ran through the thousands of undead facing her. The Tsar might not be able to speak any longer, but he could still hear her – or was he hearing her through the ears of his undead slaves? Gwen knew next to nothing about how ears actually worked, but the Tsar's ears appeared to be gone. Could he still hear? She looked at his eye sockets in genuine curiosity. Could he still *see*?

She recalled Olivia's description of how the undead perceived the world around them and shivered. It was quite possible the Tsar *couldn't* see her – or that he was reduced to seeing through the eyes of his slaves. And what did that mean? Was he no longer even remotely human? Whatever his state of awareness his decision to unleash necromancy, to unleash a plague of undead creatures, had condemned him to death.

Gwen had always felt sorry for the Necromancers condemned to death under the Demonic Powers Act, merely for being born. None of them had willingly committed any crime. It was one of the reasons she'd adopted Olivia and convinced Lord Mycroft to support her. But the Tsar was different. He hadn't been born a Necromancer, he'd made himself one – and he'd unleashed the necromantic plague on his own people. Gwen had no legal authority in Russia, but she knew the Tsar had to be condemned to death. Besides, she doubted that many Russians would object once the truth sank in.

"The Father Tsar offers you the word of a prince," the Talker said, finally.

Gwen narrowed her eyes. It had taken him a surprisingly long time to respond. Was he linked – mentally – to the Tsar? The part of Gwen that was intellectually curious – partly because she'd been brought up to believe that aristocratic women weren't supposed to be intellectuals – was curious, curious enough to suggest that further study was necessary. But the rest of her knew the Tsar had to die.

She looked back towards the airship in the distance, then turned to face the Tsar. "You have visited a nightmare upon your own people," she said. "You have condemned your country to utter destruction at the hands of the monsters you have unleashed. You have imperilled the entire continent through your selfish desires and utter madness. Why would I want to do anything to help you?"

The Tsar rustled angrily, but said nothing. Gwen couldn't tell if he was reluctant to answer her charges, if he knew they were accurate ... or if he'd lost the intellectual capability to even consider before rejecting her accusations. She was tempted to try to touch his mind, but she knew it would be a mistake. The Tsar might manage to overwhelm her and make her one of his slaves.

"The Father Tsar would ally himself with your country," the Talker said. "His armies would descend upon the French, destroying their homeland. The endless series of wars between Britain and France would finally come to an end."

Gwen shuddered. It was her duty to ensure the British Empire came out ahead, whatever happened – and they were on the very brink of war, once again. But she knew the offer was madness. The French might be destroyed, but the Russians would pose a far greater problem, particularly if they ruled an army of undead soldiers. Besides, as much as she disliked the French, there were Frenchmen and women she respected – and ordinary people who didn't deserve to be killed, only to rise again as undead monsters. If she could reject the idea of using Necromancy herself, even on behalf of Britain, she could reject the idea of allowing someone else to use it.

"No," she said, softly. "It would be utter madness."

OBEY! The command thundered into her head through her weak link to necromancy, sending her stumbling to her knees. There was nothing *subtle* about it, just brute force, powered by the collective mind of the Tsar and thousands of undead. It wasn't Charm Charm on that level would be utterly impossible to resist but it was strong enough to stupefy her, albeit briefly. *YOU ARE NOTHING. YOU BELONG TO ME.*

Gwen staggered again, then pinched herself, hard. The Tsar was looking right at her, his dead eye sockets seeming to blaze with an eerie yellow light. But he'd played his best card, Gwen told herself, as she straightened upright. His commands were powerful and unpleasant, yet Gwen had grown up ignoring commands from her parents and an endless array of governesses and servants. And her link to Necromancy was too weak for it to be used to overwhelm her completely. As long as she didn't touch his mind herself, her thoughts would remain free.

"You are nothing," she said. "And you won't last long, no matter what happens. Your undead body is dying. *You* are dying. Your undead reign over your country will end today."

There was a surge of magic. Gwen didn't try to resist as the Mover picked her up and threw her towards the barracks. Instead, she cushioned the blow as she hit the stone building, then threw herself up into the air, heading towards the grounded airship. She felt its skin shift oddly under her feet as she landed on top of it, staring down at the Tsar. The horde of undead threw themselves forwards, right towards her. Their leader, their would-be mastermind, was in the lead.

Gwen wondered, briefly, what he was thinking, if he was thinking at all. Smart military commanders led from the rear, she'd been told, although the British Army had more than its fair share of brave idiots who led the charge, resplendent in their red uniforms, only to be among the first shot down by the enemy. Maybe the Tsar just wanted to crush her and was past thinking of anything else. Or perhaps he'd finally lost his mind completely.

The Mover reached for her again, magic crackling through the air. Gwen took a breath and shot herself upwards, ducking the waves of magic following her. And then, bracing herself, she shot a pulse of fire down towards the airship, putting as much power into the blast as she could. The airship exploded, followed rapidly by the fuel storage depot and the explosives the Russians had left behind. Gwen felt the wave of heat shove her even further into the air as the fireball rose up in the sky, burning through the horde of undead monsters. The whispering seemed to grow louder, but the Tsar's commands were gone.

She braced herself, then dropped down as flames tore through the remainder of the airstrip, burning the undead to ash. There was no sign of the Tsar and no sign of the undead, apart from a handful of shambling corpses that had been on the edge of the blast. Gwen targeted them from high overhead, picking them off with pulses of magic, then incinerated the undead who had been stuck in the ditch.

And let that be an end to it, she thought, as she looked around for more undead. None seemed to be moving, as far as she could tell. *Please let it be the end.*

But it wouldn't be, she knew. Moscow had had a huge population – and not all of them had burned to death. The Tsar hadn't led them all to the airstrip. She hesitated, then flew back over the city, staring down at the buildings and the hordes of undead swarming over them, then summoned fire for the final time. Enough buildings were wooden, she knew, for the flames to spread quickly. The undead wouldn't try to put out the fires; hell, it was quite possible they wouldn't even realise the city was on fire. They had none of the sensitivity of living humans.

She watched for nearly ten minutes as the flames spread, then turned and directed her flight back towards the airship in the distance. They would have seen the explosion, she knew, as she passed over the remains of the airstrip. There was no sign that the Tsar and his army had ever been there. What, she wondered, would they make of the whole story? She drew on her magic, pushing herself faster and faster, until she finally landed on the airship's gondola. The hatch opened, inviting her inside.

The Russians hadn't designed the airship for luxury, she noted, as she stepped into the craft with a flourish. There were only a handful of compartments, none of them designed to separate aristocrats and servants, but no one seemed to be complaining. Romulus greeted her with a tired smile, while Raechel wrapped her in a tight hug. Lord Standish merely nodded. The cynical part of Gwen's mind suspected he was trying to decide how best to write his report to present himself in a good light.

"It's good to see you again," Raechel said. She held Gwen tightly for a long moment, then relaxed and released her. "Is it over?"

Gwen hesitated, looking towards the smoke rising from Moscow. "The Tsar is dead," she said, slowly. There was no way anyone could have survived the blast that had ripped the airstrip apart, burning the Tsar and his army to ash. "The Russians will have a chance to destroy the remaining undead before they can spread any further. And we're on our way home."

She rubbed her eyes, exhaustedly. "But we'll have to write reports of just what happened and why," she added. "And we have to hope Talleyrand will keep his word. If the French refuse to let us cross their territory ..."

"We're heading for St Petersburg," Romulus interjected. He nodded towards the map on the bulkhead. "We can take a boat from there if we can't take an airship."

Gwen sighed. The Tsar was dead and his heir was a minor child. British history suggested that regencies were inherently unstable – and Russia, she suspected, would have a far harsher time of it. There was so much unrest on the streets of St Petersburg that, when the truth leaked out, there might well be a revolution. And who knew what would happen then?

"True," she said. Romulus probably knew it wasn't over – at least, not yet – but Raechel deserved a chance to relax and catch up with her sleep. "What happened to Lady Standish?"

"My Aunt is currently sleeping it off, under Janet's watchful eye," Raechel said, darkly. She snickered, unpleasantly. "I think I should have waved a sword in her face years ago."

Gwen shook her head. Before going to Russia, Raechel had been a brat, a rebel without a cause. Breaking free of her family wouldn't really have *helped*. But now, she had a cause and something to live for beyond endless partying. Gwen knew she could find a use for someone like Raechel, particularly if she knuckled down and *worked* at becoming an intelligence operative. And even if she didn't ...

She *liked* Raechel, Gwen knew. Perhaps she would be her first true friend.

But the Royal Council will have a fit, she thought, with some amusement. Gwen had worked hard to be taken seriously, to avoid the impression of being a frivolous and fallible woman, not an easy thing to do when the councillors were each old enough to be her father or grandfather. *If we were to start going out every night ...*

"Maybe," she said, finally. "And where's Olivia?"

"She wanted to be alone," Raechel said. She, of all people, would have understood the impulse. "We gave her the rearmost cabin."

Gwen nodded, then yawned. "I need to talk to her," she said. Part of her wanted to put it off, but she knew she shouldn't do anything of the sort. "Give us some privacy, please."

"Of course," Romulus said. "And Lady Gwen ...?"

Gwen turned, lifting an eyebrow.

"Thank you," he said. His dark eyes were warm with relief and private amusement. "Without you, we would all have died."

"Just remember to put that in your report," Gwen said, aiming her words at Lord Standish. He looked as if he had decided to forget about Gwen completely, unsurprisingly. In his world, maids didn't turn out to be sorceresses, or butlers, secret agents. "Lord Mycroft is very good at sniffing out untruths."

Lord Standish snorted, but said nothing.

Chapter Thirty-Nine

he sun was setting, Olivia noted, as she struggled to open the window on the airship. It hadn't felt like they'd been running and hiding and fighting all day, but she couldn't deny the physical evidence staring at her. She cursed the ship's designer under her breath as she finally managed to pull the window open, sending in a blast of cold air. Outside, there was nothing but a long drop towards the ground.

It was her fault, she told herself, as she started to scramble through the window. If she hadn't been born, if she'd died during the Swing, the nightmare the Tsar had unleashed wouldn't have happened. Uncounted thousands, perhaps even millions, would still be alive, while Gwen and the rest of her party wouldn't have been in deadly danger. Gwen had come countless thousands of miles to save her life, only to be almost captured and reprogrammed herself.

And she'd lost control so quickly! Ivan had Charmed her into obedience, then Gregory and the Tsar had forced her into compliance ... and then the Tsar's makeshift Necromancy had almost allowed him to control her. No, it *would* have allowed him to control her. If Gwen hadn't snatched her away from the Tsar, Olivia knew, she would have become his slave once again. The magic she had been born with, her curse not her gift, had become a weapon to be used against her. She had been helpless against the Tsar and the monster he'd become.

Gwen had given her so much. She'd taken her from the streets, made her a lady, even promised Olivia an inheritance that would make her *very* desirable among the young bucks searching for a suitable marital partner. And how had she been rewarded? Her adopted daughter had been turned into a weapon aimed at the country she served, while her desperate attempt to *rescue* the child had almost resulted in her own death. And soon she would have to watch as her ward was executed on the orders of her own government.

Olivia had few illusions. Those who had illusions on the streets died. She had become a liability; in truth, she'd been a liability from the day she'd discovered her magic. Gwen might argue against her execution, but the Privy Council was unlikely to heed her pleas, particularly after the disaster in Moscow. Olivia would be taken to the hangman, a noose would be put around her neck and she would die. And she couldn't really argue that she didn't deserve it, either. Her mere existence was a deadly danger to the entire world.

She poked her head through the window, then paused. Suicide was wrong, she'd been told, but if she was going to die anyway ... she pushed forward, then jumped as she felt a hand snatch hold of her trousers. Moments later, she was pulled back into the room and found herself staring into the eyes of a panicking Gwen. Her adopted mother, who was – in truth – only three or four years older than her – looked terrified and furious at the same time.

"You ... you shouldn't kill yourself," Gwen said. She sounded too shocked to make a better argument. "You have a whole life ahead of you."

Olivia opened her mouth to snap out a sarcastic response, then hesitated. She could be rude to anyone else – social graces were not something she'd taken to easily – but not to Gwen, not to the person who had travelled thousands of miles to save her life. Instead, she felt her legs buckling and sat down hard on the deck. Gwen sat down next to her and put an arm around her shoulder, holding her tightly.

"I won't be alive much longer," she said, feeling her entire body shaking with bitter self-hatred and rage. "They'll kill me when I get home."

"They won't," Gwen said. "None of this was *your* fault."

"I could be forced to work for someone else," Olivia pointed out, sharply. "My mere existence is a major problem. What happens if the French get their hands on me?"

"We can take precautions," Gwen countered.

"But not enough," Olivia said. "They took me from Cavendish Hall, the very heart of the Royal Sorcerers Corps. Where could I go that would be considered *safe*?"

She shook her head. "You should just pitch me out of the window," she said. "End the threat ..."

Gwen slapped her. Olivia stared at her in shock. Gwen had *never* lifted a hand to her.

"Do you think," Gwen snapped, "that there are people in this world who won't miss you when you're gone?"

Olivia rubbed her cheek, wordlessly. The streets had taught her that someone who was a friend today might betray her tomorrow, that everyone looked out for themselves first and foremost, that those who put their trust in others were doomed to lose control of their own lives. But it had been different at Cavendish Hall ... she might not have fitted in well with many of the younger magicians, yet she had had some ... *acquaintances*. Maybe they would have become friends if she had been able to relax and open up to them.

"You've become very dear to me," Gwen said. "Do you think I wouldn't miss you after you'd killed yourself?"

"I ... I don't have a choice," Olivia said. "They will kill me anyway."

She looked up at Gwen, feeling tears prickling at the corner of her eyes. "I don't want to live any longer."

Gwen's hand twitched, then fell still. "Everyone feels the same way at one time or another," she said, instead. "But you can't give in to it."

Olivia snorted. "How many of them were indirectly responsible for unleashing an undead plague and slaughtering millions of people?"

"You were not responsible for what the Tsar made you do," Gwen said, firmly. "The law is on your side in this matter. If someone is Charmed into servitude, they are not responsible for what they do under the influence."

"You know what I mean," Olivia snapped. "What have you done that is remotely as bad as assisting someone to slaughter so many people?"

Gwen took a long breath. "No one realised I was a magician," she said. There was a bitter tone in her voice. "It was fashionable, when I was born, to have male children tested for magic, but female children were generally overlooked. No one realised that I might develop magic until I was six years old and a very spoiled brat."

Olivia nodded. Lady Mary had accepted Olivia into the family, but veered between treating her as something tainted and as a living doll, to be dressed in pretty clothes and put on display. It was easy to imagine her doing the same with the young Gwen, dressing her up from the very start and showing her off to her friends, then handing her back to the nursemaids and governesses. Many of the aristocratic girls she'd met at Cavendish Hall had barely any contact with their parents, their upbringings vested in their caretakers. She'd met enough of their parents to know it wasn't actually a bad idea.

"I was ... bratty at the time," Gwen continued. "I liked playing in the garden, even after rain, despite the mud. They'd given me a new dress, but I didn't care. I ran out into the garden and got it thoroughly covered in mud. The new governess was horrified and screamed at me, unsurprisingly. But I didn't see it that way."

She stared down at her hands, guilt running through her voice. "I was angry at her for spoiling my game," she admitted. "It never occurred to me that she might have a point. Instead ... something cut loose within me, the first surge of magic. I ... I *humiliated* her so completely that she never recovered."

Olivia looked up, sharply. "What did you do?"

"I Charmed her," Gwen said. She paused, long enough for Olivia to tell that she was debating if she should admit the full truth. "I made her do things."

She shook her head. "It took me years to understand just how badly I'd hurt her," she added, slowly. "My magic ... I thought it would help my parents love me. Instead, everyone called me a devil-child. Even now, the guilt gnaws at me from time to time."

Olivia reached out and squeezed Gwen's hand. "You could find her now," she said. "I bet you have enough money to make amends."

"She died in a bedlam, three years ago," Gwen said. "Her mind broke, eventually. And how much of her losing her mind was my fault?"

"You didn't know what you were doing," Olivia said.

"I was *six*," Gwen said. "I *know* I didn't know what I was – or what I could do. But that doesn't stop me feeling guilty over my actions, however accidental."

She patted Olivia on the head. "I can't undo what I did to her," she added. "All I can do is make sure it doesn't happen again."

Olivia sighed. "But you didn't kill millions of people ..."

"I was guiltier than you," Gwen said. "You didn't want any of this to happen."

She stood up, closed the window with a snap, then turned to face Olivia. "If worst comes to worst," she said, "I will take you with me and we will go to the colonies, or somewhere else where we won't be recognised. I've always wanted to travel the world. I believe we can probably fake our deaths and then vanish into the shadows."

Olivia stared at her, feeling an odd twinge in her heart. "You would give up your dream of being the Royal Sorceress?"

Gwen laughed, not unkindly. "I wanted to be someone significant," she said. "But I assumed obligations to you when I adopted you. I won't put them aside for the sake of my career."

"I ..." Olivia shook her head, fighting down the urge to cry. "You'd do that for me?"

"Yes," Gwen said.

Olivia couldn't keep the tears back any longer. Gwen could have killed her or had her thrown back to the streets. Instead, she was offering to take Olivia and run, to hide her from her enemies and everyone who felt a Necromancer was too dangerous to be allowed to live. It would mean the end of her life as she knew it – and Olivia knew that being the Royal Sorceress was important to Gwen – and yet she was prepared to give it up for Olivia. She felt herself lose control and begin to sob helplessly, burrowing into Gwen's arms. Her adopted mother wrapped her hands around Olivia and held her, tightly.

"I want you to sleep," Gwen said, as the tears finally came to an end. Her outfit was drenched, but she didn't seem to care. "I need to sleep too. Afterwards, we can talk about the future when we're in a better state of mind."

"Thank you," Olivia said, blearily.

Gwen levitated Olivia onto the bed, then wrapped the blankets around her and gently kissed her forehead. For once, Olivia didn't feel any alarm or inclination to panic at the unwanted intimacy. Instead, she closed her eyes, gripped Gwen's hand tightly and went to sleep.

***

"I will honour my agreement, of course," Talleyrand said. "I am indebted to you, Royal Sorceress."

"Thank you," Gwen said. She understood just how tempted Talleyrand had to be to arrange an accident somewhere along the airship's path back to Britain, but – oddly – she knew him to be a man of his word. "And yourself?"

"We will stay in St Petersburg," Talleyrand said. "I believe that Lord Standish wishes to remain too."

Gwen nodded. The first reports had been sent to London through the Talker at the British Embassy. Lord Mycroft had ordered the party to return home at once, with the exception of Lord Standish. Gwen had a feeling that this was to keep an embarrassment away from London until the government could decide what to do with him, but Lord Standish had accepted his orders with good grace. Once the Russians put together a new government, he could start negotiations with them on behalf of the British Empire.

If they do, Gwen thought. Word of what had happened at Moscow had leaked out onto the streets and tensions had risen sharply. Civil war seemed a very real possibility. *The Russians might kill both Lord Standish and Talleyrand.*

"I would wish you luck," Gwen said. She allowed herself a smile. "I trust you understand?"

Talleyrand gave her a cold smile in response. "Of course," he said. "I would wish you luck too, of course."

"Lord Standish might prefer it for himself," Gwen observed. "His household has been badly dented, his wife is on the brink of madness and his niece has declared her independence."

"There are worse things that can happen in life," Talleyrand said. He winked at her. Gwen remembered that he was a womaniser and shivered. "I dare say he will find comfort in Moscow and separation from his wife. A madwoman is *so* inconvenient."

Gwen made a face. It was rare, but not uncommon for someone to be shut up on charges of madness, when the truth was that they had simply become inconvenient. A husband might have difficulty divorcing his wife, particularly if the marriage contract included terms stating her dowry had to be returned to her in the event of a separation, yet locking her up was much easier. As annoying as Gwen had found Lady Standish, she promised herself that the woman would receive the best medical care available. It was the least she could do.

"Yes," Gwen agreed, flatly. She'd been called a madwoman often enough herself. "They can be very inconvenient."

Talleyrand smiled. "I understand the Russians have been trying to handle the remaining undead," he said, changing the subject. "Do you think they'll succeed?"

Gwen shrugged. According to the reports she'd heard, in the two days since they'd reached St Petersburg, Moscow had largely burned to the ground. Fortunately, the Russians weren't pointing fingers at her; instead, they seemed to believe there had been an accident with a cooking fire, which had spread out of control in the absence of any attempt to control it. It was true, Gwen knew, that most of the undead had been burned in the fires. But it would be a long time before anyone felt safe near Moscow. There might have been entire nests of the undead making their way out of the city before the Tsar's power collapsed.

"It will keep them busy," she said, and smirked. Even if the Russians didn't collapse into civil war, they'd have too many worries of their own to think about supporting the French, at least for a few years. "I dare say the Sultan will be pleased to see the end of the threat."

"For a while," Talleyrand said. He gave her a smile of his own. "I dare say that it wasn't *that* long ago when we were gleefully considering the prospects opened by the death of the Ottoman Empire."

Gwen nodded, conceding the point. Everyone had *known* the Ottomans were on the verge of disintegration. Egypt was effectively independent, piracy was rife, revolts and insurrections were common and Greece had secured its freedom with the help of France. The outside powers had licked their lips at the thought of seizing territory with very little risk ...

... And then the new Sultan had taken over, smashed the established interests, brought Egypt firmly under his control and executed the rulers of the Barbary States. If the Ottomans could reverse their near-complete decline, why not the Russians?

But the Romans failed, she thought. *Why did one succeed and not the other?*

"We will see," she said, rising to her feet. "I hope we will meet again in better circumstances."

"I do hope we shall," Talleyrand said, rising himself. "And please give my regards to your lovely – and useful – *daughter*."

Gwen pressed her lips together, fighting to keep her face under control. Talleyrand knew what Olivia was now, she knew. It would cause problems, particularly if he used the information to alert MPs or some of more stiff-necked Lords in Britain. But, at the same time, he also owed Gwen his life. She would just have to hope that he would keep his silence, at least long enough for the first reactions to Moscow to fade away.

And if he doesn't, she thought, as she took her leave, *I'll kill him*.

She kept her thoughts to herself as she made her way up to the roof, then launched herself into the air, flying over St Petersburg towards the airstrip. The small army of soldiers that had garrisoned the city seemed to be weaker now, after half of them had been withdrawn to help reinforce the soldiers sweeping the remains of Moscow. She looked down at the sullen population and wondered, inwardly, if any of them would survive the coming war. Even if Britain and France managed to step away from war, Russia was about to go through a long period of bloody upheaval.

"Gwen," Raechel called. She was standing by the airship, waiting for her friend, wearing a dress she'd begged from a Russian noblewoman. The white silk would be faintly scandalous in London, although it set off her red hair nicely. It showed far too much of the shape of her breasts. "What did the Frenchman have to say?"

"We can cross French territory," Gwen said, shortly. Part of her still wanted to go the long way home, but that wasn't an option. Lord Mycroft wanted them home as quickly as possible. "And you should behave yourself on this trip."

Raechel blushed. "Tell that to Romulus and Janet," she said, as she shifted her cloak to cover her chest. "I saw them kissing after they finished helping the ground crew load the airship."

Gwen laughed – she'd been right; they were sweet on each other – then she led the way into the gondola. "You have a new life ahead of you now," she said, flatly. "I don't think you want to waste it."

Chapter Forty

he issue of Olivia's status has been put before the King," Lord Mycroft said, once Gwen had been shown into his office and served a cup of excellent tea. "I believe he will not insist she be ..."

"Put down?" Gwen asked, tartly. "Or simply *murdered*?"

Lord Mycroft met her gaze evenly. "You of all people ought to know that magic poses new problems for us," he said. "The stories from Moscow are quite worrying."

Gwen nodded, bitterly. Thankfully, most of the survivors had been quarantined as soon as they reached London, allowing the government to put out a version of the story that glossed over Gwen's role in the affair and ignored Olivia altogether. The newspapers would be told that Olivia had been kidnapped for ransom and that Scotland Yard – or Mycroft's brother – had successfully tracked down their hiding place. It was a lie, but as long as it was believable, it would keep attention away from Olivia's magic.

But enough had had to be told to start questions being asked in the Houses of Parliament. No one liked the idea of what had happened in Moscow, particularly after the Necromantic outbreak during the Swing. It was likely the MPs would press for tougher measures against Necromancers, which would be difficult. Quite apart from Olivia's existence, even *finding* a Necromancer was impossible unless they used their powers. How many people, Gwen asked herself, had no idea they were magicians until their powers broke free? There was no way to know.

"However, I have confidence that we will survive a challenge," Lord Mycroft continued, complacently. "The Government is assured of a firm block of supporting votes, particularly with the build-up to war. We should remain in place until after the war is concluded."

Gwen gave him a sharp look. "Why didn't you tell me about Romulus?"

She paused. "And why was he even *there*?"

"Lord Standish ... has an aristocrat's view of the world," Lord Mycroft said. "He believes that gentlemen are always gentlemen, no matter where they are born. It is an attitude that is only workable when the rest of the world's aristocracy are also gentlemen. He would approach a Turkish aristocrat, secure in the delusion that the Turk views the world in the same way he does. But the word of an English gentleman cannot be compared to the word of a Turkish gentleman."

"I see," Gwen said, carefully.

"Lord Standish might have weakened us, in a belief that the foreigners would never take advantage of such a weakness," Lord Mycroft added. "It was deemed ... a wise precaution to keep an eye on him. Romulus was inserted into his household as one set of eyes."

"And Sir Sidney was there to override him if necessary," Gwen added. She frowned. "But why send him at all?"

"The Russians like high-ranking negotiators," Lord Mycroft said. "They believe it shows that we are taking them seriously. But I have always preferred to use less ... flashy ambassadors for the truly important talks."

Gwen remembered Sir Travis and nodded.

"But I didn't tell you about Romulus because it was important you reacted normally to him," Lord Mycroft added. "He had to know about you ... if you made a serious mistake, he could cover you against Lady Standish."

"She wanted him to beat me," Gwen recalled. "I think we have to do something about that."

"She's in a madhouse," Lord Mycroft said. "One of the decent ones. What else do you want to do to her?"

"Not that," Gwen said, shaking her head. "About the way servants are treated in London."

Lord Mycroft lifted one eyebrow, then waited.

"I worked as a maid for ... around three weeks," Gwen said. It felt as if she'd been a servant for much longer. "If Lady Raechel hadn't seen through my disguise, I would have found it completely unbearable before too long. I might well have lost control and seriously hurt Lady Standish."

"You would hardly be the only person forced to work hard," Lord Mycroft observed.

"I had something to use as a weapon, if necessary," Gwen said. She would have been a laughing stock if she'd taken the case to court, but she wouldn't have needed to do anything of the sort to extract revenge. A few words in the right ears would have forced Lady Standish into exile, either in the countryside or in France. "How many other maids have that sort of power?"

She pushed on before he could answer. "The Swing changed some things for the better," she admitted. "But other things have gone on as before, without any change at all."

"It takes time for change to percolate through society," Lord Mycroft pointed out, evenly.

"If Janet had gone to court to complain about Lady Standish, she would have lost her job and all prospects of getting another one," Gwen snapped. "I don't think the police would have taken seriously any charges levelled against Lady Standish, even if she had Janet beaten to within an inch of her life. And even the best-trained servants can be treated like slaves, if their employer has enough political clout. Something has to be done."

Lord Mycroft frowned. "We cannot afford a major political struggle, not now," he said. "And it will take such a struggle to change the law and actually make it *work*."

"Then, after the war," Gwen said, unwilling to give up. "If nothing else, this is a major crack in our defences."

She met his eyes, willing him to understand. "Howell used dissatisfied and vengeful servants as his sources," she said. "What's to stop the French or Russians doing the same?"

"Point," Lord Mycroft agreed. He'd done the same himself. "But we still need to wait until after the war."

"I won't let this go," Gwen warned, flatly. "My experiences were hardly the worst anyone ever experienced, My Lord. The abuse of servants has to stop."

Lord Mycroft smiled at her. "And how much of your feeling comes from having to act as a servant yourself?"

Gwen felt her skin heat, but kept her voice under control. "I should have realised that servants were mistreated," she said. She'd certainly known her mother hadn't been the kindest of mistresses to her servants. "And I should have done it before I had to play the role of a servant myself. But it doesn't matter, in the end, where I had the insight. All that matters is that something has to be done before this situation blows up in our face."

"True," Lord Mycroft agreed. He took a long breath. "After the war, you may seek political support for a reform bill. I dare say there are other issues that could be tackled at the same time. Slavery, for example. The growth of cotton farming in the Southern Colonies is going to pose a major challenge, sooner rather than later, as is the treatment of all who are not lily-white. The French will take advantage of that, I fear."

Gwen nodded. The Franco-Spanish Empire had managed to become more racially integrated than the British Empire, a reflection of the simple fact that large parts of their Latin and South American populations were hardly *white*. They'd even banned outright slavery and offered negroes citizenship, which had ensured that Mexico became the preferred destination for runaway slaves. It would be easy for the French to stir up slave revolts across the American South, tying down local militia and redcoats while the French were crossing the Rio Grande and mounting an invasion of British-ruled territory.

Lord Mycroft sighed. "But any reform bill will meet considerable opposition," he added. "The war may cripple some of it, but it will strengthen others."

"Yes, My Lord," Gwen said. "But it has to be done."

"You're as idealistic as Lord Standish," Lord Mycroft said, dryly. "In your own way, of course."

"Thank you," Gwen said, equally dryly. "And Raechel?"

"Will be offered the chance to train," Lord Mycroft assured her. "And even if she doesn't make it through the course, she will be emancipated from the terms of her father's will. I believe that is what you wanted, isn't it?"

"Yes," Gwen said. Raechel would be pleased. And also no longer likely to use violence to break free of her aunt and uncle. "I think she will serve the Crown well."

"Good," Lord Mycroft said. "And now ..."

There was a sharp tap at the door, which opened to reveal a young clerk. "My Lord," he snapped, "urgent message from the Admiralty. There was an encounter between one of our squadrons and a French fleet!"

Gwen felt her blood run cold. A shooting engagement meant only one thing.

The long-dreaded war had finally begun.

The End

Elsewhen Press

a small independent publisher specialising in Speculative Fiction

Visit the Elsewhen Press website at elsewhen.press for the latest information on all of our titles, authors and events; to read our blog; find out where to buy our books and ebooks; or to place an order.

Elsewhen Press

an independent publisher specialising in Speculative Fiction

Bookworm
Christopher G. Nuttall

Elaine is an orphan girl who has grown up in a world where magical ability brings power. Her limited talent was enough to ensure a magical training but she's very inexperienced and was lucky to get a position working in the Great Library. Now, the Grand Sorcerer – the most powerful magician of them all – is dying, although initially that makes little difference to Elaine; she certainly doesn't have the power to compete for higher status in the Golden City. But all that changes when she triggers a magical trap and ends up with all the knowledge from the Great Library – including forbidden magic that no one is supposed to know – stuffed inside her head. This unwanted gift doesn't give her greater power, but it does give her a better understanding of magic, allowing her to accomplish far more than ever before.

It's also terribly dangerous. If the senior wizards find out what has happened to her, they will almost certainly have her killed. The knowledge locked away in the Great Library was meant to remain permanently sealed and letting it out could mean a repeat of the catastrophic Necromantic Wars of five hundred years earlier. Elaine is forced to struggle with the terrors and temptations represented by her newfound knowledge, all the while trying to stay out of sight of those she fears, embodied by the sinister Inquisitor Dread.

But a darkly powerful figure has been drawing up a plan to take the power of the Grand Sorcerer for himself; and Elaine, unknowingly, is vital to his scheme. Unless she can unlock the mysteries behind her new knowledge, divine the unfolding plan, and discover the truth about her own origins, there is no hope for those she loves, the Golden City or her entire world.

Bookworm was Christopher's second fantasy novel to be published by Elsewhen Press, and won the Gold Award in the Adult Fiction category of the 2013 Wishing Shelf Independent Book Awards.

ISBN: 9781908168320 (epub, kindle)
ISBN: 9781908168221 (368pp, paperback)

Visit bit.ly/Bookworm-Nuttall

Elsewhen Press

a small independent publisher specialising in Speculative Fiction

A Life Less Ordinary

Christopher G. Nuttall

There is magic in the world, hiding in plain sight. If you search for it, you will find it, or it will find you. Welcome to the magical world.

Having lived all her life in Edinburgh, the last thing 25-year old Dizzy expected was to see a man with a real (if tiny) dragon on his shoulder. Following him, she discovered that she had stumbled from her mundane world into a parallel magical world, an alternate reality where dragons flew through the sky and the Great Powers watched over the world. Convinced that she had nothing to lose, she became apprenticed to the man with the dragon. He turned out to be one of the most powerful magicians in all of reality.

But powerful dark forces had their eye on this young and inexperienced magician, intending to use her for the ultimate act of evil – the apocalyptic destruction of all reality. If Dizzy does not realise what is happening to her and the worlds around her, she won't be able to stop their plan. A plan that will ravage both the magical and mundane worlds, consuming everything and everyone in fire.

A Life Less Ordinary was Christopher's third fantasy novel to be published by Elsewhen Press. Chris is currently living in Borneo with his wife, muse, and critic Aisha.

ISBN: 9781908168337 (epub, kindle)
ISBN: 9781908168238 (336pp, paperback)

For more information visit bit.ly/ALLO-Nuttall

Elsewhen Press

an independent publisher specialising in Speculative Fiction

Jacey's Kingdom
Dave Weaver

Jacey's Kingdom is an enthralling tale that revolves around a startlingly desperate reality: Jacey Jackson, a talented student destined for Cambridge, collapses with a brain tumour while sitting her final history exam at school. In her mind she struggles through a quasi-historical sixth century dreamscape whilst the surgeons fight to save her life.

Jacey is helped by a stranger called George, who finds himself trapped in her nightmare after a terrible car accident. There are quests, battles, and a love story ahead of them, before we find out if Jacey will awake from her coma or perish on the operating table. And who, or what, is George? In this book, Dave Weaver questions our perception of reality and the redemptive power of dreams; are our experiences of fear, conflict, friendship and love any less real or meaningful when they take place in the mind rather than the 'real' physical world?

Dave Weaver has been writing for ten years, with short stories published in anthologies, magazines and online in the UK and USA. Jacey's Kingdom is his first published novel. He cleverly weaves a tale that takes the almost unimaginable drama of an eighteen year-old girl whose life is in the balance, relying on modern surgery to bring her back from the brink, and conceives the world that she has constructed in her mind to deal with the trauma happening to her body. Developing the friendship between Jacey and George in a natural and witty style, despite their unlikely situation and the difference in their ages, Dave has produced a story that is both exciting and thought-provoking. This book will be a must-read story for adults and young adults alike.

ISBN: 9781908168313 (epub, kindle)
ISBN: 9781908168214 (272pp paperback)

Visit bit.ly/JaceysKingdom

Elsewhen Press

an independent publisher specialising in Speculative Fiction

TimeStorm

Steve Harrison

In 1795 a convict ship leaves England for New South Wales in Australia. Nearing its destination, it encounters a savage storm but, miraculously, the battered ship stays afloat and limps into Sydney Harbour. The convicts rebel, overpower the crew and make their escape, destroying the ship in the process. Fleeing the sinking vessel with only the clothes on their backs, the survivors struggle ashore.

Among the escaped convicts, seething resentments fuel an appetite for brutal revenge against their former captors, while the crew attempts to track down and kill or recapture the escapees. However, it soon becomes apparent that both convicts and crew have more to concern them than shipwreck and a ruthless fight for survival; they have arrived in Sydney in 2017.

TimeStorm is a thrilling epic adventure story of revenge, survival and honour. In the literary footsteps of Hornblower, comes Lieutenant Christopher 'Kit' Blaney, an old-fashioned hero, a man of honour, duty and principle. But dragged into the 21st century… literally.

A great fan of the grand seafaring adventure fiction of CS Forester, Patrick O'Brien and Alexander Kent and modern action thriller writers like Lee Child, Steve Harrison combines several genres in his fast-paced debut novel as a group of desperate men from the 1700s clash in modern-day Sydney.

Steve Harrison was born in Yorkshire, England, grew up in Lancashire, migrated to New Zealand and eventually settled in Sydney, Australia, where he lives with his wife and daughter.

As he juggled careers in shipping, insurance, online gardening and the postal service, Steve wrote short stories, sports articles and a long running newspaper humour column called *HARRISCOPE: a mix of ancient wisdom and modern nonsense*. In recent years he has written a number of unproduced feature screenplays, although being unproduced was not the intention, and developed projects with producers in the US and UK. His script, *Sox*, was nominated for an Australian Writers' Guild 'Awgie' Award and he has written and produced three short films under his *Pronunciation Fillums* partnership. TimeStorm was Highly Commended in the Fellowship of Australian Writers (FAW) National Literary Awards for 2013.

ISBN: 9781908168542 (epub, kindle)
ISBN: 9781908168443 (368pp paperback)

Visit bit.ly/TimeStorm

Elsewhen Press

an independent publisher specialising in Speculative Fiction

THE RHYMER
aŋ Heredyssey
DOUGLAS THOMPSON

The Rhymer, an Heredyssey defies classification in any one literary genre. A satire on contemporary society, particularly the art world, it is also a comic-poetic meditation on the nature of life, death and morality.

A mysterious tramp wanders from town to town, taking a new name and identity from whoever he encounters first. Apparently amnesiac or even brain-damaged, Nadith Learmot nonetheless has other means to access the past and perhaps even the future: upon his chest a dial, down his sleeves wires that he can connect to the walls of old buildings from which he believes he can read their ghosts like imprints on tape. Haunting him constantly is the resemblance he apparently bears to his supposed brother, a successful artist called Zenir. Setting out to pursue Zenir and denounce or blackmail him out of spite, in his travels around the satellite towns and suburbs surrounding a city called Urbis, Nadith finds he is always two steps behind a figure as enigmatic and polyfaceted as himself. But through second hand snippets of news he increasingly learns of how his brother's fortunes are waning, while his own, to his surprise, are on the rise. Along the way, he encounters unexpected clues to his own true identity, how he came to lose his memory and acquire his strange 'contraption'. When Nadith finally catches up with Zenir, what will they make of each other?

Told entirely in the first person in a rhythmic stream of lyricism, Nadith's story reads like Shakespeare on acid, leaving the reader to guess at the truth that lies behind his madness. Is Nadith a mental health patient or a conman? ... Or as he himself comes to believe, the reincarnation of the thirteenth century Scottish seer True Thomas The Rhymer, a man who never lied nor died but disappeared one day to return to the realm of the faeries who had first given him his clairvoyant gifts?

Douglas Thompson's short stories have appeared in a wide range of magazines and anthologies. He won the Grolsch/Herald Question of Style Award in 1989 and second prize in the Neil Gunn Writing Competition in 2007. His first book, *Ultrameta*, published in 2009, was nominated for the Edge Hill Prize, and shortlisted for the BFS Best Newcomer Award. Since then he has published more novels, including *Entanglement* published by Elsewhen Press. *The Rhymer* is his eighth novel.

ISBN: 9781908168511 (epub, kindle)
ISBN: 9781908168412 (192pp paperback)

For more information visit bit.ly/TheRhymer-Heredyssey

About the author

hristopher G. Nuttall has been planning sci-fi books since he learned to read. Born and raised in Edinburgh, Chris created an alternate history website and eventually graduated to writing full-sized novels. Studying history independently allowed him to develop worlds that hung together and provided a base for storytelling. After graduating from university, Chris started writing full-time. As an indie author he has self-published a number of novels, but this is his sixth fantasy to be published by Elsewhen Press, and the third in the Royal Sorceress series about Lady Gwendolyn Crichton. The first was *The Royal Sorceress*, followed by *The Great Game*. *Necropolis* continues Gwen's story. Chris is currently living in Borneo with his wife, muse, and critic Aisha.